COLD HARD NEWS

by

Maureen Milliken

S & H Publishing, Inc.
Purcellville, Virginia

Maureen Milliken/S & H Publishing, Inc.
P. O. Box 456
Purcellville, VA 20134
www.SandHpublishing.com

Cover photo by Scott Monroe

Note: While *Cold Hard News* is set in Franklin County, Maine, Redimere is not a real place and any resemblance of the town or its people to any real places or people, living or dead, is a coincidence. While most of the geography is real, some liberties have been taken, so if things aren't where they're supposed to be, or there are rivers or highways in the book that don't exist, it's simply because it's a work of fiction.

Cold Hard News/ Maureen Milliken. -- 1st ed.
ISBN 978-1-63320-024-1 – print edition
ISBN 978-1-63320-025-8 – ebook edition

TO MOM AND DAD

Acknowledgements

A lot of people played a part, too many to mention, but special thanks go to Mike Cousineau, John Radosta, Maureen Mullins, Dan Fitts, Carol Robidoux; and especially my family Anna Marie Milliken, Jim Milliken Sr., Nicki Milliken Beauregard, Liz Milliken, Jimmy Milliken and Bill Milliken. Nancy West, Kathy Marchoki, Kaitlin Shroeder, Roberta Scruggs and Cara Courchesne all gave me tidbits that made the book better; Ed Shamy opened his heart; Lorna Colquhoun helped clarify what it meant at one time, and maybe still does, to be a journalist.

Also, my long-ago writing group June Lemen and Lisa Jackson; Sherry Wood for the first "final" edit, Scott Monroe, for the "final" edit and the picture on the cover; my in-depth readers, Rebecca Milliken, Kathy McGrath Fitts (who came up with the title) and Brenda Buchanan. And Dixiane Hallaj for having faith in me and, most importantly, liking my book.

It's no coincidence that most of the people I've cited here are journalists or former journalists. More than a mystery novel, *Cold Hard News* is a love letter to the industry that has sustained me for more than three decades. Those people I've shared so many newsrooms, tight deadlines, late-night beers, bad jokes, fights, laughter, heartache, passion for news, and everything else that goes with it are the backbone of this book. I can't imagine life without it. We really were the lucky ones.

CHAPTER 1

The snowbank had a gash in it. A bright white bite in the gray.
A body-sized bite.

Bernie O'Dea skidded her car to a stop on the mud and half-frozen puddles that passed for the road's shoulder. She'd barely opened the door when Rusty Dyer leaned in, eager, almost triumphant.

"It's Stanley Weston."

Bernie looked down the road at the lumpy tarp, way too clean next to the moldy snowbank and mud-streaked pavement. The only other clean thing was that bite. She grabbed her notebook, pencil and camera from the passenger seat. Rusty moved back as she stepped out of the car straight into an ankle-deep ice puddle.

"Bad day for sneakers," Rusty said.

"Thinking spring," Bernie said. She headed toward the action, trying to zip her jacket without dropping her gear, doing her best to ignore her quickly numbing wet foot and Rusty as he nipped at her heels, more like an annoying overgrown puppy than middle-aged police officer.

"Entombed. Looks like all winter," he said.

Bernie nodded as she took in the scene, already writing in her head. Dead quiet, she thought, feeling the gray end-of-winter

1

stillness. Naw—she'd have to think up something less of a cliché. A huddle of vehicles was scattered on the otherwise deserted road. The town's cruiser, two from state police, a Warden Service pickup, the town public works truck. She knew them more by their colors— navy blue, robin's egg blue, hunter green, bright orange and brown—than by their seals, mostly invisible under the chalky film of salt and sand that March throws onto every piece of metal that gets near pavement in this end of Maine.

"Newspaper's here," Rusty shouted, sprinting ahead of her to get to Police Chief Pete Novotny before she did.

The state troopers and warden were a few feet from the tarp, talking quietly as a woman wearing rubber gloves—Bernie figured from the state medical examiner's office—poked through the remains of the snowbank. Pete stood off to the side at the edge of the dense pines that kept the thin mid-afternoon sun from breaking through, hands shoved deep into the pockets of his heavy police jacket. Bernie stopped next to him, giving up on her zipper, wishing she'd remembered gloves.

"Stanley. Shit," she said, the weariness in her voice surprising her. She didn't realize she felt it until it came out.

Pete gave her a sad smile and cocked his head. He'd heard it, too. "Yeah. Stanley."

"A hit and run that got plowed in?" Bernie said, trying to picture how that would happen. "When, even? How?"

"The injuries look pretty extensive. Hard to tell if it was a car or something else that killed him."

"Something else?" Bernie jotted the spare facts down in makeshift shorthand. There were surprisingly few possibilities for the something else. A Massachusetts yahoo up here for some gun fun and Stanley hit by a stray bullet? Maine's lax gun laws inspired that sort of thing, even when it wasn't hunting season. Or maybe, more likely, a heart attack in the road with no one to help? Or a drunken stumble? Then the plow? She could feel Rusty next to her, practically bouncing with his need to get into the conversation.

"Can't think that'd be anything but a car accident. In the dark,"

2

he said.

Thanks for that in-depth analysis, Bernie thought. She looked at Pete. He shrugged. Pete was a thinker, not a talker like his predecessor Cal. She knew there were things he wasn't saying, could feel it, but damned if she could penetrate the force field and figure out what it was. Once in a while she felt like they were on the same wavelength, but not today. Today any answers were going to take good old-fashioned Bernadette O'Dea persistence. "Whatever it was, obviously a plow played a part? Given he was in the snow like that."

Silence.

She tried again. "When, I wonder?"

"Dunno." Pete looked at the gritty pile of snow. "Months, maybe."

Bernie felt the weariness again. She'd covered plenty of bodies as a reporter in Massachusetts and Rhode Island. This felt different. She pushed it away. "How was he found?"

"Jogger," Pete said. "Saw part of his arm."

She'd run on this road all winter herself. Right by Stanley, apparently. She realized where some of that shaky feeling was coming from. "No one noticed he was gone?"

Pete took a deep breath, was about to say something. Stopped.

"Wasn't he gonna go south, visit his cousin for the winter?" Rusty said. "Stan wasn't feeling good. Cal'd been taking him to the VA all fall. Cal was working on sending him somewhere warm for a few months."

"South? Like New Hampshire?" Bernie asked, still thinking about the snowbank, the plow. Stanley often helped at the paper sorting postal labels, but only when he showed up for the once-a-week chore. When he didn't, she didn't think twice. Right now, that was making her hate herself a little.

"Like Myrtle Beach," Rusty said. "South Carolina?" Rusty didn't have to add "you moron" to the end for her to hear it. Usually she was in more control of her interviews, but despite two decades of reporting, most of it in much bigger cities with tougher cops than this, she couldn't get a feel for the undercurrent today. She'd dealt with Pete enough to know sometimes he was "just the facts, ma'am," but this felt like something else. Stanley, always alert and purposeful as he marched down the street—that image didn't jibe with him being plowed in, helpless and alone. She tried to stop thinking of Rusty as an annoying mosquito buzzing into her thoughts and focus more on what he was saying.

"Cal always looked out for him in the winter," Rusty said.

"Not this year," Bernie said.

Pete, who'd been watching the medical examiner and state cops, turned to her, glared.

She felt heat rise up the back of her neck, realized she better spool back in before her mouth shut things down for good. "I didn't mean because Cal died," she said. "I meant because Stanley's right here."

"Cal never said anything to me about sending Stanley somewhere," Pete said to Rusty.

"Can't account for that," Rusty said.

"Someone should have told me, let me help," Pete said. "Cal wasn't doing well either."

"Maybe we should get back on the record," Bernie said. "Can I get the name of the jogger?"

"Not much for the record right now," Pete said. "I'll get you that later, when the report is done."

The three stood in silence, watching the state cops pick through the crap that had come out of the snow with Stanley. Leaves matted together with frozen mud, crushed soda bottles, indefinable road kill. A hearse had pulled up while they were talking, and the murmurs of the state cops were punctuated by doors opening, the metal creak of a gurney unfolding.

Bernie put her hands, still gripping notebook and pencil, in her pockets, pulling her jacket around her, trying not to care how cold it was. "It was a long winter," she said. It had been, even for here. Everyone was just trying to get somewhere warm. "I bet no one really expected to see Stanley around whether they thought he'd gone away or not."

"I should have known what was going on," Pete said. "With Cal, with Stanley."

"Kind of a domino effect," Bernie said. "Cal wasn't doing well. Cal was taking care of Stanley. Cal died. Stanley wasn't doing well. He falls through the cracks. No one's fault really." She wasn't sure if she was trying to make Pete feel better or herself.

In either case, it didn't seem to be working. "So nothing else on the record?" Bernie tried to pull the conversation back from wherever it had careened. She still had a job to do.

"Not right now," Pete said. He turned and walked over to the other cops.

"Should we have noticed we didn't see him around?" Bernie asked Rusty, not sure what he'd have to add, mostly just looking for reassurance.

"Like you said, no one's fault." He followed Pete.

She took some pictures and hit up the state troopers, who echoed Pete—sorry, no information. It was Thursday and the *Peaks Weekly Watcher* had come out that morning, so she had almost a week to get the story together. Walking back to her car, she pictured Stanley, a familiar sight on the road most of the year, pushing his shopping cart, stopping in at the paper to do the postal labels for a few bucks and a sandwich. He wasn't her friend. She didn't even know him that well. But there he'd been all winter, entombed, as Rusty had put it, and no one had ever given him a thought.

Earlier, when the scanner had played a bar or two of tuneless static before its feedback-punctuated voice spit out 10-47 and Pond Road, what she heard was a seductive whisper, "Bernadette, baby, you've got a story." She hadn't needed to look at the grubby paper taped to the wall to know 10-47 meant call the medical examiner. She wasn't ashamed to say her heart raced with anticipation.

After nearly two years running a weekly newspaper in Maine's northwestern Franklin County, Bernie was still trying get used to the slow pace. Maybe it's what she deserved after screwing up her career so badly. She may be in High Peaks country—and the name of her paper, the *Peaks Weekly Watcher* was a daily reminder—but sometimes she felt like she was in a low valley of gloom. She should be happy here in her home state, the same paper she started at two decades ago, fresh out of Boston University. She had no one else in the newsroom elbowing her out of the way for the big stories. The problem was, aside from Cal's death a few months before, there hadn't been any big stories. And she spent a lot of time doing things that as a hot-shot reporter she never dreamed she'd be doing. Payroll, circulation, appeasing advertisers and the garden club president, paying the bills and cleaning the coffee pot. So yeah, the scanner had stirred that story-chasing buzz. She was pissed at the fates that the buzz was now mellowed by, ugh, feelings. Well, Bernadette, she told herself, that's another tool in the old tool box.

The late afternoon sun was burning off the clouds, almost warming up the bright penny March day. A slight smell of mud and decay, a sign things were thawing, hung in the air. Winter wasn't really over, but maybe it would be soon. She got in her car and pulled onto the road behind an old pickup truck toddling down the center line about ten miles below the speed limit.

Feelings. Got 'em? Then use 'em. She knew the best thing she could do for Stanley was to figure out the truth.

"Out of my way, gramps," she grumbled, leaving the pickup in her wake. "I've got a story to write."

CHAPTER 2

"Watcha got?" Guy Gagne called from his desk back in the corner.

"Stanley's dead," Bernie said, taking off her coat. "They found his body in a snowbank out on Pond Road."

"So I heard." Guy stubbed out his soggy unlit cigarette in his ashtray. "Lots of people going to feel bad, not that they gave a fig when he was alive."

"Yup. Lots of people feeling bad already," she said. "Maybe the not giving a fig thing has something to do with it."

"What did the chief say?"

Bernie sat down and opened her notebook. "Not much. He had a bee in his bonnet."

"Bee in his bonnet? Robocop?" Guy said.

Bernie felt her cheeks get hot. She'd shared her secret nickname for Pete with Guy, and he always looked for a chance to have some fun with it. She didn't mean it in a bad way. Pete wasn't emotionless, just in control—calm and measured. It seemed to be her day for sounding glib when she was feeling pretty damn un-glib.

"Sorry. I'm trivializing," she said. "He seemed to feel responsible that Stanley was dead. I don't know if that was the cause or the symptom. Sometimes he's Dudley Do-Right, not Robocop. Although there might have been a little Prickly Pete thrown in."

"You have that effect on people."

"I'm not proud of it." She meant it as a joke, but it came out a little shaky.

"Just teasing," Guy said, turning back to his keyboard. "I'm sure it had nothing to do with you."

"What are you doing in here today anyway?" she asked him, tired of the topic.

"Figured I'd get the About Town column out of the way. Help you out, with town meeting and all."

"Too bad you're about seventy-five percent retired. I could use more of you."

"I'd be one hundred percent retired if you'd let me," he said, still typing.

"Harry never told me he was including me as part of the furniture when he sold you the paper."

"I know you never would've let Harry leave this paper in my hands alone. You still think I'm that twenty-two-year-old kid I was my first time here."

"Prove me wrong."

"I just might yet," she said, glad the mood had changed. Even though they'd had the same conversation a hundred times over the last couple years, she knew he was happy she'd bought the paper, happy it wasn't some stiff corporate type who would've made him retire. "Anyway, joke's on me, too. When I left here for the big time, I said I'd never cover a town meeting again."

Bernie sifted through the page dummies. "Can't think of a better way to spend a Saturday than listening to the town folk grouse about money. Stanley's obviously the lead story. Town meeting the off-lead. Nothing new on the garbage strewer this week."

"Thank god," Guy said. "I'm getting tired of that idiot."

"You know you live in a safe town when the biggest story is some asshole taking people's garbage and tossing it around the streets," Bernie said. "Looking forward to Pete solving that one."

Guy didn't answer. She knew she was talking too much. She started typing her Stanley notes. She was looking forward to figuring out how to flesh out the story: get more details from the cops, find out more about Stanley. But she had to get the payroll out of the way first. She hated dealing with numbers. It took every ounce of her mental energy for them to make sense and now, with Stanley on the brain, focus was just wishful thinking. She was still trying to rustle some up when the front door of the office crashed open.

"Ought to get that fixed," Guy said, the stock staff response every time the door banged.

Bernie shrugged. Another thing way too low on the priority list to spend the money on, each crash a reminder that yes, she was back in the small time.

Ike Miller stood at the front counter, tipping his cowboy hat and giving her his Fake Texan smile. She almost expected him to say, "Howdy, ma'am."

Bernie wished Annette were there. The receptionist-slash-circulation clerk was much better at customer service. Besides payroll and administration, Bernie had to learn patience when she took over the paper. It was a steep learning curve.

"Can I help you?" She tried her best bright, happy-to-see you voice.

Ike upended a heavy-looking garbage bag. Out spilled a winter's worth of newspapers, bundled in rubber bands, unopened, soaked, black, and covered in mud.

"Found these at the end of my driveway when the snow melted," he said as the slimy mess slid onto the floor. "Bernadette." Still smiling. "You seem to be under the impression I have a subscription to your newspaper."

She matched his smile, fake for fake. Not good customer service to get in pissing matches with people, even ones who'd canceled their subscriptions out of spite. She glanced past him through the window to his pickup, caught a glimpse of Dubya, his dog, sitting in the front seat, gazing at his master with a crazy doggie grin of love. You'd expect a guy like Ike Miller to have a pit bull or something, but Dubya was some kind of mix—she'd heard Ike describe him as corgi-gone-crazy—and he looked like an oversized teddy bear. Dubya made her like Ike just a little bit.

"We didn't stop delivering it when you canceled?" She realized it was a stupid question the minute she asked it.

He smiled wider and lifted the cowboy hat slightly in what she knew was a fake gesture acknowledging her brilliance. Fake fake fake. She wanted to tell him that real gentlemen took off their hats indoors. She knew some nuns back in grade school who would've knocked it off his head for him despite his John Wayne size.

"I don't want to see another *Weekly Watcher*"—he said the name of the paper the way a Red Sox fan says Alex Rodriguez, but still smiling—"on my goddam property."

He marched out the door without waiting for her answer. She watched as Dubya did a happy polka in the front seat as Ike approached, and then get an affectionate ear-tug as Ike got in. The truck skidded away from the curb and down Main Street.

"Make a note," Bernie said to Guy as she looked at the clump of soggy newsprint on the floor. "Mr. Miller has not changed his mind about home delivery."

"That seems to be the case," Guy said.

"Fake Texan," she muttered as she went to the supply cupboard to get a garbage bag.

"Hey, he lived in Texas," Guy said.

"He was born here, raised here and now he's back here," Bernie said. "Redimere born and bred. That Texas act gets old."

The papers were disgusting. She started throwing them into the garbage bag.

"You're just sore because he canceled his paper on you in the middle of the Country Grocer with everyone watching."

Bernie burned with embarrassment just thinking about it. How she'd stood there like a dope with her bag of Meow Mix while he berated her. True, she'd done a story in the paper that led to the conclusion that, as chairman of the planning board, he had a conflict of interest voting on the wind farm, since it abutted his property. True, it got him kicked off the planning board. But still.

She was dumping the last of the rotting mess into the garbage bag when the door crashed open again.

"Can I help you?" she asked Loren Daggett, her daily customer service patience quota long past its limit.

"Speaking of the wind farm," Guy said.

"Doing a windmills story?" Loren asked, leaning on the counter. Loren, unlike his neighbor Ike, was still a subscriber, proud as punch about every story about the wind farm, even the stories that called him names.

"Not this week."

Loren looked uncertain. "I heard Ike's raising hell again about the windmills, thought you might be doing a story."

"Is that what you're here about?"

"No. Was over to the police station, but couldn't find nobody."

She wiped her muddy hands on her jeans. No surprise the police station was empty—Rusty and Pete were probably still at the scene.

"And?"

"Stanley Weston? I heard he died. Found his body in a snowbank."

"Yup."

"I figured next to police, you'd know the most about it."

"Nobody seems to know anything yet," Bernie said, hoping her impatience for him to get to the point wasn't showing. She watched him turn his John Deere cap over in his hands, suck on his droopy mustache. Neither of them said anything, the only sound the clack-clack of Guy's keyboard.

"I was gonna wait until Stanley got back from Florida, but I guess he didn't go there," Loren said.

"South Carolina. No, he didn't," Bernie said. "Wait for what?" She tried harder for concerned and sympathetic, though nosy and hopeful was beginning to make an appearance, edging out impatient.

"You know his trailer that he lived in?"

Bernie nodded.

"It was just an old trailer that some loggers used to use." Loren had a thick central Maine accent, the kind they could never get right in Stephen King movies—not the sound of the vowels as they split into more syllables than they should, or the cadence—"on oil-eld tray-lahh thit some luggahs."

She nodded encouragement.

"Downwind—the wind company?— has that easement so they can get up the mountain and they need that land. Thought it wasn't going to be until later, after the public hearing and whatnot, but they want it ASAP. I was gonna wait 'til Stanley got back, cause I thought it would be soon, before I gave him the bad news." He looked at her hopefully.

"And you want me to what?" She could feel impatience zip back through her, a physical presence.

"I want to get rid of the trailer, 'n wondering about his belongings. Don't think he has any family but that cousin down in Florida. Don't want to dump 'em. He worked for you."

Worked for me for half an hour on occasional Wednesday afternoons sorting postage labels, Bernie thought. Then again, Loren didn't have to know that. Who was Stanley? What made him tick? She needed some juice for the story that the dailies wouldn't have.

"South Carolina."

"Hmm?" Loren asked.

"The cousin's in South Carolina, I was going to call him anyway. I'll make sure it's okay," she said. She tried to ignore Guy clearing his throat in an obvious way behind her.

"Thought Cal said Florida. But same difference," Loren said. He looked relieved.

"I just have some things to finish up here. I'll go over around five or so, if it's okay with his cousin."

"No problem," Loren said. "It ain't locked."

After the door crashed shut, Guy, who hadn't been typing for a while, cleared his throat again.

"Can I help you?" Bernie asked.

"Don't you think that's overstepping? Going into Stanley's place?"

Bernie wasn't going to let Guy dampen the buzz, which had gotten buzzier the minute Loren mentioned the trailer. She might find out something no one else knew. Her hunger for it overrode any, or at least most, pangs of conscience. "If not me, then who? Anyway, if the *Lewiston Sun-Journal* or the *Sentinel* is going to do something on this, I need some exclusive stuff. I know they're dailies, but I can't get scooped in my own back yard."

Guy shook his head and bent back to his keyboard. "Don't say I didn't warn you."

"I know what I'm doing." Stanley wasn't here. He wouldn't care if she went through his stuff. Would anyone? She doubted it.

. . . . .

For the second time that day, Bernie navigated the pot holes and frost heaves down Pond Road, her Subaru shuddering with every bump and plunge. It would be summer before some of the roads in town flattened out. Some never would. The afternoon sun had done a job on the snowbanks in town. They didn't really melt anyway, more like evaporated through the spring into black piles of crust, kind of like a fast-food milkshake that had been left in the cup. Farther out, once she was in the woods, the banks still rose high, little miniatures of the mountains that towered to the west and north. There was no sign anything had happened earlier in the day at the spot where the body was found except that body-sized white gash and a tangle of muddy tire tracks. No memorial for Stanley had sprung up—the crosses, flowers, candles, teddy bears that seemed to grow right out of the ground when the victim was a child or the fun guy everyone liked down at the Little League field. She knew that none would.

She passed Rusty Dyer off on the side a little farther down the road in the police department's Suburban. She checked her speedometer. Safe. As she passed him she could see it didn't matter anyway. He was engrossed in a cellphone call. He looked up as she drove by, so she gave a wave. No reaction. Cellphone coma. Typical Rusty, Bernie thought. Our tax dollars at work.

She turned off onto the road leading to Stanley's trailer. It was one of a zillion dirt tote and logging roads that crisscrossed the state, the highways of hunters, hikers and people who were looking for a secluded place in the woods and mountains to get up to no good. Plenty of places like that in this wilderness. Her car rattled and shook over the ruts and hillocks—the frost-heaved main road was as smooth as the interstate compared to this. The setting sun elongated the shadows as she left an overgrown meadow and the trees began to take over. The funeral home didn't have a number for a relative. She'd called Pete to see if he or Rusty knew who the cousin was, but the chief said he didn't have a clue and no one else at the station did either.

"Guess Cal was the guy who knew," Pete said. "We're going to take up a collection for the funeral, and there's some VA money, since we can't find his relative."

She was beginning to think she'd turned down the wrong road when she finally came to the trailer, one of those teardrop-shaped tin cans made to pull behind a pickup truck or station wagon. Rust on top of traces of silver and pink. The shopping cart Stanley used to collect bottles and cans was parked in the dooryard by a battered fifty-five gallon drum half-filled with returnables. Another can had a neatly tied garbage bag. Bernie lifted it out and put it in her car's hatchback. Stanley used to leave his garbage in the Dumpster behind the *Watcher*. She'd dump this one, too. It was the least she could do.

She took some photos, then went out back. A lawn chair and charcoal grill that looked like they'd been pulled from the dump were still half-covered in snow. The remains of last summer's vegetable garden peeked from melted patches that overlooked a meadow stretching from the trees around Stanley's trailer down to the marshy land and then the bog—Ike Miller's land. Pond Road

14

was visible off to the south, an occasional car flashing by. The mountains loomed in the other direction. Despite the snowmobile tracks that crisscrossed what snow was left and the far-off whine of the machines, it was a surprisingly nice spot for old Stanley.

Inside, the trailer was cramped but tidy. A bunk neatly made up with old blankets. A pot, plate, and utensils piled in the tiny sink next to a half-filled plastic gallon water bottle, dented and cracked from years of use, that took up all of what might be called a counter. A makeshift bookshelf crammed in the one remaining foot of floor space held a couple dozen paperbacks. She poked the cigarette butts in an ashtray on the bookshelf with her finger. Looked like someone had smoked more than just tobacco. She could barely take a step or two in either direction. Stretching her arms out, she could almost touch both walls. Cozy, or claustrophobia-inducing? She wasn't sure.

She didn't see what Loren was so uptight about; all this stuff could have just gone into the trash. Well, maybe not all of it, She picked an Audubon field guide from among the paperbacks. She'd keep that one. She started going through the other books, but they were too dog-eared even for the library book sale. She began putting them into the garbage bag, first leafing through each book to make sure Stanley wasn't one of those people who hid things between the pages. One of them, a Lee Child book, fell open, the binding cracked, to a couple pages turned down at the corner. She always liked seeing what people noted in books, interested in what they found important. In this case, it was a sequence where a guy mailed himself a flash drive so the bad guys who were after it wouldn't find it. She vaguely remembered reading this book, also impressed with that simple, yet effective, trick. "Stan, we speak each other's language," Bernie said as she tossed the book in with the Audubon guide for another read.

She opened the trailer's only cupboard. Inside was a pile of wool socks, clean and darned, but well beyond use, and a flannel shirt in similar condition. Into the garbage bag they went. Underneath was a bulging manila envelope full of newspaper clippings, mostly from the *Bangor Daily News*. They were old, yellow. She held a couple up to the cloudy window, so she could read them better. Stanley's exploits on the high school baseball diamond and cross-country team. His parents' obituaries, both from the 1970s. A story from 1966 about his service in Vietnam, on how he'd earned a Purple Heart and a commendation for bravery. "Stanley has the ultimate respect for human life," his father said in the story. She sniffed the clippings and drank in the odor of ancient newsprint. Newspapers didn't smell like that anymore.

There was also a sheaf of newer clippings, mostly from the *Watcher*, about the wind farm. Under those clippings was a pile of check stubs, VA disability payments, the address a Redimere P.O. box. Underneath that, the key to the P.O. box itself. She'd give the key to Bev Dulac, the postmistress. Let whatever was in the P.O. box be someone else's problem. She'd poke around some more, but there was nowhere to poke and it was getting too dark anyway.

In the short time she'd been there, dusk had fallen outside. The mustiness was more than a smell now, it was a feeling. The trailer was getting dark. And cold. It creaked, maybe from the slight wind outside? The buzz had ramped up, that familiar over-the-top feeling when it turned from a high to anxiety. She heard her mother's voice, "Bernadette calm down and take a breath."

She took a deep breath. Stopped and listened. Her heart banged in her throat. A squeak, then a crunch. Footsteps in the frozen grass and crusty snow outside? She held the breath mid-inhale and listened. Nothing. She couldn't see much through the scratched, dirty window, but she felt eyes on her. Felt exposed. She had a sudden and desperate need for fresh air.

Outside, the temperature had dropped with the sun. She flinched as she stepped down the rusted metal step out the door, prepared to be surprised, ready to swing the garbage bag full of paperbacks. An engine whined in the distance, but up close all she could hear was the breeze in the grass and a flock of Canada geese squawking overhead. She took a deep, shaky breath. She laughed. All was fine. No need to create drama where there wasn't any. Still, she wanted to get away from the sad little trailer and get home.

She threw the returnable bottles in a garbage bag, and put them in the back with the bags she intended to throw in the Dumpster. She took one last look around. Dark, quiet and desolate. The view down to the bog was no longer pretty, but faded into inky shadows. The geese were gone, their squawks faint. The whine of snowmobile engines had disappeared, too, but she couldn't remember when. She felt that exposed feeling again. A little rise of panic.

She got in the car and turned the CD player up loud, just so there'd be some noise. Once she hit the pavement on Pond Road and was out of the woods and off the bumpy dirt road, she sighed and began to sing along, making up her own words. "Stanley is dead dead dead. A plow hit him in the head head head." Usually she could make herself laugh, but it just made her feel worse, so she shut up. She passed Rusty, still on his cellphone. This time their eyes met. She waved—the old friendly Maine hello—but he didn't wave back. She wondered how much help he'd have been if there'd actually been a dangerous trailer lurker. Now that made her laugh.

As she neared town, the buzz ramped back down to normal story-chasing excitement. When she worked for a daily, Bernie had been a champ at pumping stories out on deadline. You want that story in half an hour? No sweat. Twenty inches coming up. She craved those moments, lived for the adrenaline rush. And she was good at it. The best. She even had a plaque on her bedroom wall that said so. But the *Watcher* only came out on Thursdays. Stories had to be massaged so they were still interesting days later. Something happened too early, and it was old news. Too late and she barely had time to write it up because she had to put the paper together. And with the Internet, the twenty-four-hour news cycle, if she didn't find a new way to tell a story, she was going to get beat bad in many different ways around the clock. She always felt like she was in the slow lane. But she could see some angles on this story. Human interest, the details about how he'd actually died. Even if it was a hit-and-run, it was still poignant, interesting. She could give it a ride.

She stopped at the office to finish up some bookkeeping odds and ends and took another look at the decades-old clippings. Gold. She knew the dailies wouldn't do much searching in their clip files—even if they were going to go big guns on this remote corner of their circulation areas, Bernie knew that these days reporters' research usually stopped with Google, and they weren't going to find many newspaper clippings from the 1970s there.

She locked the door behind her. She usually parked out front, parking not being hard to find in Redimere in March. But the street was deserted. Where'd she leave her car? Busy brain, busy brain, she told herself and closed her eyes, shutting off the other running commentaries long enough to focus. Yes. She'd parked in the alley out back so she could toss Stanley's garbage. She walked down the steep dirt driveway by the side of the building into the lot. Her car was there, but no garbage bags inside. The returnable bottles were scattered through the wayback. Had she left the bag open and the bottles spilled out? Did she throw the garbage away when she first got there? She looked in the Dumpster. Empty. Maybe she was the latest victim of the Redimere garbage-strewer. So why wasn't the garbage strewn? Even in the dark, lit only by her car's dome light, she could see that the pot-holed dirt parking lot was garbage-free. She felt that same chill that she'd felt in the trailer, but this time it didn't feel like she was making it up.

. . . . .

When she got home, she plugged the USB cord from her camera into her laptop and looked over the pictures she'd taken. She'd never been the world's best photographer, but had to get skilled at it fast, since she was the only one the *Watcher* had unless her friend Carol had some free time. Digital cameras should have made things easier, but they didn't—what they made up for in convenience, they lost in richness and clarity. Tonight was no exception. She'd had the settings wrong and the pictures were too dark to use. Bernie was about to click the file off in disgust when she caught something in one of the photos that had caught the far off edge of the bog. She zoomed in, but it became pixilated. It was impossible to tell, but it looked like a person. Couldn't say if it was a man or a woman, or standing or sitting. To be honest, she really couldn't say for sure if it really was a person, but it had a little oval of pinkish white where a face would be and something dark, possibly a body, or something bigger, beneath. Bernie zoomed in and out, but it didn't help. She was making herself crazy. She turned off the computer.

She made herself some rigatoni and sat down to eat, taking Stanley's Audubon book out of her bag. When she leafed through, the book fell open to the back, just like the Lee Child novel had. This one had a neatly penciled list, turned to so often the binding was cracked. Letters and numbers, no words. Maybe a birder's code? If it were her, she'd just write down "great blue heron" or whatever.

She put down the book and scraped the sauce off her empty plate with a piece of bread. She usually enjoyed her food, but the Stanley questions distracted her. It had been a long day and she was tired and getting buzzy. That's what she'd called it for as long as she could remember. Buzzy. Totally different from the story-chasing buzz. This one was more like a million bees swarming in her head, dozens of thoughts racing at the same time, jostling for position so it was hard to grab one and hang on, backed by growing, unspecified anxiety. When she couldn't tell if she was making stuff up just to feel some excitement—Was it really a hit and run? Do the numbers in the book mean more than great blue heron?—or if she was onto something. All perspective gone. That stupid song kept playing in her head. "Plow hit him in the head head HEAD." Had anyone even said that? She couldn't remember. And how does a plow hit someone in the head, anyway? Someone had been watching her, sneaking around the trailer? Maybe. Someone took the garbage bags out of the back of her car. Definitely. That book with the turned down pages kept sneaking in. What if that meant something, too? The guy in the book mailed something to his P.O. box. Stanley had a P.O. box. What if he mailed himself something? But what? And why? Maybe nothing. But through all the buzz, one thought kept coming back: it was goddam *something*.

CHAPTER 3

Friday morning, the day after Stanley's body was found, was overcast and cold. Bernie took a deep breath as she stepped out into the dawn, the sun just beginning to peek over the trees, and the cold air seared her throat. Most mornings, towering Mount Abram, fat and round Mount Wesserunsett and stubby little Patten Mountain usually greeted her, glowing in the reflected sunrise against a backdrop of the bigger, darker western mountains. Not today. The forecast was for several inches of snow by nightfall.

Bernie had a friend, a fellow New Englander, who'd lived in northern California for a year. She said the days were beautiful and unchanging, each one like the day before. "And you know what?" she said to Bernie with wonder. "No one ever talked about the weather."

In New England, the weather was like the grown son living in the basement. Sometimes you loved him, sometimes you hated him, but he was always there, going through the refrigerator, watching TV with the volume up at three in the morning. Can't move around the house without tripping over his stuff. Can't get dressed, can't plan the day, can't go on a trip, without consulting a forecast. "Hot enough for ya?" "Cold enough?" "Whadaya think it's gonna do tomorrow?" "How 'bout this rain-wind-snow-fog-heat-sun-whatever?"

Bernie could smell the storm coming, sharp and wet. In December a coming snowfall makes everyone giddy with anticipation. By March it's a disappointment.

She walked down her narrow street, lined with old capes and bungalows and one or two impressive Victorians. Rounding the bend where the hill got steep, she could see downtown below her in all its brick and sagging clapboard glory. She had to admit that despite her frequent funk about her job, she was still happy to be back in unmanicured, unadorned Maine, with her back against the edge of the country, keeping an eye on the rest of the lower forty-eight from this distant corner. There were times she worried if she thought too much about how she ended up here or the crazy responsibility of having her own newspaper with no safety net, she'd just go spiraling out of control, so she tried to focus on the tasks at hand. That wasn't easy this morning. She'd lain awake most of the night, going over her Stanley questions, coming up with no answers. Was it a big story? Or was she playing a game, distracting herself so she wouldn't worry about payrolls and advertising? Was she worrying too much about worrying? Plow hit him in the head, head, HEAD. She knew she needed to tell herself Stanley's death was as good a story as she believed, chase it, and not question it too much before the creeping anxiety she'd felt last night formed into the paralyzing and dreaded anxiety spiral.

"Hi dear," Annette chirped from behind her counter as Bernie walked into the office. "Storm's coming."

"Morning," Bernie said. She took off her coat and headed for the coffee pot. When she'd taken over the *Peaks Weekly Watcher*, she'd inherited the staff. She was glad they all knew what they were doing, the front line on circulation, selling ads and anything else to do with business. Annette, Shirley, Paul, and Guy kept the balls in the air. Still, after two years, other than with Guy, she felt like the butting-in stranger who didn't know the language and customs.

"Leave me some room between the ads, Shirley," Bernie said, booting up her computer. "Between Stanley and town meeting, we've got plenty of news."

Shirley gave a thin smile without looking up from her computer.

"Too bad about Stanley," Annette said. She didn't look at Bernie either, but her voice had an edge and Bernie knew the comment was a holdover from a few months back, when Cal Littlefield, the former police chief, burned his house down with himself in it. It was tragic, but it was a story and Bernie covered the hell out of it, much to the discomfort of the staff. It was a big reminder though, that little-town journalism was more nuanced than big-town journalism. She knew sometimes she just ought to shut her pie hole and keep her thoughts on the quality of the story to herself.

"Yeah, too bad about Stanley," Guy said. He winked at Bernie, waggling the unlit cigarette clamped between his lips, then looked back down at his keyboard. Bernie knew he was on her side, but, as he'd said to her during the Cal fiasco, "I gotta work with these folks."

"Definitely too bad," Bernie said, sitting down at her desk. The office's pleasant working hum picked up again—Annette on the phone, the click of keyboards, the classic pop of WMTN (A mountain of music for you!).

She felt at home in a newsroom, even the tiny *Watcher*'s. Aside from the lack of a blue cigarette haze and new computers, it was the same as when she first worked in it twenty years before, including Guy. He made her smile the same way the teetering stacks of old newspapers did, the mismatched, battered file cabinets, the wooden desks and chairs. The papery, inky smell comforted her, almost every day bringing her back to the year she'd spent here fresh out of college, learning more than she had in the four expensive years that went before it. Any time she started feeling the floor slipping out from under her, she'd bang on one of the old IBM Selectrics back in the corner. The clatter of the keys and the ding as she threw back the carriage was her way-back machine, reminding her that all the things she'd thought about journalism as a fresh kid, and all the stuff she'd learned from Guy and her boss, Harry, were still true. It was up to her to get her shit together, and focus.

Even so, she missed the big city dailies where she'd spent the last couple of decades—the push-and-pull, the arguments, the black humor and the inappropriate jokes. The shared excitement when there was breaking news. Everyone wanted in when there was a big story—everyone shared that rush when it's big and it's yours, even if it's heartbreaking. Bernie had no patience for reporters' hand-wringing and platitudes about how tough some stories are to cover. The best of her colleagues at the daily got that it wasn't about them, that they could save their crying for later. Big stories were made to be covered, and they were the people to do it—a special band, a club, and regardless of the squabbling, they had each other's backs.

When she bought the *Peaks Weekly Watcher* from Harry, he told her a lot of things, but he never told her how lonely it was going to be.

She poured some more coffee and got to work.

Friday mornings were devoted to a little bit of newsgathering and a lot of administrative work. Bernie hated doing the stuff she couldn't pass off to the staff. It took a focus and attention to detail that she couldn't muster, particularly when she had something more interesting to think about. After a couple hours, she'd had enough.

She leaned back and put her feet up on her desk. The glass front of the office offered a great view of the Country Grocer and she enjoyed watching the show.

"Lots of bottled water coming out of there today," Annette said.

Bernie nodded. A storm staple—when the power went out, as it often did in Redimere, the well didn't work and you didn't have water. She'd learned that the hard way.

"There's the chief," Annette said.

Yes, there he was. Pete stood in front of the store talking to Bev Dulac. He threw his head back and laughed. What the hell could the crusty old postmistress have said that would make Robocop laugh? He had a great smile, his square face breaking into laugh lines and dimples. His eyes had a tilt that made him seem amused even when Bernie knew that he sure as hell wasn't. When he laughed, his eyes squeezed into half-moons. So different from yesterday.

A boss once told Bernie—she guessed it was supposed to be a criticism—that she didn't like any conversation that she wasn't a part of. Damn right she didn't.

"I'm going across the street for a sandwich. Anybody hungry? It's on me."

She caught Shirley and Annette exchange glances. She knew they suspected she had a thing for Pete.

After taking sandwich and drink orders from the crew—one truth for newsrooms everywhere is that no one turns down a free lunch—she threw on her coat and skipped out the door.

She was too late to horn in on the Pete and Bev confab. Bev was nowhere to be seen and Pete was coming out of the store with a sandwich-shaped brown paper bag.

She'd chalk one thing up for working in Redimere: there weren't any annoying levels of bureaucracy to navigate to get information. At her last paper, reporters had to find the approved officer of the day so he could read them a prepared press release and then say he didn't know more. In her last year, the police department had started blogging its information on its website. The stock response to reporters looking for crime information became "check the blog."

She thanked the newspaper gods that Pete Novotny didn't have a blog.

"Chief."

He smiled. A good sign. "Want to hear about the medical examiner's report?" he said.

"That was fast."

"We're going to get more details in a few weeks, but preliminary cause of death is blunt trauma to the head. He also had broken bones, consistent with being hit by a snowplow."

"Head?" Head, HEAD!

Pete nodded. "That's what I said."

Said said. Bernie shook the stupid song aside. "How does that happen with a plow?"

"I know. The first point of impact by a plow hit wouldn't normally be to the head. And it's to the back of the head at that. But if someone gets rolled around into a snowbank by a plow, there's a lot of damage, so it's hard to say. And the shape seems wrong."

"Wrong how specifically?"

Pete shrugged. "Can't say right now."

Okay. He wasn't going to elaborate. She'd back up then flank it from another angle. "Could he have still been alive and died in the snowbank? Suffocated?" A terrible thought that had just occurred to her.

"I don't know."

"So what happened? He was hit by the plow, then plowed in?"

Pete gave her his inscrutable straight-in-the-eye green-laser look that made her feel like he could read every bad thought in her head. She tried to nonchalantly gaze back, but it was hard. She stared at his nose, concentrating on a faint row of freckles. She felt Annette and Shirley across the street, watching through the window. Light snow had started falling. Her coat was unzipped and the cold had seeped in. She shivered. His coat was unzipped, too, but he looked totally comfortable. It annoyed the hell out of her.

It didn't seem like he was going to answer that question, either. So she'd try the other one again. "So what's with the injury to the head?"

He waited a beat and she felt the same frisson of irritation rise off him she'd felt at the scene the day before. "I don't know. I'm waiting for the full medical report."

"So what would that mean? If it's odd?"

"I don't know." He paused, irritation level ramping. She could feel it. "Can you keep that part to yourself? On the record, you can say head trauma appears initially to be the cause of death. The odd parts? Off the record."

Damn. That was going to be her lead. "I guess so." She hated it

25

when people tried to tell her what to print. But she wasn't going to argue with Pete. She hadn't known him for long, but knew to pick her battles. "What were you and Bev Dulac talking about?"

"This and that."

She had a plan for something she wanted to do with the key to Stanley's P.O. box, but it hinged on no one knowing for the time being that she had it. If he and Bev had been talking about the box, she hoped Pete wouldn't say, because then she'd have to tell him about the key and scuttle her plan. The angel on her shoulder said tell him about the key anyway, but the devil was as interested as she to know what was in the box. "You were laughing."

He smiled—not the face-cracking laugh Bev got, but it was much better than the mind-reading green-laser gaze.

"You're not the only funny gal in town."

"Bev's not a funny gal."

"Give her a chance," Pete was in a full-blown grin now, teasing her. His irritation seemed to have blown away in the cold wind.

Bernie wasn't going to give Bev a chance. Bev scared her a little—she acted like her role as postmistress gave her authority over all town actions, including Bernie's. Many conversations they had began with Bev saying, "Of course, you can do what you want, but Harry always…"

It made Bernie want to do the opposite just to prove Bev didn't have the upper hand.

"She did mention she doesn't know Stanley's cousin. He never got any mail from anyone in South Carolina. We were talking about making arrangements for a memorial service and burial."

"I'll put something in the paper if it's going to happen after next Thursday."

"Yeah, paperwork will take a few days. We'll get him buried at the VA cemetery in Augusta and have some kind of service here. All set? I have to go work on the budget." He was giving her the green laser stare again.

She felt the guilt about the post office box. Almost said something. Brushed it away. "Yep, thanks."

She watched Pete as he made his way down the street, blue police coat flapping in the wind, oblivious to the snow and cold and waited for the guilt to subside. As she went into the store, she thought how Harry would've beheaded her if she'd pulled a stunt—because that's what he'd call it—like she planned with the key. But Harry wasn't her boss, hadn't been for twenty years. She was the boss. Was she breaking the law? Yeah, maybe. Technically. But she was just going to look, not take anything. After all, no one else cared. And besides, she had the key. And Stanley was dead. She was just going to look.

CHAPTER 4

Pete leaned back, took off his reading glasses, and rubbed his eyes. No matter how much he went over the budget numbers, he still couldn't make them stretch. He understood the recession, understood why the budget couldn't go up. People were strapped. Every penny counted. Hell, half the folks in town didn't have enough heating oil to make it through the winter. But using out-of-date, broken equipment felt like an accident waiting to happen. It was his first town meeting, but he'd heard enough to know he was probably going to have to explain every cent in excruciating detail. After which, the department still wouldn't get the money it needed to replace the safety vests and failing radio. It's hard to explain, when the biggest crime of the year is the garbage strewer, that real safety equipment was necessary. Hard to explain that everyone thinks they're safe right up until they aren't. And then it's too late.

"Hey, Chief," Rusty appeared in the doorway.

"You're off tonight, right?" Pete asked.

"Just leaving."

"I need you to take a look at Stanley Weston's trailer tomorrow morning."

"What for?"

"Just to tie up the loose ends."

"It was a hit and run. Or he just passed out in the road and got plowed in."

Lazy bastard. The last thing he needed was the constant resistance he got from his two senior officers. Ray and Rusty, different as hell in looks and personality, but united when it came to being pains in the ass.

"Just covering the bases," he said, trying not to sound as irritated as he felt. "I'd do it myself, but I'm going to be up all night going over the budget. Ray and Jamie are going to be out straight with the snow tonight." Pete wondered why he was explaining himself. "A guy from the state crime lab will meet you there at eight."

Rusty nodded and shrugged. "Whatever."

"So you're going out tonight?"

"Yeah. Waterville. To that place my wife likes. She's not going to let the snow stop her, it's her anniversary."

"Yours, too, right?"

Rusty blushed. "Twenty-five years."

"Congrats. Drive safe."

Pete watched Rusty leave. He knew Rusty was probably right about Stanley's death being exactly what it looked like, but he couldn't shake the feeling he needed to do more. Maybe it was guilt that once Cal died, he should have made sure Stanley was taken care of. And then there was the head injury. It didn't seem right. It was a gut feeling. Hard to explain. He'd figure it out. It was the least he could do. Just as soon as the budget passed. He turned back to his computer.

. . . . .

By late afternoon the snow was falling steadily. Everyone in the newsroom had gone home early. Bernie had been itching for them to leave. She wanted to take a look at her contraband haul from Stanley's trailer.

Her visit to the post office had worked as planned. Well, kind of. She hadn't planned to actually take something. Bev always closed the counter between eleven-thirty and one for lunch, leaving the lobby empty; in fact, she'd been going home for lunch when Bernie saw her talking to Pete.

When Bernie dropped off the sandwiches in the office, then said, "Shoot, I forgot to go to the P.O.," no one even noticed. She quickly found Stanley's box—the number had been on his VA checks, after all—and opened it up. Sure enough, there were three envelopes from the VA. Bernie left them alone and took out the one odd piece of mail. It was a fat, grubby security envelope addressed to Stanley in pencil with no return address. Postmarked December 12.

When she'd formulated her plan, she'd wondered how she'd open whatever looked like it ought to be opened and then reseal it without it looking tampered. She knew Bev was way too nosy not to remember putting it in the box in the first place, and nosy enough to notice if it looked different. But Bernie was in luck: the envelope was old and the glue hadn't held. One flick of her finger, and it opened without a rip. Inside was a small notebook. Fingers trembling and heart pounding, one ear listening for the door, she opened it up. The pages had lists of dates, numbered. She needed time to look it over, figure it out.

The new plan was to look at it over the weekend—just borrow it—and put it back before Monday. But she couldn't take it and leave the envelope empty. If Bev looked, she'd notice. Conscious of the glass door that opened onto the passing sidewalk, sure it would open any second, she sifted through the trash, looking for something the same size as the notebook. But that wouldn't work. Too obvious if someone opened the envelope before she replaced the notebook. Why would he have scrap in an envelope? She sifted through her bag, full of tools of the trade, needed accessories and junk—aha!—her Dennis Kucinich autographed copy of the Constitution. He'd given it to her after she interviewed him before the New Hampshire primary a few years back. She wasn't special. He gave them away like candy. Just signed, not a personalized autograph. Same size, same basic heft as the notebook. If she didn't get the notebook back in time and someone opened the envelope, the Constitution would hopefully be written off as an eccentricity.

Now, alone in the office, she took the notebook out, the now-familiar guilt rising. Stanley was dead, no one cared what was in his mail. She'd told herself that over and over. If worse came to worst, she could give it to Pete and say she found it in the trailer.

The penciled notations made no more sense than they had in the post office. A numbered list of dates, some with an asterisk. But no key to what the asterisk meant. Staring at it didn't help. Bernie put it in her bag and threw on her coat.

As she locked the door, a car screeched past in the snow, fishtailed around the corner, and turned up School Street. The town's police cruiser pursued with lights flashing. Another chapter in the Ray Morin and Dragon Dube saga.

Bernie wished she had her camera with her, but she'd left it at home. One of these days the feud was going to erupt into violence and she wanted to be prepared.

Dragon's Dodge Neon was having a hard time getting up the snow-covered hill. Ray caught up and pulled in front of Dragon, blocking him.

They weren't very far from Bernie, just about twenty yards up the hill, but dusk was falling and with the snow she could only see silhouettes in the cars. Neither got out. As she got closer, she saw Ray was on his radio. Calling Pete, no doubt. After a particularly nasty confrontation a couple years ago, Cal convinced Dragon to leave town. When Cal retired, Dragon came back. Pete got Ray to agree that whenever he pulled Dragon over, he would call for backup.

There was no sign of movement from Dragon's car, just the orange glow of a cigarette.

They were waiting. Bernie waited too.

After a few minutes, Jamie Paradis' pickup truck came down the hill. Dragon rolled down his window and threw the cigarette out in the snow. "I want the chief, not some kid half-cop," he yelled.

"The chief's busy. And I'm a full cop, just like Ray. I just work part-time." Jamie gave his usual calm smile. Same age as Dragon and he never lost his cool. Bernie couldn't figure out if he had nerves of steel or was just too young to know any better.

Ray got out of the cruiser. "He pulled out of the Pour House at about seventy. I had to chase him all the way here before he stopped. Wouldn't have stopped either, if it weren't for the hill. I'm going to have him blow a Breathalyzer and bring him in."

"The hell you are," Dragon yelled. "I ain't getting out of this car. I had one beer on my way home from work."

"Now Double D," Jamie said, using Dragon's high school nickname, "if you're okay, the Breathalyzer won't make a difference. Then we can all go home."

"It's the principle," Dragon said, staring straight ahead.

Ray started to say something, but Jamie put out his hand to stop him. "C'mon D, the press is here," he said, gesturing at Bernie. "We don't want a scene."

"I welcome the press, man," Dragon said.

Bundled in her parka, with snow piling up on her ski hat, Bernie didn't think she looked very imposing. She shrugged, hoping the attention would focus somewhere else.

"You gotta write about what a Nazi this guy is." Dragon gestured toward Ray. "This is a fucking police state."

"That's crap," Ray said.

Jamie took the Breathalyzer from Ray's hand. "Just blow it."

Dragon gave Jamie a meaningful stare. Jamie smiled back, still holding out the Breathalyzer. "I ain't got nothing to hide," Dragon said, and blew it.

Jamie looked. "He's okay, Ray. Let's go home."

Ray looked at the Breathalyzer, his face reddening. "He was still driving erratically."

"It's snowing and he's got crap tires," Jamie said. Then turned to Dragon. "Hey, D, you're going to drive like a little old lady all the way home, aren't you?"

"I can go?" Dragon asked.

"Better, before I change my mind." Jamie put his hand on Ray's arm.

Dragon backed away from the cruiser and fishtailed back down the hill.

Ray yanked his arm away from Jamie. "What the hell? I don't need a kid like you—"

"We don't need that kind of trouble tonight, you know that. Chief called me up and wants me on, too, with the snow. Accident patrol," Jamie said. "Anyway, the press was watching." He winked at Bernie.

"Nothing to write about," she said. The Ray-Dragon feud wasn't going to be news until something bad happened.

"That's good," Jamie said. "See Ray? All good. I'm going back home to dinner. I've got to come on in an hour. You okay?"

Ray looked at him, then at Bernie. Without saying anything he got in the cruiser and slammed the door for an answer.

"You need a ride up the hill?" Jamie asked Bernie.

"No, thanks. I need the exercise."

"Okay, have a good night. Be careful in the snow," he said, getting into his pickup. Bernie watched him watch Ray's cruiser disappear down the hill and turn in the opposite direction from where Dragon had gone. Then Jamie roared back up the hill and was gone, too.

Bernie felt sorry for Ray. He never seemed to hit the right note with people. She had some empathy for that. When she first came to town, she used to get him and Rusty mixed up because their names were similar. That didn't last long. They were far too different. Rusty was Goofy, Ray was Charlie Brown. He even looked like him.

Night had fallen fast. Aside from two blocks downtown, there were no sidewalks or curbs in Redimere. Between the darkness and the snow it was hard to see where the side of the road was. Bernie wondered if this was what it was like when Stanley took his final walk home months earlier. The night was quiet, muffled by snow. The only sound was a plow in the distance somewhere, beeping as it backed up. She gave a shiver and hurried toward home.

CHAPTER 5

"Someone hit him on the head or something, and left him there," Bernie said. "Someone was watching me yesterday. Maybe. Someone took the friggin' garbage bags from my car."

Bernie was sitting at the scarred wooden table in Carol's kitchen. They were working on their second bottle of wine and what was left of the pie they'd had for dessert. Bernie made it a point to have dinner at Carol's often, ever since that first week in Redimere, when Carol stopped in the office to introduce herself, took one look at Bernie, exhausted from learning the job and feeling like she'd just landed on Mars and said, "You need a home-cooked meal." Carol's kitchen was the closest thing Bernie had to her large family—the good parts, not the aggravating wish I were an only child parts.

Carol was one of the few in town who knew the whole story about how Bernie had been fired and how Harry convinced her to come back to Redimere. Back home where you belong, as Carol put it, even though Bernie would always interject "I'm from Augusta." Carol was as warm as her house. But not very warm to Bernie's wine-fueled Stanley Weston foul play theory.

"Just because Pete Novotny made a remark about the head injury being odd, doesn't mean it wasn't caused by an accident,"

Carol said. "He was a homicide cop in Philly. How many accident scenes has he ever been to? How many people get hit by plows in Philly?"

"He seemed to know what he was talking about," Bernie said. He'd looked so intense, Bernie had no doubt he knew what he was talking about.

"For a prize-winning investigative journalist, you are very easily charmed. Don't let a crush cloud your judgment. Anyway, you're not even his type. Isn't he supposed to be dating some lawyer from Portland?"

"Supposedly," Bernie said. "I'm sure she's everything I'm not. I heard she's young, tall, blond and thin."

"You're not fat."

"I'm not thin." Bernie stuffed a piece of pumpkin pie in her mouth. Point made. "Anyway, it's not a crush. He's just, I don't know, interesting. I'm not trying to lasso him. If nothing else, it would cause serious ethical problems."

"Right." Carol gave a little snort into her wine.

Carol's husband, Vince, clomped into the kitchen with a load of wood in his arms, smelling like the barn, wood smoke and the cold night. "What guy wouldn't be nuts about you? You're a Botticelli angel. I curse the fact that I'm married every time I see you."

"Ha." Bernie wasn't in the mood for teasing. "What do you think about Stanley?"

"Everyone's saying that Don Littlefield probably got him with the plow," Vince said, shaking snow off the end of his long gray ponytail before helping himself to a glass of wine. "Don wouldn't even know he hit anything. That plow's a Sherman tank. So what's suspicious?"

"Circumstances," Bernie said. "I just have a feeling. Things seem off."

"This is Redimere. When are things ever on? Like someone ran him down on purpose?"

"I haven't figured it out that far."

"Why don't you talk to Bev? Her and Stanley were tight. Maybe she has some off feelings, too."

Bernie felt a clutch of anxiety at the mention of Bev. She hadn't told Carol about the notebook, the P.O. box. They were becoming the goddam tell-tale heart.

"He's quite a gardener. Was," Vince said. "He even talked to me about sitting in on my class at the college. The sustainable gardening one. So she and him were always trading compost secrets and whatnot."

"Boy, he got around," Bernie said. "Talking gardening with Bev, monitoring classes at Redimere College."

"Smoking dope with Dragon Dube," Vince said.

Carol and Bernie looked at him.

"You didn't know? Dragon used to go over to his trailer and they'd get high."

"That would explain the roaches in Stanley's ashtray," Bernie said. "You know this because?"

"D did a little work for me around here." He turned to Carol. "When I needed help with the chicken coop? People tell me things."

"Bernie thinks someone was watching her when she was over at the trailer yesterday," Carol said. "She thinks someone took his garbage from her car."

"They didn't necessarily know it was garbage."

"That's right," Carol smiled at Vince. "Bernie the spy thinks Stanley was part of a secret conspiracy. Now the bad guys are after her."

"You're making me sound silly."

"Isn't it a little silly? C'mon."

"When I was out at the trailer it didn't seem like it. Someone was outside. Garbage or not, someone took stuff from my car."

Carol sighed. "It was probably the garbage-strewer. Don't go getting all paranoid. Someone was hunting in the bog, saw you at Stanley's and was nosy. Anyway, couldn't some of this be, you know," she trailed off.

Bernie felt herself grow hot. "My ADHD? It doesn't make me hallucinate. I'm not a crazy person."

"I know, but you want some excitement, or you get an idea in your head and sometimes you get fixated —"

"Focused. I hyperfocus. Fixated makes it sound like I'm crazy."

Carol held up her hand. "Okay. Sorry, sorry. Don't get worked up. But I think you need to look at this from angles that are believable, too."

"What about the garbage?" She wanted to add "and he mailed himself a notebook" but she didn't.

"Sometimes a cigar is just a cigar. Who knows how long he's been dead? Why would this mysterious person suddenly be interested in his stuff now?"

"Because they didn't know he was dead until yesterday."

"Okay, then they didn't kill him. Or whatever you think happened."

Carol refilled their wine glasses and the trio mulled that over for a minute.

"He was missing for months, maybe, and no one even knew. How sad is that?" Vince said. "He was dead all this time, right under our noses. All these people who were his friends, but nobody noticed."

"Someone did," Bernie said.

Carol smiled tolerantly and raised her eyebrows. "Who?"

Bernie raised her eyebrows right back. She was being stubborn, but she didn't care. "The guy who killed him."

. . . . .

Bernie woke up before the alarm the next morning with a slight hangover. She and Carol and Vince had sat around the old farmhouse kitchen for hours, drinking wine and debating. They hadn't reached any conclusions. Driving home on the snow-covered country road, Bernie had tried to sort things out, but just felt more confused. It irritated her that Carol had brought up the ADHD. Like getting fired, it was something she'd just as soon not discuss.

She had a long day ahead and she wasn't looking forward to it.

She took medication for ADHD, but it only lasted eight to ten hours. It was great while it lasted, dimming the irritation, the racing thoughts and lack of focus. Sometimes it slowed her brain down enough that it took her head a while to catch up with a thought or a word, but it was worth it. The problem came when it wore off. The doctor called it rebound. Bernie called it re-entry. Like when a rocket re-enters the atmosphere, all fire and turbulence. ADHD on steroids. For about an hour her mind raced and danced and patience and focus were just pleasant memories. On some really fun nights, she'd get heartburn, a headache, blurry vision, hot flashes. On long days like this, with town meeting ahead of her, the question always was, when do I take the pill? She could take it now and hope it wouldn't wear off before she was done working, when re-entry would make finishing the job a huge pain in the ass. Or she could take it later and be bitchy and irritable for the next few hours.

Whenever she took it, it always took a lot of coffee and some time to herself before she could gear up to deal with people.

She pushed aside the curtain and looked out the window. The snow was already melting even though the sun wasn't up yet. The power hadn't gone out either. Maybe that would be the last of winter until fall.

She decided on the no-pill-until-later option. She put the coffee on. If she was going to sit through a day of earnest townsfolk wrangling over whether or not to spend $1,200 on a copier for the clerk's office, she was going to need a lot of coffee.

Her three cats were curled up on the couch in front of the pellet stove, not a worry in the world.

"What's the secret, guys?" she asked. No answer, just a steady triple purr. Typical.

Her coffee and newspaper reverie was interrupted a few minutes later by a knock at the door. The cats jumped and tumbled down the hall, one big ball of fur.

Bernie looked at the clock: six-thirty. Way too early for the morning bitch to have visitors.

Pete Novotny.

"Hey," she said, pretending she was as at ease in her sweat pants, T-shirt and sweater as he was in his running gear. His running glow—flushed face, short brown hair curly with sweat—made her feel woolly and gray.

"I was just finishing my run and thought I'd stop by."

"Huh," Bernie said. Pete never "stopped by." His predecessor, Cal, did once in a while. That's the way people did business in Redimere. More happened in casual conversation than in the meeting rooms. But it didn't seem like Pete's style. And six-thirty in the morning sure wasn't her style.

"Come on in and have a cup of coffee."

"Sounds good." He stepped in, looking around her small kitchen and living area. He wasn't a big guy, a little more than half a foot taller than Bernie, but her bungalow shrunk with him in it.

"I'd give you the tour, but you just had it," she said, turning her attention to the coffee.

"Cozy. Nice."

"I'm sure you didn't come over just to say hi." More small talk was beyond her. "Do you take anything?"

"Black's good."

Of course.

He prowled the living area, touching books and knick-knacks. He lit on a picture of Bernie and her siblings.

"Is this you?" he asked. They were lined up, eight in a row, in order of age. His finger was on twelve-year-old Bernie, third from the top, beaming out at the world, one braid coming undone, her sweater—complete with quarter-sized hole near the collar—buttoned crooked.

She handed him the coffee. "Yeah. I'm not hard to pick out. Just find the biggest slob."

"It's cute."

"It's a family joke. My mom had to work, she was a second-shift clerk at LaVerdiere's drug store, so she had my dad take us for the picture. When the prints came back, she yelled at my dad, 'What's wrong with you? You know you have to clean Bernadette up!' Thirty years later, my brothers and sisters still say, 'Don't forget to clean Bernie up!'" She shrugged, embarrassed.

Pete smiled. "Big family," he said, putting down the picture.

"And everything it's cracked up to be. You?"

"One brother. I heard there was a little incident up the hill last night."

Bernie wanted to hear about Pete's family, but he obviously wasn't going to offer. "Ray and Dragon? Not newsworthy. Is that why you're here?"

He took his mug of coffee over to the couch, sat down and took a big sip. He looked up at her as she leaned against the counter. "I was up all night with the budget and riding herd over the snowstorm fender-benders. Haven't talked to Ray yet. Jamie told me." He turned his attention back to his coffee.

"And?" Bernie asked. If this was going to go on much longer, she was going to need another pot.

"Glad you're not putting anything in the paper."

"Despite appearances, I'm not some buzzard that feeds on the petty personality clashes of this town. I have better things to write about."

Pete cocked his head, eyes crinkling and dimples showing. "That's not what I meant."

"Sorry. I'm not a morning person."

They both sipped in silence.

"It's funny though," Bernie said after a minute. "It's one of those things in town where everyone knows the whole story, talks about it. It's a thing. But it's not news. Not yet, anyway."

"Not ever, I hope. I don't want anyone to get hurt. My guy or the kid. By each other, or by you."

"It could hurt me, too," she said. She knew she sounded defensive again. "I'm not from this town. A story on something like this by an outsider could rub people the wrong way. Unless something newsworthy happens, I'm keeping my distance."

Pete nodded. "At least you grew up in Maine. I'm from Wisconsin by way of Philadelphia. Might as well be from outer

40

space."

Bernie nodded. "I guess it's no secret to you that Ray thought he was going to be chief when Cal retired. With the force for more than twenty years, then suddenly a guy from away gets the job."

Her remark got no reaction, so she kept going. "I never bought the official line that the town needed a fresh perspective. Towns like Redimere don't like change, and they don't seek it. But Cal really pushed for you, and the selectmen agreed. Like Cal had some issue with Ray."

Pete still didn't react. She wondered if she'd offended him, and again she wished she'd just shut up. She knew she talked too much, especially when she hadn't taken her pill. "Ray's a good cop, just kind of uptight."

"He *is* a good cop," Pete said. "Kind of lacks the shades of gray you need in the job sometimes, but he's by the book."

"He thinks you take it too easy on Dragon."

"I saw some really bad kids in Philly. Dragon isn't a bad kid." He drained his coffee and brought the mug over to the sink and rinsed it out.

He turned around and leaned back against the sink facing Bernie, pinning her with the green laser glare.

Here we go, Bernie thought, the real reason he's here. Nice touch rinsing out the cup. Soften me up, then lower the hammer. She was still propped against the counter. They were squared off like two gunfighters. Only in sweats and all she was armed with was a coffee cup. Okay sheriff, draw.

"I hear you were over at Stanley's trailer, going through his stuff," he said. Ouch, right between the eyes. He didn't seem angry, but it was hard to tell. Stupid small town news traveling fast. His eyes held hers as she tried to figure out whether to be contrite or blustery. She opted for something in between.

"Loren Daggett wanted the stuff out of there. I told him I'd help out. It's not like it's a crime scene, right?" She felt an anxious spasm. The notebook was on the coffee table among her magazines, books and newspapers. He couldn't have seen it, wouldn't know what it was. Still, she tried not to look over there. She should tell him though. Now would be a good time.

They had a staring contest for a minute.

"Find anything?" Pete finally asked.

Ha, sheriff, I win. Bernie mentally blew smoke off the barrel of her gun. "Socks. Paperbacks. Bottles and cans. Oh, and this." She reached over and picked the key off the counter. "Key to his post office box, I think. Looks like." It was an impulse and she wasn't sure why she did it. But why not at least give the impression of honesty? She felt a guilty blush start up her neck.

"You know, police like to have the first shot going over a guy's place when he's been the victim of unnatural death," he said, looking at the key and putting it in his windbreaker pocket. His breezy conversational tone didn't fool Bernie. The duel wasn't over after all.

The edge of the counter against her back was uncomfortable, but shifting position would give him a psychological advantage. "Even if there is anything funny about his death, like how you said the head injury was odd?" she said. "I didn't find anything there out of place. I just looked around and cleared up his belongings. Odds and ends. No one could find the cousin. It's not like he has any other family. I thought it was okay. I mean, you obviously can have it if you want it. It's at my office." She paused. "I did give you the key."

He smiled. Halfway, kind of.

She just realized since she'd given it back, she wasn't going to be able to return the notebook to the post office. She felt her neck get hot, followed by her face. Her words tumbled out as she tried to cover up. "I had some bags of garbage in my car, I was going to throw them in the Dumpster, but someone took them."

"Took them?"

"Yeah, from my car. It was parked behind the paper."

"You didn't report it?"

"It was garbage. I thought maybe it was the garbage strewer. The car wasn't locked. I'm going to report bags of garbage missing?"

He studied the floor for a minute then pushed himself away from the sink. "I guess the garbage is gone, unless it turns up somewhere. Strewn." He gave the halfway smile again. "Thanks for the key, but Bev already gave me the things in his P.O. yesterday after she locked up. I've got Rusty going down to the trailer this morning. A crime unit from state is going to help out."

He trained those green lasers on her, smile gone. "You're right, it's not a crime scene. But someone's dead, and it was none of your business."

Her cheeks burned. She was always amazed at how fast a pleasant conversation could deteriorate. She'd already wrecked her plan to put the notebook back. Now that she hadn't told him about it, her plan B, to say she found it in the trailer, was also trashed.

Pete walked to the door. "Guess everyone feels bad about not paying more attention about Stanley. Bev said she was beginning to wonder if she should do something about the VA checks in his box. She thought he went South, too. She figured he forgot to have them forwarded. But she didn't think it was her place."

Bernie felt her face burn hotter. She had to stop thinking he could read her mind.

"Thanks for the coffee. See you at town meeting." He turned as he opened the door. "Try to stay out of trouble."

. . . . .

Pete left Bernie's and jogged down the hill. Stopping by Bernie's wasn't planned—he was running by and saw the lights on. He'd been chewing over her trip to the trailer in between chewing over the problem of Ray and Dragon. He didn't like it when things were off. Kind of like wrinkles in the rug. He wanted to smooth them out. Ray and Dragon was one wrinkle. Stanley, another. Then Bernie nosed around where she shouldn't have. Three wrinkles. That garbage thing didn't make sense. Four wrinkles. Way too many.

He liked reporters. They were like cops. Bernie also reminded him of his ex-wife, Karen, who was without bullshit, smart as hell and could always laugh no matter how bad things were. Even when he was laying down the law about the trailer to Bernie a few minutes before, those giant brown eyes were laughing. It was easy to pick her out of that photo—the sloppiness had nothing to do with it. She popped right out of the frame, grinning out at a world that she seemed sure was happy to have her there, full of energy and ready to go. He felt like maybe she was someone he could talk to. Two strangers in a strange land. He liked Redimere, but he'd been out of sorts since he'd arrived and discovered Cal's good-buddy friendliness didn't extend to being a confidante. Cal had been a friend before Pete moved here, but avoided him after he arrived. He'd talk to Pete about department stuff, but it seemed like he didn't care anymore. Then came the fire and Cal died, so Pete didn't even have that connection. When he stopped by Bernie's this morning his plan had been to ask her about Ray and Dragon, and the trailer, too. But also to see if she had any insight on the Stanley thing, an off the record conversation with someone who maybe thought the same way he did. But that got derailed somehow.

He turned the corner toward home, picking up his pace to a full-on run until he stopped at the front steps, out of breath and covered in sweat. He took a few deep breaths before going up the stairs to his second-floor apartment. She'd derailed him all right. There was something she wasn't telling him. He knew she was too much of a straight arrow for it to be anything serious, but it was another wrinkle in the rug.

He hoped it didn't screw things up before he figured out what it was.

Chapter 6

The conversation with Pete left Bernie unsettled. At her last paper, she would have laughed at a cop's disapproval, but Pete was different. She knew sooner or later she'd piss him off and they wouldn't be friends anymore. It had happened to her often enough that she was braced for it. She never pleaded with anyone, "Give me a break! My brain is firing dopamine like a Gatling gun on steroids. It's the ADHD, not me." Never. She was who she was, no matter what the reason. It was a non-starter to tell people anyway. She got used to a certain look when she mentioned it—the listener's gaze would freeze into "I'm feigning interest but hoping you'll stop talking about this." Sometimes she could see condescension mixed in. Once she learned she could expect that look, she was careful who she told. The last person in the world she wanted to get it from was Pete. Let him think she was obnoxious all on her own.

The walk down the hill in the chilly morning air perked her up. She could only spend so much time beating herself up before she got tired of it. The sun was coming up and the street was wet with melting snow. Why did the air always smell so good this time of morning? It tasted fresh and full of a new day. The steamed-up windows of the old clapboard building that housed Choppy's promised warmth, good food, and day-after-a-storm bonhomie. The restaurant was packed, the post-snowstorm bustle in full swing, everyone relieved the storm had been quick, not as bad as forecast, and most of all, that the power hadn't gone out. The smell of bacon and coffee mixing with the wet wool of hats and gloves made her almost giddy.

She was attacking some scrambled eggs when Dragon sat down next to her.

"Hey, news lady," he said with a grin. Dragon could be a pain in the butt, but Bernie knew a lot of it was bluster. In her persona as small town newspaper owner-editor she tried to be friendly to everyone. Some of the folks made it pretty damn hard, but Dragon was easy, and right now he was smiling at her like a kid. "That was a scene last night, huh?"

"Good morning, Dragon. You're up bright and early." She couldn't help but smile back.

"I was plowing all night." Dragon worked for a landscaping company part of the year, and then plowed when everything that could be landscaped was under snow. "It's melting anyway, seems kind of pointless."

He ordered coffee and blueberry pancakes. "Anyhow, I'm getting out. I'm gonna buy an ice cream truck. We don't have one in town. I think I can make a lot of money. I'm tired of digging in the dirt and staying up all night plowing. I want to be my own boss."

Bernie must have looked as dubious as she felt.

"I'm serious, Ms. O'Dea. It's going to be a going concern."

"Well, good luck with that," she said, trying to cover up her grin with a sip of coffee.

"My brother said I can come to work for his insurance company. But, man, I'm no suit and tie guy, you know? But I gotta do something new."

"I feel you," Bernie said. "I'm no suit and tie guy, either." She raised her coffee mug in a toast and they clinked cups.

"Anyway," he said, leaning close and keeping his voice low, "I wanted to talk to you about something. I was serious when I said you should do a story about Ray Morin. That guy is no good and you need to do an investigative story."

Ah, the burden of the journalist. It didn't matter if you worked for the *New York Times* or the *Watcher*. Everyone had a story you should do. Once in a while there was something there, but most of the time no one would give a damn.

"You know, I think Ray's a pretty good cop, he's just got a thing about you."

"Well, doesn't that make him a bad cop? Aren't cops supposed to be objective?"

Bernie laughed. "I don't know about that."

"I know you know there's bad cops. He's one of them. There's just nobody here to call him on it. That started with the last chief. He didn't care what Ray did. Or any of the other cops, for that matter. You should know that there's some things —"

The door of the diner swung open and Ray himself, in street clothes, walked in. He gave Dragon a look of disgust and sat down at the other end of the counter.

"Hey, Ray, did you hear Dragon's buying an ice cream truck?" asked Debbie Mitchell, Choppy herself, as she turned over some pancakes on the grill. She winked at Bernie. She was a big woman who liked to laugh and loved to tease. Guys like Ray with no sense of humor were her favorite targets.

Ray snorted. "Yeah, it won't be ice cream he'll be selling from that," he said, miming someone smoking a joint.

"Hey, man, I don't have to listen to that shit," said Dragon.

"Settle down," Debbie said as she put his pancakes down in front of him. "Eat your pancakes." Debbie was as tough as ten miles of Maine road in March. She was legendary for the time a trucker took a look at all two hundred-fifty pounds of her standing under her "Proud to be a Passamaquoddy" bumper sticker behind the counter and said, "Feeding you pretty good since they let you off the reservation, huh?" He ended up wearing a pot of coffee. Cal, police chief at the time, was in the diner and saw the whole thing. When the trucker tried to press charges, Cal said, "The girl tripped and spilled the coffee. It was an accident."

When Debbie talked, people listened. Dragon was no exception. He took a bite of his pancakes.

"So you were friends with Stanley Weston?" Bernie asked Dragon.

"I guess." He didn't take his eyes off his plate, his long hair flopping forward, so Bernie couldn't see his face. She wanted to see his expression, get the information she could from it.

"Did you see him this winter?"

Dragon shrugged. "Nah. He was going to his cousin's. At least that's what I heard. Didn't see him after the snow started. I used to give him a ride home if I saw him walking, stay and visit a bit. Wish I had seen him whatever night he got hit, maybe he'd still be alive." He glanced at Ray, who was making a point of not looking at their end of the counter. Dragon pushed back his hair and looked meaningfully at Bernie, adding quietly, "On the other hand, maybe it just would have happened on a different night."

"What do you mean?"

He shook his head.

"I'm trying to figure out if anyone knows what happened," she said.

"Good luck." He attacked his pancakes.

Bernie waited, hoping he'd say more. "C'mon, you can tell me," she said when she realized he was done talking.

"Nothing to say."

It pissed her off when people reeled out a tidbit of information, then pulled it back. Sometimes it was a power trip, sometimes it was a test. Sometimes they wanted to talk but were afraid. She'd have to try to figure out where Dragon was coming from, but until then, she knew when to give up.

"So what do you know about owning an ice cream truck?"

He shrugged, his attention still on Ray. "What's to know? You buy the ice cream wholesale, you drive around town with the music—you know 'Turkey in the Straw'—"

"I like the theme to 'The Sting' better," Bernie said.

"Yeah." He grinned. "Anyway, then you sell the ice cream. It can't lose. A guy I know in Bangor knows someone who's selling a truck. It's sweet—a 1983 Chevy, bright green, with all the equipment included."

"So you do that for a couple months out of the year, then what do you do?"

"I've got some other irons in the fire. A pretty big iron." He glanced over at Ray again, then drained his coffee and got up from his stool. "Hey, remember what I said." He inclined his head toward the other end of the counter. She wanted to tell him he never finished his thought on that, but she could feel Ray's eyes on them.

After Dragon left, the cop looked down the counter at her. "I don't know what line of bullshit that kid's feeding you, but don't believe a word he says."

"Don't worry, Ray, I didn't fall off the turnip truck yesterday."

He snorted and went back to his coffee.

"Morning, Debbie baby." Rusty Dyer had come in while they were talking. He put his police hat on the counter and sat on the stool Dragon left empty.

"You're starting early today," Debbie said, handing him a mug of coffee.

"Boy, that tastes good, especially when it's free," he said, winking at her. Then to Bernie, "One of the perks of the job. Get it? Perk?" He waited for Bernie to react. She gave a pretend smile.

Back to Debbie, he said, "Yeah, doing another double shift. Did one Thursday, with Stanley and whatnot. Now I'm doing one today. I'm heading over to Stanley's trailer. Guy from the state crime lab is meeting me there. We're going to check things out. I mean, who knows how Stanley really died, right? Big mystery."

"So do you think it was more than a hit and run?" Bernie asked, pretending she didn't notice his sarcasm.

"I think a drunk walking home in a snowstorm got hit by some poor son of a bitch who just didn't see him. And I think our chief's been watching too much CSI or something." He gave Bernie a big toothy smile. "I hear your prints are going to be there. Hope you don't become a suspect." He winked again.

Bernie wasn't a big fan of people who wink all the time. Not that she was going to answer him anyway, but he was already scanning the counter, looking, she assumed, for someone more interesting to talk to.

"There's my fellow crime stopper," he crowed at Ray. "How'd shift go last night?"

Bernie could see Ray's scalp turn red under his thinning hair. He pushed his glasses up his nose and didn't say anything.

"Ray worked the night shift for me last night," Rusty said to Debbie. "I had to take that cousin of yours out for our anniversary."

Debbie rolled her eyes. "Heard she might finally divorce you over that stupid truck. She don't know how you're going to pay for it."

"Work double shifts." His grin had lost some of its luster. Then he turned to Ray, "Heard you mixed it up with the kid again."

Ray ignored him.

"Why isn't the chief going to the trailer?" Bernie asked Rusty, who'd finished his coffee and was heading toward the door.

"He's gotta be at town meeting. Anyway, he probably knows what a waste of time it is. Leave it for the little guy. Don't see why the trailer matters. Think we'd have better things to do in this town."

. . . . .

Bernie walked into an empty newsroom. As much as she enjoyed the bluster, she also liked it when she was there by herself. She kept the lights low and could get some work done without distractions. The calm before the storm. Not that she wouldn't trade the quiet for more of a news staff. When she got out of college, a reporting job on a weekly newspaper was considered a good gig and she was thrilled to be on the *Watcher*'s small staff. Now in what very well could be the dying days of newspapers, kids didn't want to work for them and they didn't want to work for peanuts. Repeated offers of an internship to the University of Maine journalism department, to University of Maine Farmington and Redimere College, got no takers. Bernie figured the kids going into journalism all wanted Internet blogging jobs. She shuddered. Carol, who used to work for a magazine and was a hell of a writer, helped out, but she was busy freelancing and helping Vince run the farm. Guy did an occasional feature and his column, helped with layout and put together the sports pages, but made it clear that at his age, he wanted to spend what time he had left fishing, too. That left Bernie to do most of the heavy journalistic lifting.

She looked over the town meeting warrant, wondering if the police department would get its equipment. Everything was always a big question in tough economic times, which they always seemed to be in Maine. Great Recession? It's been going on here since Maine broke off from Massachusetts in 1820. Police budget requests were no exception. Bernie figured they would get slashed at today's meeting. One of the budget committee members, Bud Carrier, was quoted in the *Watcher*'s latest edition calling the new public safety complex a Taj Mahal and saying police were lucky there was even a department. A lot of the towns in Maine, some bigger than Redimere, some smaller, didn't have police departments. They relied on the state police and county sheriff, proud and secure that their town had virtually no crime and they were saving the taxpayers money.

Bernie knew better. After all, what was a crime rate? It was the amount of reported crime in a community. Those towns that didn't have a police force had crime, all right. There were things no one bothered to report because they knew it would be half an hour before the cops showed up and there was no point. Then there were all the little things. Even the most law-abiding citizen knew there was no one to enforce the school speed zone or two-hour parking sign or the guy running a chainsaw at two in the morning. No one to keep anyone from swimming off the dock that was posted no swimming. Filling up the tank with gas and driving off while the owner was in the back stocking shelves or ringing up someone's order.

Then there were crimes no one even knew were happening.

The entries through unlocked doors, the rifling through sheds, barns, garages and basements while the owner was at work. The forgotten prescription bottle in the medicine cabinet that disappears. The missing wad of bills from the cookie jar or the missing old hunting rifle from the barn. Because, in their pride and security, the people of small-town Maine didn't lock the doors and windows of their homes. The barns, sheds and basement bulkheads didn't need padlocks, because their town had no crime.

And what about those people who lurked and prowled through the cold, dark nights, when everyone was bundled into their nice warm homes? Those people who knew there'd be no cruiser slowly rolling down the street, no nosy cop wondering why someone was out in the cold instead of at home in the warmth?

No, Bernie never bought the "our town doesn't need a police department" philosophy. She'd been a reporter in both small towns and big cities for a long time and knew darkness lurked everywhere. What does a criminal look like? A hell of a lot of them looked just like the guy next door. Sometimes it *was* the guy next door. Doesn't matter where you live. Redimere was slightly more prosperous than the surrounding towns, thanks to the college and the luck of geography that made it a four-season playground for rich out-of-towners who liked police to keep an eye on their camps when they weren't here. So it had its police force, small as it was. She'd pay the extra taxes and feel better knowing Pete and his crew, even Rusty, were around.

Annette bustled in to the newsroom, shaking her curly gray perm out of her hat—poodle-do, Bernie called it, not out loud, of course. She was followed by Carol.

"Hey," Bernie said.

"Hey yourself," Carol said handing Bernie a Dunkin' Donuts coffee and dropping a bag that sounded plump with doughnuts on her desk. "Thought this might take the edge off."

"So much for my diet. I just had breakfast at Choppy's."

"You can start the diet Monday."

Bernie nodded and looked in the bag. Chocolate frosted. Her

favorite.

"I not only bear doughnuts. I bear info. What if I told you I could pinpoint what night Stanley died?"

"I would say you're a genius. And you're hired. And, oh, I guess we should share it with the chief."

"I think he already knows."

"Scooped again."

Carol laughed. "Vince ran into Gary Lambert at the dump this morning and he said the last time he saw Stanley was the VFW Christmas party on December 14."

Bernie thought a minute. "That's the night we had that big storm, when the power was out for two days. How does he remember that's the last time he saw Stanley?"

"Hardly anyone showed up because of the storm. Gary even sent the other bartender he hired for the night home. Handful of guys were there. Stanley, Ike Miller, Cal, Loren Daggett, Rusty, and a couple other guys. Gary was bummed because his wife made a big lasagna and nobody was there to eat it."

"Wish I'd known. Hate lasagna to go to waste."

"He was going to serve the lasagna the next few days, figured Stanley would eat it if no one else did. He never came in, and Gary ended up throwing it away."

"Oh the humanity."

"Focus," Carol said. "Gary said he realized that he hadn't seen Stanley since. Kept waiting for him to stop in and have one for the road before he went south. So he thinks that must be the night Stanley got hit. He used to return his bottles there weekly."

"There were a ton of bottles and cans at his trailer."

"There you go. Gary said Stanley, Ike, and Cal stayed the longest that night. Ray Morin also stopped by on patrol. Had some lasagna and cake. He took the night shift because Rusty wanted the night off for the party."

"In fact," Carol paused, making sure Bernie was paying attention, knowing where lasagna and cake could lead her. "Ray and Stanley went outside together for a few minutes."

"Really?"

"Yeah, but then Stanley came back in. Gary said Stanley was more talkative than usual that night. He and Loren got into it over the wind farm. He had some rambling argument with Ike and Cal that Gary can't even begin to recreate. It got pretty heated. Something about guys getting killed in Vietnam. I guess they all had a lot to drink."

"Gary told all this to Vince this morning at the dump? And Vince told it all to you? Boy, a lot can happen before eight in the morning."

"You know those guys. They both love to talk."

"If Vince ever decides to become a reporter, he's got a job here," Bernie said. She could go to the VFW and talk to Gary on Monday. Now she would know what to ask. "And you said Pete knows?"

"Gary told Vince he was going to tell him this morning."

"Goody. I can get some quotes from him at town meeting."

. . . . .

A little while later, Bernie found Pete just inside the entrance of the community center. She gave him a big smile, ready to talk about Stanley's last night, but he didn't smile back. Now in uniform, he looked no-nonsense and official. And angry. He looked like a man with something on his mind, something Bernie had a feeling she wasn't going to like.

"Let's talk outside," he said, steering her out the door by her elbow. She was confused. What could have changed in the two hours since she saw him at her house? Did he know about the notebook? If so, she had to think up a cover story. Fast.

"The trailer's gone," Pete said. Not what she expected at all.

"Gone?"

"It's not there. Turns out Loren Daggett was just waiting for the go-ahead to get rid of it so Downwind could take over the easement. For some reason he thought you gave that go-ahead."

"Me?" asked Bernie. "I just told him I'd clear up Stanley's stuff. I didn't say anything about what to do with the trailer."

"Well, whatever you told him—"

"I told him what I just told you I told him," said Bernie. She was trying to figure out how this was her fault.

"Whatever you told him, he couldn't wait to get rid of it."

Bernie, for a change, didn't know what to say. She wanted to protest more, but knew that would be a wrong move. "I'm sorry."

He glared at her. So much for apologies.

She heard the moderator call the meeting to order. She glanced at the door, then looked back at Pete, not sure what she was supposed to do.

"Go on in," he said, disgusted. "Nothing can be done now."

CHAPTER 7

Break-ins weren't unheard of in Redimere. In fact, in recent years, they paralleled the uptick in prescription drug abuse in rural Maine. The occasional break-in, store, bank or pharmacy holdup, and what Bernie called—though not in the paper, of course—dirtbag on dirtbag violence, was a fact of life. Still, when she walked through the wide-open front door of her house after town meeting to find her belongings scattered across the floor, Bernie's first reaction was confusion—did I do this? Did the cats? It took a tick to register. Then she was pissed off. She felt sorry for anyone who thought he was going to get much robbing her place. She'd had her laptop with her, and if someone thought her ancient TV and out-of-date electronics were worth stealing, they were worse off than she was.

Then she started feeling creeped-out. Someone had been in her house, going through her stuff. Actually, she was more than creeped-out. She was flat-out scared.

Confused, pitying, angry, creeped-out, and scared: the five stages of being broken into. She almost laughed.

She tracked down two of the cats—Billy and Becky were outside under the hedge by the front door; she didn't find Poopoo until hours later at the back of her bedroom closet—then she called

911. At that time on a Saturday night, the Franklin County regional dispatch center took Redimere calls. They sent Rusty over.

"Anything missing?" he asked as they surveyed the mess. It really wasn't that bad—mostly overturned drawers, including her file cabinet and the dresser in the small bedroom at the back of the house. All the books and CDs from the bookcase were on the floor. Her CD player was still there, as was twenty dollars she had left on the kitchen counter. She checked the medicine cabinet and was relieved her ADHD meds were still there. If whoever broke in had been looking for drugs, the bottle would be gone. Last she'd heard, she could sell those babies on the street for forty bucks a tablet.

"Missing? I can't tell." It wasn't until right before Rusty arrived and she noticed that the money was still on the counter and the meds still there that it occurred to her this wasn't an ordinary break-in. Someone took those garbage bags out of her car on Friday— now this. We're back to creeped-out, she thought. "Doesn't look like anything's gone," she told Rusty. "Probably just kids."

"You sure? Any prescription drugs missing from your medicine cabinet? Painkillers, opiates, narcotics, stimulant-type stuff?"

"I don't have anything stronger than Advil. Nothing's missing that I can tell." Her meds were none of Rusty's business. Bernie wanted him to leave so she could see if Stanley's notebook was gone. She'd stuck it with the giant rubber-band wrapped pile of used reporters' notebooks in her file cabinet. Purloined Letter style. The fact that Rusty kept poking the pile of notebooks and folders that had been spilled from the file cabinet with the toe of his boot didn't help.

"Chief told you Stanley's trailer was gone?" he asked her.

Startled, she had a momentary fear that he knew what she was thinking. Then she realized he was making conversation.

"Loren Daggett couldn't wait to get rid of it," he continued. "Scrap guy from Massachusetts came and got it. You believe that?" He gave her a big grin. "Boy was the chief pissed off at you."

"I know. Look Rusty, I'm beat. I've had a long day. Are you done here?"

"I guess," he didn't seem to want to leave. "Want me to help you go through your stuff and see if anything's missing?"

"No, it's fine." She hated it when people touched her stuff, but the thought of Rusty pawing through it was even worse, especially since the notebook she stole—yes, she admitted to herself, stole—was about two inches from his boot toe.

"You sure? It's a quiet night and you've got a mess here."

"I'm good, really."

He shrugged. "Okay. I'll ask your neighbors if they saw anything, but don't expect much. Must've happened after dark for whoever it was to come right through the front. With those pines all over the yard, can't see the house good from the street. You're the last one before Route 145. Easy target, getaway. Probably looking for drugs and stuff to steal to buy drugs. Jewelry and whatnot. Not much we can do now."

Bernie realized that was going to be the extent of Rusty's investigation. Regular Sherlock Holmes. Maybe she'd have to rethink that whole better-off-with-our-own cops philosophy where he was concerned. "Guess you're going to be the star of your Crime Beat this week." Another toothy grin.

"Guess so." She hadn't thought about that. The police log ran in the paper every week—disorderly conduct. Suspicious activity. Car accidents. Fights. Domestic violence. Even the most mundane calls were listed—"Resident reported vandals had peppered her car with paint. Police responded and determined the car was parked under a tree and 'paint' was bird waste." Readers ate it up. She couldn't leave herself out, it was a rule of journalism. Leave it out, how could she ever print anyone else's bad news? She'd seen it countless times in her career: fellow reporters' and editors' drunk driving arrests. One guy busted for shoplifting. One glorious moment when a former editor everyone hated was busted for child porn. In Redimere, where everyone would know anyway, her first-hand brush with burglars had to be printed.

She finally shooed Rusty out. She waited until she saw his headlights turn from her driveway onto the street. She picked up the bundle of notebooks, and there was Stanley's, still bound with the others, just like she'd left it. Either her Purloined Letter method worked, or the burglar wasn't sure what he was looking for. Assuming, of course, that whoever broke in was interested in Stanley's belongings at all.

She thumbed through the notebook again. It was intriguing, puzzling, but maybe meaningless. A list of dates, some with asterisks. She sat down on the floor, surrounded by her scattered CDs and books and began at the beginning. The dates started about three years ago, all of them numbered beginning with 1 and ended with 81. There didn't seem to be a pattern to the dates, some repeated, bunched together, then big gaps between others. Page after page. She waited for it all to form itself into a pattern that made sense, but it didn't. Or if it did, she didn't see it.

But the last page with writing on it was different. Bernie hadn't noticed before, because it was on the back of a page, near the end of the notebook. A list—a checklist like the ones Bernie made to remind herself of errands, calls she had to make, her daily schedule, things she had to ask someone in an interview. She had them scattered all over the kitchen counter, some days. This one Stanley had topped with "Talk to Cal." Then "1/18/08, shelter, negligent?, R, J!, bridge 'coyote bait'."

Bernie stared at the page the way she had at the dates, but it didn't make any more sense. A list of nonsequiturs. Quotes around coyote bait. She wondered if Stanley was as serious about quotation marks, as annoyed by unnecessary ones, as she was, because that would mean coyote bait could mean something else. The items all had checks next to them. As a serial list-maker she knew the list, the check-offs, probably made sense to Stanley, but he wasn't here to ask. Cal wasn't either.

She fired up her laptop, the mess in the house forgotten for now. Googled January 18, 2008. It was on that checklist, but wasn't one of the dates in the long list in the notebook. Google loaded, and of course she remembered that night. There had been a fatal snowmobile accident in the bog. How could she have forgotten?

She scanned the story that came up. She remembered most of it. She'd written it herself, after all. Two local teens, Evan Wentzel and John Carrier, were riding a snowmobile down the road that went through the bog at the back of Ike Miller's property and went off a bridge and into the water, the sled crashing through the ice. Evan, the driver, died. John was badly hurt. Conclusion was speed and alcohol. She Googled the other stuff on the checklist, but nothing helpful came up. Googled various combinations. Still nothing. Curse Google. Time to use my brain like we did in the old days. But her brain was wiped out and her meds were wearing off. Thoughts were running around in her brain, leaping and jumping over each other and not stopping long enough for her to grab hold of one and think about it. She made a stab at cleaning the living room, had a beer, tried to read a little, made sure the doors were locked, then went to bed.

She couldn't sleep. She couldn't stop thinking. Most of the town knew by now she had been to Stanley's trailer. Anyone could have been her burglar-wanna-be. She was sure there was something to it. But hell if she knew what.

Right before she finally went to sleep, another date popped into her head. December 12. The postmark on the envelope the notebook had been in. Two days before December 14. The last night anyone had seen Stanley alive. "What's this all about, Stanley?" she said out loud. "Was it big enough to get you killed?"

. . . . .

Monday morning, she was the unintentional highlight of Town Administrator Dave Marshall's weekly press conference.

Every Monday at ten, she and Jeff Lydon, who worked for a struggling news website, sat around the conference table in Dave's office as he went over town government news for the week. He always had a fresh pot of coffee and a dozen doughnuts in an open box on the table, like he was expecting the rest of the press corps to show up at any minute. Once in a while the Farmington reporter for the *Morning Sentinel* would come, or someone from the *Lewiston Sun-Journal*, but mostly she and Jeff had Dave to themselves. Bernie

60

enjoyed it, if for no other reason than the free coffee and doughnuts and an hour or so of mostly gossip and small talk. Jeff had been a radio news reporter until that profession became even rarer than Bernie's. They spent a lot of time talking about the good old days.

This morning, there was a crowd. Pete, Fire Chief Sandy MacCormack, and Don Littlefield were all gathered around the conference table eating doughnuts with Jeff and Dave when Bernie arrived.

"Wow guys, what's news?" Bernie asked.

Jeff gave a "your guess is as good as mine" shrug.

"So, you got broken into," Sandy said before Bernie could sit down. The big blue eyes of the best-looking man in Redimere, and possibly all of Franklin County, were fixed on her, round with concern. Bernie melted.

"Must've been kids or someone looking for drugs. Nothing's missing. It's just kind of creepy."

"Are you okay?" Pete asked. Unlike Sandy's, his eyes, Bernie couldn't help but notice, were squinty with annoyance.

"Yeah, I wasn't home." Bernie couldn't tell from his tone if he was still mad at her about the trailer, but at least he was talking to her.

"Rusty says you don't lock your door." Pete again.

"I do now," Bernie said. "Who in Redimere *does* lock their door?"

"I do," Pete said.

"Flatlander," said Don Littlefield. The other guys snickered.

"Why do you think they picked your house?" Sandy asked.

Bernie could feel Pete waiting for her answer. Rusty asked the same question Saturday night. She didn't have a better official for-public-consumption answer now than she did then.

"I don't know. Maybe they think I'm a rich newspaper magnate. Joke's on them, huh?"

Everyone laughed except Pete. He looked at her, green eyes unwavering. Right into her soul.

She was relieved when Dave Marshall got down to business.

"You are probably wondering why I have half the town payroll here," he said, pulling at the sleeves of his polyester suit coat. Bernie's private name for him was Disco Dave. With his blown-dried hair and wide ties, he'd stalled somewhere in the 1970s. "Don has something he wants to say."

Bernie had a fleeting thought that maybe Don Littlefield was going to fess up to hitting Stanley with his plow, but realized just as quick that the news certainly wouldn't be announced in this easy-breezy atmosphere.

Don, in mid-doughnut, began chewing rapidly. Everyone watched and waited. His face reddened all the way through his bald spot. He swallowed with a little choking noise, then cleared his throat. A mist of doughnut crumbs blew out. "As you know, Cal was my cousin. He was a big presence in this town for a long time. On the police force for forty years, chief for almost thirty. He did a lot for this town and everyone loved him a lot. So the bunch of us have asked the town that the public safety complex be named the Calvin L. Littlefield Public Safety Complex. And, um, they're saying yes. So this is the official press conference to announce it."

He looked at Dave for reassurance and Dave nodded.

Bernie had liked Cal, despite his old-school ways. In other words, blatant male chauvinism. He was big, friendly, funny. He always said in a fake brogue and with a wink, "Ah, Bernadette, the Italian girl with the Irish name. Or are you the Irish girl with the Italian eyes?" Hard to dislike. She'd been shaken by his death. But still, she wondered if anyone caught the irony of the town's public safety complex being named for a guy who'd drunkenly burned down his own house, killing himself in the process.

She looked around at the other faces, trying to catch anyone's eye. Jeff intent on taking notes. Sandy and Dave were both looking at Don, who was grabbing another doughnut.

Unfortunately she caught Pete's. He raised his eyebrows as if asking, "You've got something to say?"

She looked down at her notebook and began writing, her cheeks hot.

"Pete?" Dave was looking at the chief.

"Sandy and I are proud to be housed in a building bearing Cal's name," Pete said. Bernie tried to concentrate on her notebook, but she could feel his eyes on her. "His dream was getting it built. It took him ten years to do it. This is a great way to honor a good man."

"Ditto on all that," Sandy said.

Dave clapped his hands together —okay we're finished. "There'll be a dedication ceremony Saturday at 10 a.m. Who wants another doughnut?"

Bernie wrote down the day and time and reached for a doughnut, trying to look like she wasn't aware of Pete's steady all-seeing gaze.

Local Man Found Dead

Stanley Weston started out with a promising future. He was a high school track and baseball star. He volunteered for duty in Vietnam before most people even knew there was a war there, and came back a hero, with a Purple Heart.

But after Vietnam, Weston's life went off track and he spent the past several decades in and out of the VA hospital, living on the street.

The final blow came Thursday, when the body of Weston, 63, the apparent victim of a hit and run, possibly by a town snowplow, was found at the side of Pond Road by a passing runner.

His body was in a melting snowbank and police can't say how long he may have been there, but he was last reported seen on Dec. 14 at the VFW Christmas party.

The preliminary cause of death is blunt force trauma to the head, according to Police Chief Pete Novotny. The official cause of death had not been released by the state medical examiner, and Novotny said that information may not be available for weeks. Weston suffered multiple injuries to the body and head, which are consistent with being hit and rolled by a plow, Novotny said.

"Our theory is that he was walking during a snowstorm, and was hit, either by a plow or a motorist," he said. State police are leading the investigation, as they do with all major crimes.

Public Works director Don Littlefield would not comment on whether he thought it was one of the town's two plows that hit Weston. He acknowledged that a driver of the bigger plow, a Kenworth T470, could hit a person and not know it. He was driving that plow on Dec. 14.

Lance Berube was jogging on Pond Road around 1 p.m. Thursday when he saw an arm sticking out of the snow.

"Grisly as hell," Berube said. "Straight out. I knew right away what it was."

He called 911 from his cellphone, waited for the police to arrive, then continued his run.

Weston lived alone in a mobile home off Pond Road on property owned by Loren Daggett.

"We all thought he went south to his cousin's," said VFW bartender Gary Lambert. "No one gave him a second thought."

Weston was born in Bangor, and was a 1964 graduate of …

Peaks Weekly Watcher, March 26, 2009

When the paper came out Thursday, Bernie wasn't satisfied with her Stanley Weston coverage. After the particulars of the accident, the story had meandered off into the background of his Vietnam heroism, his high school sports success in Bangor, his troubles after he came back from Vietnam. The usual stuff. It lacked something. She felt in the very pit of her gut that the real story had yet to be told.

The VFW bartender, Gary Lambert, when she interviewed him, didn't help flesh out the story much. Stanley was ornery that night. Just as he'd told Carol's husband, Stanley got into an argument with Loren about the wind farm, then he, Cal, and Ike Miller mixed it up about Vietnam.

"Stanley said something like, 'when innocent people die, that's when you stop,' or something like that. I'm not sure of the exact words," Gary told her. He was one of those guys who talked a lot, but rarely had anything useful to say. This time wasn't an exception. "You know how those drunken arguments are. I hear them all the time, being a bartender. You know Cal and Ike served together? Ike even talked Cal into enlisting out of college. He had that baseball scholarship at Maine. Cal did. But anyway, they were kind of ganging up on Stanley. He was there a lot earlier. In Vietnam. He got a medal. Anyway, they were all really drunk. Don't put that in the paper, okay?" he added. "Off the record. Some of them were driving. Don't want to lose my liquor license."

Nothing about the night at the VFW, aside from the fact that it was the last time anyone admitted to seeing Stanley, made it into the story, simply because she couldn't pin down any useful information. Not because Gary told her not to put it in.

Ditto on the topic of Ray Morin walking outside with Stanley for a minute. Bernie asked Ray about their last conversation.

"None of your goddam business." It didn't really make for good copy.

So when Bernie clicked the cursor on her computer to send the pages to Waterville to be printed Wednesday afternoon—no rumbling presses like her old daily, just a PDF file winging its way through cyberspace—she felt empty and dissatisfied.

She was going over bills in the empty newsroom Thursday morning, trying to get past her unhappiness with the Stanley story and wondering what to do about it when the door opened with its usual crash. "Gotta fix that thing," she muttered.

"Can we talk?" It was Pete, all business. But he had two takeout cups of coffee. A good sign.

"Sure."

"Do you have someplace more private?" he asked, gesturing with one of the coffee cups at the big front window.

"My office, I guess." Bernie led him to the back. She sat down behind her desk, pushing the mountain of papers and files to the side, so she could see him.

He shut the door with his elbow, then put a coffee on the desk in front of her before lifting some files off the only other chair. He looked around for a place to put them, before setting them on the floor. The process didn't seem to please him. She didn't use the room much, mostly because it was so small and full of junk. With both of them squeezed in and the door shut, she had a fleeting image of one of those old college pranks where frat boys see how many of them they can stuff in a telephone booth. She figured she could always stick a leg out the window to give them both more space, assuming she could get the window open. Actually, that wouldn't be a bad idea. With the door shut and the steam radiator under the window pumping hot air mixed with the simmering tension rising off of Pete, who she was sure had yet to forgive her for the trailer, she felt the walls closing in. The closeness magnified the musty radiator, inky paper and ancient wood odor of the building, tempered slightly by the smell of whatever soap Pete used— Dove? Ivory?—familiar and comforting.

"The state is officially classifying Stanley Weston's case as 'cause of death: undetermined,'" he said.

"Okay." Bernie perked up. "What can you tell me?" She pulled a legal pad out from the pile of stuff and searched the debris for a pen.

"Not a lot. The state doesn't see a reason to continue the investigation, so they're handing it over."

"Okay."

"What we know is that he died of blunt trauma to the head. The ME has determined his injuries aren't necessarily consistent with being hit by a vehicle, but not totally inconsistent either."

She wrote "not consistent but not inconsistent," on her legal pad, then realized how ridiculous it looked.

Pete had paused while she was writing, but started up again. "It looks like he was hit on the head more than once. There were a lot of small skull fragments, some overlapping, which means repeated hits." He demonstrated, overlapping the fingertips of one hand on the fingers of the other. Bernie tried to picture his strong, tanned fingers, the nails neatly trimmed, as skull fragments. She had an urge to touch them. Focus.

"Some of those fragments were embedded in the brain. That doesn't happen with one hit to a head. The overlapping fragments. You need repeated hits. But, his head could have bounced on the pavement several times, if the plow rolled him. Even with the snow, it'd be damn hard."

Bernie looked up from Pete's fingers. He was looking at her. Inscrutable, as always.

"Is that what you think happened?"

Pete shrugged. "There's another issue. Usually when someone is hit by a vehicle, the point of impact is clear from the injuries. There's no obvious point of impact on Stanley."

"I thought you thought it was his head?" The song came back to her: Plow hit him on the head head head.

"Well, that's undetermined now."

"So it's the cause of death but not the point of impact?"

"There were a lot of injuries to his body consistent with being rolled by the plow. Then he was all folded up, scrunched, packed into the snow. It's conceivable the point of impact got lost in all that. It's a big vehicle."

That behemoth plow truck was Don Littlefield's pride and joy. Don had told her earlier in the week that if he hit something that night, he never felt it. He told her, off the record of course, that he once hit a deer in his driveway with the plow during a blizzard and didn't know until the next day, when he saw the dead deer in his yard. "But don't put that in the paper," he added. "I'm not supposed to be using it on my own driveway." Pause. "Um, don't put that in the paper, either." Bernie could see how something that big could inflict so much injury it would be hard to tell where it started and where it finished.

"Stanley was well-preserved," Pete continued. "Frozen into the snow. That's a first for me. In Philly they just used to leave 'em cooking on the pavement. Or a Dumpster." He paused, looking into his coffee cup. "So the ME got a good look at everything before he started to decompose. But once he started thawing, he might as well have been in a Philly Dumpster. It happened fast."

His voice was calm. If she didn't look at his face, all tense lines and laser green eyes, she could act like all was normal. But she knew he was still mad at her, and more to the point, bothered by Stanley's death. Still, she had to ask questions. It was her job.

"So if the state police are handing it back, are you still investigating? Do you still think the head injury's odd?" State police handled homicide and other major crime investigations in every Maine community except Portland and Bangor, but Bernie knew local police could still pursue leads. "Do you think there was foul play?"

Pete barked a laugh. "Even if I thought there was foul play"— he said foul play all drawn out and exaggerated, making Bernie feel like a dope—"this is a town of two thousand people. Everyone already knows what I ate at Choppy's this morning. So I wouldn't be saying. I've given you all I'm going to for now. For the record, just say he died of head trauma. Inconclusive. The state is handing it over. Period."

She wrote that down. It looked so lonely there in her notebook.

"Tell me about what you found."

She felt a jolt. He knew about the notebook. "What?"

"You said you had clippings and some other things here at the office."

"Oh yeah. They're right here in my desk." The manila envelope was jammed on top of all the other things in the deep wooden drawer, she leaned down to pull it out, hoping her face wasn't as red as it felt.

She handed him the envelope. "It's his parents' obits, sports stuff, Vietnam service. I used it as background for the story. Some newer clips about the wind farm."

He looked it over and shrugged and handed it back. "This is scrapbook stuff."

She took the envelope back. He was looking at her expectantly. "What?"

"Is this it?"

She felt her face begin to burn again. "Well, they took the garbage bags and I gave you the P.O. key." The angel on her shoulder was saying "Tell him about the notebook. TELL HIM ABOUT THE NOTEBOOK!" but she couldn't. She could feel guilt written all over her face. She shrugged, trying to get that angel off her shoulder because it wouldn't shut the hell up. The radiator clanked and squeaked. She felt the heat start creeping up her neck again and sweat forming on her back and under her arms. She knew he didn't believe her, but she couldn't make herself confess. Divert. Divert. Divert. "So does this mean you're still investigating?"

He sighed. Shrugged. "Maybe. But I don't think the answer to what happened to Stanley lies with the trailer anyway. If there's anything to answer, it'll be somewhere else."

Was she off the hook? At least she was for now.

"Okay. Cal." He had that squinty intense look again.

"What?" she said, feeling like an idiot. The conversation had already gone off the rails, and now she felt like she'd missed a huge chunk of it.

"Cal's death wasn't a joke."

She took a big gulp of coffee as she tried to think of how to respond. It took her a few seconds to make the mental transition. The public safety complex thing? Had her mental smirking been so obvious Monday? She still felt shitty about not bringing up the notebook, now this. She wanted to say "I'm not an awful person, really." But people who had to say that usually were, and anyway, it's a pathetic thing to say.

"I don't think Cal's death was funny. It was the opposite of funny. Give me some credit." It was true. She didn't think Cal's death was funny. She knew it had hit Pete hard. God was an idiot.

He looked at her for a long minute. She couldn't tell if he was going to give her credit or not. In her experience, it usually fell on the not side. She put down her coffee cup and tried to look as sincere as she felt.

"I want to get along with you," he said. His mood shifted, it seemed for the better. He smiled, totally unexpected, just for a second, then it was gone again. "Cal's death is a sore spot with me. When I thought you didn't take it seriously Monday, it hit me wrong. Sorry. I know you liked Cal."

"I'm sorry, too, if I seemed insensitive. I know that was a rough night for you."

"Rough." He seemed to consider the word. "Yeah. I should have done more. Just like I should have with Stanley."

"Pete, you ran into a burning house—"

He held up his hand, "He was drinking too much. I should have talked to him, something."

"It wasn't your fault."

Pete shook his head. "He was there for me when I needed him. Bailed me out of Philly."

"Okay," Bernie said, not sure what was expected of her. The tension that had boiled under the surface between the two of them since he'd found out she'd been to Stanley's trailer, along with the guilt about the notebook, was beyond her comfort zone. Now here he was baring his soul, which was unusual and unexpected. "He liked you a lot," she said, mentally wincing because it sounded so lame.

He shrugged. "Yeah, maybe he just liked having someone listen to his bullshit."

There were plenty of people around who listened to Cal's bullshit. "I'm sure there was more to it than that," she said.

"You're square on all this?"

"On?"

"You. Me. Stanley. Cal. I know I've been irritated the past week." He paused. Then he broke into one of his face-cracking grins. "It's me baby, not you."

She laughed. It was always a sweet surprise when he made a joke and it was the last thing she expected out of him today.

"So we're square?" he asked.

No. "Sure," Bernie said. Nice of him to say it wasn't her. He didn't have to. He wasn't the first person to be irritated by her. Not even this week. Not even today.

He shot his empty coffee cup into the wastebasket and stood up.

"Anything else you can remember about the trailer, anything you've found out, be sure you tell me."

She nodded. He locked eyes with her again, held the gaze. When the front door crashed closed behind him, she was still sitting at the desk, trying to make the guilt go away.

. . . . .

That Saturday, a colorless cold end-of-March day, the town held the dedication for the public safety building. Bernie hadn't talked to Pete since he'd been in her office two days before, and she avoided him at the ceremony, afraid she wore guilt like a scarlet letter. It was easy. It was a crappy day and the event didn't last long. Since the metal letters the town had ordered to affix to the side of the building hadn't arrived yet, a temporary sign was unveiled, stenciled by Don and his boys at the Public Works Department: Calvin L. Littlefield Public Safety Complex. A few of Cal's friends talked— Pete, Don, Ike Miller.

No one rehashed the ugly details of Cal's death. Why would they want to? He'd been drinking a lot in the months since his retirement. On Christmas Eve he knocked over a bottle of vodka while sitting in his recliner, spilled it all over the floor and fell asleep smoking a cigar. The wooden lakeside camp ignited like a summer bonfire. Cal had enough time to grab the phone on the table by his chair, but that was all before the smoke got to him. The call came in as a 911 hang-up. Pete heard it on the scanner at his place and got there first, dragging Cal out into the snow. Rusty showed up minutes later—dispatch had alerted him to the hang-up call. He told Bernie later he'd found Pete, coatless in the sub-freezing weather, performing CPR on Cal's lifeless body.

When Bernie arrived, most of the excitement was over. The ambulance was still there, always a bad sign. Pete, wearing a too-big fire department coat, was leaning against the pumper truck, head bent, as Sandy talked quietly to him, leaning in close with his hand on Pete's shoulder. Bernie stayed away. She didn't feel like eavesdropping for once. The conversation just seemed too intimate. She took a picture of the pair, but surprised herself by not using it in the paper. Anyway, the photo of the charred remains of the camp encased in ice as the water from the fire hoses froze was better.

Bernie didn't try to interview Pete that night.

Christmas Day, only hours after the fire, when Bernie went to the police station for the official press conference, Pete looked shell-shocked, but he was rock steady with the press. Despite the holiday, the conference had drawn half a dozen TV and print reporters, even a crew from Boston. Big news on a slow day. Pete stuck to the facts, as sparse as they were. Since Christmas was on a Thursday and the paper didn't come out for another week, she interviewed him a couple days later, hoping for more, but he didn't have much more to say and she didn't push him.

At today's dedication, everyone talked about what a great guy Cal was. How much he had done for the town. His unheroic death, though, hung over the ceremony like the March weather. Everyone seemed in a rush to get it over with and out of the cold and wind.

Bernie, dissatisfied and guilty, needed some carb therapy. Looked like everyone else had the same idea. Choppy's was almost full, and the only seat available at the counter was between Ray Morin and Ike Miller. Fun. She sat down on the stool, trying to look as inconspicuous as possible, hoping Debbie would notice her so she could order, while also hoping Ike, who was talking to the guy on his right, wouldn't notice her at his elbow.

No such luck.

"Hope you're not planning to misquote me."

Bernie turned, ready to do battle, but she saw he was smiling.

"We'll see how interesting the story is with the real quotes. If not, I may have to."

He guffawed. "I like a person who can take a joke on herself."

"No problem," Bernie said as she watched Debbie fill her

coffee cup. "You said some nice things about Cal, anyway."

Ike sighed. "Yep, he was my buddy from way back. Ran with each other in high school, went to 'Nam together. Partners in crime. I miss him like hell, like he died yesterday not three months ago. I keep expecting him to walk through that door. Call me up and say 'Hey buddy, the fish are biting.' Life's no fun when your friends start going."

"He was a good guy."

"Yeah. Better man than me," Ike said, smiling again and getting up from his seat. "Anyway, he liked you. So does my dog." He put a ten dollar bill on the counter. "No accounting for taste, I guess."

Bernie looked up from her bagel, expecting to see another smile. But Ike was going out the door.

"Whoa, truce with you two?" Debbie asked, picking up the money and wiping down the counter.

"Nah," Bernie said. "I think losing his buddy has just softened his cold, cold heart a little for the day. He's okay, anyway. Just one of those good old boys, you know? Not much use for a gal like me and I don't have much use for him."

"He's a good customer and tips well, that's all that matters to me," Debbie said.

"The Calvin L. Littlefield Public Safety Complex."

Bernie had forgotten Ray was to her left. Now she turned to him. He was staring into his coffee.

"Calvin L. Littlefield Public Safety Complex," he repeated, shaking his head. "Never got the point of naming a building."

"Lots of people loved Cal," Bernie said. "It's a way to honor him. If it weren't for him, you guys would still be in the basement at town hall."

"Doesn't matter to me, I spend most of my time in a cruiser. Guess it's a good thing your buddy Ike there helped Cal out on that before you got him booted from the planning board."

"He got himself booted." She was good at her job. Why the hell did she always have to defend herself? "He had an obvious conflict of interest, trying to block the wind farm, when he was an abutter. Don't kill the messenger."

Debbie came over with the coffee pot and refilled Bernie's mug. "Anyway, he's still got the biggest farm in the county, that must keep him busy," Debbie said. "He'll find another hobby if he needs one."

"I think guys like him like to be in a position where they're calling the shots. He's got a lot of friends," Bernie said. "He'll definitely find another hobby. I hope it's not too much of a pain in my ass."

Ray sputtered. "Everyone thinks Ike is such a big shot, but he's just another blowhard. All them guys—Ike, Cal and all their buddies—throwing their weight around, forcing everyone to do things their way and everyone just lets them."

"That's not true," Bernie said. "No one let Ike get away with blocking the wind farm. Right? Justice was served. So see? The truth is power, even against the old boys' club."

Ray snorted. "Truth my ass. Look at the way everyone just let Cal anoint Professor Pete police chief. Guy is from away. Spent a few weeks here two years ago on some fucked-up Philly case. What the hell does he know about this town? After I put in twenty years, working my butt off, never saying no. Nights, weekends."

"Come on, Ray," Debbie said. "Stop your griping. Cal's gone, anyway. Not much you can do now."

"That's true," Bernie said. "Might as well give Pete a chance."

Ray turned to her. "Where's the truth there? You knock Ike off the planning board, but where's your story about the chief? Seems like a double standard to me."

"How so? What's the story? You know something?"

"He doesn't belong here," Ray said, more to his coffee than anyone else.

"I think he's a living doll," Debbie said. "And you'd be one, too, Ray, if you'd just lighten up a little bit."

. . . . .

As Maine's version of spring slid in muddy fits and starts toward summer, the town moved with it. The fields and lakes and bogs thawed. The mountains to the west and north turned from white and brownish-gray to green. The last shards of ice in the Wesserunsett River thawed or drifted down toward the Kennebec. People began to venture out, blinking and stretching in the thin spring sun. The last snow along the roads melted, leaving behind a winter's collection of crushed soda bottles, leaves, dead squirrels, odd bits of clothing and all the other detritus the plow pushed from the roads.

Pete thought about Stanley every day. Since he came to Redimere, two people had died from unnatural causes. In Philly there was more than a murder a day in his last year as a homicide cop, so he was used to unnatural death. But the two Redimere deaths in less than a year gnawed at him.

Pete could still feel the searing heat and taste the smoke as he dragged Cal's heavy, already dead body out of the house. Cal had been drinking too much and made a fatal mistake. No mystery there, just a world of pain and regret.

And then there was Stanley. He hadn't died in an accident. Pete was sure of it. But hell if he knew where to go from here. He should have checked out the trailer himself the day they found the body. He couldn't shake the feeling Bernie wasn't telling him something. On the other hand, he knew she wasn't a game player. Wouldn't she have told him if there was something to tell? The answer to Stanley's death was somewhere. He just had to figure out where to look.

. . . . .

Bernie thought about Stanley every day, too. She had a copy of his high school graduation picture from that sheaf of clippings in her desk drawer. He'd been a jug-eared kid with a crew cut and a gap-toothed smile on his way to college, then ended up in Vietnam. He survived that, more or less, only to be left dead on a snowy country roadside in the middle of Maine. Sometimes she'd look out the back door of the office, expecting to see him down by the river fork past the parking lot in his favorite grassy spot, but of course, that was silly.

She'd puzzled over his notebook so much she knew it by heart. She'd Googled every single date and nothing that seemed significant came up. It didn't keep her from checking further though. She went through every single *Watcher* in the yellowing piles on the metal shelves upstairs, looking the dates up, seeing if there was the tiniest connection between them. If there was, she couldn't figure it out. She Googled that stuff in the list in the back, but of course nothing came up. Coyote bait? No point Googling "talk to Cal." Nothing spurred a sudden memory or thought. Nothing.

She asked Pete every week if there was anything new. He always said, "When there is, I'll let you know."

She intended to sit down and really figure it out. Working fourteen-hour days, trying to fit life in when she could, never really off the clock, time slipped away and there was a lot of stuff she didn't get to, not just that. She just had to focus on each day sometimes to keep her head together. Weeks passed. Months.

Still, almost every day, she'd look at the picture and wonder what happened to Stanley Weston.

Chapter 8

S top the presses, stop the presses." Paul Libbey panted the words as he barreled through the front door of the *Watcher*.

He leaned on Bernie's desk, gulping air, his soft pink face and hairless head bright with sweat. Since there were no presses, Bernie waited and hoped her best and only ad salesman didn't stroke out before he could tell her what was going on.

"Cruiser's in front of Redimere Drug," he said. "State police too."

"You sure Ray's not just picking up some Pepto Bismol?" Bernie asked, amusing only herself. Paul sold a lot of ads, but he'd yet to show any news sense.

"Lights flashing."

For the past few weeks as May morphed into June the rain had dominated the news—how it was affecting crops, the opening of the farmers market, logging, fishing, the ATV trails, the summer people from out of state griping, like the weather should bend to their will and it was everyone in Maine's fault if it didn't. It was mid-June, and the rain, to use the old-time newspaper cliché that Bernie hated, had put a damper on the beginning of Redimere's summer. State police? Lights flashing? It was the most interesting news she'd heard in weeks.

Bernie shot an accusing look at the scanner, which had been mostly spitting out strings and blobs of static all day, and grabbed her notebook and camera.

Sure enough, the town cruiser and two from state police were parked at angles, partway onto what passed as a sidewalk in town, lights pulsing. One state cop did sentry duty, standing in front of the glass door. The windows of the low-slung brick building were covered with signs for everything from discount bath products to what her dad called five and dime gee-gaws. The summer stock was in, the signs announced in a burst of optimism. Sun block $4.99! Beach hats, sandals and towels! 12-pack of Pepsi 5.99! It's a wonder there was any room for pharmaceuticals. The signs made it impossible to see inside.

"What happened?" she asked, a general appeal to the gathering crowd.

"Kenny Paquette. Robbed the place then took off. On his sister's bike. Pink," someone said.

"I heard he went up to Herb Beedy, pointed a gun at him and said, 'Sorry, Mr. Beedy, but I need all your oxycontin,'" said a teenage girl, not looking up from her phone, texting the news, no doubt. Or just texting.

Bernie wrote that down. Good stuff, if it was true. Pharmacist looks down the barrel of a gun.

Ray came out of the store and headed toward the cruiser. Bernie intercepted him.

"What's going on Ray?"

"Robbery. Chief's still in there with state police. He'll give you the details."

"Are you looking for Kenny Paquette?"

Ray looked surprised, then laughed. "Don't worry, he won't get far on his sister's bike."

Pete joined them. "What's funny?"

"The getaway car," Ray said, then turned to Bernie. "Had a pretty serious gun with him. A Glock."

Pete had been friendly to Bernie since that talk in her office in

March, but she still couldn't shake the notebook guilt. She knew it was a dead end, that she'd never crack its code without more information. So why not just give it to Pete? Because she still hadn't figured out what to tell him that wouldn't make her look bad. The time never seemed right. And now so much time had passed, it seemed impossible. And he was being so nice. They'd gotten into the habit of chatting in his office or hers nearly daily when she stopped by the station, at the store, the post office, the gym. Wherever. They talked about the Red Sox, town events, books they were reading, things in the news. He wasn't just another bullet-headed cop, or a blowhard like Cal. He actually had interesting things to say. But she always felt the notebook hovering behind it, making her feel like a phony.

Today, as he stood squinting in the rare June sun, his arms folded across his uniform shirt, he looked all business. Bernie pulled her pen cap off with her teeth and got ready to take notes.

"He must be pretty desperate, robbing a store on his sister's bike," she said around the cap. Pete didn't respond. "How much did he get?"

"Undisclosed amount of drugs and cash. Class A felony. State police will issue a press release once we're done here."

Bernie had seen Kenny around town. A skinny kid on a skateboard with hair in his eyes. She took the pen cap out of her mouth. "I can't see him shooting anyone. Was the gun even loaded?"

Ray's smile turned into a tight line. "Herb was scared shitless."

"I bet Kenny was scared shitless, too," Bernie said.

"That doesn't make it any better," Pete said. "That was a serious gun. It doesn't matter if it was loaded or not." Ray now had his arms crossed, too. They both stared at her. Stonefaced.

"Two sides to every story," Bernie said, smiling to show she wasn't really arguing. Even though she kind of was. She wasn't sure why.

"Not in an armed robbery," Pete said.

"Breaking the law is breaking the law," Ray said, his voice

rising. "Guns like this are showing up more and more often. I know everyone in town has a gun, but they're for hunting. Not this shit. Where in the hell does a kid like Kenny get a Glock? Don't make excuses."

"I'm not," Bernie said. She knew she was just trying to get under Pete's skin for no good reason. Instead she'd made Ray mad and made Pete—what? It was hard to tell. Pharmacy robberies were epidemic in the state, though this was a first for Redimere Drug. The gun angle was something new and would juice the story up. Maine was a gun-lovers state, but there was also a certain respect for them. They were tools, not political statements, and had a purpose. No one liked it when people broke the rules, but they still got broken because guns were so easy to get. She made a mental note that maybe there was a gun story. She knew better than to ask more now, though.

"I'm gonna go look for Kenny before he ODs or something," Ray said, turning toward the cruiser.

Pete and Bernie watched him drive off.

"Sometimes, Bernie, you're too much, you know that?"

She knew all right. She shrugged.

He shook his head and turned to walk back to the station.

He called later to tell her Ray tracked Kenny down at a friend's house, his sister's bike propped against the front steps. The kid wasn't even smart enough to get out of town. Now he was cooling his heels in the county jail in Farmington. The gun was unregistered and they didn't know where he got it. Kenny said he didn't remember. She asked Pete if he wanted to talk more about guns and he sighed heavily and told her he'd talk to her about it later, too busy. So the armed robbery was wrapped up with a nice, neat bow. Too bad it all happened on a Thursday and would be old news when the next paper came out in a week.

Bernie locked the door at the end of the day and stepped outside. The afternoon's sun was gone and the rain had started up again. Was it ever going to be warm and dry? She began the walk to her clammy house. Everything was damp—the sheets, the couch, her clothes. Books and papers curled with it. Salt clumped in the salt shaker, impossible to use. And the news? That was damp, too. The armed robbery sounded good at first, but it ended up a sad story that more or less fizzled. By the time the next issue of the paper came out, everyone in town would know more about it than she could possibly learn in the next few days. She knew she didn't have any time to pursue the gun thing as in-depth as she'd like.

She felt as limp and soggy as the sad little American flag on the pole in front of town hall. I need something to happen, she thought. Something good. Something big enough that I can kick some journalistic butt.

She barely heard the little voice that added, "Be careful what you wish for."

CHAPTER 9

Bernie visited the police station almost every day. She'd get the police log on Mondays and Wednesdays, but also stopped in on other days to touch base and see what was going on, like all good reporters do. She'd park herself in Pete's office and chew the fat if he didn't seem harried. But mostly she chatted with her secret weapon, Dawna Mitchell. Dawna was a younger, slightly softer, slightly smaller version of her sister Debbie, the owner of Choppy's. She was smarter than Rusty and Ray combined.

When Bernie stopped in Friday, the day after the drugstore robbery, Dawna, as usual, was focused on her computer screen.

"Hey Bernie," she said without looking up. "I have some stuff for you."

Bernie sifted through a bunch of faxes and computer printouts in the wire basket on Dawna's desk. Mostly from the state. Awards, workshops, procedures. Yawn. Snore.

"Did he tell you about the press release?" Dawna asked, nodding toward Pete's office. "Stuff from the gun task force."

"He didn't say anything about it. He said he was too busy to talk about guns yesterday. But I'm thinking about a story, if I can think of something to say that hasn't been said already. Is he here?" Pete's door was shut. Why didn't he tell her he had a press release? He could have said that on the phone quicker than saying he was too busy to talk. A few months ago, he'd said it wasn't her, baby, it was him. They'd both laughed. Right. She was pretty sure by now it was her.

"He had to go to Augusta for something. It might have to do with Stanley. He didn't say, but that's the impression I got."

"He didn't tell me about that, either."

"He didn't tell anyone," Dawna said. She blushed. "I overheard him on the phone. Hey, let me show you something. You're going to like this."

Bernie pulled a chair from the empty desk next to Dawna's and sat down. A Google map of Redimere filled the computer screen.

"What is it?"

"It's called Crimetracker." Dawna typed and icons appeared on the map, some in clusters, some all alone. "I input all the police reports for the last two years, and it all comes up on the map." There were icons for break-ins, car thefts, car accidents, OUIs.

"Look, there's your break-in," Dawna pointed to a lone icon on School Street, a cartoon burglar with a black mask and bag over his shoulder. "I did the icons myself. Safe neighborhood otherwise." She hovered the cursor over the icon and a balloon popped up with the time, date and details of the March burglary.

"Cool."

"The really cool thing is that people can go on this—anyone, citizens—and check out their street. Or if they're moving to town, check out neighborhoods."

"Do you think Redimere really needs this? It's not like there's a crime problem."

"Yeah that's what Chief, I mean Cal, always said. He wasn't interested. But Pete said go for it. I've been working on it on my downtime."

"You've got downtime? What between doing this, being an EMT, going to school, solving world peace and curing cancer?"

Dawna blushed again. "Turns out my Marine medic training wasn't adequate for the cancer-curing thing. Or the world peace thing. They're on the back burner."

"Two tours of duty in Afghanistan makes up for it."

"Can we get back to this?"

"Show Pond Road, down near the bog, that snowmobile

accident last year," Bernie said. One of the things that had stood out in that list of dates in Stanley's notebook was January 18, 2008, the night of the accident. Maybe this would yield a clue.

Dawna manipulated the map so it showed the west end of town. There were a handful of icons there. A row of half dozen scattered along the shore of Patten Pond, Stanley's hit-and-run, and, down the bog road, the snowmobile accident. She hovered the cursor over the accident icon. The balloon said, "January 18, 2008, 9:09 p.m., one vehicle snowmobile accident. One dead, one injured. Officers reporting, Rusty Dyer and Ray Morin."

That didn't tell Bernie anything she didn't know. She stared at the map.

"What?" Dawna asked.

"I don't know. Don't you ever have anything on Pond Road? There's not much showing there."

"I only put in reports where a crime was committed. See those ones along the pond? Those are off-season break-ins. We're getting more of those. Or when someone gets a ticket for something more serious than speeding, if there are criminal charges. Aside from Daggett and Miller's farms, the state and a couple logging companies own most of the land. Not much there. It's pretty quiet."

"May I?" Bernie nodded at the mouse. Dawna moved back a little and Bernie took over, hovering it over the snowmobile accident icon, as though it would tell her something. It didn't.

Dawna watched the screen, too. "Rusty patrols the Pond Road at night. You know he always takes the Suburban instead of the cruiser? My guess is it's so quiet down there he can take a nap and no one will bug him. Easier to nap in the Suburban. Dispatch says there's times they can't even roust him." Dawna blushed. "Don't tell Chief I just told you that, okay?"

Bernie laughed. "Our little secret. Knowing Rusty, I'm not surprised. Maybe that's one reason no crime shows up down there. He's always asleep and doesn't notice it." She got up. "I can do a nice story on Crimetracker."

But it was the bog, Stanley and the snowmobile accident that were on her mind. Stanley's body emerging from the snow was the only interesting thing that had happened in ages and she'd dropped the ball. Hard to justify hanging onto that notebook if she wasn't going to do anything about Stanley.

"Do you get any calls from that area that don't result in arrests? Things that wouldn't go on Crimetracker?"

Dawna shrugged. "Ike Miller calls to complain about trespassers once in a while, but no one ever gets arrested. Usually it's hunters or kids who wander onto his land, people on four-wheelers or snowmobiles, and we just shoo them away if they're still there. I think he chases most of them away without calling us. Once in a while, a hunter calls complaining about him. I mean, the guy's got a lot of land. It's posted, but you know people are used to being allowed on land and don't always pay attention. Rusty sends people away without arresting them. Sometimes we call the Warden Service if a hunter was involved and it was getting heated. Chief Cal would go down and calm him down if he got worked up about something, too. They were in Vietnam together. Miller's not a fan of the Warden Service, either. It was a hassle last fall with Pete new and Cal gone. Expect it'll be one again when fall comes and hunting season starts."

"Do you keep track of the dates on that stuff?"

"No, why?"

"Just thought about something, but it's probably nothing. That snowmobile crash, both Ray and Rusty responded. How did both of them end up down there? Who was on duty?"

Dawna studied her computer keyboard.

"So what was the deal with that?" Bernie pressed.

"You know how it is with a crash, especially a fatal one involving kids, everyone wants to be in on it," Dawna finally said. Her round open face looked, what, guilty?

"Who was on patrol that night?"

"I assume Rusty, but you never know. Sometimes Ray or Jamie takes the night shift."

"Can I see the full accident report? That Crimetracker blurb doesn't tell me much."

Dawna looked uncertain. "Why are you so interested?"

"Just curious." Bernie smiled. Nothing going on here, folks.

Dawna found the report in the file cabinet and handed it to her. Rusty had been the one to fill it out. Pretty straightforward. He had radioed dispatch. Ray heard it on his scanner at home and showed up, as well as the fire chief and the rest of the fire department, Warden Service, state police. Even a Border Patrol agent from up Route 27 had wandered down.

"Quite a crew out there," Bernie said, remembering the scene. She had been stunned at the vastness of Ike Miller's property—the accident had been down his road more than a mile into the bog, and if it hadn't been for the police and rescue crews, floodlights, and accident scene hubbub, she would have thought she was a thousand miles from nowhere.

She and half the responders had rushed down there from the planning board meeting, including Miller, who was still chairman. That's the other memory that stuck out in her mind about that night: Ike looking more human than usual, concerned about the kids, not a word about the trespassing. Although why should that surprise her? He's human too, as much as she'd like to make him a cartoon character.

The kids—Evan Wentzel and John Carrier, both eighteen—had been drinking, snowmobiling where they shouldn't have—and went off a wooden bridge. Evan was driving. The bog was frozen, but the ice was thin, and the sled crashed through it, nose-first. Two drunk kids in boots, helmets, and snowmobile coveralls in twelve feet of freezing water. It's a miracle one survived.

The report said the boys swerved to avoid an animal.

"It doesn't say here how Rusty heard about the accident in the first place."

"Doesn't it?" Dawna took the report. "Maybe John had a cellphone on him and called it in. Hard to remember. It *was* a year and a half ago."

"In the water with a broken leg? And he called? Anyway,

wouldn't there be a record?"

"County dispatch would have it." Dawna put the report back in the file folder and back in the drawer. Bernie didn't remember saying she was done with it.

"Usually it's in the report," Dawna continued. "But Rusty hates paperwork, he never does a very good job with it. Cal was still chief back then. He never got after him about that."

"Do you remember seeing Stanley down there that night? Or did he ever say anything to you about it?"

"Stanley? No. But I was pretty busy with the kids."

"Yeah, I didn't see him either," Bernie said.

. . . . .

When Bernie stepped out of the office that afternoon, the sun was struggling through the drizzle and mist. Maybe summer will come after all. Her foot slipped off the uneven granite curb into a puddle and her sneaker was instantly soaked. Or maybe not. She was doing yet another story on how the rain was affecting the farmers market. It operated year-round in the old brick mill on the bank of the Wesserunsett next to the falls, but when it moved outside into the parking lot in mid-June, coinciding with the yearly influx of summer people, it brought the town to life. This year, the rain was making that hard. The town was almost panicking that if the weather didn't improve, the rich folks from Connecticut and New York, from New Jersey and Virginia, would stop showing up with their money. Don't worry, Bernie wanted to reassure everyone, they've been coming for decades, they're not going to stop now. Maybe she'd do a story about it.

She was hit with the usual assault on the senses when she pushed open the big wooden doors of the renovated mill—food, music, warmth. No matter how cool and damp it was outside, the Redimere Public Market was always warm, its old board floors and brick walls practically glowing. A few people sat at the café tables near the riverside windows, drinking coffee. Felt kind of like an indoor summer.

Sure enough, Denise Carrier was presiding over her organic

bread, pies and jellies. She was vice president of the Wesserunsett Association of Crafters and Organic Farmers. The ying to president Bev Dulac's yang.

"Bernie!" Denise always shouted. "You look like you could use a jar of jam. Keep Wackoff in business." Denise always pronounced the acronym of the group the way the rest of the town did, despite Bev's attempts to twist it into something that sounded like way-cove. Or maybe a cat coughing up a hairball. Bernie felt bad for Bev. You can't fight something like that.

"You read my mind," Bernie said as she picked through the breads. "I'm all out of strawberry preserves."

"Well, you better take two jars, my supply is running low. Strawberries gonna be late because of the rain." Denise shook her head in despair, the rain a personal affront.

"You guys moving outside this weekend? I'll come over and take some pictures for the paper."

"Yes we are! Rain be damned! Can't wait for the weather here or you'd never do anything!" Weathah! Nevah! Denise always talked in exclamation points and Bernie felt bad that her quotes in the paper never matched the full flavor of talking to her.

"How's John doing?"

"Oh, he's great! He's down at USM. Loves Portland," she said. "You know, after that broken leg, he can't play baseball anymore. But he likes school, anyway. Thank the lord. I don't know what I'd do with that boy if he was just going to sit around the house and mope."

With Denise, asking one question was like tipping the first domino in a domino train—you really didn't need to tip any more to get all the information you needed, and a lot you didn't.

"So he's recovered okay from the snowmobile accident? It's been almost a year and a half. That was a long haul, huh?"

"Pretty much. That leg will never be the same, but he's getting a degree and hopefully he'll find something to do with himself. It's not like he was ever going to play for the Red Sox anyway, no matter what he thought!" She guffawed. "That would have helped my retirement! Move out of the trailer and eat bon bons all day!"

"That must have been a hell of a shock when you got the call that night."

"Oh, it was. Ray called. From the hospital. In Farmington. Poor Evan. His folks moved to New Hampshire after. Just couldn't take living here anymore."

"You know, I always wondered, did John call the police? How did they know about the accident? Hard to imagine he'd be able to call it in."

"Oh no, Rusty was right there. John says they never saw him before it happened, but he was right there. Rusty managed to pull him out pretty quick, then he called it in. Tried to get poor Evan, but it was too late." Her round face deflated.

"How did Rusty know they saw an animal? Did he see it?"

Denise shrugged. "I don't know. He must know somehow, right? He's the police!"

"Did Stanley Weston ever say anything to you about that accident?"

"Stanley? Lord no!" She laughed, her face round and happy again.

. . . . .

Outside, it was raining again, but Bernie didn't really notice. The news crawl was circling through her head, a dozen separate lines of thought at once. Once she was diagnosed, she had an official name for it. Racing thoughts. She liked news crawl better. Liked to pick through it and see which one took hold for a few minutes. Stanley and his broken head head head. The accident. Did Rusty know something he wasn't saying? What did Stanley know? What did he talk to Cal about? Why was Dawna so antsy about her looking at the report? She sifted through, trying to figure out what was important. Figure it out, smart girl, because Stanley isn't with us anymore to help you out.

CHAPTER 10

Bernie clutched her notebook and camera to her chest and looked for a spot along the back wall of the community center, which vibrated with a high-pitched buzz. Wow, she thought as she threaded through the crowd looking for her spot, cabin fever must be epidemic. When she covered meetings like this, she liked to stand in the back so she could keep an eye on the crowd, see who was talking. Exchange snide remarks with the other people who preferred the back wall, mostly town department heads and other cynical types. She liked to think that was where all the cool people hung out. She'd die of boredom otherwise.

She found a spot and propped herself up.

Downwind Energy Corporation's plan for the wind farm on Patten Mountain was practically a done deal. She cringed remembering how fast Loren got rid of Stanley's trailer so the company could start site work. Done deal or no, the public still had to be heard before the official stamp could be put on it.

Neighbors whose land abutted the property in question were the only ones who were officially notified for planning hearings, but most of the town was crammed into the room, as well as the first wave of the summer population. She could always tell the summer folk—they must all stop at L.L. Bean to stock up on duck boots and fleece vests on their way north. The town was nestled at the foot of Maine's western mountains in a valley right above where the Wesserunsett River joined the Carabassett and the Sandy, and the three went tumbling together south and east to the Kennebec. The land in the river valley was punctuated by lakes big and small left behind when the glaciers scrubbed Maine's rocky terrain on their retreat north, and hugged on two sides by the two-lane highways, 27 and 16, that brought skiers, fishermen, hunters, outdoor adventurers and those just looking to get remote. For ten or so months out of the year, the town forced a smile, tugged its forelock and tried to be Disney cute for the people whose money kept it afloat. From the end of March to the end of May, Redimere rested. In June, it got up and did it all over again.

Bernie had seen a lot of the summer regulars at Saturday's farmers market grand opening, many toting umbrellas despite the fact the rain had let up for the afternoon. Cooing over the few early strawberries. Calling jars of jam precious and smelling the homemade bread with big, exaggerated sniffs. Now they crowded with the year-rounders into the public hearing. Summer people were human, too. This was the only show in town.

Bernie had a love-hate relationship with public hearings. They usually made for decent stories. Hell, the story practically wrote itself: he said, she said, he yelled, she accused. On the other hand, she knew who was going to speak and what they were going to say. The issue didn't matter: raising fees at the dump, buying a firetruck, building the Dunkin' Donuts—the same dozen people had to have their long-winded say.

Most of the town's meetings were held at the conference table in the town office. The selectmen rarely had more than an audience of two or three. But big meetings took over the community center hall. Tonight they'd really taken over. People squeezed in on benches and wooden chairs. She checked the room. Her quick estimate—reporters become experts at crowd estimates, and hey, if they're off, who's going to prove them wrong?—was about two hundred. More than March's town meeting.

"We should have charged admission."

Bernie wrote her estimate down in her notebook before looking up to see who was reading her mind.

Pete leaned against the wall next to her. He wasn't wearing his uniform, just jeans and a short-sleeved cotton shirt. But he had his duty belt on—handcuffs, badge, billy club, mace canister, radio. No gun, or even a Taser, Bernie noticed. Unlike Cal, he was judicious about bringing out the artillery.

"Are you on duty?" she asked. She wished she could just relax around him, because she was always happy to see him. But that notebook of Stanley's still beat like the tell-tale heart. If there could only be some closure on what happened to Stanley, she could forget about it and wouldn't ever have to reveal what she'd done. Pete was giving her a big crinkly, full-dimple smile. She tried to bat away her anxiety and enjoy it.

"I'm always on duty." She'd almost forgot she'd asked the question. "Rusty's off and I didn't want to pull Ray off patrol to keep an eye on this mob."

"They are a pretty wild group. Are you expecting trouble?"

"I hear the organic farmers are going to take on the summer theater troupe. Rumble out behind the mill. Weapons of choice tomatoes, green strawberries and some dog-eared copies of 'Our Town.'"

She loved it when Robocop—man, she rarely even thought of him as that anymore—made a joke. "Dangerous."

"We're going to counter with Big Macs and our most over-the-top Olivier impressions."

She laughed, her anxiety gone for a moment. "Good, some news besides the weather for the front page."

"Speaking of news, can we talk after? I have something for you. It's not about the weather, I promise."

"I was going to go back to the office. Wanna talk there? I heard you were in Augusta Friday. Stanley news?" Maybe this was the break she needed to ease her guilty conscience.

He gave her another big smile and shrugged. "See you then." He tapped her on the arm before walking away, unaware, she was sure, that she'd feel the little burn from his warm finger for the rest of the night.

A gavel banged and the meeting got underway.

. . . . .

Outside the theater, Dragon Dube pulled up in his ice cream truck, "Turkey in the Straw" playing from the loudspeaker. He bought the truck in April and it took him and his buddy Justin, who worked at the Irving garage, almost a month to get it in working order. But now he was up and running. It was a sweet ride. Fully loaded and lime green. He even had a soft-serve ice cream machine. Popsicles, Choco-Tacos, Nutty Buddies and ice cream sandwiches were okay, but he knew the big bucks were in ice cream in a cone. Maybe he'd get a hot dog cooker once he made some dough. If only the rain would stop he knew business would be fantastic. He was tired of working for other people. They wanted too much, bugged him when he wanted to think. Assholes. Now he was his own boss. Future's so bright I gotta wear shades, man, even with the rain, he thought with a chuckle. He filled the coffee maker. Another bright idea. He saw how Dunkin's did. Look out, there's another DD in town. The night was warm, but misty. If they weren't in the mood for ice cream, he had them covered.

The big black wooden front doors of the former school were propped open. He could see the backs of people crowded in the entrance. Standing room only. A bunch of smokers stood outside on the steps getting their last puffs in.

He cranked up the music and stood in the serving window. C'mon people, he murmured. Buy something.

"Music's too loud." Ray Morin was in front of him. Shit, Morin usually worked days.

"Hey, Officer Morin." Dragon tried a smile, the price of being a businessman. "You can be my first customer of the night."

"Turn off the damn music."

"I have a permit, man. You can ask the chief. He was over at town hall when I got it." Ray was like a mean dog as far as Dragon was concerned—don't let it see how scared you are.

"I don't give a damn." Ray's voice was calm, but Dragon felt the menace behind it. "It's a public nuisance. They're trying to have a meeting in there."

Dragon saw Pete appear in the doorway of the theater. Good. He was a businessman now, he should be above being hassled by Ray Morin.

"Hey guys," Pete said, strolling over to the truck. "Give me a medium chocolate-vanilla twist."

Dragon grinned triumphantly at Ray. "Sure Chief, you're my first customer of the night. One twist, coming up."

Pete turned to Ray. "Problem?"

"Just trying to get him to turn off the music so they can hold their meeting in peace," he said, looking at the community center door instead of Pete, the last of the smokers just going in.

"Well, that makes sense, doesn't it, Dragon?" Pete asked as he took his ice cream cone. "You can turn that off if you want to stay out here. But better yet, why don't you go over to Bigelow Park? Probably more of an ice cream crowd at the Little League field."

Dragon hesitated. He hated to be the one to back down. Ray fumed, arms crossed, shaking his head. Pete licked his ice cream cone, eyes steady on Dragon. What the hell, with the meeting started, he wasn't going to get much action, anyway.

"Sure, Chief." He reached up to close the window. "That's on the house," he added, refusing Pete's two dollars. "Cops eat for free." He couldn't resist. "Some cops."

Ray's eyes, still focused on something past Pete's shoulder, narrowed. Pete looked engrossed in his ice cream.

"Okay, over to the ball fields. See ya, Chief." Dragon acted like he didn't notice when Pete tucked the two dollars into the napkin holder.

Pete and Ray watched the truck go, trailing a tinny "Turkey in the Straw."

Pete turned to Ray. "I've got the meeting covered."

"I just thought that music was a little loud, Chief."

"All taken care of now."

"I don't know why everyone gives that kid so much slack."

Pete knew that by everyone, Ray meant him. "He's trying to make a living. You should be relieved he's doing something honest. I've told you before to lay off him and I mean it."

Ray shook his head. "I think you're gonna be sorry. The kid's no good."

He got in his cruiser and drove down the street in the opposite direction from the one Dragon had taken. Pete watched him go, then turned around and went back inside.

. . . . .

Dragon gripped the steering wheel hard to keep his hands from shaking as he drove off. He was scared of Ray Morin. He tried not to show it, but he couldn't make it go away.

He swung by the Irving station, where his buddy Justin was getting off work.

"Hey man, how's the first night of business?"

"I'm going over to the Little League fields."

"What happened to the wind farm meeting?"

"That fucking Morin was hassling me. I didn't need to take it, so I made like a bird and flew."

"Someone call the Chief for backup?"

"Didn't have to. He was there. I like that guy, but he's from away, you know? I don't think he knows how things are here. He's nicer to me than old Cal was, but he doesn't have any clout. Sooner or later, me and Morin are going to have to have it out."

"That'll be the day."

"Whatever. Pretty soon it won't matter anyway. I've got something. Something good. I just need one final piece. That'll show those cops. Or it'll make me some money. Us, if you want in."

"What is it? I'm trying to stay out of trouble."

"Tell you later. But look at it this way, we can have the last laugh. Show everybody."

"I'll think about it."

"No need to be scared, my man. Take a look at this." Dragon opened the glove compartment.

Justin turned white. "That's one mean-looking gun."

"Bet your ass it is."

Dragon didn't blame Justin for being chicken. Hell, everyone in town would be if they knew what the cops here were really like.

. . . . .

Loren Daggett had prepared his remarks. He fumbled with his index cards when it was his turn at the microphone, which didn't help his reception from the crowd.

"I think the plan by Downwind Energy Corporation could be a big boom for Redimere and the area," he read with the stiffness of a third-grader made to stand up in class.

Bernie wondered whether she should quote him directly—boom instead of boon. Would the readers think it was her mistake? Would they even notice? She'd have to paraphrase him and use boon or everyone would think she was the moron. If people only knew, she thought with a mental sigh, the decisions reporters had to make to get things right.

"Big boon for you, Loren!" someone yelled from the crowd.

"How much you get for that easement, Loren?"

The crowd was getting ugly.

Loren turned around.

"Now you just wait a minute," he said, his voice wavering. "Any one of you would take the money for a bunch of land I ain't using anyway."

"Stanley was using it!" another voice chimed from the back of the room. The room went dead silent.

Bernie strained to see if she could tell who had yelled, but from the back it was hard to tell.

"Now let's all calm down and only speak when you have the mike," said Dave Marshall. The town administrator looked nervously from the crowd to the wind farm officials.

The next speaker was Ike Miller. He didn't need any notes.

"With due deference to my neighbor," he drawled as Bernie wrote "Fake Texan" in her notebook. "I don't think this is something Redimere needs. Don't we all love our woods and farmland? There's a lot of wildlife in my bog, my woods. Now, as former chairman of the planning board, I can tell you..."

Bernie wrote down "not in my back yard." She'd heard it all before.

She stared out the window. Dusk was falling, but she could still see the outlines of the trees, the ragged line of mountains rising beyond them, a little glow of orange behind, despite the mist. The leaves were out, more or less. The Wesserunsett, charging down the falls, faintly rumbled just out of sight. She wished she was on her porch having a beer and listening to the Red Sox on the radio. How many meetings had she daydreamed through in her early days? Meetings were mind-numbing, no matter what the topic. Afterward, she had to go back to the office, write her story and begin putting the pages together. At her old paper, she would have been chasing stories, tracking down leads, talking to sources. When she hit the big time, she told herself she'd never have to cover another municipal meeting again. Yet here she was in this humid hall, listening to the same old blather.

A low groan from the crowd brought her back to reality.

Loren Daggett's brother, Wayne, was getting up to speak. Wayne was the Billy Carter of the Daggett family, only nuttier and grubbier. He'd be a nut even if it weren't for the fact that every square inch of his yard was loaded with trash, old lobster traps, rusted cars, appliances—but that certainly added to the theme. Some of the locals called it a Yankee dooryard. Cute name for a severe case of hoarding. He had a big sign out front, Down East Curiosity Museum. She couldn't imagine what admission was; he was even less hospitable to trespassers than Ike Miller. And news flash, Wayne, Down East is about 200 miles to the east.

Bernie wrote the word "rambling" in her notebook after his name, journalistic code for "the person being quoted is crazy."

"I want to speak about individual rights, property rights, and this fascist, socialist government's trampling of our rights and taking away our freedoms…"

. . . . .

After the meeting, Pete caught up with Bernie out on the front steps. The warmth of the day was gone and the mist that had been hanging in the air all day was cold. She wished she'd brought her fleece, like the summer people she'd been mocking a couple hours earlier.

Pete, in his short sleeves, of course, didn't look the least bit uncomfortable.

"You on your way over to your office?" he asked.

"Yeah, I have to get this written tonight."

"You want a coffee?"

"You read my mind."

Pete turned right to go to Dunkin's, Bernie went left to the newspaper office.

It was Monday. She already had what her front page was going to look like in her head and she hated changing course. There was too much work to do before she finished up the paper on Wednesday and sent it to Waterville. Still, she hoped Pete had something good for her.

She dropped her notebook and camera on her desk and booted up her computer. The office was empty and humid. Its small shabbiness depressed her and made her long for the good old days, even though they hadn't been good for a while. It was nights like this, boring, depressing, that she almost wished things had gone differently at her old job, even though she knew she didn't really feel that way. The paper had been going downhill for a while. The whole newspaper industry was going to hell. Her job was secure, she'd been there forever, but it was changing. As friend after friend got laid off, quality, ethics, and good journalism had given way to the desperate scramble to keep the paper afloat. So when her boss, who she never liked much anyway, spiked a story she'd been working on for weeks because it would piss off an advertiser, she took a stand. Fifteen minutes later she was out of a job. That satisfying moment when she told her editor he could shove her job up his ass was almost worth him agreeing. Fine, she told him, she didn't want to work for a place that hadn't been a real newspaper for years anyway. Then she turned and marched out.

It wasn't until she got out to her car and saw how much her hands were shaking that she realized what she'd done.

Her boyfriend wasn't the supportive rock she was looking for. Steve was a software designer, an industry that was also pretty shaky. "Do you know there are no jobs in journalism right now? *No jobs!* How the hell do we pay the rent? You were *fired*, how the hell are you going to get a new job? Do you ever think before you open your mouth?"

She didn't regret quitting—okay, getting fired from—her job. Steve and a few members of her family thought she should go back and plead impulsive behavior brought on by stress and ADHD. Forget it. She was never going to use that excuse. It had nothing to do with it. She couldn't work for a paper that cared more about pleasing an advertiser than telling the truth. Why be a journalist if you weren't there to tell people the truth? Whether anyone liked it or not. Steve said that, too, was the ADHD talking. Bullshit! That's me talking! Sometimes she felt she was the only one in the world who gave a shit about what was important.

When Steve asked for the zillionth time in the week after she was fired "What the hell are you going to do?" Bernie realized exactly what she was going to do. Their relationship had been going the way of the newspaper industry, including the quality and ethics part. So she quit that, too.

Both the job thing and the Steve thing felt good at the time. Freeing. Full steam, fueled with a good dose of stubbornness. When she was a kid, her big line when she got into an argument with her parents or one of her siblings was, "I'm right and God knows I'm right, and that's all that matters." She learned early on never to use it with the nuns, who made it clear they had a more direct line to God than she had. As an adult, she became less certain that God, or whatever deity may or may not exist, would have her back, but her inner Bernie was always clear: "I'm right, and *I* know I'm right, and that's all that matters." Sometimes that voice seemed more whiney than confident, but it was all she had.

No looking back. She was where she was, and she had a paper to put out. She tried to shake off her funk, knowing most of it was just re-entry as her meds wore off.

Pete came in with two coffees. "Coffee," he said, sitting down in the chair next to her desk. "What did you guys ever do in this town before Dunkin's? Surprised there wasn't a movement to get Choppy's to stay open past three."

"It was brutal," Bernie said. She didn't want him to see how greedy she was for the coffee. Coffee and alcohol both worked to take the edge off re-entry, and she had to keep herself from grabbing the cup like an addict desperate for a fix. "I'll give credit to Ike Miller and Dave Marshall. Coming up with that land swap with the Dunkin's folks to get the public safety complex built was the best idea those guys ever had. Sure made Cal happy. He'd tried for years to get the police department out of the town hall basement."

"Those months I spent in town hall before the safety complex opened were hell. The rats kept eating my lunch."

They both laughed. Bernie couldn't remember seeing him in this good a mood in, well, ever. She took the plastic lid off her coffee, and willing the caffeine to work its magic as fast as possible, took a sip she hoped was properly demure, not the giant slurp she would have taken if she were alone.. "What's up?"

"There's a break in the Weston case."

"Knew it." She hoped her inner yes yes yes! wasn't as obvious as she feared her greed for the coffee was.

"There was some skin under his fingernails—along with a lot of other stuff—and they did some DNA testing on it in Augusta. You know that takes forever."

"Three months in this case."

"They came back with a DNA profile. Unfortunately, they didn't find any matches in the data base."

"What does that mean?"

"It means we hope that somewhere down the road we get a match. I can't make all the guys in Redimere give DNA samples."

"Assuming it even belongs to someone in Redimere. Or a guy. All it proves is there was some kind of human contact."

"It was embedded pretty good under the nails, not something you get from casual contact."

"Is this is on the record?"

"That's the thing." He gave her that crinkly smile again. "I need a favor. You can say we've got DNA. Leave it at that. A fishing expedition. Maybe someone will get scared and do something incriminating."

"So you don't want me to say you don't have a match."

"Right." He shrugged and smiled, all crinkly and cute.

There he went again, telling Bernie how to do her job. She hated that. But Pete, even when annoyed with her, was always straight with her. Why not help him out? Then maybe he could help her out sometime. And how could she resist that smile? Best of all, with the DNA, that friggin' tell-tale heart notebook might not matter anymore.

· · · · ·

Bright and early the next morning, Bernie laid out the page dummies on the big table in the center of the room. With computer pagination, there was really no need to draw the page design, but it helped her picture everything better. She liked to get things sorted out early on Tuesday, the beginning of the big two-day push to get the paper together.

The breaking news of the DNA information in Stanley's death wasn't that hard to fit onto the front page. Bernie drew a spot for it across the top. She'd put in the same high-school picture of him she'd used in March. The only other picture the paper had of him was from Veterans Day, when they'd gathered all the town's vets they could think of from all the wars, and lined them up for a photo at the memorial.

It wasn't a great shot, the light was all wrong. But it seemed more interesting now than it had in November—Cal, hanging on the fringe with his big smile, looking healthy and happy, before he started going downhill. Ike at attention, right in the center, cowboy hat in place. A handful of younger guys, the Iraq and Afghanistan group. Dawna, the only woman. Stanley, at the other end from Cal, hands in pockets, looking down. No, not a good picture at all. Certainly not of Stanley. She felt a stab of guilt. The centerpiece was a not too bad shot from the public hearing, Bev Dulac standing at the microphone pointing a crooked finger at the Downwind flack. Bernie could feel the guy's fear. She knew what it was like to be at the end of Bev's pointy finger.

"Jody!"

Bernie looked up from her computer at the sound of Annette's singsong greeting. The *Watcher* got a lot of walk-in traffic, unlike the industrial park location of her last newspaper. Want to stay in touch with the community and keep people reading the paper? Stay on Main Street and keep the door open, Bernie wanted to tell the rest of the industry. Newspapers started making mistakes long before the Internet, and moving out of town was one of them. Downside is, you have to deal with a lot of interruptions.

Jody Mercier adjusted his work apron and settled his bulk on the corner of Guy's desk. It was hard to ignore the plea to buy Blue Seal Feeds when it was screaming at you from his huge stomach. Bernie always wondered if his parents, when they named their cute little pink bundle Jody so long ago, ever pictured him as a forty-year-old three hundred-pound man. Some names just weren't made for grownups.

"How's my paper going today?" he asked. Jody worked down the street at the hardware/feed/hunting store, but Wednesday nights he was Bernie's. He drove his truck to Waterville, picked up the papers, and even though, as they say in Maine, you can't get there from here and the round trip could take ninety minutes or four hours, depending on the weather, he did it cheerfully and unfailingly every week.

"We got some good stuff for you this week," Guy said.

"Do you have the latest on Ike Miller?"

Bernie looked up from her dummies.

"What's he done now?" Guy asked. Guy and Jody spent a lot of time hashing over the doings of the good old boys club. Neither was a member. "Built an airport?"

"Smaller. Bigger than a breadbox, though. You want to guess?"

"No," Bernie said.

"Let's see." Guy stretched and rubbed his chin. "I haven't heard anything about him giving away all his millions, so I guess it's not that, because you'd be over there getting some. If he shot someone, we would've heard about it. I guess if he blowed somethin' up, we would've heard about that."

Jody looked as deflated as a three hundred-pound-plus man could. "Nothing that exciting. But might be worth a story anyway."

"I'm waiting," Bernie said.

"He's put a gate up on conservation land," Jody said triumphantly.

"Boring," said Guy, going back to his computer.

"Elaborate," Bernie said.

"There's that strip of land the state owns along the Pond Road, along the bog? Ike put a gate up right at the parking patch, where the road goes into the bog. Ned Silsby went over to do some turkey hunting the other morning and parked in front of it. Ike was there twenty minutes later telling him to get out. Well, Silsby said he wasn't on Ike's land, and they got into a kerfuffle. Ike threatened to shoot him."

"He doesn't like people on his land," Bernie said.

"Didn't turkey season end at the beginning of the month?" Guy asked.

"Ned's gotta feed his family, Guy," Jody said. "Anyway, that wasn't Ike's issue. He just didn't want Ned out there. Even though he grew up here, he acts like he's from away."

While being from away was only a venial sin—after all it's hard to control an accident of birth—being from here but acting like you're from away was a mortal sin. In a state where most of the land is privately owned, Mainers had a four-century-old tradition of letting people use their land to hunt, fish, ride, whatever. In Redimere's part of the state, letting people do that was vital to the economy. Ike Miller's parents were like most others as far as that was concerned, but when they died several years ago, and he moved home to work the farm, Ike shut it right down. Mortal sin.

"He's been more antsy about it ever since the snowmobile accident," Guy said. "Surprised he didn't put one up sooner."

"Speaking of that, there's another thing." Jody said. "Justin told me that Kenny Paquette got that gun he used in the robbery from Evan Wentzel."

"Evan's been dead a while," Guy said.

Judy shrugged. "You know kids. Kenny probably didn't intend to use it at first, told himself he was just going to have it. Then events took over."

"The police told me Kenny said he found the gun, but didn't remember where," Bernie said. "Did Justin tell the cops?"

"Who knows? You know kids," Jody repeated. Justin was a good kid, but Bernie knew he'd been in teenage trouble. Jody seemed to read her mind. "He steers clear of the cops, and I just stay out of it. Anyway, you know kids. Probably just a story."

"Yeah." She'd file it away in her brain, under the snowmobile accident and related issues label.

Jody turned back to Guy. "That bog used to scare the hell out of us when we were kids. Like a Grimm's fairy tale. When we got older we used to hunt there and whatnot, but that's back when his folks owned the land."

"Did you know Ike's folks had a bomb shelter?" Guy asked. "We did a feature on it, back after the Cuban missile crisis. Bet it's still there. Guess Ike comes by that paranoia honestly, but he's less picky than his folks. They were scared of commies, but Ike doesn't trust anyone."

"Well, Cal kept him normal. Now he's getting worse, seems like," Jody said.

"Crazier," Guy agreed.

"You guys are worse than the Gossip Girls," Bernie said. "I'm assuming he didn't shoot Ned Silsby."

"Did not."

"Too bad," Guy said, winking at Bernie. "Would've made a good story."

CHAPTER 11

After pushing the button to send the paper to Waterville on Wednesday, Bernie drove out to the bog. She'd been tempted to take a run down there once or twice when she was out on Pond Road. The soft old dirt tote road leading into the dark, wet interior looked cool and inviting. But she never did, because it was only superficially inviting. Like Guy said, it was more like something out of a Grimm's fairy tale, a primordial tangle that seemed to stretch to the mountains. Bernie always half-expected some Sasquatch-like creature to come slinking out of the ooze and start eating the town's chickens and cats.

For all the inroads Redimere's generations of farmers, loggers, and builders had made, they'd never been able to tame the bog. Nature saying screw you. After the snowmobile accident, when she realized most of the bog was part of Ike Miller's property—and after they'd had their dust-up over the planning board story, she lost all desire to explore it. Sasquatch wasn't the only thing that might come slinking out of the ooze.

She passed the spot where Stanley's body had been found. It was overgrown and weedy, like every other patch between the crumbling two-lane road and the woods. She'd run by it a few times this spring, but mostly found herself taking her runs to other roads where thoughts about the snowbank and trailer, the notebook, the unanswered questions, weren't as insistent. When she did come this way, though, she always gave a nod to Stanley. The place where his body was found had become part of her decades-long list: the highway where a teenager committed suicide by driving head-on into a tractor-trailer, the house where two little girls were found dead in a fire on New Year's Eve—turned out they'd been murdered—the interstate rest area where a dad shot his two kids, then drove all night and buried them in a Midwestern field. All places where the ghosts of Bernie's stories lived.

Bernie turned onto the bog road and crossed the state land, a strip of meadow a quarter-mile wide between Pond Road and where Ike Miller's property began, lined by an old stone fence. Across the meadow, to the west, was Loren Daggett's property, where Stanley's trailer had nestled on its little rise below the mountain all those years. Farther down, closer to the woods, was a dirt patch that hunters, snowmobilers and off-roaders used as a parking lot, and generations of kids went to neck. It was exposed in winter, but at this time of year there were parts where a car pulled farther in among the birches and overgrown brush would be mostly invisible. Someone would have to be halfway down the dirt road to see it. The gate was just beyond the parking area, a swinging metal affair that looked like it could cause some damage if someone ran into it with a snowmobile or ATV. Shiny. Definitely new. Monstrous next to the old wooden rail fence that leaned into the weeds by the parking area. The no trespassing signs nailed to the tree trunks were new, too. No trespassing my ass, the dirt patch was public. Those damn trees were, too.

The gate was the type to keep out vehicles, but not people. Bernie slathered on the mosquito repellent she kept in her car. She was going to take a walk.

The snowmobile accident had happened in the dead of winter, when the land was more open and exposed. Now in June, after the rainy spring, the road disappeared into a green and brown tangle. The bog was hundreds of acres, fed by streams that came down out of the mountains and the west fork of the Wesserunsett, which snaked through marsh grass for miles past the bog before emptying into the Sandy River down by Phillips.

As Bernie started down the road, the wall of vegetation separated into thick stands of trees: pines, birch, giant swamp maples, both dead and alive, twisted and mangled by decades of wind, ice and snow. The trees, some posted with bright orange "no hunting" signs, sheltered reeds, pussy willows, shrubs—plants Bernie couldn't even begin to identify—and marsh grass taller than Bernie and coarse to the touch. The smell was almost as thick as the vegetation, earthy, full of mud and decay.

The night of the snowmobile accident had been lit by a full moon, and the bog had been forbidding and stark. Bernie tried to convince herself the sporadic light of the summer sun coming through the branches made it more welcoming, but it didn't erase the uneasiness she'd always felt about the bog. She had a flash of Snow White in the haunted forest, the branches reaching out to grab her. But a cheerful chorus of frogs and buzzing bugs called out, "Why so nervous? Why so nervous?"

Really, why so nervous? Honestly. It was Maine on a beautiful, almost-summer day. She knew Ike Miller's house was on the other side of the bog, nowhere near her, at the other end of the road, probably a good two miles through the bog and across the hay fields and pastures of his dairy farm. The gate down here wasn't really a surprise—the front of his house, on Beedy Mountain Road, had a ten-foot high stockade fence.

Ike hadn't been happy the night of the snowmobile crash, beyond his obvious concern for the injured kids. He was okay with Rusty and Ray and the rescue crew, but not so much with Bernie and the crowd that had followed him out of the planning board meeting. The rescue crews got the kids out of there fast. Ray, irritated as usual, rode herd over the accident scene, the investigation, the ambulances and overseeing towing the snowmobile out of the frozen swamp double-quick while Rusty played Ike-whisperer, soothing him, shooing onlookers away, standing in for Cal, who was on vacation in Florida, visiting Bernie's old boss Harry, and looking for retirement property.

The cops, Ray in charge and everyone on guard with Cal gone, didn't want to talk afterwards. Ike had no quotes for Bernie. It could have been a good story, but it wasn't. She remembers wishing Cal had been around. Since she'd seen Stanley's notation about it in his notebook, she tried to remember if Stanley had been there, too. She was pretty sure he hadn't. The night, the story, the bog, Ike, Rusty and Ray—the whole thing made her feel like she was missing something. She'd chalked it up to still being new in town when the accident happened, getting her sea legs. Now she wondered.

She felt a stinging pain on her calf, then another one. Black flies. A mosquito dive-bombed her. So much for the repellent. Nothing to fear down here but the bugs, she told herself. She gave up slapping and tried to ignore them. The zen of bug bites—they only bother you if you let them. The bridge where the accident had been was a little more than a mile in. Stanley's notebook had said "bridge – 'coyote bait' " She knew what coyote bait was, usually a dead deer or some other animal bloody and hanging. She hoped there wasn't anything like that down there. It still wouldn't be there now, so long after whenever he'd written it anyway, right? Coyote hunting was legal, with the permission of the landowner, and usually done at night. Ike didn't like anyone hunting on his land, so unless it was his bait, maybe there was something to that. What the hell was she going to do when she got there? She had come down here with no plan, without even a camera or a notebook.

The tote road, more like a causeway in some places, was well maintained. A rise that traversed a creek had been laid with logs for traction. The logs looked new, stripped of their bark and still white, crisscrossed with muddy tire tracks. Ike must use the road for farm access. She was glad it wasn't deer season. She had a flash of Ike Miller shooting her and claiming he took her—a short, pale, slightly round female human—for a deer.

She rounded a curve and almost stepped into a roaring creek. Part of the road was washed out. No surprise, the rainy spring had washed out roads all over the state. Another pile of fresh logs and some lumber lay by the side of the road, ready to repair it.

Bernie took off her sandals and waded in. The water, bone-aching cold as it rushed down from the mountains, wasn't the calf-depth she'd thought, but more like thigh-high. So much for thinking her Capri-length pants were going to stay clean. The bottom wasn't firm, but oozing mud that sucked at her feet with every step, making it hard to pull them out. Rocks, sticks, and other unidentified objects tripped her up and grabbed at her ankles. The washout was several yards wide. When she climbed up the embankment on the other side, her legs were covered with black mud that smelled like something dead. She put her sandals back on her wet feet and kept going.

The bridge had changed since her last visit here. For one thing, there was a gate at the near end of it, just like the one out by the road. The bog water on either side looked deep, a riot of tangled shrubs growing out of it. No way a vehicle could get around the gate, even an off-road one. Similar gates, maybe with a little less hardware, but similar nonetheless, crossed roads like this all over Maine. Most of those, however; are marked with fluorescent tape so that snowmobilers and off-roaders don't crack their heads open. She guessed Ike didn't care about that. The steel-pipe gate was elaborate, reinforced. It looked like it could stop a tank. She could just see him: "What? The guy's head split open like a watermelon on my gate? Not my fault. Didn't he see the no trespassing sign?"

There were no signs of the crash, but she didn't expect there to be. It had been a year and a half ago. To her relief, no coyote bait, either. The bridge was weathered planks, no rails, Chappaquiddick-style, about fifty yards long, almost seemed like a boardwalk, until you looked over the edge at the oozy brackish bog where Evan Wentzel had met his death. Again she was struck by what a different place it had been that night.

Even this early in summer, the bare branches that in winter poked out of the ice were now heavily tangled trees and shrubs. She'd seen the huge swath of Milky Way that night, but today the afternoon sun filtered through the canopy, the sky barely visible. Twisted mossy limbs stuck out of the water, like arms reaching for a lifeline. Bernie wasn't sure if they were trees or parts of trees. There was a rusty iron eyelet, a big one, sticking out of one of the swamp maples next to the bridge, about hip high. She'd turned to see if there was a corresponding one on the other side when she was stopped cold by the roar of an engine. Before she could decide whether to turn and run, Ike Miller himself was in front of her on a four-wheel ATV.

"Hello Bernadette. Can I help you with something?"

"Sorry. I'm looking for an off-road place to do my runs. I thought I'd take a look down here." Shrug.

"This is private property, little lady." He was smiling, but she didn't trust it for a minute. "Didn't you see the signs? Or the gate?"

"I thought that was just for hunters. Posted, you know?" She tried her best self-effacing smile, the one that always got her out of speeding tickets. Or did until she moved to Redimere and all the cops got to know her too well to fall for it.

It didn't work on Ike either. "It says 'no trespassing,' too. You're lucky I didn't take you for someone causing trouble and shoot you."

He was still smiling. Bernie wished Dubya was with him. The dog always made her see Ike in a different light. She tried to see him as Dubya's dad. It wasn't working. She didn't see a gun, knew he was probably just having fun with her. It must have been the woods, Snow White, her memory of that snowmobile accident. Something sent a chill through her. "Sorry. My bad."

"Don't let anything getcha on the way out."

She gave a little laugh, turned and walked as fast as she could back the way she had come. She felt his eyes on her back and held her breath, hoping to hear his engine retreat in the other direction. After what seemed like a long time, but probably was a minute or so, she heard it start up and recede to the north. She started to run.

When she got back to her car, she didn't bother to wipe her feet or legs, soaked from her second trip through the stream. She threw her sandals in the back, started the engine and roared out of the parking lot. She didn't breathe again, or at least felt like she didn't, until she was back on the road to town.

. . . . .

"What have you been doing? Mud wrestling?" Guy was leaning back in his desk chair, drinking a soda with his feet up on the desk. Wednesday post-production mode. Bernie had taken several deep breaths in the five or so minutes it had taken her to drive back to the office. Now she felt a little silly. There'd been nothing to be scared of, just Ike Miller teasing her, as usual. She hoped she looked normal. She didn't want to say where she'd been or what she'd been doing.

"Naw, just down by the river and slipped on a rock."

"Likely story. Bet you went down to check out that gate."

She was never a good liar. Why try? "Yeah, I did. Stinky stuff."

"Knew you would." He sighed. "Anyway, that high school kid you hired to sort the postal labels never showed up. I guess the glamorous life of a journalist wasn't for her. Was about to do them myself, but now that you're here, boss…"

"Ugh." Bernie said. Who could blame the kid? It was a half-hour of drudgery that she wished on no one. When Jody brought the papers back from Waterville in the wee hours, he and sometimes his son Justin or his wife, Helene, would stick the labels on papers to be mailed for same-day delivery to nearby customers in Strong and Phillips, Avon, New Portland, and Kingfield, and to far away places like Florida and Quebec. But first the labels had to be made and sorted. She went into the bathroom and cleaned up as well as she could, then started up the machine.

"I never miss Stanley more than at times like this," she said a while later as the machine finished rumbling out the strips and she started sorting the labels by zip code. "That sounds bad. You know what I mean."

"I do," Guy said. "I think he'd go down out back on Wednesdays just 'cause he knew we'd pop our heads out the door looking for him. Best sorter we ever had and all it cost us was a sandwich and ten bucks."

By the time she finished sorting, it was five o'clock, Guy was long gone and she was hungry. She couldn't stop thinking about the bog. Her trip had renewed her resolve to get to the bottom, if there was a bottom, of the whole Stanley-snowmobile accident thing and figure out if it had anything to do with Stanley dying. She was going to start with Rusty. He'd looked pale and scared in the light of the police strobes that night a year and a half ago. She wondered if he'd tell Pete she was asking around. If he did, she'd probably have to come clean. She'd almost welcome it.

Rusty's huge, giant-wheeled extended-cab pickup was one of the few cars in the parking lot of the Pour House out on Route 27 when she pulled in a few minutes later. He'd bought it last fall and it was almost all he talked about, like a lover in the first stages of a torrid affair. The day after he bought it, Bernie watched it roar past Choppy's as she had her morning coffee.

"Damn thing's almost causing a divorce," said Debbie, whose cousin was married to Rusty. "My cousin doesn't know where they're going to come up with the payments. Rusty says it's no problem, he works a lot of double shifts. He's an idiot."

Bernie figured if Rusty had to choose between his wife and the truck, the truck had it, hands down.

A few men sat at the Pour House bar, several stools between each. The tables, tree stumps with giant shellacked tree-slice tops, were empty. Even though there'd been no smoking in Maine bars and restaurants for years, the smell of stale cigarette smoke seeped out of the walls.

Bernie heard Rusty before her eyes adjusted enough to pick him out.

"Then I said, I don't care who you are in Augusta, here in Redimere you're someone who was going twenty-five miles an hour over the speed limit and I want to see your license and registration," he was saying to the bartender.

"Hey Rusty," Bernie said as she sat down on the stool next to him. "Mind if I join you?"

"Come right up. I was just saying how I pulled over some big shot state rep or something on Route 27 this afternoon. You oughta do a story on the guy."

"Rusty, there's something I've wanted to ask you about," Bernie said after she gave her order and the bartender went to fetch her chili. "It's about the snowmobile accident in the bog."

"Why do you care about that? You doing some kind of story?"

"Maybe, some kind of story about, you know, private land rights and our outdoor culture. Haven't really nailed down the angle yet." She looked at him expectantly. Smiled.

"That didn't have nothing to do with that," Rusty said. He was all edge, his normal soft ooze gone. "Dark night, narrow bridge. Someone's had too much to drink, probably going too fast. You know the rest. Kids shouldn'ta been down there."

"Were they coyote hunting?"

He laughed. "Jesus, no. They were just riding around drunk and making trouble."

"And you were the first on the scene?"

He hesitated. "Yeah. I called dispatch got the sheriff, state police showed up. Ray heard it on the scanner. When I got there, the sled was nose-first in the drink. Gone through the ice." He fidgeted with his spoon, picking up chili, then dropping it back in the bowl.

"How did you know there was an accident?"

Rusty started to answer, stopped, then started again.

"I saw the sled turn down the bog road and went after it. Gave Ike a courtesy call on his cell about then, because I know he don't like folks on his property."

He hadn't been looking at her, but now he did. "I wasn't chasing them, I was just checking them out. I didn't know they were going to crash." His nervousness had morphed into irritation. "Anyway, it was a long time ago. No use going over yesterday's news." He put a ten on the counter and got up to leave.

Bernie had a thought. "Hey, Rusty."

He sighed.

114

"You ever see Stanley writing in a notebook? A little green one?"

She could tell it wasn't what he expected, but she couldn't gauge his response. Relief? Confusion?

He thought about it, or made a show of thinking about it. "Nah." He turned and walked out.

As Bernie walked across the dirt parking lot to her car a little while later, Dragon and Loren Daggett pulled into the parking lot, lime green ice cream truck followed by beat-up pickup.

Bernie waited for them.

"Hey, did you ever see Stanley writing in a little green notebook?" she asked Dragon.

"Huh?"

"You know writing," Bernie mimicked writing. "In a little green notebook." She held her other hand out flat and made a scribbling motion over it.

"I don't think I ever saw Stanley writing anything," Dragon said.

Loren, who'd stopped to listen, shook his head and laughed.

"Get that?" Dragon asked him, laughing too, as the two walked toward the entrance. "Grocery list? His memoirs probably. Stanley writing in a notebook."

As Bernie got into her car, she saw Dragon look back at her. He wasn't laughing.

CHAPTER 12

Pete was sifting through the way-too-thin Stanley Weston file wondering how he could know so little after three months when Dawna knocked on the door jam.

"You know you don't have to knock. That's why the door's open."

"Habit," she said, blushing. She blushed every time he talked to her. He wished she'd get more comfortable. "Cal didn't like people barging in."

"You can barge any time you want to. What's up?"

"Thought you'd like to know the biggest case of the spring has been solved."

For a fleeting moment, he thought she meant Stanley, but she was trying to suppress a smile.

"Oh?"

"Garbage strewer. Perpetrator about this high"—she held her hand down by her knee—"weight about sixty pounds. Covered in black fur. And cute as a button."

"A black bear?"

"Yup. Little one-year-old. Don Littlefield and his guys set up a sting with a dozen doughnuts and a bear trap. He's been incarcerated up north in the Bigelow preserve."

"Another case cracked."

"Speaking of cracking cases, um, I was wondering if you'd heard anything new about the DNA. Since the story was in the paper? I thought since it's Monday now maybe somebody would call?"

"Nothing. Guess we have to give it some time."

"Oh."

"Is there more?" He tried to say it gently, didn't want to cause another blush. She blushed anyway.

"I was just wondering. With the DNA and all, it made me wonder if we should revisit the Christmas party. Like maybe something happened there."

Pete had been through his notes a dozen, no probably a hundred times. He kept coming back to the VFW Christmas party, too. "Something probably did. The problem is, everyone was drunk. And how do we ask the guys there for DNA samples? Guys we see every day. I mean there was that argument with Stanley, Cal and Ike about Vietnam. But how do we go from that, to something happening to Stanley?"

Dawna sat down. "I never heard those guys talk about Vietnam much, even though I bet they thought about it all the time. I feel the same way about Afghanistan. There's not much you can say." She blushed again, the red catching up with the other blush.

"When I was up here from Philly a couple years ago, you know, Cal and I became friends." She nodded. "Cal and I were drinking one night, talking about our college baseball careers, and he told me a buddy had talked him out of going back to college for his second year, dumping his baseball scholarship at Maine, to fight in Vietnam. When I came to work here, I found out the buddy was Miller. You know Miller ended up doing three tours?"

"Yeah, he was the real deal," Dawna said. "So was Stanley. He got a Purple Heart. Do you think that argument had something to do with why Stanley died?"

"I don't know."

"I don't mean to be nosy," Dawna rushed the words out.

"You're not nosy," Pete said, laughing. "It's our job. It's good to talk it out. I'm at a dead end if someone doesn't make a move because of that DNA."

"Sorry I'm not more help."

"No, I'm glad you asked about it."

"Okay." She looked uncertain. "I'm going to lock up. You staying long?"

"Little while. Paper work."

Pete had thought about finding a way to do DNA matches on everyone at the Christmas party. More to eliminate them than anything else. But he rejected it. How the hell do you ask for something like that in a town this size without pissing off people you'd have to see every day after? Anyway, he bet it was someone Stanley met on the road, after the party, but he didn't think it was random. He'd talked to Rusty and Ray about that night. Rusty had been at the party, didn't remember much. Ray talked to Stanley in the parking lot, invited him over to his family's house for Christmas. He said he didn't want to do it in the bar and embarrass Stanley in front of everybody.

"He said he'd think about it. Never said he had plans to go south," Ray told Pete, hurt. It was snowing so hard, Ray said, no one else was around. There was hardly any traffic at all that night.

That damn trailer nagged at him, too. It had been towed to a scrap yard in Massachusetts the day after Stanley's body was found. When Rusty called down to ask them to hold onto it, they'd already crushed it. Case closed. He wished he'd stop thinking about it, because if it had anything to say, it wasn't going to now.

Don Littlefield drove the plow that cleared Pond Road the night Stanley died. He said he didn't remember seeing any cars, or people. Not even Stanley. Stanley had obviously been plowed in— dead or alive. Don bristled at Pete's questions.

"Thought we were buddies, Pete. You think I would hit someone with my plow and just drive on if I knew about it? Cal wouldn't be asking me questions like this."

Pete sighed. He was tired of everyone telling him what Cal

would or wouldn't do. When Pete first met Cal a couple years ago, in town on a case and running away from himself, too, Cal was easy to talk to, a real cop, but one who, even after Pete told him what had happened to him, didn't treat him like he was a piece of shit or a coward. They kept in touch. Cal knew Pete was sinking at his desk job in Philly and knew Redimere would be a good fit even if nobody else could see it.

Cal had warned him that in this small town, he'd have to learn to do some glad-handing. And Cal downplayed just how little information people wanted to share with someone "from away." He felt like there were things going on under the surface that no one was telling him, including Rusty and Ray. What *would* Cal do? He knew everyone, knew where they were and knew what they knew. Pete never felt at more of a disadvantage. He'd felt like talking to Bernie about that the other night when he went over to tell her about the DNA. When he saw her through the window of the newspaper office, pushing her damp hair out of her face, glowing in the desk lamp, he felt the same pull that he had with Cal. Someone who cared, who'd listen to him, who he could tell how lost he felt. Actually, to be honest with himself, it wasn't the same pull with Cal. There was more to it with Bernie, some physical, some more. He had to fight the urge to ask her what she thought about Stanley, about everything. He couldn't, though. She was too good at her job. It would be a mistake to start confiding, because he could end up going too far. Because what he really wanted to do was feel how she felt with his arms around her. What those lips—when they stopped talking, he thought with a laugh—tasted like.

"Okay Chief, heading home."

He looked up at Dawna's smiling face and smiled back. "Thanks for being a sounding board."

She shrugged. "Sorry I didn't help much. Don't stay too late." She disappeared into the hallway.

His best cop. His brightest cop. Cool as a cucumber in times of crisis. Just the person you want in your foxhole.

"Hey Dawna."

"Yeah?" She popped her head back in.
"Got another minute?"

. . . . .

It was close to seven and still hot and muggy as hell out. Bernie's run hadn't gone well. She still wasn't used to the warm weather. Just when you get acclimated to one season, it ends and a new one starts and you have to get acclimated all over again. She sat on the screen porch drinking a beer. She'd spent the entire run chewing over recent developments. They clanged around in her brain and she had trouble sorting them. Usually runs were when she did her best thinking. But not tonight. Everything was a jumble. Rusty's nervousness, or even fear, when she talked to him earlier. The DNA. The snowmobile accident—what wasn't she seeing that Stanley had seen? The notebook. She'd tried everything she could think of to figure out those dates, that weird little list. Now she had to figure out how to get it to Pete. Fess up and have him hate her forever? Or even arrest her? Make up some flimsy story? Drop it off in the police station's mail slot, anonymously, like some thief in the night? That seemed the best idea, but it was chickenshit. Anyway, it would raise a lot of questions and it would eventually come back to bite her. She needed to come clean.

She held the beer to her forehead. Her cats purred and snored nearby. The soon-to-set sun trickled between the trees. In the winter she could see all the way down the slope to Little Pond. Other seasons, she was closed in by the woods. Her green oasis, little piece of paradise. Maine felt more like the real world than the frantic paved cities she'd lived in, the slow easiness made everyone relax and take more notice. Still, having this puzzle to sort out felt like something she needed to get her old big-city adrenaline going again. It had occurred to her since March that maybe she was making a mystery where there wasn't one, just to give her life some excitement. Another ADHD symptom. Gotta add some drama just so you don't get bored and cranky. She often played that game: Is it Bernie? Or is it ADHD? Carol pointed out to her that they were interchangeable, she was who she was and why didn't matter. But why did matter. It mattered if you wanted to separate truth from fantasy.

A huge bird landed in the clearing in front of the thick pines that ringed her yard, almost close enough for Bernie to reach out and touch if she'd had the energy to get out of the chair. It cocked its head, looking at her out of one eye.

"What are you looking at bird?" she said out loud. "You think I'm a crazy-ass drama queen?"

The bird flapped its wings.

"Do you know what happened to Stanley?"

The bird shook its head, then, wings churning the evening air, took off. It had a huge wingspan, long legs hanging down, long beak. Bernie tried to remember the little she knew about birds. She knew it wasn't a loon. Those she recognized. Was it a crane? A sandhill crane maybe? Or a cormorant or a heron? Actually, were cormorant and herons the same bird? Or were cormorants and cranes the same?

It circled, riding the wind currents, then swooped beyond the trees down the hill to the lake.

What a life, Bernie thought. Nothing to do but ride the wind and look for fish.

She started obsessing. Cormorant? What was a cormorant even? She thought about booting up the computer and Googling, but it seemed like too much work.

Then she remembered Stanley's Audubon field guide. Trees, flowers, critters, birds. Her mind started singing. Trees, flowers, critters, birds, oh my.

She dragged herself off the chair and went inside to the bookcase. She scanned her shelves. Where did I put it? Mysteries, histories, old college textbooks, trees, flowers, critters, birds. The field guide wasn't there. She knew she put it on the shelf. Her books weren't in any order. She ran through the bindings again. She hadn't looked at it, hadn't given it a thought since she brought it home that night in March and put it on the shelf. After the break-in, all the books had been scattered across the floor. Couldn't remember if

121

she'd seen it or if it was gone when she loaded the books back onto the shelves. She went through again, touching each binding, making herself read the titles out loud.

The book wasn't there.

CHAPTER 13

To get an air conditioner or not to get an air conditioner? That was the question. It happened last June, too. No one could argue that Maine was hot, but the endless cold and damp months ended with a thud and the warmth that would be laughed at by the rest of the country hit like a hammer. The newspaper building's spirits—piles of newspaper, ink, cigarette smoke and everything else that had settled in to the soul of the walls for the past one hundred and fifty years—crept out as the heat baked aging wood walls. After a few weeks, Bernie got used to it. Thoughts of air conditioning faded when she thought about how much it cost and how it was only needed a few weeks out of the year. Anyway, who knew if the wiring system in the building could handle the load? So she made do. But boy, those first hot weeks of June were a killer.

It was Tuesday night. Darkness had fallen hours before, but Bernie was behind getting that weeks' paper together. The front and back doors were propped open and moths and mosquitoes buzzed and dipped in front of the black night. Two creaking ancient fans ran at full speed.

In the twenty-four hours since she'd realized the bird book was missing, she'd wracked her brain trying to remember what had been written in it. She thought it was code for birds Stanley had spotted.

She'd never even bothered to ask anyone if he was a birdwatcher. There were letters and numbers, but she couldn't remember what they were. She hadn't taken any notice or notes, they'd just all flown past her without leaving an imprint. Some hot-shot reporter you are, she told herself. One thing her dim brain had figured out—whoever broke into her house in March had recognized it for something she hadn't and taken it.

She was trying to not let it distract her from getting the layout done. She was rushing to get as much finished early as she could because she was covering the final meeting of the Old Home Days committee in the morning. It wasn't often she'd take off in the middle of production Wednesday morning to cover something, but her role as the town's only reporter required it.

She was making progress, too. Editing stories, getting them ready to put on the pages. A finely tuned machine. Shirley had put the ads on the day before and Bernie was figuring out how everything was going to fit. It's amazing, she thought, how much I can get done when no one's around and the phone's not ringing. She opened another page on the computer. What was this one? She glanced over at her dummies on the table in the middle of the room. She'd anchored them down with old dictionaries and staplers so the fans wouldn't blow them around. Garden page. Uh oh. Sudden sinking despair. The kind that can only hit the editor of a weekly when she realizes she has two extra hours of work ahead of her that she hadn't anticipated. The club notes column hadn't been written and input. Usually Shirley did that, but she left Monday afternoon for her yearly trip to Old Orchard Beach and Bernie assured her she'd take care of it. What a pain—all the women's clubs, garden clubs and other social clubs in the area submitted notes about their activities with no regard to sentence structure, grammar, or punctuation. They had to be retyped, cleaned up, shortened. Some came by email, but others were old-fashioned hard copy.

Bernie tried to remember what she'd done with the folder with the hard copy. She'd been so obsessed with that stupid bird book she'd forgotten all about it. She had a vague memory of leafing through the folder while in the back office eating lunch the day before. She went into the office and looked at the pile of debris on her desk. The little room was bypassed by the breeze from the fans and the thick close air landed on Bernie and wrapped around her like an itchy blanket. The window had never been opened in the time Bernie had been there, but Bernie felt a huge need to open it now. She pulled and tugged. Of course, it was painted shut. That wasn't going to stop her, she was determined. She realized she was just putting off dealing with the dreaded club notes, but she didn't care. After a couple minutes of sorting through the desk drawer, she came up with a screwdriver and turned toward the window.

She could hear papers blowing around the outer office. What the hell? What about her paperweights? Whack! The door to the room slammed shut. Damn fans. She'd worry about the papers in a minute, she was focused on the war with the window. She jammed the screwdriver into the pitted wooden casement. Nothing. She jabbed harder, trying to get some leverage. The pane was stuck. Dammit! The screwdriver slipped and nicked her finger. She stuck her finger in her mouth. Shit that hurt. She heard a crash from the outer office. A familiar sound. The front door. It had been propped open with a cast-iron door stop. How could it shut?

"Who's out there? Paul? Guy?"

She turned to open her office door and tripped over her open desk drawer, cracking her shin on the radiator. She let out a stream of expletives as she limped to the door. She turned the knob. The door wouldn't give. Every inanimate object in the little room was conspiring against her. Bernie banged the door with her hip and it gave an inch. Something was blocking it from outside. She reared back as far as she could—the desk took up most of the room. She braced herself against the desk and kicked the door with the bottom of her foot. It gave enough that she could get out. She squeezed through.

The oak cabinet that held the coffee maker and microwave was blocking the door. That didn't make sense.

The dummy sheets on the table were scattered across the floor. The front door was shut, the doorstopper feet away. It took Bernie a couple seconds to notice the drawers to her desk were open, the contents scattered in a fan-blown mess across the room.

Her stomach churned. Someone had been in the newsroom, went through her stuff, blocked her in her office. Forget the fact that she'd been too moronic to notice it was going on, battling with the stupid window. Someone was looking for something and she couldn't rationalize it away. She'd cast the bait about the notebook to Rusty, Dragon, and Loren. Who knew who they told? Whatever. She'd been having fun with her own secret investigation, but it wasn't fun anymore. The time had long gone by when she should have told Pete about the notebook, the post office box, the bird book, and everything else. Things were getting out of hand. She'd tell him everything. If he was mad at her, arrested her, treated her like she was an idiot, whatever, so be it.

. . . . .

Wednesday morning's gathering of the Old Home Days committee had the inevitable Dunkin' Donuts assortment, but that didn't ease the pain of having to sit through a meeting. Bernie hated sitting while other people droned on, all the things she had to do running round in her mind on a speeded-up never-stopping carousel, that day's office chores competing with the Stanley mystery. More like a Tilt-A-Whirl than a carousel, she thought, as she ate doughnuts and took notes. She'd spent most of the night and morning trying to rehearse what she was going to say to Pete, but couldn't come up with the right words. Maybe she'd figure it out on her run later, once the paper was done, jiggle some brain cells free.

As she was leaving the meeting—it had gone on longer than she thought it would and she was under the gun—Bev Dulac cornered her. The Crow, Bernie called her. To herself, of course. She was always strutting around, cawing about something.

"I'm worried about Stanley."

Bernie's gut reaction was "you're too late." She bit her tongue. "Huh?"

Bev, impatient, rattled on. "I thought someone would find out something by now. I don't believe that hokum about an accident." Even with her Maine accent, Bev always sounded like she was reciting lines from a play. Pronouncing. She didn't have an indoor voice. Bernie looked around to see if anyone was listening, but the room had emptied. "I thought our new chief had something on the ball, but he's not doing anything," Bev said, annoyed as she caught Bernie's wandering eyes.

"That's not true. I know for a fact he's investigating."

"It's been months. You're the newspaper. Hold his feet to the fire. Like you did with Ike and the windmills."

Thanks for reminding me, that worked out great. Bernie batted down the devil on her shoulder. "What makes you think it wasn't an accident?"

Bev lowered her voice. "He was worried about something. I know he was. He almost told me, but said he had to talk to Cal first. Then he went south. Well, I thought he did."

"Have you told Pete?"

"It's more a feeling. He never said much. I don't want to seem silly." Her crow face melted a little. Bernie knew how she felt, and knew it had to take a lot for Bev to ask. "There was something else. He, well I shouldn't be telling you this, but, well, he mailed himself something. I put it in his box, but I could tell it was his own handwriting. At first I thought he was getting a little eccentric, but now I think he had a purpose."

Bernie swallowed. Oh guilt, you are a cruel mistress. "Did you tell Pete that?"

Bev was back to her usual bossiness. "He took the items from the P.O. box. I'm sure he's aware of what was in it."

"Right." Bernie felt the sweat under her arms. Shit.

"And one other thing." Geez, Bev had as many secrets as Bernie.

"Yes?"

"I don't know if this is anything."

"Okay."

Bev took a big breath. "I don't want to seem nosy." Okay. "But I overheard Stanley talking to John Carrier, the boy who survived that awful snowmobile accident last year? And it was fairly heated. This would have been in December. And that's what got Stanley agitated, I believe. That's when he told me he had to talk to Cal."

Talk about burying the lead. "I thought John was down in Portland at USM."

"He just got home for Christmas break. That day. He came into the post office to mail some packages for his mother. Stanley was getting his VA check."

"So what did they argue about?" Bernie tried to sound professionally interested, rather than hopped-up excited.

"Well, I don't usually eavesdrop, but as I said, it was heated."

Bernie nodded. Come on, come on.

"I couldn't hear everything. It had something to do with coyotes and one dying, I think. At the bog."

"Do you know the date?"

"Yes I do. December 11. That's the day of the month Stanley's VA check came and he always came right in to pick it up. I should have known when his checks started piling up, something was wrong." Her voice, querulous at "Yes I do" had softened, but it became brusque again. "Then he mailed himself that envelope December 12. Very odd. Very odd."

Caw caw caw, Bernie thought. Very odd, indeed. "Well, I know Pete is determined to find out what happened."

"Help him."

"Pete?"

"Yes, Pete," she snapped. She softened again. "And Stanley."

. . . . .

Bernie finished her run and still hadn't figured out what she was going to say to Pete. It was dusk, but the humidity hung in the air. By the time she walked the half-mile down the hill and through Redimere's little grid of streets to Pete's, she was almost as sweaty and drained as she was when she finished her run an hour before.

128

She slapped at a mosquito as she went down the driveway of the two-family where Pete lived upstairs. Hot, humid, buggy, guilty, annoyed, nervous. Bernie wished she were home on the porch with a cold beer. She walked past Pete's car and the sagging doorless shed that housed his landlord's aging Ford, and up the wooden stairs to the second-floor porch, where a lawn chair and a recycling container full of beer bottles took up most of the space.

Music came through the screen door from somewhere in the apartment. Pete, his back to her at the kitchen counter, in a T-shirt, shorts and sandals, his hair damp and curly in the humidity, was singing along. Some Van Morrison tune. He sounded good, chopping vegetables in time to the music. She paused before knocking, enjoying the suspended-in-time moment. Unaware of her watching, he looked sweet, unguarded. Definitely not Robocop. Her heart leapt a little, followed quickly by the ever-present guilt and backed up by the knowledge that she was going to piss him off and wreck the whole scene. She tapped on the door. "Hey."

He turned around, a smile, happy to see her. Ugh. "Hey, hi. Come in. What brings you here?"

The kitchen was old, with tin cupboards, linoleum floor. Apparently the landlords didn't watch much HGTV. The kitchen fit him. Comfortable, functional, neat and clean, no fuss, the table and counter spotless, no residue in the coffee pot, no dishes in the sink. She plopped down in a chair at the table. The humidity had soaked all the energy right out of her, nervousness didn't help, annoyance at her nervousness adding to the mix.

"I had some stuff I wanted to talk to you about. I didn't want to do it at the shop."

"You look like you could use a beer." He took one out of the fridge, popped it open, and handed it to her, still smiling. It was cold in her hand, already covered with condensation. She hadn't realized how thirsty she was.

"What are you making?" she asked. The beer was cold and fizzy and tasted good. It brought her back to life a little.

"Gazpacho. For the organic homemade contest?"

He turned from his chopping to look at her when she didn't answer. "For Old Home Days?"

It took her a moment to get what he was saying. "I never took you for a cook."

"I'm a man of many talents. Learned to cook when I was a kid. If I didn't cook, I didn't eat." She waited for him to elaborate, but he didn't. "No bites on our DNA bait, if that's what you wanted to talk about." He took a sip of his own beer before scooping up the cucumber he'd been chopping, dumping it into a bowl.

"Where'd all the vegetables come from?" Bernie asked, stalling. "Little early in the season for cukes and peppers."

"The Dosties, my landlords?" he turned around and she nodded. "They let me take my pick from the greenhouse. They plant way more than they can eat. Garlic's from last year," he said as he pulled apart a head of it and began chopping the cloves.

"You're going to put that whole thing in?" She really wasn't interested in the gazpacho-making so much as putting off the inevitable.

"Lots of garlic, that's part of my secret recipe. I intend to win. Bev Dulac, look out."

She took a long swallow of beer. "Speaking of secrets." She waited as Pete stopped chopping and turned around. "There's something I've been meaning to tell you."

"Okay."

Just pull off the Band-Aid. "You know that post office box key that I found in Stanley's trailer?"

His put down the knife and crossed his arms. There was still a trace of a smile, but she knew she was about to wipe it away.

"I used it."

He didn't say anything. She wasn't sure what she wanted him to say, anyway. Something to make this easier. Another dumb idea. Nothing was going to make this easier. She took a deep breath. "I looked in the box."

"Before I took his mail out?"

"Yeah."

He was stone-faced now, the laser glare at its most intense. She drank some more beer, trying to figure out how to say what she had to say.

He wasn't going to give her the time. "You found something in there."

"Yeah."

"I'm guessing Stanley didn't mail himself a copy of the Constitution autographed by Dennis Kucinich."

"No."

"Well?" His voice was level, but a flush traveled up his neck to his face.

"It was a notebook. Like a diary, with dates, numbered dates." He just stared, no more help, so she kept talking. "So not really a diary. Just the list of dates. He has the date for that snowmobile accident in it, though. Evan Wentzel died? It happened before you got here, but you probably heard about it."

Still nothing. She stumbled on.

"Um, and there's a like checklist in the back. That's where the date of the accident is, actually. And it says 'talk to Cal' and then lists a bunch of things, about coyotes and stuff. It could mean anything. Probably nothing. You know, Cal kind of took care of him, so, um. That accident, though, it's given me a funny feeling. I looked at the report and —"

"Stop."

She stopped. Drank more beer, afraid he might take the bottle away from her. Slap it right out of her hand. She would've deserved it.

"Anything else you haven't told me?"

"The bird book."

His jaw muscle twitched, laser eyes not moving from her face. "The bird book."

"Not so much a bird book. An Audubon field guide. In the trailer, I took it and put in on my shelf because I figured I could use it because I can never figure out what birds are what and animal prints, you know, in the snow, and trees and stuff, and it was in

131

good shape and it would come in handy and I didn't think anyone else would want it—"

"And I would care about this because?"

"I realized the other day someone took it when they broke into my house in March."

The jaw muscle worked again. "And?"

"Well, he'd written notes in the back. I thought they were bird sightings or something it was like numbers and letters and I feel like a dummy because I don't even know if he's a bird watcher or if they list them that way and never bothered to—"

"And?"

"Someone was in the newsroom last night while I was in my office the window was stuck and I was trying to get it open. They blocked the door and I couldn't get out and they looked through my desk, ransacked it really, the papers were scattered all over the place and I think they were looking for the notebook—"

"You didn't report that."

"Yeah, um, the door was open and they didn't take anything and I was way behind in the production I forgot about the garden notes and that's why I was back in the office I was looking for them and I'd decided by then I was going to talk to you anyway—"

"Anything else you haven't told me?" Still level, but a low, angry level.

"I guess that's all." She hadn't realized there was so much.

He stared at her, arms still crossed, chopping knife gripped in his left hand. A little tight, it seemed to Bernie. "You should have told me this. All of it, back in the beginning."

"I know. I thought you would think it was dumb. You know, Sherlock Bernie with her theories about foul play." She tried a grin.

"That's why you didn't tell me you went into his P.O. box and stole something? Because you thought I'd think it was dumb?"

"That, well, I was going to put it back but then you went in and I didn't know how to tell you and I thought I could figure out what the dates meant then as more time went by I planned on telling you but didn't know what to say and I knew you'd be mad—"

"Mad? Mad?" The last one was a strangled cry. "Do you know what that could mean to my investigation? My goddam investigation that has been going nowhere? You steal something from a P.O. box and don't put it back because you're afraid I'm going to be mad?"

He turned around and tossed the chopped garlic into the bowl and took a two-cup measure and started scooping the contents of the bowl—it looked like tomatoes, peppers, onions, Bernie couldn't tell what else—a profusion of red, green, and white—into a blender. Poured in some tomato juice from a bottle on the counter, then some vinegar. Turned the blender on. Watched it with his back to her. The bright chunks of vegetable churned into a muddy soup. He left the blender on a lot longer than Bernie thought he needed to. She wasn't going to point that out, though. She waited. The blender was loud, really loud. He wouldn't have heard her even if she could think of anything to say.

Pete finally stopped and poured it back into the bowl.

"Jesus Christ." He still had his back to her, but she felt the anger simmering off of him. He turned around and there was no doubt. "Were you playing a game? In what world don't you tell me this?" He wasn't yelling anymore, back to level. But it was worse than the yelling. Cold and flat.

Heat traveled up her neck to her face. Pete's eyes were locked on hers. A vein in his temple throbbed and his jaw twitched. His face, already flushed, had grown darker. Forget Robocop, he was the Incredible Hulk. Not funny. Shut up and fix this. Or at least rise to the occasion.

"I'm telling you now."

"Did you bring it?"

She reached in her shorts pocket and took out the notebook. She'd almost forgotten it was there. He took it without looking at her and leafed through it. "I'm not sure what all the stuff in it means," she said, hoping to move him past his anger. "I mean those numbers don't seem to have a pattern. Some are repeated and the snowmobile accident date I know that's probably important you know I've been thinking about it and it seems like—"

"Okay." Dismissed.

She wasn't going to give up. "I was thinking about the snowmobile accident, how the report didn't say Rusty called dispatch, even though he says he did."

The music had ended and Bernie wished there were some other noise in the hot apartment besides her voice.

"Anyway, everything seemed dumb when I said it out loud. And the trailer didn't seem important. This stuff? You said you thought the DNA was the key—"

"Don't tell me what I said."

"Bev thinks there's something wrong with Stanley's death, too."

"You told all this to Bev Dulac?"

"No. But she's worried because —"

"Are you done?"

"I guess so." She burned with shame. The only thing keeping her from running out of the kitchen right then was the fact that it would make her look even more like an idiot.

His voice was a low rumble, his glare unbearable. "Did it ever occur to you that, if someone hurt Stanley, maybe they'd hurt you, too?"

She looked at her now-empty beer bottle. Interesting label. She picked at it. "Are you going to arrest me? Because of the P.O. box thing?"

"Jesus," he said. "Go home." He turned back to the counter and put a plastic lid on the bowl of gazpacho.

"So how much trouble am I in?"

He tamped down the lid. Forcefully. "Go."

"Okay. But Cal would have —"

Pete went over to the back door and opened it. "If you haven't figured it out by now, I'm not Cal."

CHAPTER 14

Every day threatened rain the week leading up to Old Home Days. In true Redimere style, all conversation was about how rain would ruin the weekend. But Saturday morning, the Fourth of July, dawned about as perfect a summer day as Bernie could imagine.

Thursday and Friday she'd spent a lot of time at the office, wrapping up business and taking care of chores like planning feature stories and cleaning the bathroom. They were things that had to be done and she'd been putting them off. She was also avoiding Pete. She guessed she wasn't going to be arrested. She wasn't sure what was going to happen, but she knew she didn't want to see his anger, his disgust. She was used to people getting annoyed with her, the novelty of her wore off pretty fast. She'd experienced it enough in her life, seeing people she thought were friends roll their eyes when they thought she wasn't looking, overheard conversations about what a pain in the ass she was, how annoying. She expected it. She knew deep down it would happen sooner or later with Pete, too. But it still hurt. Not that it wasn't her fault. Because it was. In the week since their talk in his apartment, she'd managed to stay out of his way. She wondered if he was avoiding her, too.

The memory of his anger still burned her. She wasn't sure what she had been planning to say about Cal. That he'd laugh it off? Yell at her? Who cares what Cal would have done? Why'd she even bring him up? Desperate to find a common thread, she guessed. Distract Pete from the subject at hand. Great plan. She's glad he didn't let her finish the sentence, because she had no idea what her stupid point was going to be. She'd just been trying to fill the angry, angry air.

She never used to care much if cops were mad at her. In her old life, some were friends and sources, and some hated her guts. It went with the territory. The problem with Pete was his opinion meant too much to her. That was bad journalism. She had to get back to her roots and remind herself why she was doing this. She hadn't been a good Catholic for a long time, but she still felt the burden of penance. Losing Pete's friendship was penance for the journalism sins she'd committed since Stanley's body was found. Some venial, some mortal.

Back to basics. She was even more fired up to get cracking on the Stanley stuff. The right way. Now that the albatross of the notebook no longer weighed her down, she actually felt renewed. She'd called Denise Carrier to ask if John had said anything about an argument with Stanley. Denise was flummoxed. "I didn't even know they knew each other," she told Bernie, but gave her John's cellphone number. He was spending the summer in Portland, working. Bernie tried the number repeatedly, left a few messages, but he hadn't called back.

Today she was going to not let any of it bother her—Pete, the fact she was a shitty journalist, the questions about Stanley. It was a warm, sunny day. The Fourth of July. She strolled the midway at Bigelow Park. It was noon and already there were a lot of people around—holding hands, eating cotton candy and hot dogs, smiling and greeting one other, the mountains in the background against a cloudless blue sky, the river gurgling nearby. It was almost too nice. Like a movie. *Picnic*? No, that was dark and ended badly. More like some kind of overly sentimental Disney flick.

It finally felt like summer after the never-ending months of cold and wind and ice and snow and rain, of sand and salt all over the car, the coat sleeves, the shoes, and the kitchen floor. Followed by months of mud and damp clothes, damp house, wet sneakers. Suddenly it was a perfect day. She knew to enjoy it while she could. The weather and her moods were a lot alike, no telling when things would go south.

There were splashes and laughter from the river as people got ready for the canoe and kayak race. Bernie sat under one of the massive willows that lined the bank, a big chunk of fried dough warm in her hand. She could sit here all day and look at the river, the mountains. The fried dough cheered her up. She'd run five miles that morning, so she deserved it. Hard not to love fried dough. Part of it, of course, was because it was dough, fried, covered with sugar and cinnamon. What's not to like? Then there was the name: fried dough. No need to pretty it up, make it sound like health food. It was what it was. She took a big bite, scattering powdered sugar and cinnamon down the front of her shirt.

"In Philly we called that funnel cakes."

Bernie looked up from trying to wipe her shirt clean. Pete, in uniform, stood above her, the sun behind him, making it impossible to see his expression.

"I've had funnel cakes and they're a sorry second," Bernie said, trying to gauge his mood. She felt at a disadvantage sitting on the grass while he loomed over her, but standing up would have meant acknowledging that.

He squatted down.

"How are you?"

"Good," she said, wary. "You?"

He smiled, a mild shadow of the big crinkly dimpled one. And only for a second. "Wanna talk?"

"Okay." She wondered if he was going to yell at her again. It didn't seem like it, but you could never tell. Or maybe this was her arrest, but he was doing it in a good-cop kind of way.

"Explain why you didn't talk to me." His voice wasn't angry, more curious.

Bernie's shame and embarrassment, which had returned the moment she saw him, paralyzed her. She couldn't think. The little bit of fried dough in her mouth turned to sand and she felt tears building. She shrugged and looked at the river, away from Pete.

"I know you're not stupid and you're not dishonest," he said. "I know you know that was a really bad error in judgment to go into that box, even though you had the key, even though you thought no one would care, if that's what you thought. I know you wouldn't deliberately keep information important to a police investigation from me. I'm not going to get into why you had so many lapses in judgment. That's for you to figure out. But I want to know why you didn't trust me."

"It's not that." Stricken, she turned to look back at him, despite the fact she hadn't managed to blink back the tears and felt them on her cheeks, tasted them. "I trust you."

"Do you?" His voice was level, obviously unmoved by her tears. That was fine with her. Her rule that female journalists could never cry was a solid one and she felt like a dope for doing it now. Better to pretend it wasn't happening. She'd turned her face back to the river, but could feel him watching her, waiting. No, she didn't have a good answer for why she hadn't told him. She wasn't sure. Couldn't remember all her rationalizations. So she didn't say anything.

"You need to let me do my job and respect my position," he said after a long minute.

"I know. Sorry."

"Look at me," he said, more softly than she deserved. He waited until she was looking at him. "I'm not going to pursue the P.O. box thing, but you ever do something like that again it won't end with me." His eyes searched hers, she nodded in acknowledgment, wishing the tears would stop.

"This isn't a game. You could get hurt. Okay?"

"Okay."

He got up and left.

Bernie let out her breath. She got up after he was a good

distance away and threw the rest of her fried dough in the trash. She wandered the midway, the smell of fried food and animals from the farm exhibits a nauseating mix. She had a sudden memory from last year's Old Home Days. Stanley going through trash cans, picking out bottles and cans and putting them in his shopping cart as the fair swirled around him. The sight made her sad at the time. Poor Stanley, grubby and out of place and scrounging for bottles as everyone else had fun, oblivious. Then she hadn't given it a second thought. Until now.

She felt queasy. The humidity was picking up and the warmth was uncomfortable. The sunlight, which had seemed like a gift from Disney a little while ago, now a harsh glare, uncomfortable and cloying. Someone had killed him and no one cared. Poor Stanley. Poor me. Screwed things up again. She felt a grip in the pit of her stomach that she knew was more than the fried dough. There was nothing she wanted to do here now. Didn't want to run into Pete again. Wasn't hungry. Not interested in rides or games. She went home.

· · · · ·

Bernie walked back to the park after supper, carrying a portable lawn chair over her shoulder and twenty dollars in her pocket for the beer tent, clipped to her driver's license with a bobby pin. It was a trick she used when she ran. A regular Hint for Heloise. Why lug a purse around when you didn't have to? She'd felt better after taking a nap, though even the nap and a cool shower hadn't managed to soften the edge of the conversation with Pete.

She settled in on the grass, picking a spot with easy access to the beer and porta-potties, but close enough to the stage to enjoy the music. Carol and Vince would find her when they showed up later and she could pour her heart out to Carol, who would only say "I told you so" a little bit and mostly make her feel better. A country band was solidly into its act and a dozen or so fans who seemed to know the words to every song were lurching around in a drunken dance in front of the stage. Most of the town was at the fair. The stage was set up along the river. The midway was across the parking lot. She could hear the barkers and music from the rides. Just upstream from the dam, where the rocky, speedy Wesserunsett widened out into a flat expanse, was the barge that held that night's fireworks. Over in the parking lot, it looked like Dragon Dube was doing a brisk business from his ice cream truck. She was beginning to feel all was well with the world again.

To the side of the stage she could see the next band getting ready to start. She looked at the program, Dermot McHugh and the Mountain Ramblers. She looked again, jolted. How had she not noticed Pete's name among the list of band members? Sure enough, there he was standing with the others, wearing Levis and a white short-sleeved shirt, holding a banjo, drinking a beer and laughing, talking to a big guy with steel-gray curls. Dermot McHugh himself maybe? Would wonders never cease, as her dad always said. Bernie settled in with her beer.

. . . . .

As dusk fell, Dragon Dube sold a final ice cream and shut his window. Business was good, but he had better business of a different kind somewhere else. Something that was going to make the ice cream truck look like chump change.

He turned to Justin, who'd been hanging with him. "You coming?"

"I don't know, dude," Justin said. "I don't know if you oughta be getting involved in this shit. Remember what John told us? Hell, he's so nervous, he's spending the summer in Portland."

Dragon laughed. "C'mon, we're gonna have some fun and make some dough. If you're scared, you can stay in the back of the truck. Just back me up if I need you."

"I'm not scared," Justin shot back. Then, "I'll stay in the back of the truck."

Dragon checked his glove box to see if he had everything. He did. He was all set. He touched the gun for luck, then roared out of the parking lot.

. . . . .

Ray Morin sat in his patrol car near the intersection of Route 145 and Pond Road. He didn't really like working nights, but everyone did extra duty Fourth of July weekend. If there was one thing worse than working a Saturday night shift, it was working Saturday night Fourth of July. Everybody was a cowboy. A cowboy with twelve beers under his belt and a box of illegal fireworks in his pickup.

His cellphone rang. It was Rusty. "What's with the phone?"

"Friggin' radio's on the blink again," Rusty said. "Saw Dube speeding in that damn ice cream truck toward the Pond Road. Check him out and I'll be out to back you up."

Ray sighed and started up the cruiser.

. . . . .

Pete put his beer down on the edge of the stage and plucked at the strings of his banjo, checking to make sure it was in tune, even though he knew it was. He didn't usually play in front of people he knew. In Philly, he was in a bluegrass band and there was rarely anyone he knew in the audience. He liked it that way. He could be someone else—not the cop. Here, he was The Chief. He hadn't even told anyone in town he was in a band. It wasn't his idea that the band play at Old Home Days. Dermot had set it up, "Hey, it's a gig, right?" he said in his Irish brogue, playing it up. "We never turn down a job, Petey me boy."

Pete saw Bernie sitting in a lawn chair, drinking a beer and bobbing her head to the music. He'd been so pissed last week, but at himself as much as her. He should have followed his instinct months ago that she was holding something back. He let those big brown laughing eyes keep him from thinking straight. There was the cold stab of betrayal mixed in, too. Why didn't she tell him? He knew she was honest, wasn't a bullshitter. When he saw her earlier under that tree, eating fried dough, with her ponytail and shorts, he was surprised that he was happy to see her. He'd been all set to read her the riot act that he'd been too pissed off to read her the week before, but he just couldn't be as mad as he should've been. Hell, it was all he could do not to hug her when she started crying. Chump, he said to himself. He drained his beer and was thinking about getting another one when his cellphone rang. County dispatch.

141

Weird. Ray, Rusty, and Jamie were all on patrol, if there was something going on, one of them would call.

"Novotny," he answered it. Then listened.

Dermot nudged him. "Hey man, put away the mobile. We're on in five."

"Gotta go. Sorry." Pete had already forgotten the show, Bernie, and everything else. He left Dermot staring behind him as he ran across the grass toward the parking lot, not realizing until he got to his car that he was still clutching his banjo. He threw it into the back of the car, jumped in, and was moving before the door shut.

. . . . .

Bernie saw the flash of white as Pete ran across the grass to his car. Something was going on. She grabbed her chair, rolled it into its case, hoisted it over her shoulder and started jogging home to her scanner, her phone, and hopefully some information. She was huffing up the hill to her house wondering why they made portable lawn chairs so darn heavy and why she didn't bring the office keys with her when Carol pulled up in her van.

"I was looking for you. Hop in."

"What's going on?"

"Shooting. Heard it on the scanner. On that tote road off Pond that goes into the bog." She was breathless. "Two down, one's an officer."

"Jesus," said Bernie. Rusty, Ray, or Jamie? Neither she nor Carol said anything in the five minutes it took to get there.

As fast as they were, the state police were faster. There was already a cruiser blocking the dirt road.

"We're press," Bernie said, showing the trooper her ID, the one she made when she bought the paper and hadn't had a chance to use until now.

"Law enforcement only."

She cursed the time she had wasted jogging around with her stupid chair.

"Can you tell us what's happening?" Bernie asked.

"Sorry, ma'am. You have to move out of the roadway."

Bernie and Carol stepped onto the grass and leaned against the stone wall. Carol put her giant shoulder bag on the ground and rooted through it, bringing out two notebooks, one of which she handed to Bernie, pens, her camera and a telephoto lens.

A couple hundred yards down the dirt road, they could see the police department's Suburban and cruiser, two state cruisers. Pete's car. Farther down, just visible in the twilight, a lump of lime green showed above the shrubs.

"Tell me that's not the ice cream truck," Bernie said to Carol, who had started taking pictures with the telephoto lens.

"It is."

"I wonder what that means?"

"Nothing good."

Behind them, the state police mobile crime lab—a converted RV—approached. The trooper waved it through and they watched it bump down to the waiting police.

Carol looked through the viewfinder.

"Can you see anything through that?"

"Not much, people milling around, it's at the edge of the woods, hard to see much."

"You know, this is the second incident to take place on this road since I've come to Redimere."

"The snowmobile crash."

"They let me go down the road for that one. Once there's a cop involved, they shut things right down."

Carol and Bernie jumped as the portable spotlights from the mobile crime lab burst alive, even though it wasn't dark out yet.

Bernie was glad she was wearing an unhealthy slathering of mosquito repellent. The bugs were merciless. While they waited, she told Carol about her conversation with Pete.

"Could've been worse," Carol said.

"I guess I got off easy."

"Don't take this the wrong way, but I hope you've learned your lesson."

Bernie sighed. "I have. Until next time."

Another vehicle roared up and skidded to a stop near them. A van from Channel 14 in Lewiston. As a videographer started unloading his equipment from the back, a reporter Bernie recognized as Trish LaBrie—could that possibly be her real name?—picked her way through the knee-high grass. She wore a dress and high heels. Not exactly what you want to be wearing on a July night in rural Maine.

"Hi, guys. Any idea what's going on?" she asked with a TV smile, waving at the bugs.

"Not yet, and we've been here over an hour," Bernie said. Reporters at scenes like this usually bonded while they waited for information. It was when the information finally came that they stopped being friends.

As the hours passed. Bernie, Carol, and Trish were joined by a college-age kid from the *Lewiston Sun-Journal* and the Farmington reporter for the *Morning Sentinel* in Waterville. Jeff Lydon was the last to appear.

"I was on a date at Sugarloaf. We were going to watch the fireworks when my boss called," he said. "What did I miss?"

The answer was nothing. There was a lot of activity down the road. Cruisers and other official-looking cars coming and going. Cops standing in groups, some chatting, some scurrying around with purpose, some doing nothing. All lit up in the eerie glow of the strobe lights. The reporters waited and watched for something to happen, nursing sodas Carol dug out of her van and trading war stories—the older ones at least—about similar scenes they'd waited at over the years. The calm before the storm they all knew was coming when the story broke.

A loud boom split the night. Everyone jumped.

Bernie looked at her watch. Nine-thirty. "The fireworks."

They turned and looked. Above the tree line to the south, they could just see the multi-colored bloom. Then, as the fireworks exploded behind them, they turned their attention back to the shooting scene.

Sometime past eleven one of the state cruisers came up the dirt road, followed by two ambulances. No lights flashing, no sirens. The cluster of reporters watched. No one asked what the slow, silent ambulances meant. They knew. It was just a matter of time before someone would come and tell them officially.

They didn't have long to wait. Pete and a state trooper walked up the road behind the ambulance convoy. The Channel 14 videographer switched on his light and a thousand mosquitoes and moths dove in for the kill.

"For those of you who don't know me, I'm Lieutenant Sean Leary from the Maine State Police," the trooper said. "We have two subjects deceased. One a police officer, one a citizen. We are not releasing their names until we notify next of kin. The incident is under investigation."

Pete stood next to Leary, his hands behind his back, staring beyond the reporters, his face white in the glare of the TV light.

Bernie had to ask. She hated to, but she had to. "Chief, we know the officer is Ray Morin, Rusty Dyer or Jamie Paradis. Can you confirm which one?"

"We can't tell you until the family is notified. We're doing that shortly," Pete said.

"Is Dragon Dube involved?" Carol asked. "We saw the ice cream truck."

"No comment."

"What happened?" Bernie asked.

"We're still trying to sort it out," Pete said. "Two people were shot. A third person was involved—"

He stopped a second as the reporters, as one, began writing.

"You might as well all go home, because we're not going to release any more tonight."

Leary added, "We're going to have a press conference tomorrow. You're all on our email list, right? We'll let everyone know where and when."

. . . . .

At the office, Bernie started typing her notes into the computer before they got overtaken by whatever she learned tomorrow. She'd been wishing for a big story to break. She'd also warned herself to be careful what she wished for. Bingo on both counts. Her meds had worn off and she was in major heat, hunger and adrenaline fueled re-entry. Two bodies. A cop. Rusty, Ray, or Jamie? Who else? Her conversation with Pete. The bog. Two people dead. Third person involved. The ice cream truck. Stanley. John Carrier. Pete. Focus. Think about one thing at time. Who? What? Why? She typed a little, then stared at the screen as if it would give her the answers.

The front door was propped open to catch any cooling stray breeze. She didn't realize Pete had walked in until he was standing next to her.

"Saw the light on and wanted to let you know the press conference is tomorrow at ten in front of the police station," he said. "I figured I'd tell you in person, since you were here."

"Thanks."

"We're still gathering the information. I was just getting some air."

"What happened down there? You okay?" She hoped she didn't sound too much like a reporter. She was asking as a friend. Her discomfort and embarrassment of earlier was gone. So was all the guilt from the past few months. Here was her conversation buddy of before, her Red Sox pal, stunned and broken.

He looked at his hands and then wiped them on his white shirt. So clean hours earlier, now covered with grime and soaked with sweat. "I guess I can tell you. We're going to release it at the press conference anyway. It's not like you're publishing in the morning."

Okay, so he was going to take it as a reporter question, not a friend question. They probably weren't friends anymore, anyway. She was lucky he was even talking to her.

"Dragon shot Ray," he said, his voice rising, as if just realizing, and not believing, what happened. "Ike Miller was there. Dragon was reloading, was going to shoot again, so Miller grabbed Ray's gun and shot Dragon."

He looked at the ceiling and closed his eyes a second, then back at her. "Ray and Dragon are both dead."

146

He sat down as if the weight of the night had finally dropped him. "What the fuck?" He almost whispered it, looking at her with the same white-faced shellshock he had the night of Cal's fire.

"What was Ike Miller doing there?"

"Checking his gate."

"Are we on the record?" She realized that might sound jerky. She was stunned, too, but she had a story she had to hit hard. One of the biggest she'd ever covered and it was right in her backyard. Her territory. If this was on the record, she could use it. There'd been too many other reporters there tonight to go easy.

"Sure. Whatever." He dropped his gaze, stared at her desk. Was he pissed? Thinking? She couldn't tell. He took a deep breath. "You're going to hear this soon enough. Justin Mercier was there, hiding in Dragon's truck."

"Holy shit. Is he okay?"

"He's shaken up."

Pete took another deep breath. "I had to tell Annie about Ray."

"Sorry." Bernie wanted it to make sense, grab the pieces out of the air and put them together. Impossible, the pieces flew and danced around, out of reach.

"What charges are being brought against Ike?"

Pete didn't respond and she thought she'd have to ask again, but then he looked up from the spot on her desk he'd been staring at, the first time she'd seen the green laser look since he came in. "None. Dragon was reloading. Miller told him to drop the gun and he didn't. Ray was still alive at that point. Four bullets in him. Miller thought Dragon was going to keep shooting, so he shot Dragon."

She wrote that down, hoping her face didn't give her away. No charges? Fucking Wild West out there.

"I'm responsible for this, Bernie," he said, looking straight into her eyes again, green lasers full throttle.

At first she thought he meant Ike not being charged, but his face told her no, it was everything. Dragon. Ray. Everything. "Pete, you can't—"

"The hell I can't." His voice rose and cracked. "It happened on

147

my watch. I was way too easy on Dragon. Should have backed up Ray more. Let my feelings get in the way of doing my job." He kept his eyes on her, searching, willing her to understand. "I screwed up. Two people are dead, one of them is one of mine. It's all on me."

He put his hands on his knees in preparation to get up, looked away. "What a waste," he said, almost a whisper. He was out the door before Bernie could answer.

Bernie's mind spun as she walked home an hour later. Ray and Dragon dead. Dead. She couldn't believe it. Pete shell-shocked, beating himself up. Ike shot Dragon, but wouldn't be charged. As soon as she latched on to one thought, another one crowded it out. She tried to slow down her head, took a deep breath. The wet blanket of humidity that had been hanging over the town for days that seemed to be gone that morning at the fair—was it really the same day? No, yesterday actually—was back in force. The early morning was quiet, dark, without even the pop of firecrackers that usually punctuate every hour of Fourth of July weekend. Moths danced in the streetlight at the corner as she turned to go up the hill. Lightning flashed to the west, out toward the mountains. She wished for a storm. A big one. Torrents of rain and wind that would wash away the dead, dead air.

CHAPTER 15

Some things percolate. They fester. The volcano builds up deep in the Earth's core for centuries before it blows. The ocean changes color, the waters recede, before the tsunami hits. The forgotten cigarette between the couch cushions sizzles and glows for hours before the fire starts.

Not in Redimere.

The day after Ray Morin and Dragon Dube died dawned hot and muggy. The town was dizzy, airless, that feeling that comes when something unimaginably bad has happened. But under that vacuum was a hurricane force wind of horror, anger, grief, frustration, pointing fingers and accusations.

At Choppy's before the press conference, the shooting was the only topic of conversation.

You'd think it was simple: screwed-up kid shoots cop, passerby shoots kid. But this was Redimere, and it wasn't simple. Some people thought Dragon had it coming. Some thought Ike was trigger-happy. There was a faction that felt Ray was playing with fire, the way he tormented Dragon.

Bernie tried to stay out of the rolling, restaurant-wide argument and look like she was concentrating on her coffee and eggs.

"Everyone's going to that press conference," Debbie said as

she refilled Bernie's coffee mug. "You'd think it was the Little League championship game or something. A little sick if you ask me."

Bernie nodded and gulped some coffee.

"My cousin says Rusty is a mess. He got home around six a.m. and just sat up in a chair, moaning and groaning, crying his foolish head off." Debbie snorted. "He always was a pussy."

Bernie nodded again. She didn't really blame poor Rusty, he and Ray had worked together for a long time.

"What do you think of all this?" Debbie asked.

Bernie looked around to see if anyone was listening, but they were all busy with their own debates, the woman on the stool next to her with her back to her, chewing it over with the guy on the other side. Ditto for the guy on her left.

"I don't know. I liked Dragon. You know, a little stoned, a little flaky, but big-hearted. Sweet."

Debbie nodded.

"I liked Ray, too. He was a hardass, but he used to help me out when I needed it, at least before Pete came to town."

"Ray was a good egg," Debbie said as she went down the counter to fill more coffee mugs.

Bernie didn't say the biggest thing she felt—it pissed her off that Ike had been judge, jury, and executioner, but was off the hook. Was she letting their mutual dislike get in the way of seeing him as the hero, the guy who tried to save Ray, that a lot of people thought he was? She didn't know. Didn't care either. She hoped the press conference would help her put it into some kind of perspective.

. . . . .

The courtyard outside the police station was crowded with media, not only Trish and her crew from Lewiston, but TV stations from as far away as Boston. Bernie also recognized newspaper reporters from all over the state and a bunch of people that she didn't recognize at all. The nervous *Lewiston Sun-Journal* stringer from the night before had been replaced by an older guy, a staff writer.

"Andy Horgan," he said, sticking his hand out. "Who you

with? *Bangor Daily News? Sentinel?*"

"Bernie O'Dea, *Peaks Weekly Watcher*," she said, pressing her take-out coffee cup against her boob with her notebook and pencil hand so she could return his handshake. It was limp and clammy, like grabbing a bag of hot dogs that had sat on the picnic table in the hot sun too long.

"This'll be nice for a Monday front, usually we've got nothing from Sunday," he said. "Looks like all the vultures are out. Must be slow all over," he added, with an air of seen it all before. She wanted to tell him to get over himself, but didn't have the energy.

The microphone squealed as the official state police spokesman stepped up. The townsfolk behind the mob of press chattered, drinking coffee and talking on cellphones, but the reporters settled in, shushing the crowd.

Besides a heavy state police presence, officials included a guy from the attorney general's office Bernie had dealt with a few times, and a bunch of other guys in suits with short haircuts and bull necks she didn't recognize. Pete was clean and fresh in his dress white uniform shirt, but looked like he didn't get much sleep. A piece of toilet paper clung to his jaw where he'd cut himself shaving. Bernie wished she could go up and gently take it off, kiss the cut, still gripped by his pain from the night before. And as bad as last night was, she had a feeling his hell was just beginning.

Rusty, Jamie, and Dawna huddled in the doorway, kids trying to shelter themselves from a storm. Sandy MacCormack and Don Littlefield were off to the side near the firetruck bays, fire chief and public works director, leaning against the brick wall, arms folded, protecting their fortress.

The gathering felt like a wake.

The state police spokesman took the lead. Same guy from when Bernie was a rookie reporter twenty years before. He had the routine down pat. They'd reviewed Ray's cruiser tape and interviewed Rusty and Ike Miller, and once all the official cop speak was sorted through, it boiled down to this: Ray saw Dragon drive down the road toward the bog and followed. He pulled up and parked behind the ice cream truck and asked Dragon to get out.

Dragon became belligerent, so Ray pepper-sprayed him.

Dragon shot Ray four times.

Ike Miller saw it all, yelled for Dragon to put away his weapon. Dragon ignored him. Then, he told police, his military training kicked in. Dragon's gun jammed, so Ike ran to Ray, who was slumped against the rail fence, grabbed his service revolver, told Dragon again to drop the gun. Dragon was sitting in the driver's seat trying to unjam it and reload. Ike stuck Ray's gun in the window and told Dragon to put down the gun a third time.

When he didn't, Ike shot him.

That was the summary. It had been a long and complex recitation and when the spokesman paused, most of the reporters were still writing. He waited for them to catch up. "As far as the state is concerned, Mr. Miller is a hero. He saw an officer attacked, he felt there was threat of further attack and he stopped it. No charges will be brought against him."

A buzz went through the crowd.

"It was an execution," someone behind Bernie said. She turned around to see if she could tell who, but all she saw was a sea of shocked faces.

Someone else said in the crowd behind the press said, a little louder, "Cop killer got what he deserved."

The spokesman turned to Pete. "Chief?" Then he said to the press, "Redimere Police Chief Pete Novotny."

Pete was pale, but his voice was strong and steady. "A police officer—a good man—is dead. He was a brave and good cop. Our heart goes out to his wife, Annie, and his daughters, Ashley and Brittany. Redimere has lost an officer, but they've lost a husband and father.

"Our hearts also go out to the Dube family. They've lost someone, too. But Ike Miller did what he had to do. He tried to save Officer Morin's life."

"Chief Novotny," it was TV Trish. "How do you feel about your officer's death?"

Pete's eyes met Bernie's for a second. Bernie couldn't believe reporters still asked that lame question. What the hell do they expect the answer to be? I feel great! Like dancing! Someone had asked Pete the same thing after Cal died and Pete had fielded it gracefully. But later, simmering with anger, he told Bernie what he really thought. Bernie wondered if Pete was going to take Trish's head off.

Of course, he didn't. "I feel like this is a tragedy for everyone involved."

Trish nodded in full TV frowny face, waiting for him to elaborate.

"What was the role of Justin Mercier?" Bernie asked, knowing that was all Pete was going to say about his feelings.

Pete hesitated. "No role. For those of you who don't know, a fourth party, Justin Mercier, age twenty-two, was in the back of Mr. Dube's ice cream truck. He didn't see what happened, but what little he heard corroborates the facts. As far as we're concerned, he had nothing to do with it."

Justin didn't see anything. That means the story police got was from the only living person who actually saw what happened, Ike Miller. Could that really be classified as "the facts"? Bernie considered asking that, but knew it was wrong time, wrong crowd.

The state police spokesman said, "We have some loose ends to tie up. But it's pretty cut and dried. We'll have an official report sometime in the near future." He began to turn, conference over.

"Chief," said Bernie. Everyone looked at her. "Is your department satisfied with those findings?"

She concentrated on the piece of toilet paper on Pete's jaw as it worked for a couple seconds. "Yes."

She tried to decipher his look. Was that a yes yes? Or a yes for the crowd, we'll talk later?

"Why wasn't Officer Morin wearing a bullet-proof vest?" Trish asked.

Way to go, Trish. Bernie gave her a telepathic high-five.

"Officers aren't required to wear one," Pete said. "It's their choice. Officer Morin did most of the time, but not always. Ours aren't in the best condition, we haven't had replacements in years and they're uncomfortable."

"Why didn't Ray call for backup? Wasn't that procedure when Dragon was involved?" Bernie asked.

"I don't know why he didn't."

"Is it common for someone who's been pepper-sprayed to be able to almost immediately shoot four shots from a gun?" asked the *Morning Sentinel* reporter, Nick. He had cowlick-happy red hair and freckles, and Bernie always wanted to call him Opie, but he was also a smart kid who gave her a run for her money. She gave him a telepathic high-five, too. Let's not let these guys off the hook.

"People react to pepper spray in different ways," Pete said. "We know he was pepper-sprayed and we know he shot Officer Morin. So in this case, the answer is yes."

"When do we get to see the videotape from the cruiser?" asked Andy, the clammy *Lewiston* reporter. Good question. Bernie gave him a telepathic high-five, too, despite the telepathic grossness of his fingers.

"We're not releasing that," the assistant attorney general said.

Sentinel Nick caught her eye and mouthed "FOIA." Bernie nodded.

"Okay folks, is that it?" asked the spokesman. Everyone looked done. Fine with Bernie. Let them do their TV reports, their blog posts, their daily paper stories. Put 'em on the web. She didn't care. She had inside access. She'd have more than all of them when the *Watcher* came out Thursday.

The law enforcement group filed back into the police station, Pete holding the door open for the others. She hoped he'd look back, catch her eye. He didn't.

She turned to walk the block and a half back to the newspaper office, already writing the story in her head. She heard a huffing behind her and felt clammy hot dogs on her shoulder.

"Hey, Bernice." It was Lewiston Andy.

"Bernadette. Bernie."

"Right," he said, unimpressed. "Wonder if I could use your

office to call my newsroom? My cell's dead."

"Sure."

"You know," he said, wheezing as he tried to keep up. "We need to file a right-to-know request for that cruiser video."

"My thoughts exactly."

"Hey." It was Sentinel Nick. "You want to file that FOIA together?" He was talking to Bernie. The more news organizations involved with a Freedom of Information Act request—FOIA—the better.

"Definitely," Bernie said. "We need to know what happened. Not just what Ike Miller and the state police said happened, but what actually happened. I can do the paper work."

He nodded. "Right. Talk to you later. Gotta let the office know what I've got." He trotted away, punching at his cellphone with his thumb. Lucky kid, working for a daily. But it didn't matter. Her news machine had kicked in—that engine that went on when she got hold of a big story and focused on it like a missile. Daily, weekly. Whatever. She was charged up. All the spinning puzzle pieces from the night before were arranging themselves in her head in 9-point Courier. She hadn't felt like this since before she came to Redimere.

"So you guys are gonna handle it, right? The right-to-know request?" Andy asked.

Bernie nodded and walked faster, wishing he would go away and stop interrupting her brain at work.

"I know where I know you from," he said, cutting the story in her head short. "Drega."

Carl Drega. Colebrook, New Hampshire. 1997. Crazy malcontent shot a judge, a newspaper editor, and two cops, all dead. Wounded two others.

"Who'd you work for?" Bernie asked. She didn't remember him. But there'd been a lot of press there. For days. Reporters wearing the same clothes, begging telephones from local businesses as the story unfolded. No cellphones back then. It was the biggest thing she'd ever covered. But this was just as big, and it was in her town.

"Stringing for the *Herald*," he said. *"Boston Herald."*

Big whoop. "Right."

"Didn't you win some kind of award for your Drega stories?" he asked.

"Yeah."

He looked at her.

"New England Press Association Breaking News Coverage Reporter of the Year." She didn't say it with any sense of pride. All the stories related to Drega, awful as they were, wrote themselves. It was the story that launched her to bigger and better things. The story, not the award. By the time she won it, she'd moved on up to another paper, a bigger job.

He sighed. "Yup, those were the good old days."

She didn't want to give him the satisfaction, but they were. As horrific as that story was, she always thought of it as the last gasp of good old-fashioned journalism. Reporters talking to people, digging out the details. Being horrified—stunned—but doing their jobs. Because they knew the story had to be told and they wanted to be the ones to tell it. She thought of all the reporters these days, tied to email and Google and their desks, who probably wouldn't feel the thrill of what used to go into the chase on a big story.

"We were the lucky ones," he said, making a nod to where Nick had run off, echoing her thoughts.

"We were." She couldn't help herself.

"So what are you doing here? In Redimere? Kind of a step down."

She turned around and started walking again, trying to pick up the thread of her thoughts before he'd derailed her.

"Anyway," he said, breathing heavy as he followed her. "Anything you can tell me that wasn't covered by the suits? Anything special? Any color? You know these folks, right?"

Bernie wasn't going to help him anyway, but "what are you doing here" sealed it.

"Not that well. I'm new here."

He shrugged. "I get it. You're gunning for another award. But throw me a bone."

She felt her irritation begin to boil over. Jesus buddy, do your own damn work. "Honest, they're just a cop, a kid, a farmer. Just folks in town."

"Have it your way."

Just folks in town. Folks in town who'd killed each other. Screw awards, they were bullshit. Figuring this out, getting the real story, that was the award.

. . . . .

Bernie was going over her notes from the press conference in the empty news office an hour later when Justin Mercier walked in.

"I was there," he said, standing in front of her desk.

She gestured toward a chair. He looked like he needed to sit. Justin was a nice kid. Helped his dad, Jody, pick the papers up in Waterville once in a while. Always said nice things about her car when he gave it a tune-up or oil change at the Irving station.

"So I heard. I'm sorry about Dragon."

Justin wouldn't look at her.

"We fixed up that ice cream truck over at the garage. Reworked the engine."

Bernie waited.

"People are talking a lot of shit about how he killed that cop," Justin's words shot out like he couldn't stop them.

"Well, he did, right?"

Justin looked at his fingernails, picking at the grime, and shrugged. His hands were shaking and she could tell he was trying not to cry.

"What were you guys doing down there?"

He shrugged again.

"Justin, if you want both sides of the story in the paper, talk to me," she said. Justin's mother, Helene, was a big flour-covered muffin with a heart just as soft. Bernie tried to say it in the tone that she imagined Helene would. "The more we know about what happened, the more truthful the story is, the better it will be for

Dragon's memory."

He sighed. "We were looking for a place to smoke some weed. The bog's a good place, once you're down by the trees, no one can see you that good from the road."

"Okay," Bernie said, knowing that the lime-green ice cream truck could not only be seen from the road, but looked as out of place as a circus clown at morning Mass.

"So right after we got down there, that asshole Morin pulls up."

"He's dead. A little respect."

"Officer Morin," he spit out. So much for respect. "I was in the back, so I just stayed there. He started giving Dragon the usual shit. Then he pepper-sprayed him for no reason."

"No reason?"

"No reason, dude. Then I heard, I don't know, a lot of shit. I couldn't see anything. Then shots." He shrugged. "That was that."

"Just shots? No talking? Yelling? What about Miller? When did he show up? What did he do? Did he say anything?"

"I don't know. I was, um, after Morin sprayed him, I ducked behind some stuff in the back. I didn't know what was going on. It was a mess. I can't remember what anyone was saying. It happened so fast."

Tears streamed down his face. "He was so scared," he said, his voice shaking.

It took Bernie a second to realize he was talking about Dragon, not Ike Miller.

"He was just so scared. When Morin showed up. I've just never seen anyone so scared." He covered his face and started sobbing.

Bernie didn't think Justin had told her the whole truth. But there was no doubt in her mind that he was telling the truth about that.

. . . . .

Bernie was still putting her notes together from Justin's visit when Carol stopped in. She heaved a sigh as she sat down and kicked off

158

her high heels.

"I hope God appreciates that I still get all dolled up for church," she said.

"Coffee?" Bernie asked, getting up to pour herself a mug. Carol nodded.

"Church was chaos. People going at each other like you wouldn't believe. Such a horrible tragedy and people have to attack each other. At church, no less."

"A town divided," Bernie said, trying out headlines.

"Bernie, be careful. This is really sensitive."

"We can't ignore the fact that the population of the town was 2,017 yesterday and it's 2,015 today because of the gunfight at the OK bog."

"I know, but your circulation could go from four thousand to zero in a week if you handle this wrong. Anyway, what do you mean 'we'? As Tonto said to the Lone Ranger when they were surrounded by Indians."

Bernie gave Carol what she hoped was her sweetest smile.

Carol sighed. "I'll help you, but I'm going to opt out of anything I feel uncomfortable with. I live next door to Dragon's aunt and uncle. They're good people. And I don't want to have to move."

"I'll do all the heavy lifting."

"What do you think of it all?"

"Two guys were being assholes and it went too far. Then a third guy joined the asshole parade and it went way too far."

"Have you heard what Ike Miller's telling people? 'When I shoot, I don't miss.' That's what he told the cops when they interviewed him."

"Nice. I want to see the cruiser video. See how necessary it was for him to shoot Dragon. Okay, the kid shot a cop. So put him on trial and let him spend the rest of his life in Warren. Don't execute him on the spot."

Carol shook her head. "Cops said Dragon was reloading."

"The operative words there being 'cops said.' Since when do

we take anyone's word for something that we can find out ourselves?"

"Bernie."

"Journalism. That's the point, right? Someone has to tell the truth. Keeps everyone honest."

"Don't get carried away. Keep some perspective."

"I'm not some crazy person. I'm actually good at what I do. This is what I do." Bernie could feel heat creeping up her neck. "There's no one better equipped to tell this story than me. It's my town. My story. It's gotta be told and I have to be the one to tell it."

Carol didn't say anything.

"I'm not a crazy person," Bernie repeated, trying to sound more reasonable than defensive.

"I'm not saying that. But I can see you really want the big story. Remember, this is Redimere. Yes, your town." Carol held up a hand, halting the interruption that was bubbling up. "But you're going to see these people in the Country Grocer for the rest of your life."

Bernie laughed. "I'm on the side of the angels. Geez Carol, you sound just like Harry when I was a rookie reporter."

Carol got up and slipped her shoes back on. "Harry's a wise man."

. . . . .

Bernie didn't waste any time making the request for the cruiser video.

Under the state right-to-know law, all she had to do was ask for it. But it was never that easy. She'd ask, she'd get no for an answer. Then she'd file the paperwork and force it.

The day was even hotter and muggier than the day before. Walking into the air-conditioned police department Monday morning felt like walking into the ice cream cooler back when she was a teenage waitress. She'd go in there some times to literally chill out when things got too busy and hot out in front. She knew this cooler was going to have the opposite effect.

She found Pete at his desk, his hair sticking up in little tufts as

160

though he hadn't combed it after his shower. He looked like he hadn't slept for days. He usually finished his morning run with a swim across Patten Pond. She wondered if he'd done that since the shooting, or was just camped here picking up the pieces.

"Why?" Pete asked when she made her request.

"It's not just me," Bernie said. "I'm asking on behalf of the *Morning Sentinel, Lewiston Sun-Journal,* Jeff Lydon, AP, and Channel 14, too. Two people are dead and we want to know what happened."

"Well, aside from the fact that you've already been told what happened, I think it's a pretty grisly request."

"I can outline the reasons that you can refuse to give it to us, but I don't think any of them apply." She began to recite: "All public records can be inspected and copied by any member of the public—"

He held up his hand. "I'm familiar. The video is in Augusta. You're going to have to make your request to the state."

He looked back at the papers on his desk. Bernie guessed the meeting was over.

"Bernie." She was on her way out the door when he spoke.

"You know that damn thing is going to be all over YouTube the minute it gets released."

"I know."

"Ray getting shot. All over the Internet. All those idiots making their online comments." He looked at her for a response. The appeal in his eyes broke her heart a little bit.

She didn't have anything to say that would make it any better.

"I know," she said, and left.

. . . . .

As the week wore on, things in town got worse.

Someone spray painted "cop killer" on the side of the Dubes' barn.

Someone egged the town police cruiser while it was idling in front of Pondside Convenience.

In any corner of town any time of day or night, there was an argument. Most of the town's merchants tried to keep their mouths shut. No one wanted to be labeled pro-Dragon or pro-Ray and lose business.

Debbie put a sign up on the front door of Choppy's: "This diner's for eating, not fighting. Any discussion of Saturday's events stays outside."

The diner was full every day, but boy was it quiet.

Bernie got more letters to the editor in two days than she'd got the previous year, many dropped off at the front desk to make sure they got in Thursday's paper. She had to add a couple extra pages just to accommodate them.

Nothing new had been released about the shooting since the press conference Sunday.

"It's a lot of work preparing a cop's funeral," Pete said when Bernie called for an update Tuesday afternoon. Terse. He didn't have any more to add.

On top of it, Jody and Helene Mercier were beside themselves. They hadn't seen Justin since Sunday. He left a note saying he needed to get his head together.

"I hope he's back for Dragon's funeral. He'd never miss Dragon's funeral," Jody said through tears to Bernie before he left to get the papers Wednesday night.

Bernie went over that last conversation she had with Justin and how he cried when he told her how scared Dragon had been. Justin had seemed pretty scared, too.

. . . . .

Ray's funeral was going to be at Bigelow Park Thursday at four. It was originally going to be at Ray's church, but the guest list got too big for the little building and its grassy narrow parking lot. Police from all over New England were coming. Bernie was impressed and annoyed at the same time. Of course, they wanted to pay tribute, but she hated police-killed-in-the-line-of-duty hoopla. At her last paper, a cop had been killed and his funeral was a circus. The solemn sadness was overrun by overblown pomp and clichés. By the end of that week, if she heard—or read—the phrase "fallen hero" or "one of their own" one more time, she was going to puke. Underneath it all, the self-righteous vindictiveness fueled by the fact that everyone wanted to be part of the drama gave a nasty edge to what should have been a tribute. She didn't advocate cop killing, but she wasn't a big fan of lynch mobs, either.

Bad luck for her, too, that Ray's funeral was going to be on a Thursday. Bernie could already see her front-page picture of the parade of cops marching behind the hearse down a flag-lined Main Street. Cliché or not, it would be a great shot. She hoped it would still pack the same punch once it was a week old. Her front page this week would pack a punch anyway, though. Nearly a week after it happened, the entire page was the shooting and she had an exclusive.

TWO DEAD IN SHOOTING
CHIEF TAKES RESPONSIBILITY
AFTER OFFICER, RESIDENT DIE

The town is reeling after police Officer Ray Morin and resident Dragon Dube died in a shooting Saturday night off Pond Road, an incident the police chief takes responsibility for.

Dube shot Morin after a traffic stop, then was killed by bystander Ike Miller, near whose property the shooting took place, according to police.

"I'm responsible for this," Police Chief Pete Novotny told the *Watcher* the night of the shooting. "I screwed up. Two people are dead, one of them is one of my cops. It's all on me."

Morin and Dube had a history of clashes...

Peaks Weekly Watcher, July 9, 2009

163

CHAPTER 16

The newsroom was busy for a Thursday in the summer. Shirley and Paul were in to get the books ready for the annual audit. Annette was there, too, to lend a hand.

Bernie had her back to the front door, head bent to her computer screen, and only realized something was up when the familiar door crash was followed by silence, the low chatter and plastic clack of keyboards gone like a switch had been hit. The only sound was Kenny Rogers on the radio.

Something told her she didn't want to turn around.

When she did, she saw Pete, holding that morning's paper. He looked like he wanted to hit something—her?—with it.

"Your office." His voice was barely audible.

Bernie led the way.

He shut the door behind him and slammed the paper down on her desk. The effect was lost because the mountain of debris, some of it shifting and drifting to the floor, kept it from making a satisfying smack. She got the picture anyway.

"What the hell is this?" His voice was strained, about to crack wide open. Every vein in his head and neck stood out. It hurt to look at him.

In times of real crisis—and she'd had a few—Bernie resorted

to smartass. Her parents and countless nuns, coaches, and bosses had been driven to fury by the Bernie O'Dea wise-guy crisis response. The smartass in her wanted to say "A newspaper?" Drum roll. Big laugh. Pete's wrath, though, rendered her mute.

When she didn't say anything, he picked the paper up and threw it at the wall. It opened and its pages cascaded onto the floor, a pathetic gray pile.

"What the hell were you thinking?" His voice rose with each word.

"Pete, we were on the record. I even asked." She tried to sound calm, professional, but her inner Bernie was scrambling for a foothold.

"You know better than that," he said. Or rather, bellowed. Bernie was painfully aware of the ancient wooden door, the open transom over it, the two-inch opening at the bottom, and Paul, Shirley, Annette and Guy all sitting silently on the other side. All that broke the silence was the crackle of Kenny on WMTN. *Gotta know when to hold 'em, know when to fold 'em...* Thanks for the advice, Kenny.

"There's on the record, and there are things you know are not," he said. His voice, low and strained, hurt more than his bellowing. "In a moment of pain, I confided in you. I told you I screwed up. As a friend. You splash it all over your goddam front page."

Bernie was stunned. Sure, she'd had a quick second thought or two about putting Pete's quotes in. But then, he *had* said on the record. She'd even asked. And no one else had it.

"You think you're this great journalist," he spat, his hands balled into fists. "But you're a joke. You're not professional. You're not great. You're not even good. You've been doing this, what? Twenty years? But you run around acting like some kid just out of college. You're a fucking joke. I don't know why I didn't learn my lesson from the last time."

His words stung. Most of the time when, as a reporter, she made someone mad it meant she was doing her job. This was different. The reality of it, that she'd really screwed up, knocked the wind out of her. Heat ran up her back, through her neck and across her face. She wanted to jump out the window. Anything to get away from his anger and her humiliation. She concentrated on the spray of freckles standing out like punctuation across his bright red nose and cheeks.

"Do you even know what you've done?" he asked, his voice cracked, so low it was almost a whisper.

She looked down at her desk. She was painfully aware. She tried to form the words that would make an apology, but couldn't find any.

It didn't matter, he was opening the door.

"From now on, when we talk, it's purely professional. You won't have to ask me if it's on the record, because it will be. That's all it will be."

As he strode through the newsroom, Bernie could see the blurry pink ovals of her co-workers' faces, their mouths open in little Os. At least that's what she thought she saw. She couldn't be sure because of the tears. She pulled herself together and put a smile on her burning face.

"Okay folks, show's over. Nothing to see here. Move along."

The four exchanged glances and bent back to their work.

Bernie gave a shaky sigh and went back to her computer. It was several minutes before her eyes cleared enough for her to make out the figures on the screen.

. . . . .

The last thing in the world Bernie wanted to do now was to go to Ray's funeral. Pete's visit had been a little after eight-thirty. The funeral was at three. The more the day went on, the more she felt the burn of humiliation, the slow dawn of recognition that she'd made probably her worst mistake ever as a journalist. She'd been kicking herself over the notebook, then she turned around and did this. It wasn't some big city, where she could avoid Pete. Whatever impulse issues she may have didn't matter. She was a big girl and knew she had to rein herself in. In her excitement over her story and her smugness—yes, she admitted, it was smugness—over having something the dailies and TV stations didn't have, she crossed a line. Sure, she had a right to print what she did. But she shouldn't have. There's a saying journalists have, only partly in jest: "Sometimes it's worth burning a bridge just to see the fire." Well, when you're on a tiny island and there's only one bridge on or off, that fire will burn you right up.

At two-thirty she walked down Main Street toward the park. She knew the funeral would be crawling with reporters and cameras. The media loved a cop-killed-in-the-line-of-duty funeral. She wanted to get her spot early. If nothing else, she could at least get the best photo.

"Good story today." It was Sentinel Nick. "Good angle. No one else had that."

"Don't I know it," she said. "Chief is ripshit." It felt good to talk to a fellow reporter about it, even though she knew there's no way he could understand what really happened.

He shrugged. "Doing your job, right?"

"Right." Right. The validation didn't help.

Bagpipes wailing hushed the crowd, and she and Nick turned toward the road. Despite the muggy heat, a slight breeze whipped the American flags that Don Littlefield and his crew had spent all morning putting up on the telephone poles.

In the haze, like a scene from a movie, a police cruiser came shimmering over the rise in the hill, headlights and blue lights flashing, Jamie at the wheel. The Suburban followed, Rusty driving and Ray's wife and kids in the back seat. A police bagpipe line out of Boston and then the hearse. She could see the flag-draped coffin inside as it passed. Bernie felt a lump in her throat.

Behind walked Pete and Dawna in full dress uniform, both with heads up, chins and eyes forward. After them, line after line of police.

Bringing up the rear was the fire department's ladder truck, driven by Sandy MacCormack. Sandy gave a half-wave at Bernie as he passed and she held up her hand in greeting.

The crowd filled in the rows of metal seats, family and special guests in front of the stage still set up from Old Home Days. Hundreds of police behind, everyone else scattered around the sides, all the way out to the road and to the river bank.

After all the official speakers—everyone from the governor, a state senator, a representative from the state police, down to the president of the Maine Brotherhood of Police Officers—Ray's oldest daughter, Ashley got up.

"Most of you know my dad as a police officer," she started out, her twelve-year-old voice ringing across the silent park. "He's the guy who stops you for speeding or the one you see drinking coffee at Choppy's." She looked up and smiled, "He liked his coffee and doughnuts, just like a good cop should." This brought a laugh from the crowd, almost of relief, as if everyone was hoping what Bernie was: maybe this wouldn't be so heart-wrenching after all.

"But to me, he was Dad," Ashley continued. "I bet you didn't know that every Saturday since I was six we went bowling. He called it the Morin bowling challenge. Loser had to buy the sodas. It took me a couple years to figure out he was letting me win. He let me win every single time." She paused. "And I bet you didn't know that he used to bring home stray cats he found on his patrol, because he couldn't bear them being out in the cold alone without a family…" She faltered, then started sobbing. Bernie's heart sank.

"Now all two thousand of us get to stand here and watch a twelve-year-old cry for her lost father," she whispered to Nick.

Pete, sitting nearest to Ashley on the stage, got up, whispered in her ear, and gently took the piece of paper out of her hand. He continued her speech in his strong, low rumble, "And I bet you didn't know he didn't mind playing dolls with Brittany. And that he said girls could be just as good at baseball as boys and was teaching me how to hit a curveball." Pete put his arm around Ashley's shoulder, hugging her to him as she sobbed against his uniform jacket. From where Bernie stood, she could see his knuckles were white where he gripped her.

"He was a good policeman and a good man. But he was the

best dad any girl could have and me and Brittany will miss him forever." Pete gave Ashley back her speech and hugged her, kissing her on top of the head. The crowd, silent for a second, began thundering applause as Ashley ran down the steps of the stage into the arms of her mother. Pete sat down, expressionless, as the minister got up for the final prayer.

"Okay," Nick said. She looked up from her notebook, where she'd been staring, hoping her tears would dry before she had to wipe at them. He was rubbing his eye.

"That was sad," he said with an apologetic smile.

She nodded, not trusting herself to say anything.

As she walked back to the office, she thought, yes, she felt profoundly sad. Sad for the Ray she realized she had never bothered to get to know. Sad for the little girl who was going to miss her father for the rest of her life.

Sad, too, for Pete, whose pain she'd added to.

And sad for herself, because she'd begun to realize that nothing good she'd done or could do would make up for her screw-up. What a mess she'd made. Both with her career, that, face it, was already halfway down the shitter, and with any friendship she might've had with Pete.

. . . . .

She was glad the office was empty. The gang had spent the morning and early afternoon after Pete's visit sending each other wordless eye messages and treating her with kid-glove awkwardness. The past couple years had been a big learning curve for them, too. They'd been used to Harry. Good old easygoing Harry. Good journalist, but everyone's buddy. He'd run the paper for decades and everyone was used to him—not only used to him, but actually liked him. Now Harry was in Florida and they had Bernie. The jury was still out on whether anyone liked Bernie. She'd never felt that more than today.

She didn't feel like writing the funeral story. Hell, she had a week to do it. She got a beer out of the refrigerator at the back of the office and sat with her feet up on the desk, looking out the window. People from the funeral drifted by, mixing in with the tourists and summer people, heading for the town's few restaurants, the gift shop, the theater. Just another summer night in Redimere. It depressed her.

She considered going over to the Pour House getting really drunk and getting her karaoke on. Nah. She'd been enough of an idiot for one day.

On an impulse she picked up the phone and dialed.

"'Lo," a cheerful, raspy voice said after one ring.

"Harry, hi. It's Bernie."

There was silence for a second. "Hi, sweetheart, how're you doing?"

"I really screwed up." Her voice cracked.

"Yeah, I talked to Guy." She could feel his disappointment through the phone wires, all the way from Florida. "Well, keep your chin up. Is that why you called me?"

"Yeah. I wanted to hear a friendly voice."

"What about all those sisters and brothers you have? Your mom and dad?"

"I don't think they'd understand." Bernie pictured her family of doctors and lawyers, the unwanted advice, the expert opinions, the admonishments. Exhausting to even think about it.

"Well, you can't unring a bell. You're the best reporter I've ever known. Just keep doing what you do best."

She couldn't believe him. "Thanks for not saying I told you so."

"You know me better than that. Speaking of reporting, anything new on Stanley?"

"Not really."

"I haven't seen any stories recently, but thanks to the U.S. Postal Service my papers come so late I thought maybe there was something new I'd missed."

"Stanley's kind of got lost in the shuffle."

"That DNA come to anything?"

Bernie had to think. Had that really been only a couple weeks ago?

"Non-starter."

"You know, there's something I —" He stopped.

"What?"

"Never mind. Senior moment."

Bernie didn't believe him, but she was too wiped out, too dispirited, to care. "Okay."

"Keep fighting the good fight, kiddo. You're doing a great job."

After they hung up, she wished she'd pushed him more. That's what a good reporter would've done.

. . . . .

It was close to dusk and Pete had been running for an hour, his second long run of the day. He wanted to be exhausted so maybe he could sleep. He felt like he hadn't slept for a week. He pounded out Route 145, sprinting. The night was unbearably muggy. The setting sun was searing. Sweat stung his eyes. He could feel it dribbling through his hair. He didn't care. He needed to be really, really tired. Too tired to think.

The shooting was his fault. He cringed—had he really used the phrase "a moment of pain" with Bernie this morning? It was his fault, and he felt it deeply. He should have taken better care of the people he was responsible for.

It turns out he wasn't the only person who thought it was his fault.

What Bernie didn't know, and what Pete wasn't about to tell her—certainly not now—was that he started taking the heat for the shooting hours after it happened. A not-too-pleasant phone call from Selectmen Chairman Lew Kinney in the wee hours Sunday was followed by a less pleasant meeting with Kinney and Town Administrator Dave Marshall Monday.

Lew and Dave were full of questions about training and procedures. Why wasn't Ray wearing a vest? Why hadn't he called for backup? Why didn't the department do anything about Dragon carrying an unregistered gun? That last one was news to Pete. Rusty told them the whole department knew. The town was going to take a closer look at how the department was run. A much closer look.

That was Monday. He'd spent the days since planning the funeral, trying to figure out what the hell was going on in his department, being badgered by Kinney and Marshall, and fighting off nightmares. When the paper came out this morning, it was like a punch in the gut. He must have stood there at the bottom of his stairs on the front porch for five minutes staring at it. Dripping all over it from his post-run swim until the letters screaming out his shame started to disintegrate.

He'd been a fool. Bernie had charmed him with those big eyes. So open, so warm. Made him feel like he could open up and she'd understand. Why why why when he knew he couldn't trust her, did he trust her?

He pounded along the pavement. He couldn't stop thinking about how Ashley had clutched him, sobbing, while he'd read her sad little eulogy. Jesus, he'd barely been able to keep it together himself. Two little girls who don't have a dad. My fault.

He picked up his pace. Then there was Dragon. He should have handled him differently. He was too much like Pete's brother, Joe, who, high on who knows how many different kinds of drugs, and a little booze to wash them down with, had run a stolen motorcycle full-speed into a brick wall back home in Milwaukee after Pete had escaped to Penn. *My fault.*

He ran faster. His chest was tight. It was hard to breathe in the heavy, sticky air. But he pushed harder. Dragon, getting his life together, then one brutal, idiotic mistake. Why'd he shoot Ray? Doesn't really matter. *My fault.*

His feet pounded a rhythm on the uneven pavement. *My fault. My fault. My fault.*

It was getting dark. No streetlights out here in the country. Hazy moonlight, the nearby mountains a silhouette against the few stars visible through the muggy air. Just the sound of crickets, bullfrogs, and cicadas. An owl. Somewhere a loon. An occasional car or 18-wheeler careening out of Canada barreled by, roaring around the curves and up and down the hills, the sharp little dips and the long, steep climbs. Pete was nearly invisible in his T-shirt and shorts. He didn't care.

My fault. My fault. My fault. My fault.

. . . . .

Harry had been Bernie's biggest fan since that first day after college when she'd walked into his newsroom. He always had her back. She never knew how special that was until after she left the *Watcher* for bigger and better things.

When she was fired two years ago, and reeling from it, and thinking of packing it in and trying some other career, she'd called Harry for a pep talk. It had been twenty-plus years since she'd worked at the *Watcher*, but he was still the guy she turned to when she needed a smart journalist to talk to or a little support.

"Don't suppose you'd want to buy a paper of your own?" he'd asked her. Harry wanted to retire, but didn't want to sell to just anyone. Own her own paper? Where would she even begin? But she didn't know what else she'd do. Couldn't conceive of being anything but a journalist. And at least, for the first time since Harry, she'd have a boss who appreciated her.

One SBA loan, and the deal was done.

She'd called him the afternoon of the funeral to reassure herself. The newspaper had been his baby for four decades. Could she have destroyed it with one impulsive bad move? Her confidence was rattled and this time she wasn't sure she'd be able to get it back. After talking to him, she still wasn't sure.

She dialed Carol's number.

"Can you add one for dinner?"

"I already have your plate on the table."

Like Harry, Carol wasn't going to say I told you so. Bernie knew she had the right to. Instead she greeted her at the door with a glass of wine and "I made meatloaf."

It didn't make Bernie feel better, but it was a start.

"I think I should sell the paper, do something else," she said as she downed her first glass of wine and poured herself another.

"That's crazy talk," said Carol.

Bernie shrugged. "I'm embarrassed, ashamed. I made a huge mistake and didn't even realize I was doing it. I'm a loose cannon. I can't be trusted with journalism."

"You made a mistake. Dial down the drama and learn from it."

"You don't get it. This is who I am and I fucked it up. So what does that make me?"

Carol made a motion like she was turning a dial. "Down," she said.

Bernie shrugged, swallowed more wine.

"I know why you're so upset. Pete will get over it."

"I don't think so," Bernie said. "You should have seen him today. Venomous."

"Well, you hurt his feelings."

"Hurt his feelings?" Bernie laughed. "Pete Novotny's feelings run the gamut from uptight to angry. I don't think hurt is in there."

"That's unfair. Don't assume because he's not always talking about them that he doesn't have feelings. You saw him at the funeral, how he was with Ashley."

"It wasn't hurt feelings this morning in the office. He was mad. Really, really mad." She poured more wine. "I can't really say I blame him. My instincts told me what he said was between the two of us. But I asked if we were on the record and he said yes."

Carol shook her head. "The guy was in shock."

"I didn't misquote him. I quoted him accurately."

"I didn't say you did. But you were impulsive."

"Right. And that's the problem. Sometimes the problem with impulsivity is you don't recognize it when it's happening," Bernie said. "Things seem like a perfectly good idea at the time. I even ask myself sometimes, 'Is this impulsive?' And then I say, 'No, it's a fantastic idea, totally not impulsive.' Then I get up the next morning and say, 'Holy shit, how did I think that was a good idea?'"

Carol gave Bernie a knowing look. "Maybe you should tell him, you know, that sometimes that happens with you. The A word."

Bernie glared at her.

"D," Carol said, smiling. "You know. H."

Bernie couldn't help but laugh. "No."

"D!"

"No way," Bernie repeated. "Anyway, it's no excuse. I'm a big girl. I know better. I'm dangerous. To myself. To Pete. To journalism."

"Move on, drama girl. And apologize. It would go a long way."

Vince broke in. "You know they want to fire him, right?"

"You gotta be kidding me," Bernie said. "For what?"

"He said it best, right there in the *Watcher*. He screwed up."

"Where did you hear that? About them wanting to fire him?"

"It's around town."

"How do I not know about that?" If the police chief was going to be fired over the shooting, she should know. But she didn't. "I guess I'm out of the loop now." She wondered how much her story that morning fueled the fire against Pete.

"I heard the selectmen already have the ball rolling," Vince said.

"They didn't waste any time," Bernie said. She chewed her meatloaf. It didn't taste very good. Tasted like fucking up. Like shame.

CHAPTER 17

Thunder and pounding rain woke Bernie at six the next morning. For the past week the storm had been building. It had finally come.

Dragon's memorial service was outdoors. Great.

The meadow behind the Dubes' farm was down the road from Carol and Vince's. Bernie went back to Carol's for a fortifying breakfast, then the three of them slogged down the road in the mud. The morning downpour had fizzled into a steady light rain. Bernie and Vince held umbrellas while Carol walked between them cradling a casserole dish.

"Circle of grief. It's a pagan mourning ritual. Non-religious worship," Carol explained. Bernie rolled her eyes. She knew that Carol thought if she explained it carefully enough, she would buy in. "It's all about people and the earth."

"People and the mud, today."

"Anyway," Carol went on, "they'll probably have a fire pit, candles. Each guest can place a gift on an altar, where they'll have a photo of Dragon. When you do that, you bow. Did you bring something?"

Bernie nodded and waggled a dragon finger puppet that one of her brothers had put in her Christmas stocking a couple years ago.

It had clunked around in the junk drawer in her kitchen, just waiting for something like this.

"Then we do the circle of grief," Vince said as they joined a quiet parade of mourners filing down the muddy path that led past the Dubes' barn to the meadow out back.

"Good grief," Bernie muttered.

"Everyone sits in a circle and shares a story about Dragon. Then we hold hands—"

"Ugh," said Bernie. "Too much like the sign of peace. That's why I stopped going to Mass."

"We have a moment of silence during the hand-holding, think you can handle that?" Vince asked. "Then everyone throws a coin into the middle of the circle for good fortune. Then there's some music, some dancing. We eat."

The rain was letting up. "I guess that last part doesn't sound too bad."

The service was about what Bernie would expect from Dragon's parents, Fred and Sarah. Fred taught with Vince at Redimere College. Sarah ran the farm stand and made quilts that she sold at the public market and craft fairs. They had both blown into Redimere in the 1970s to attend the college, which opened in the 1960s as a place for boys to avoid the draft. It had grown into a well-respected school that specialized in the environment, organics, and sustainable energy. But it still carried a certain cachet in Redimere.

"What do people major in there?" Cal had growled to her once, repeating her question after police found a thriving marijuana farm behind some student housing. "They major in hippie."

Today's ceremony had its share of hippies as well as run-of-the-mill Redimere folk, not that you could always tell the difference.

After the circle of grief was formed, actually more of a giant egg of grief, Fred got up to say a few words.

"We want to thank you all for coming. Dragon would be really flattered and pleased. His mother, Sarah, and his brothers and sisters—" he nodded toward the family, "Heron, Penobscot, Aurora

177

and Borealis."

Aurora and Borealis. The twins. "Do they call them Northern Lights for short?" Bernie stage-whispered to Carol.

"Hush."

"—want to tell everyone that, even under these trying circumstances, we know Dragon was loved. And he loved. Dragon wasn't a killer, he was a peacemaker. We'll never know what went wrong down at the bog, mostly because The Man doesn't want us to. But we'll always know in our hearts that Dragon must have been driven to do this awful deed in some way, or he never would have done it."

"Hold on." Loren Daggett stepped forward. "Dragon was decent, but he wasn't no victim."

"This is our son's memorial service," Fred said, putting an arm out to stop Sarah, who had stepped forward, too, and looked like she might be thinking of doing something non-peaceful with her rolled-up umbrella. "We appreciate you being here. Especially since we all know how busy you are spending the money from your windmill farm." There were snickers from the circle. "But we're here to honor Dragon, not crap on him."

"I'm just sayin' " Loren said. "We laid Ray to rest yesterday and nobody said nothing bad about Dragon. I'm here to pay respects to your son, because he worked for me sometimes, but he shot a cop. Four times."

"Don't do us any favors," Penobscot said. "Get the hell out of here."

"Let's all calm down." Sandy MacCormack, handsome as ever in a suit instead of his fire chief's uniform, stepped between Penobscot and Loren. No one was holding hands anymore and the crowd had moved toward the center. So much for the circle of grief, Bernie thought. More like a scrum of anger.

"We've been listening to this all week in town," Sandy said. "If there's anywhere to take a break from it, it's here." He put one arm around Penobscot's shoulder and one around Loren's. "You guys are both fire volunteers. You've both been on the line together.

Let's not say things here anyone's going to regret."

"But, Ray was—" Loren started.

"This isn't Ray's rodeo, buddy," Sandy said, leading Loren back to his place. The circle haphazardly redrew itself. "Okay?" He shined his thousand-watt smile at Fred and Sarah.

Penobscot opened his mouth, but one of the Northern Lights said, "C'mon, Pen. Dragon wouldn't want fighting."

So the circle continued, but with everyone on guard, fellowship and compassion blown away with the rainclouds.

As the line formed for the buffet, Bernie noticed Jamie, the only member of the police department she'd seen there, standing to the side. She went over, but he didn't greet her with his usual smile.

"I'm just here as a civilian. I don't have anything to say for the paper."

Bernie felt slapped. "I just wanted to say hi. It's nice to see someone from the PD here."

Jamie shoved his hands in his pockets. "Chief was here, too. Kept a low profile and left early. I've known Dragon all my life. He wasn't a bad kid. But that's not for the paper, okay?" He wouldn't look at her. "You know, after what happened with the chief and all."

"Okay."

He waved. It was apologetic, but the message was clear. Bye-bye.

. . . . .

The town was divided over Dragon and Ray and Ike, but one thing everyone seemed to be in agreement on, at least it seemed to Pete, was that he was to blame. Well, what do you expect? I said so in the paper, he thought a hundred times a day. Still, as much as he blamed himself, he was frustrated by the town's lack of faith.

After his run the other night, he'd collapsed, soaked with sweat, in the lawn chair on his back stoop. He drank beer and stared at the mountains, black against the starry sky. When he woke up the next morning in the chair, he didn't feel any better.

After Dragon's memorial service, which he'd watched from the edge of the meadow and left when the shoving started, he spent the day in his office with the door shut, catching up on paperwork and letting Dawna handle the phone. He tried not to think about the shitstorm he was in, but that was impossible. He'd let his feelings rule his head, but that didn't mean he ran a slipshod department. His self-blame was personal, not professional. He wondered if Lew and Dave and the rest of town government would get that. Redimere cops were good cops. He didn't let criminals get away with anything, Dragon included. He'd be damned if he was going to let the selectmen or anyone else lay the blame with his department.

On top of it, he sure as hell didn't have anything to do with the state letting Miller off without any charges. It wasn't his call, it was the attorney general's. It wasn't his place to publicly dispute it, so the anti-Miller crowd assumed he was all for it.

Saturday morning as he walked into the Country Grocer, he wondered when time was going to start healing all wounds. Obviously not today. The group of guys hanging around the front stopped talking as he went over to the cooler and got a gallon of milk and took it up to the counter.

"Hey, Chief, when we gonna hear some answers on how you let this happen?" Bud Carrier leaned against the counter next to him, close enough so Pete could smell the cow manure on his overalls.

"Everything's been answered," Pete said, fishing his wallet out of his jeans.

There was a group snort.

"Is that police procedure? Let some half-baked kid careen around town in an ice cream truck high on drugs and packing a loaded gun? Someone was bound to get shot sooner or later."

Pete wanted to say that no drugs were found on Dragon and he didn't know about the gun, but he kept his mouth shut. He wasn't going to get into a pissing match with a bunch of assholes.

"Thanks, Walt," he said, taking his change as the store owner gave him a sympathetic smile.

"Chief." Bud blocked the door. "How'd you let that situation get so out of hand? Ray was out there all by himself. A sitting duck."

The group of men closed in. "Excuse me," Pete said. Bud moved enough for him to get out the door. Just barely. Their shoulders smacked, but Pete kept moving.

"Cal would've been on top of that," Bud called after him as Pete stepped out into the bright July sun. He kept walking. All he wanted to do was get back to his apartment with his milk without talking to anyone else and spend a quiet Saturday afternoon watching baseball and drinking beer in peace.

"Hey, Chief." It was Walt, the store owner. Now what?

"Hey, I wanted to ask you," Walt said, catching up with him.

Pete looked past him to the group of men standing on store's porch, watching. Pete knew Walt slightly. He didn't seem like the kind of guy who would take part in the hazing ritual. Guess you never can tell about people.

Pete braced himself.

"You play hoop, right?"

Not what Pete expected. "A little."

"I'm in the Saturday morning two-on-two league. Lost my partner this morning for the rest of the season. Kermit O'Neil? Tore his ACL. We were overmatched, probably did it on purpose just to end the game." Walt grinned.

Pete waited.

"So, anyway, I'm looking for a partner."

When Pete didn't say anything, Walt continued, "I heard down at the gym you're pretty tough on the court."

Pete appreciated the gesture, but wasn't sure if he wanted to put himself in a situation every Saturday morning where guys like Bud Carrier could legally pound the crap out of him.

"You must notice I'm five-ten," Pete said.

"Well, you must notice I ain't no six-footer myself," Walt said. "They all think I'm a threat because I'm the only black guy in town. I need a partner with game before they figure out the truth." He gave Pete a big smile.

"I don't know that I have game."

"I could really use someone I can count on," Walt said.

Pete took a deep breath. "Sure. Why not?"

Walt clapped him on the back and shook his hand. "Great. Maybe we can get in a little practice tomorrow."

"Give me a call in the morning," Pete said.

Walt walked back toward the grumbling group. "Talk to you later, partner," he called back.

Pete turned toward home, thankful that every once in a while the world handed him a little bit of grace.

CHAPTER 18

It hadn't taken the selectmen long to get their ducks in a row as far as the matter of Pete Novotny was concerned. By Monday night, a little more than a week after Ray and Dragon died, the ducks were lined up and ready for the gun.

Chairman Lew Kinney called Bernie on Friday, after Dragon's memorial service to tell her Pete's situation would be talked about at the selectmen's meeting. She'd had a sinking feeling ever since. Some of that, she knew, was guilt. Some of it was apprehension for Pete. They couldn't seriously blame him for what happened, could they?

"We haven't made any decisions yet," Lew said, when she asked him if they were going to fire him. "But that fella's got a lot of questions to answer."

When Bernie, balancing her coffee, notebook and camera, elbowed her way into the town administrator's office Monday night, the selectmen were already around the conference table even though the meeting didn't start for another twenty minutes. The room was hot and close, despite an ancient air conditioner chugging away in a window. The misty, humid night probably had something to do with it, but the anger and expectation that simmered off the audience, leaning against filing cabinets, standing in the middle of the room, even packing the hallway outside, didn't help.

Bernie looked around for somewhere to sit. Usually she just sat at one of the empty desks. It was a rare selectmen's meeting that drew more than half a dozen people.

Pete, in uniform, stood with his arms crossed next to the conference table, looking out the window, his back to the room.

None of the three selectmen—Lew, Gert Feeney, Rene Lambert—was talking. None of them looked at Pete. A jury never looks at the defendant before they pronounce him guilty, do they? Bernie thought. Lew, a mournful walrus in the best of times, looked like he was going to melt into the table. Next to him, Gert, a retired high school teacher who could shut down the room with the glare from her ice blue eyes, tonight trained them on the shuffling, mumbling crowd, ready to spring at a sign of trouble. Rene stared at his agenda as though it were the most fascinating thing he'd read all week.

Bernie lit on the corner of a desk, putting her coffee down next to her, hoping it wouldn't get knocked over.

Dave Marshall, who'd been making copies since Bernie got in, handed out agendas to the crowd, most of whom took one, but didn't bother to look at it. He started to hand Bernie one, but she waved the notated copy she'd brought. He gave her a grateful smile and moved on, pulling at his tie, his shirt damp with sweat. She bit back the urge to say, hey Disco Dave, don't you know better than to wear polyester on lynch mob night?

"Okay, we're calling this meeting to order," Lew said, clearing his throat. He reminded Bernie of that shambling Sesame Street character, the one always whining to Big Bird. Whenever Lew spoke, she always expected, "But birrrrrd…"

"Um, there's a lot of people here" was what he actually said.

"Can't hear you," someone hollered from the hallway.

"We've got a lot of people here," Lew said, louder. "I know what you're all here for, but we have a lot of things on the agenda. When we talk to the chief, we're gonna do it in executive session—" He paused. "That means in private—"

A grumble traveled through the room.

"That's how we deal with personnel issues. We do it in private and come out of session to take a vote, if we need to. Nothing we say is for the public record. So first we're going to address the agenda, and then we're going to address the chief."

Bernie could feel Pete, motionless, behind her. She didn't have to look to know he wasn't reacting. Robocop.

The crowd was, though. There was an angry shift in the crowd.

"I for one," Gert said, high school teacher's voice cutting through the crowd, "just want to say I'm gratified that this many people are interested in town affairs." Her eyes narrowed. "I hope we have this much interest when we discuss the transfer station bond issue next month."

The people nearest the conference table managed to look guilty. "We came here tonight for some answers!" someone yelled from the hallway. Several people in the room grunted and nodded.

"Well, you'll have to wait on those," she said.

Bernie hoped some would leave once they knew they'd have to wait, then maybe she could sit in a chair and be able to take notes, drink her coffee and rifle through the agenda and its attachments without having to juggle everything. No dice, everyone stayed put.

"Bernie, you come up here," Dave Marshall said, pointing to an empty chair at the selectmen's table, inches from where Pete leaned on the wall.

She shouldered her way to the front of the room, ignoring the grumbles, and sat down. She was close enough to Pete to smell him—warm soap—but he didn't look at her.

The selectmen meandered through the agenda even more slowly than usual. Lew stumbled over his words as Gert sat with her arms crossed, interjecting a comment or a correction as needed.

Pete didn't sit down, but stayed leaning against the wall, slightly behind Bernie. With her peripheral vision, she could see him glance at her once in a while, feel him inches from her, but she didn't turn around. She was embarrassed. She still burned with shame from his words on Thursday. Being called a joke by Pete was the biggest punch in the gut she ever got as a reporter. Or a person, for that matter. She felt stupid with her reporter's gear and coffee, taking notes and sitting at the selectmen's table. She'd rather sink right under it. She didn't turn her head even slightly toward him, do anything to draw his attention.

It was exhausting.

After nearly two hours, Lew cleared his throat and said, "Okay, in personnel matter involving Chief of Police Petri— Petri—"

"Finally," someone said loudly, followed by a smattering of applause.

Lew looked up, then back at his agenda. "Matter involving Police Chief Petrika—nuts."

Gert sighed and said, "Petricek Francis Novotny."

Someone in the crowd snickered.

"Police Chief Petricek —" Lew looked at Gert to make sure he was pronouncing it correctly. She nodded. "Petricek Francis Novotny, I move we go into executive session."

"Second," said Gert, stepping on the end of "session."

"Okay, everyone but Pete out," Lew said.

Bernie stepped out onto the granite steps of the town hall. After the close, humid room it was almost cool outside. The earlier drizzle had stopped and steam puddled along the top of the asphalt on Church Street. She found a dry spot on the steps under the overhanging roof and sat down to start writing up the items from earlier in the meeting, mostly to keep herself occupied.

"What do you think is going on in there?" Bud Carrier sat down next to her.

"I don't know."

"I heard he's going to get fired."

"Now that would just be stupid," she said. "We're already down one cop."

"This is what happens when you hire someone from away," Carrier said. "What does he know about us? Anyway, you had it right there in the paper. How it was all his fault. Good story."

Bernie looked back at her notes and began tapping on her

laptop, hoping Bud would take the hint.

"Now Cal, he had Dragon in hand." So much for Bud taking the hint. "He made sure that kid didn't get away with too much."

"You know," Bernie said. "Cal ran Dragon out of town. That's no solution. His family's here. Hell, Penobscot is thirty and owns an insurance company in Farmington and still lives on the farm. Dragon was going to come back. This could have happened under Cal's watch just as much as Pete's."

"Cal had things in hand," Bud persisted. "When my boy's sled went into the bog, Cal came back from Florida and got that all squared up."

Okay, now Bernie was interested. "What do you mean?" She hoped her sudden interest didn't scare Bud away, but she didn't have to worry. He actually puffed up with gratification.

"Evan Wentzel's parents made a stink, wanted to sue all sorts of people. Ike, Rusty, us, you name it. Bridge was dangerous, whatnot. Cal made it clear there was a coyote on the bridge, Stanley Weston saw it and told him. And Evan was drinking, shouldn't have been there and went into the bog trying to avoid the coyote. Case closed."

The crowd from the meeting had formed little knots of gossip and smokers down by the street and no one was within earshot. Bernie was glad, she wanted this conversation to be private. "Stanley was down there?"

"Oh yeah, he used to do a lot of bird watching and whatnot."

"It was after nine at night in January, what was he watching, owls?"

Bud shook his head in exasperation. "He was mental. He used to wander around at night. The kids would see him all the time on the trails out there. Used to say he was looking for coyotes. John says he even showed them his coyote book. Notebook he'd write about coyotes in."

"Why didn't Cal or anyone tell me back when the accident happened that Stanley saw a coyote? Why wasn't any of that in the police report?"

Bud shrugged. "None of anybody's business but ours, I guess."

"I was just talking to your wife about that accident a while back, she didn't say that either."

Bud shrugged again. "Cal told me this in his office. Said case was closed and that was that. Said he explained it to Matt Wentzel and he was okay with it, had just been upset because his boy was dead, but understood it was his boy's fault now. Matt didn't want a big deal made. Never told you any of that, did he? It was all between him, me and Cal. Can't remember if I told Denise. Probably not."

"What did your son say?"

"Says it seems like it's what probably happened."

She began to write and didn't look up again until she felt him move away. She wanted to get down everything he said before she forgot it.

. . . . .

After about ninety minutes, Rene stuck his head out the door. "Okay, people."

The crowd jostled back into the room.

Bernie caught Pete's eye. She couldn't read his expression. Full-blown Robocop. But the muscle in his cheek that twitched when he was livid—and boy was she familiar with that—was getting a workout.

Lew called the meeting back to order. It was short and sweet. The board put Pete on probation until further notice. They'd even typed up an official press release. Dave handed it to Bernie as Lew read it out loud. They were going to form a committee to review police training and "readiment." It all sounded like a load of bullshit to Bernie. She made a mental note to look up readiment when she got back to the office to make sure it was really a word.

Pete was the first one out the door after the meeting adjourned and Bernie had to sprint to catch him halfway down Church Street.

"Pete."

He stopped.

She caught up. "Can I ask you a few questions?"

"No comment," he said, turning around to face her. Circles under his eyes that hadn't been there a week ago made his face look unnaturally pale. She wanted to hug him, squeeze him tight and feel his heart beating against her chest. The unexpected urge was followed by another, stronger feeling. Painful. Bereft.

"How's it going?" she asked.

"How do you think?" The words stung. "I'm tired. I'm going to have a beer and watch the Red Sox. What's left of the game." He started walking again.

"Pete."

He turned around.

"I'm trying to do my job. I know I burned you and I'm sorry. I can't change what I wrote. But I've got a job to do, and it will help you to talk to me. I know the newspaper hurt you, but it's also there to protect you. Print everyone's side of the story."

He rolled his eyes. No sale.

"Think about it, okay?"

As Bernie walked back toward the *Watcher* office, she saw Gert walking to her car.

"What happened in there?" Bernie asked.

"You know the rules," Gert said. "Personnel issue." Gert's cool stare made it clear Bernie was smarting off in class and better give it a rest.

"Off the record?"

Gert thought for a minute. Took a pull on her cigarette and blew out the smoke while she eyed Bernie. Bernie felt scrutinized, but whatever Gert saw must have worked for her. "Off the record, this is a mess. He's a good chief. Thank God those idiots didn't fire him. The fact that we're already down one officer helped." She paused, taking another long drag. "Cal talked them into getting someone who was not part of the old boy's club, and they did. Now they want to jerk him around for it."

Bernie started forming a question, but Gert cut her off.

"We almost fired him." She shook her head. "Unbelievable. The guy is twice the chief Cal ever was. Held his own in there

189

tonight, too. These guys are lost without Cal here to tell them what to do. There were questions when we hired Pete, a problem from Philadelphia, but Cal convinced them it was okay. Now they're dredging up all sorts of crap about his past that doesn't matter. They got what they wanted when they hired him, now they don't know what to do with it."

"They? You were on the board when he was hired."

"They."

"I'm not sure I follow."

Gert gave her that high school teacher look again. "Cal was president, king and commander of the old boys' club, but he wanted them to hire someone who wasn't in it." She raised her eyebrows at Bernie. "You figure it out."

"Tell me."

Gert dropped her cigarette on the ground and got in her car. "I can't tell you, Bernadette, because I don't know. I'm not a member of the old boys' club."

CHAPTER 19

Tuesday morning Bernie woke up before dawn to what was going to be another unbearable day. Last night's heat and humidity had never abated and she lay awake most of the night in a damp tank top and underpants on her bed trying to catch a breeze from her wide-open windows.

Stanley was there the night of the accident? Why hadn't she seen him? She didn't remember seeing anything about coyotes in his notebook except that last notation "coyote bait." There were too many dates in there for them to be coyote sightings, even with the little she knew about the animals. How did all that get by her—Stanley telling the cops he saw a coyote on the bridge—when she was writing stories on the accident for the paper? Then there was the whole issue of Gert and the old boys' club. Did any of it have anything to do with anything else? The shooting. The unbelievability of it. The thoughts spun through her brain as the clock ticked toward morning. Over it all was Pete. Pete suspended. Pete mad. Pete hurting. Pete hating her. Pete blamed. Pete had a secret. How did that get past her, too?

Why did so many things suddenly have to do with Cal?

With his flowing mane of white hair and handlebar mustache, giant laugh and towering frame, Cal commanded a room. Pete was quiet, intense, short and square. Cal was a force. Pete was solid, an anchor. Odd friends. Pete said Cal rescued him from Philly. Bernie figured he meant he didn't like his job. Did Cal have some kind of agenda? An agenda that didn't have to do with "bringing the town into the twenty-first century" which is what he told Bernie hiring Pete would do?

"That implies that you weren't in this century," Bernie had pointed out.

Cal had boomed out a laugh. "There's only so much I can do. They know me too damn well here. This guy can come in here and do things I can't. We need to get away from mountain politics."

"Right." Bernie said. That'd be the day. Towns south and east accused the mountain towns — Rangeley, Carrabassett, Redimere — of having their own brand of police-politician corruption. Like Chicago or Boston, only in mud boots and with a Maine accent. The cops did small-time favors, lived to make the right folks and tourists happy.

An Augusta police lieutenant once told Bernie that no one in Redimere gave out an OUI without calling the chief or selectman chairman first to see if it was OK.

Bernie called Lew Kinney to ask about it and he just laughed. But his laugh was nervous and she always suspected there was some truth to it.

So what Cal said made sense to Bernie at the time, but now she chewed it over and it didn't go down as well. Because Cal seemed like the king of mountain politics. But how did that involve Pete?

Gert said they were dredging up stuff from Pete's past. When the selectmen voted to hire Pete, at Cal's urging, Bernie had Googled him. His name came up in a few Philly newspaper homicide stories. Nothing out of the ordinary. He'd been a desk guy right before coming to Redimere and he also headed a youth outreach program that a short article said "focused on leadership and literacy." He'd been in Redimere briefly a year before he took the job on a case out of Pennsylvania. That's how he met Cal. At the time she thought he was attractive, competent-seeming, friendly.

Then she kind of forgot about him until Cal told her he was in the running for chief. If it had been the old days, she would have made some calls and found anything there was to dig up. Running the paper, she didn't have time. If there was something juicy in Pete's past, it would've been on the Internet. Right? Shameful. She knew better than that. But if there was something sketchy in Pete's past, would Cal have pushed to hire him? Convinced the selectmen? Been his friend? Neither of them had acted like they were hiding anything.

One thing was clear. Her recent revelation that she sucked as a journalist was true.

She looked at the clock. Four o'clock. There'd be no sleep escape from the racing thoughts tonight. Bernie ran through everything she remembered about Cal, trying to look at it in a different light. He'd gone downhill fast. His drinking got bad. Hell, his drinking killed him. Retirement didn't agree with him. He always proudly wore his wedding ring, even though his beloved Celeste had died a decade ago. In the weeks before he died, Annette noticed he didn't have the ring on. That's the kind of thing Annette would notice. Fifty-plus years old and she still looks at Modern Bride magazine. She asked Cal where it was and he just shrugged, said he lost it. Annette had been friends with Celeste and was worried about Cal. Bernie agreed. He seemed dazed, lost. Bernie had gone over to his place the week before Christmas with a basket of cookies. The bluster was gone. He was old, sad, and tired. He offered Bernie a bottle of booze from the huge variety on his dining room table.

"Got all these as gifts when I retired. People should know by now all I drink is Jack Daniels." Well, he must've changed his mind on that, because he was working his way through a bottle of vodka the night he died.

She couldn't turn off the jumble of thoughts, or the anxiety that had been growing since she realized how bad she'd blown it with Pete. It wasn't just him, it was everything. She felt her foundation slipping out from under her, her belief in herself and what she thought was her reality spinning out of control. Careening toward collapse. She'd felt that a lot at her last job near the end, but hadn't felt it since she came to Redimere. The logical part of her mind told her she was overreacting, but the spinning, anxious, self-hating part of her mind told her everything could fall apart in seconds. If she sold the paper, what she could do for a living. Get a job in PR? With the state government?

In any case, she still had to get this week's paper out. She had to get a grip and she wasn't going to get it, or any sleep, lying in bed driving herself nuts. She swung her legs onto the floor and stood up. The humidity and lack of sleep made her arms and legs feel like they weighed a hundred pounds each. Like she was walking underwater. She made a pot of coffee. Nature hadn't created the humidity yet that could keep her from her morning coffee.

It was going to be a long day. She had to polish up last night's story and start work on the paper production. She'd have to corral her thoughts. Maybe if she didn't think about anything but today's work for a while, something that made sense would pop through. And she knew once she had some tasks in front of her, the anxiety would get pushed back. At least for the time being.

When she got downtown at six-thirty, Pete was sitting on the granite step in front of the door to the *Watcher* in his shorts, his hair wet and his T-shirt sticking to his chest and shoulders. It cheered Bernie that his ritual of morning run and swim seemed to be intact.

"Hey," she said. She felt her heart leap, despite the humiliation that sent her reeling every time she talked to him. "Catch the end of the Sox? Another tough one."

"Got a minute?" He got up off the step as she got her key out.

"Sure," she said, unlocking the door. "Come on in."

"No, this'll just take a minute," he said, not moving to go inside. The street, glowing in the rising sun that filtered through the pines and maples, was deserted except for the usual half dozen vehicles in front of Choppy's and Dunkin' Donuts, each a block away in opposite directions. No one was going to interrupt or overhear.

"I guess you need a quote," he said. His face was flushed from his run and swim, but the circles under his eyes looked, if anything, darker. She guessed he didn't get any more sleep than she did.

"Why did Cal tell you he wanted you here?" she asked, mentally cringing before she was even done. She hadn't meant to blurt that out.

"Wanted me here?"

"Instead of the obvious suspects. Ray."

"The town needed someone. I was looking for a change," he said, rushed, impatient. "I gotta go home and get dressed. I just thought you'd want that quote you were so anxious for."

Bernie fished around in her bag, held up her pad and pen and smiled. "On the record."

He didn't smile back.

"So, probation?"

"Yes."

"They're forming a committee and they said it's still possible they'll fire you."

He looked at her. Okay, it wasn't really a question anyway.

She tried again. "What was it like in that meeting?"

"None of your business."

"Do you have something you *do* want to say?"

"There's nothing wrong with the way I've run my department. There's certainly nothing wrong with my officers. They are pros who do an outstanding job. There's nothing wrong with their training, or their readiment, if that's even a word."

Bernie suppressed a smile. Great minds think alike.

"If they want to put this on me, fine. But I'm proud of my officers. Ray was a good cop. So are Rusty, Jamie, and Dawna. This town should be as proud of them as I am. I plan to keep doing my job to the best of my abilities."

He nodded at Bernie, *got that?*

She nodded back.

He turned and sprinted down the street.

. . . . .

When the hour got more decent, Bernie picked up the phone to do what she should have done a year ago when Pete got hired.

"I don't recall any stories about anyone of that name," said the young-sounding reporter who answered at the *Philadelphia Inquirer*. "Let me give you my editor."

A weary voice came on the line. "You want to talk to Suzy Lehane. If anyone knows anything, she would."

"When can I reach her?" Bernie asked.

"You can't. She took a buyout last year."

"Can I have her number?"

"We don't give those out." He sounded distracted.

Bernie could hear phones ringing and people talking loudly in the background. A shout of laughter. She felt a pang of nostalgia. She almost felt like asking the editor if they had any openings, although she knew no newspaper had any openings anymore and the background buzz was partly fear and desperation. Instead she gave him her cellphone number and asked him if he would contact Suzy and ask her to call.

Bernie's cellphone rang fifteen minutes later.

"I heard you're asking about Pete Novotny," Suzy Lehane said without preamble, her voice sounding like it had taken a several-decades whiskey and cigarettes beating.

"I am."

"Is he in trouble?"

"Yes and no."

"Here's the deal," Suzy said. "You tell me your story, then I'll tell you mine."

Bernie told her what had happened in Redimere.

Suzy sighed when she was done. "That poor bastard can't catch a break. Look, what I'm going to tell you doesn't have anything to do with what's going on there, so keep it off the record. Pete was always straight with me and he doesn't deserve more shitstorm."

Bernie agreed.

"I was doing an in-depth piece on homicide cops on the street."

Bernie felt her second pang of nostalgia of the morning. "In-depth. Wow, the good old days."

"You're telling me," Suzy's laugh was more of a bark. "Now if you can't research it and write it in an hour, they don't want it. Only source is Google. Interviews done by email. Newspapers are going to hell. We'll be lucky if there are any left this time next year. Anyhow, I was friendly with Pete and his partner, Sid. Good guys. Helpful. Didn't mind having me around. We were at this scene about three years ago. A drug dealer shot. Blood everywhere. The guy's still lying half in, half out of the front door in a pool of blood. Pete hears something in a closet, draws, opens the door, you know, gun first. Cowering in a corner is a little girl, maybe three, four years old. She's okay, but she's covered in her daddy's blood. So Pete picks her up."

Suzy stopped and didn't sound like she was going to keep going.

"And?"

Suzy sighed again. "And that's it. He picked her up and wouldn't let go. Wouldn't put her down. They had someone from the juvenile division, social services, everything else show up, and he just stood there with this kid and wouldn't let go. He wasn't out of control, wasn't losing it, at least on the outside. Just wouldn't let anyone take the kid."

"Oh." Bernie wasn't sure how to react.

"So Sid finally got him to let go after about an hour. There was an IA investigation—Internal Affairs —"

"Yep."

"It turned out he'd been having panic attacks and Sid was covering for him. Pete didn't even know that Sid knew. Long story short, after a suspension with pay while they determined he wasn't a psycho, they gave him a desk job."

"So there was no other issue? Corruption? Bad cop stuff?"

Suzy barked another cigarette laugh. "Pete Novotny? Hell no. Who told you that? Guy is a straight arrow. Straight as they come. Trust him with my life."

Bernie felt immense relief. "When I Googled him when they

first hired him, I didn't find anything like that. About that thing with the kid."

"Googled. Huh. Was a time we used to pick up the phone. Make some calls."

"Yeah."

"I never wrote about it," Suzy said. "Right or wrong, I don't know. It would have been good human interest, but if you had seen him with that kid, it just felt too personal. The kind of thing you have the right to write about, but don't because you know it's wrong. You know what I'm talking about."

Oh yeah, Bernie knew exactly what she was talking about.

"He's a good cop. A good man," Suzy continued. "He lost it, but didn't hurt anybody. And in the big scheme of things, this is Philly, not butt-fuck Maine—no offense—"

"None taken."

"It wasn't right to print it, so I left it alone."

Bernie rang off and sat back in her chair.

She couldn't see Pete losing it like that. Panic attacks? She wasn't even sure what those were. So was Cal just trying to help him heal? There had to be more to the story.

Bernie's cellphone rang. She didn't recognize the number, but it had the same area code. Suzy calling back?

The voice on the other end was a rich baritone.

"Ms. O'Dea? This is Sid Lincoln."

Pete's former partner.

"Suzy Lehane just called and said you're asking questions about Pete Novotny."

"Guilty."

"Is he in trouble? I gave him a call after that shit up there hit the news and he seemed okay."

"Just small-town stuff. The selectmen are antsy. You know. Or maybe you don't."

Sid huffed out a sigh. "I knew he shouldn't of gone up there. I didn't like it."

"What didn't you like?"

"That's why I called." A long pause. "You know what they used to call the two of us down here?"

Bernie murmured no.

"The Mod Squad. You know, Pete and Linc. I'm Linc. Lincoln? Maybe you're too young."

"No," said Bernie. She had loved that show when she was a kid. Come to think about it, Pete did look a little bit like a squarer, older Mod Squad Pete.

"Anyway, that was us. Brothers."

"Right." Lucky for Bernie, Sid was the talkative brother.

"When Cal started talking up that job, I didn't like it," Sid said. "Pete had been on the desk for a while, months. I guess Suzy told you what happened," he waited for Bernie to give an affirmation, then went on. "But he and I were still partners at heart. We drank together, talked to each other. Went to ball games. I didn't trust Cal."

"Why not?"

"He was laying it on really thick, selling the job hard. Told Pete all he had to do to get it was apply, Cal'd take care of the rest. He really wanted Pete up there. Middle of nowhere, you ask me. But one thing nailed it for me."

"Okay."

"Pete had said he'd put in for the job and the three of us were out celebrating. More of a wake for me, but it's what Pete wanted, so I put on a good face. After about a million drinks, I went to the men's room. Cal had gone off to make a call. He was in the hallway, on his cell, bunch of coats hanging up and he didn't see me. I heard him tell someone 'We've got our boy.'"

"Doesn't sound very suspicious."

"That's what I kept telling myself, maybe I was reading too much into it because of how I felt. But it was the way he said it, his tone of voice, it got me right in the gut. I feel like Pete got pulled into something and didn't even know it."

"That's it?"

"It's my gut. I never said anything to Pete. He needed it too much and I wasn't sure about my feelings. Take it for what it's worth."

"Okay."

"Another thing you can take for what it's worth," he said. "Pete is a tough cookie. After what Suzy told you, you may think otherwise."

"I don't get it. The panic attacks, the kid."

"He just lost it. People do. He had a rough time growing up. He keeps a lot to himself because that's how he survived. He's one of those guys with the weight of the world on his shoulders, but man, he carries it well."

"I get that."

"Don't tell him I told you any of this. I just want you to understand where he's coming from."

Bernie hmmphed an affirmative.

"Rough childhood, abusive situation. Younger brother on the wrong path who died when Pete was in college and it ate him up he wasn't there to straighten him out. He felt responsible on the job, too. Lots of sad, ugly shit. It got to him. He got divorced, that bothered him. So, you know…"

"Yeah."

"He's takes his job seriously. Takes people seriously. Takes friendships seriously. You know his given name? Petricek? It means 'rock' in Czech. That's what I used to call him. Rock. And he called me Solid. You know, Mod Squad."

"So what was the deal with the little girl?"

"Don't ask him about it."

"I wasn't planning to." The way Sid was going, she'd never have to ask Pete anything.

"He told me he could see what the rest of her life was going to be, like a movie going fast-forward. He knew what happened to little girls in that world, how they grew up. He said the minute he let go of her, he was going to start her on that life and he couldn't let go. After he gave her up, he was okay until he got into the car. Man, he lost it."

"That's sad."

"That's Rock."

Neither of them said anything for a moment.

"Pete says Cal died." Sid broke the silence.

"Fire. Christmas Eve."

"A lot of weird shit going on in that town."

"You're telling me."

. . . . .

Bernie wondered if the selectmen thought that Pete was going to go all psycho. She would love to have been a fly on the wall in the meeting last night. She bet Pete did a good job of sticking up for himself. She always thought her family was dysfunctional—mostly because it was too many people, with too much personality in too small a place with too few bathrooms. But then she'd hear about other people—like Pete—and realize no one's family was "normal." Now Pete made more sense to her. Suzy and Sid had confirmed he was the guy she thought he was. Or wanted him to be. She had that bereft feeling again. It's not like they were even that close, but she realized she thought things were moving in that direction. And that finally there was a guy in the world who'd have her back. Well, baby, you blew it because you didn't have his. And while Pete made sense to her, Pete being in Redimere, not so much. Okay he was tired out and needed a change. But where did Cal fit in? Was Sid right that something was off?

Bernie had been staring at the dummies on the layout table for minutes without seeing them. Normally they comforted her, her plan laid out neat and clean with pencil and paper. She could look at them and see a finished newspaper. She tried to push all the other thoughts away and see that now.

The shooting, week two. It still took up most of the front page.

Even though Ray's funeral would be a week old when the paper came out, Bernie was using a huge picture of the funeral procession coming up over the rise in the road, the afternoon haze making the hearse shimmer. Pete and Dawna in the foreground and an army of policemen marching behind.

Dragon's funeral was a side piece, with a picture of mourners holding umbrellas filing into the meadow.

Pete's probation went across the top with a big headline. The exact same play she gave the DNA story. Was that really only a few weeks ago? She wondered what was going to happen about Stanley's death now that the shooting was consuming everyone. Dragon and Cal had been Stanley's friends. Now all three were dead.

"Chief's here!" Annette's voice rang out. Bernie could feel the rest of the crew stir. They were probably hoping for round two of Thursday's dressing down. Bernie knew better. Pete's a pro, and he'd said his piece.

"I know it's probably too late, but I need to ask a favor," he said, brusque, professional. "With everything else, I forgot all about his." He handed her a press release. "It's no big deal, but should probably get in this week."

It was a notice about the gun trafficking task force. "Is this the same thing Dawna gave me a couple weeks ago?"

"No, a new one."

Bernie looked again. The task force was going to hold a public meeting Saturday in Farmington, at the Franklin County Sheriff's Department. Pete must have read the lack of interest on her face.

"I told them I'd get this out before the meeting, then forgot all about it. Lots going on." He shrugged and gave her a thin smile that Bernie knew took an effort.

It was way past the deadline for adding things to the paper. She pictured him holding that little girl in Philadelphia. "I have a spot for it. But you have to give me a quote so I have a better story than the dailies."

He grimaced.

Annette, Shirley, and Guy watched the exchange with undisguised interest.

"Why don't you come into my office a minute?" she asked.

He hesitated. Bernie rolled her eyes toward the watching trio.

"Okay."

In her office, Bernie fumbled for the elusive legal pad and pen. "You know what I was wondering actually?" she said as she shifted a pile of press releases. "I was wondering what might be new with Stanley's investigation." She found what she was looking for and leafed through the pad for a blank sheet. "Although I guess events have kind of trumped that."

"I'm still working on it. One death never trumps another." He looked like he was going to say more, but instead crossed his arms and wandered to the window.

Bernie turned to the window, too, and the view of the parking lot and the boulder-strewn fork of the Wesserunsett that ran behind downtown. "That was one of Stanley's favorite spots," she said. "He'd hang out on the riverbank and just watch it flow."

Pete turned. Their faces were inches apart. "That's my point."

"What?" his closeness distracted her. Warm soap again. She couldn't remember what he'd been saying.

"No death is more important than another. Stanley's still a priority. Now, gun trafficking." He stepped away and sat down.

"What's the task force's goal?" Bernie asked, sitting down too, pen poised, trying to bring herself back to the task at hand and tamp down the ever-present humiliation and longing.

"There are people making a lot of money off something that's against the law. Maine has looser gun laws than a lot of other places, so people come here to buy them and bring 'em home. They buy them under the table, don't follow the rules. People are dying because of it." He seemed more at ease now that he was talking about something official. His nice low timbre, him talking to her like a normal person, felt good. "That border guard got shot in Coburn Gore last November, just up the road from here. Guy was bringing illegally bought guns into Quebec."

When he paused, Bernie nodded to show she remembered.

"We've got a problem here in town, too," he said. "Kenny Paquette held up the pharmacy with an unregistered gun, said he found it but doesn't remember where. We don't know where the hell it came from. We're still trying to figure out where Dragon's gun came from. It's a problem."

Bernie wrote down the bones of what he said. "If it's being done illegally, then why does it matter if Maine's laws are looser? I mean, if it's illegal, it could happen anywhere. Looser laws, tighter laws. Doesn't matter."

"None of it's in a vacuum. The people selling them illegally can acquire their inventory more easily. And it's a cultural thing, too. Since guns are a way of life in the state, everyone has guns, fewer questions, fewer eyes on the problem."

She wrote that down while he watched her. "Any progress with the notebook?" She knew she was pushing her luck, pressing on a bruise.

"Notebook?" He paused, expressionless. "No."

"You know what struck me odd? The coyote reference. Don't you think so?"

"Are we done?" He got up and opened the door. She followed him into the newsroom, feeling stupid, her humiliation cloud suffocating her.

"They're releasing the records from the shooting next week," she said. "It's taking them a while to get all the stuff together, the interview transcripts, crime scene photos. Cruiser tape. I'm going to Augusta a week from Thursday to get it all."

His eyes flashed, angry green lasers, as he opened the door and stepped out onto Main Street. "Good for you."

. . . . .

Pete hadn't been gone twenty minutes when Bev Dulac dropped by the *Watcher*. Bernie briefly considered putting up a sign, "Closed on Tuesdays." At this rate, she was never going to get the paper out.

"We're having a reconciliation festival." Bev was never one to waste time on small talk when an announcement or order would do.

"Reconciliation festival?"

"Yes. Are you going to write this down?"

Bernie picked up a pencil and pad from her desk as Bev waited.

"We want to bring the town together. Bigelow Park. You need to put something in the paper." Bev watched her write it down.

"One o'clock Saturday."

Bernie already had to rearrange a page for Pete's meeting notice, so why not?

"We're going to have a band, food, clowns and jugglers, actors from the Shakespeare troupe, the usual," Bev said, as though Redimere put on reconciliation festivals every week.

"Right," Bernie said, brain trying to catch up.

"Hope you're still working on Stanley," Bev added.

Bernie shrugged. "Trying." Bev glared. "Did you ever hear anything about him looking for coyotes down at the bog?"

Bev shook her head. "That would be a stupid place to look for coyotes. They like the mountains. Anyway, he watched birds, not coyotes."

"Right. Did he ever say anything about that snowmobile accident to you? The one where Evan Wentzel died?"

Bev thought about it. "It bothered him. He was a gentle man who respected life. Be sure to give the reconciliation festival good play."

After the door crashed shut behind Bev, Annette said, "Stanley lit a candle for the Wentzel boy."

"What do you mean?" Bernie asked.

"We used to give him a ride to St. Joe's in Farmington. He didn't go to Mass, but he'd go down Saturdays when I go to confession to light candles. He lit one for that boy every time."

"So he talked about the snowmobile accident? Seeing a coyote down there that night?"

Annette frowned. "Nothing like that. But it upset him. Anyone died, it upset him."

CHAPTER 20

Today, finally, with Ray's funeral and the selectmen's meeting behind him, Pete could get back to police work. First order of business was taking care of the notice for that task force meeting. He could have emailed it to Bernie. But today was Tuesday, and he knew she was on deadline. He'd learned that much in his year here. Also, he wanted to make sure she knew he was still going to deal with her on a professional level. He'd be careful. It wasn't going to be like before. He wasn't that much of a chump. But she has a job to do, he got that.

She showed some chutzpah asking about the notebook. She was nuts if she thought he was going to discuss it with her, though. While the shooting and political fallout had occupied all of Pete's time—in fact, had devoured it—he was telling the truth when he told her he was still working on the Stanley investigation. And while he wasn't going to discuss any of it with Bernie, he had one of his best cops on it.

If people in Redimere didn't talk to Peter before, they sure as hell weren't going to now. Dawna was another story.

"We need to talk," Pete said to her after he got back from the *Watcher*.

"Yes sir." She looked stricken.

He laughed. "Nothing to worry about. Job duties."

"Sir?"

"I really need you to call me Pete. Or if you can't, Chief."

She nodded.

"With Ray gone, we need to rearrange. You're great in the office, but I think you'd be even greater out on the street. So why aren't you?"

She blushed. "Chief, um, Chief Cal thought I'd do better in here."

"Why's that?"

She blushed more. "I'm not sure."

"So, you got a criminal justice degree from Farmington and went to the police academy. Did you always want to be a cop?"

"I wanted to be a nurse. Scratch that. I first wanted to be a doctor. But Passamaquoddy girls from Redimere, Maine, don't become doctors. It didn't matter, anyway, because I joined the Marines."

"Good move."

"It was. After two tours I realized I didn't want to be cooped up all day. I liked action. I thought cop would be a good fit."

"Yet you're cooped up in here, filing papers and answering the phone."

She bit her lower lip. "Sorry, I…"

"Don't apologize. You're smart, you have good instincts. You don't belong filing papers all day."

"Sorry, sir, I…"

Pete laughed. He couldn't help it. "Really, Dawna, honest. I don't bite. I think you were underestimated before, but you're not now. Don't think of me as your boss, think of me as a fellow cop. From now on, you're on patrol."

"What about the office?"

"We'll hire somebody. Until we do, we can all pitch in."

She looked dubious.

Pete wondered what poor instincts had led Cal to keep Dawna on such a short leash. Granted, she was great at the computer stuff, great at paperwork. But she'd lived in Redimere all her life. She had served as a medic in Afghanistan, she was an EMT with the fire department. The guys considered her one of them—and with her linebacker's build and open, dimpled face, gentle nature, she could belly up to the bar and have a dozen new friends before the second round. He sure as hell wasn't going to make the same mistake Cal did.

"Tell me about the Weston investigation," he said.

"It's not really ready for a report. I kind of got sidetracked. With Ray…"

"That's okay, what's going on?"

"I keep coming back to the bog. Bev Dulac says he used to sit out behind his trailer and watch birds every day. If you look down the rise behind where he lived, you can see the bog where the road goes in. And when he walked to and from town, he'd hang out by the stone fence. Everyone saw him, just sitting there with his shopping cart, whiling the day away. There's the notebook, the dates. It's something, and what did he do all day? I don't think it's birds."

"What about the coyote reference? Just the one, right?"

"Yeah. Coyote bait on the bridge. Why?"

"Nothing. Go on."

"I don't know if there's anything to that Vietnam argument at the VFW. Cal's not here to ask." She was transformed while talking about her investigation, her inner Marine kicking in, but now she blushed again. "Not that he would've told me anything, anyway. He kind of kept me out of the loop. Sorry, I didn't mean—"

"It's okay. Cop to cop here."

"So my next move is to go down to the VFW. See if I can get Miller to talk. Vietnam argument, bog. Whatever."

"Keep me posted."

"You bet, Chief."

. . . . .

The rest of the guys who were drinking at the VFW the night of the Christmas party were useless—the ones who were still alive. Gary the bartender was no help. He'd heard too many bar arguments in his life to pay attention, he told Dawna. What a drunken mess they all must have been at that party. She had never been a big drinker and drunken male behavior was at the bottom of her entertainment list, so she didn't spend a lot of time at the VFW even though she'd earned her membership.

But now she was going there every night after work and nursing one lonely screwdriver. Ike Miller had become a local celebrity since the shooting, particularly to the boys at the VFW. Part of the problem with hanging out there, though, was that crowd wasn't happy with Pete. She hated listening to it. She noticed when Rusty was there he didn't do much to defend the chief, too wimpy to have principles.

Another problem was that no one was talking about Stanley anymore. All they wanted to talk about was the shooting.

Ike's retelling of it riveted his followers at the bar, replacing the tales of wrasslin' commies in Vietnam and oil wells in Texas. His bar buddies especially loved to hear him retell his signature final line to Dragon: "When I shoot, I don't miss."

In Dawna's experience the best warriors didn't talk much about their exploits. That went for the war here at home, too.

When she walked in after talking to Pete, Ike was the only one at the bar.

She sat down a stool away from him and ordered her usual screwdriver.

"Hey, Mr. Miller," she said, giving him her best dimpled smile.

He smiled back—a too-bright winking extravaganza that made her skin crawl.

"Hey, little lady," he said.

Dawna gave him the benefit of the doubt that his years living in Texas made that a figure of speech and he wasn't making fun of her size.

"How is everyone holding up at the PD?"

"We're okay," Dawna said, taking her drink from Gary. "We miss Cal. Kind of wonder how this would've played out if he was still around." She looked down at the bar as she sipped her drink, afraid Ike would see through her.

"I think it never would've happened," Ike said. "That college boy, he's smart, but he's no Cal. Cal was one of a kind. And he had this town by the balls."

Dawna smiled and nodded again. She took a bigger gulp and winced, offering a silent apology to Pete. "Yeah, the chief doesn't know the town."

"I'll tell you something about that chief of yours."

Gary had gone in the back room and the two of them were alone. Even so, Ike lowered his voice to a stage whisper.

"Cal told me when he hired him that he was soft. He's got a skeleton or two in his closet, too. Got into lots of trouble down in Philly. Know what else? That girl over at the newspaper, Bernadette, knows all about it. She's keeping it under her hat because she and your chief are having a secret affair."

Dawna gulped down her drink. Gary reappeared at the end of the bar and she ordered a refill.

Ike gave her another wink. "Put that in your peace pipe and smoke it."

. . . . .

The next day, Dawna caught up with Bernie as she was walking home to lunch.

"What's up?" Bernie asked as Dawna fell into step with her.

Dawna's smile had a nervous tilt.

"I need to talk to you about something."

"I'll make you lunch," Bernie said. She tried not to make her relief visible—Dawna was still her friend after all. Maybe.

"I don't know if I should even be talking to you," Dawna said. "But I can't think of anyone else to tell about this."

Bernie didn't answer.

"The chief asked me to help him look into the Weston case," Dawna said.

"Smart move." Good for Pete.

"I was talking to Ike Miller and he said some things about the chief. What bothers me more than what he said—because I know it's not true—is the damage it can do."

"What did he say?"

"He said some stuff happened in Philadelphia? And people are saying the chief's some kind of head case?"

Great. Cat's out of the bag. Poor Pete. Bernie sighed. "Something did happen in Philadelphia. It has nothing to do with what's going on here. Has he ever done anything that would make you think he can't be trusted? Or that he can't handle a situation?"

"Hell no. He's the real deal, one hundred percent." She paused. "Ike also said, um, that you know and you're not putting anything in the paper because…" She faltered.

"Because?"

Dawna blushed. "Because you're having an affair."

Bernie's laugh came out harsher than she intended. "Nothing could be farther from the truth. I'll tell you what happened in Philly, judge for yourself."

By the time they got to Bernie's house, she'd told Dawna the story.

"I know guys like that," Dawna said as they sat down to tuna fish sandwiches. "I guess Philadelphia was kind of like being in a war. He's still one tough guy."

Bernie smiled. Same thing Sid had said. "I'm keeping that information about the chief to myself, not because we're having an affair—which we're not—but because it doesn't belong in the paper. It's got nothing to do with anything. Anyway, the selectmen know all about it."

Dawna nodded. "I appreciate that. After what was in the paper last week —" She changed course. "I'm not telling anyone, either. The chief's going through enough crap. He needs people to have his back."

Bernie thought Dawna was perfect for that job.

"There's something else I wanted to run past you," Dawna said. "I don't want to keep things from the chief, but…"

"I don't know if you should. Especially if you're telling me."

"I can't tell him," Dawna said. "Something I've been thinking about ever since you came by that day to look at the report about the snowmobile accident."

Bernie nodded. Score!

"I didn't want you to look at the accident report, because I knew they'd fudged it. Sorry."

"That's okay."

"There was a meeting," Dawna said. "Right after the accident. The chief—Cal—" she looked at Bernie.

"Right, Cal."

"Cal, Rusty, and Ray," Dawna said. It came out in a rush. "He called it a staff meeting, but told me I didn't have to be there. I was pissed. I said it was okay, I'd like to be there and he told me no."

Bernie grunted in sympathy. "Jamie wasn't there?"

"No, day off. It was the day Chief got back from Florida, right after the accident. The doors to his office didn't close well back in the old department. I could hear some of what was going on. They were talking about the snowmobile crash. It sounded like they were having an argument. I heard the chief say, he sounded mad, 'I'll take care of it, but this stops here.' Stanley had come in to talk to him earlier. I didn't think anything about it at the time, but now..." She looked at Bernie expectantly.

"That's it?"

"What do you think it means?" Dawna asked. "The morning after you talked to Rusty at the Pour House, asked him about the accident, I heard him tell Ray. Ray told him to shut up."

"Why don't you want to tell Pete?"

"If the department's involved, maybe he knows about it? I mean, he and Cal were close. Maybe it was nothing." She paused, blushed. "Anyway, I don't want him to think I go around listening at doors and telling tales."

"Right."

"Can you not tell him we talked about this?" she asked.

"You bet. This is just between us."

Which, of course, didn't mean Bernie couldn't use it to pursue her own investigation.

. . . . .

As Dawna walked back down the hill to downtown she thought about how she hadn't told Bernie the most interesting information she got from Ike Miller. Nothing to do with Stanley, but still interesting. He was as concerned about the whereabouts of Justin Mercier as Justin's parents were.

He had asked her if she was a friend of "that kid who worked down at the garage."

"The one in the ice cream truck during the shooting?" she'd asked.

Ike had scowled. "Damn kid. That's the one."

She knew Justin, slightly. He was a few years behind her in school. "I know him."

"I was just wondering if you'd seen him around. He's got something that belongs to me."

Dawna filed it away. It didn't fit. It was interesting. It had to be a piece to some puzzle. It's the pieces that didn't fit that helped the puzzle get solved. If not the Stanley one, then another one.

. . . . .

Later that afternoon, Bernie was finishing up paperwork when she saw Rusty across the street at the Country Grocer, talking to Walt Pecoe, the store's owner.

She got up and crossed the street. "Hi, guys. When's this heat gonna break?"

Walt smiled at her. Rusty kept talking.

"So, I'm not sure, with the tournament starting in two weeks, that you can switch partners. The rules don't call for it. It's not fair." Rusty was pouting.

"Big doings in the two-on-two league," Walt said to Bernie. "I had to pick up a new partner and Rusty doesn't like it."

"It's not me who doesn't like it, it's the league," Rusty said.

"Look, we're not playing for world peace or something here," Walt said. "This is for a cheap trophy. We play on an elementary school playground, for chrissake. And, if you kick me out, you'll have to redo the tournament rotation." He turned to Bernie. "It's a round-robin."

"Ahhh." She had no clue what that meant.

"Don't say I didn't warn you if some of the guys have an issue. Chief might have a rough game."

"We can handle it. I gotta get back in there. Some of us have to work for a living."

Rusty sighed and turned to climb back into the Suburban.

"Can I talk to you a minute?" Bernie asked.

"I don't know, I gotta get out on patrol. Chief's a stickler." He looked around the empty street, as if Pete were going to burst out and crack a whip.

"This'll just take a minute."

Rusty looked dubious.

"It's about you and Cal and Ray and the snowmobile crash. You want to talk to me before you read something in the paper." It was a total bluff, but one that usually worked.

"Okay, what?" he asked, scowling.

"Come on, it's not that bad," Bernie said. "I just want to know what happened at the snowmobile accident that had you arguing with Cal and Ray after Cal got back from Florida."

"Who told you that?"

"Ray." Sorry Ray. She wondered how much of a sin she'd just committed. But hell, it's okay to lie about a dead guy if it helps get to the truth, right?

"I doubt that. He wouldn't say anything."

Bernie shrugged. "It was in context." She knew that didn't make much sense, but it was a phrase that worked—people didn't want to let on they didn't know what she was talking about. Another piece from her reporter's bag of tricks. "Say anything about what?" she added.

Rusty looked up empty Main Street. Redimere stuck in its usual mid-summer-day torpor. Everyone was either away, on the water, up a mountain or at work.

"The sooner you tell me something, the sooner you can get

back in that air-conditioned Suburban."

Rusty now seemed more annoyed than nervous. "Why would I trust you after you misquoted the chief?"

"I didn't misquote him. But if you won't talk, maybe I should ask the chief, he might have some ideas."

"Okay," Rusty said, looking around again. Still nobody in sight. "It's embarrassing. And it's private and I don't need to see it in the paper. So this is off the record. Totally."

Off the record, Bernie thought. I wish I had a nickel for every time I've heard that in the past week. "Fine."

"I was meeting a, um, lady friend down by the bog. So I was already down there when the kids went by," Rusty said, not looking at Bernie. "I didn't want anyone to ask why I was already down there, so I asked Ray to help fudge the report, make it unclear about how it was called in. Cal found out anyway, and that's what we were arguing about."

Bernie wondered about the likelihood that some woman would consent to an extramarital affair with goofy Rusty, who from all accounts didn't seem to know what to do with the woman he had. "What lady friend?"

"None of your beeswax."

It didn't matter. She didn't believe him, but she got what she was looking for, confirmation that the argument had something to do with the accident and that Rusty, Cal, and Ray all knew something.

"Do you know of any conversations Stanley and Cal might have had about the accident?"

"No."

"Didn't tell him he saw a coyote on the bridge? That's why the kids crashed?"

Rusty snapped his head around to look at her. "Where'd you hear that?"

"Can't reveal my sources."

"There was a critter. Don't know about a coyote. The kid, John, said he saw it. I don't know about Stanley. Maybe he saw it,

215

too."

"Where was Stanley that night? In the bog?"

"How the hell should I know?" Rusty said, opening the door and getting into the Suburban.

She grabbed the door before he could close it. She had a thought. Not about the crash or Stanley, but something about the shooting that had bothered her and she'd just figured it out. "The night of the shooting, why do you think Ray didn't call for backup when he went after Dragon?"

"We ain't talking about the shooting. No comment." He slammed the door and the Suburban leapt to life so fast Bernie had to jump back to not get sideswiped as it roared away from the curb and down Main Street.

CHAPTER 21

The reconciliation festival beer tent was hopping. Only in Redimere, Bernie thought as she looked for a place to hunker down. The tent was in a good spot, off to the side of the stage, with a good view. Perfect for when Dermot McHugh and the Mountain Ramblers started, playing for free after the shooting interrupted their Fourth of July gig. Bev had hired actors from the summer Shakespeare theater to wander through the crowd reciting passages about reconciliation, but they seemed to be staying out of the beer tent. Thank god, Bernie thought. She could think of some passages of her own. Bubble, bubble toil and trouble. I'll give them some passages. She was in a foul mood. Hoping the classic combination of beer, summer afternoon, and music would improve it. She was tired of the snide remarks about the Pete story. Tired of trying to figure out what the hell was going on. She sipped her beer. Tired of feeling like her career had passed her by and she'd starting sucking at it without even realizing.

"Hey, Bernardo, come on over here."

Sandy MacCormack was sitting on a picnic table a few feet away. Bernie's stomach did a little flip. She couldn't help it. Sandy was not only the best-looking guy in Redimere, but the sweetest. He loved women and women loved him and he had three marriages—

and divorces—to prove it. "What can I do?" he said to Bernie with total sincerity over beers one night at the Pour House. "I'm a born lover."

She sat next to him as the band began to warm up. Dermot, all steel-gray curls and twinkling Irish eyes, was strumming a guitar, singing snatches of songs and calling out to his bandmates. Professional Irishman, that's what Bernie's dad would call him. The band, there was a half dozen or more of them, laughed and chatted as they tuned up their instruments—guitars, fiddles, a stand-up bass. Pete stood off to the side, toying with his banjo strings, picking and adjusting, not joining in the chatter.

"That's our boy up there," Sandy said.

Bernie humphed through a sip of beer, swallowed. "I guess you know how pissed off he is at me."

"Yeah. He doesn't talk about it, though. The morning the paper came out, I went into his office and said, 'Man, you were misquoted bad.'" Sandy drew out all the words, especially baaaaaaaad. "He said, 'I wasn't misquoted.' And that's all he's ever said about it."

Good old Pete, Bernie thought, taking another gulp of beer.

He laughed and shook his head. "Poor Pete."

She didn't say anything. He elbowed her in the side, one of those pay-attention-to-what-I'm-saying elbows.

"Do you know what it took for him to say that to you? That stuff you quoted?"

Bernie shrugged, drank some more beer, feeling the shame and humiliation creep back in, a sudden cloud cover to a day that had been turning out to be all right.

"No one likes to talk about how they've failed," Sandy said. "Especially when friends have died."

When she didn't say anything, he added, "Maybe reporters ought to think about that a little more."

Annoyed, she said, "And yet, he did."

"And yet he did," Sandy agreed. "Think about that for a minute."

She wasn't sure she wanted to.

"I asked him about you, you know," Sandy said, all big round blue eyes.

"Asked him what?"

"If I could take you out."

"You asked him if you could take me out?" Bernie asked. Actually it was more like, "*You* asked *him* if *you* could take *me* out?" She didn't know whether to be insulted or flattered.

Sandy smiled, eyes dancing. "C'mon, it's no secret you two have the hots for each other. Everyone knows. And he *was* seen leaving your house one morning."

"When?" Bernie was about to deny, then remembered. "Back in March? He stopped in after a run." It was a lifetime ago. Eons. "I can assure you there is nothing going on between us."

"And yet, he did." Sandy repeated, then elbowed her again.

They sat silently on the table for a minute or two, their feet on the bench, sipping beer and watching the band set up.

Bernie's curiosity got the best of her. "So what did he say? When you asked about me?"

Sandy grinned wider. "He said, 'You're welcome to her.'"

Bernie felt a surge of disappointment, followed by a bigger surge of annoyance and then a tidal wave of stop being a dumbass.

"Are you asking me out?" She wasn't sure what she wanted the answer to be. On one hand, Sandy was so adorable she wanted to eat him up. Squeeze him like a twelve-pack of Charmin. Wrap her arms and legs around him and take a ride. On the other hand, it would be a fast fling and everyone in Redimere would know about it and it wouldn't solve any of her problems, except make her feel loved for a very short period of time. She also felt some loyalty to her reputation. Pat and Marianne O'Dea didn't raise a floozy.

"I think you're cute." He turned and looked at her, made sure she got his meaning. "I bet you're a lot of fun."

"I'm a barrel of monkeys." It came out about as glum as she felt.

"But, Pete. Man." He shook his head. "He may not be talking

219

to you, but that doesn't mean he doesn't like you. I don't want to interfere."

"I don't think—"

Sandy shushed her. "The band."

"Hello, folks," Dermot said into the microphone. "We're here this afternoon to heal some wounds. We lost two sons of the valley. It's not a time to point fingers. It's a time to mourn. A time to love one another and be there for each other."

Bernie was reminded how the biggest cornpone could sound like poetry when it rode home on an Irish brogue.

Dermot turned and nodded to the band and the music started.

It sounded familiar. Bernie couldn't place it.

"Love is but a song we sing," Dermot sang.

Oh my god, it's The Youngbloods, "Get Together," Bernie realized. A 1960s peace and love song. Every cynical bone in her body wanted to mock the corniness. She looked around for someone's eye to catch. Sandy was singing along. The crowd, both those in the beer tent and the few hundred on lawn chairs and standing in front of the stage, were singing too, swaying and nodding.

What the hell, she was on her second beer and she was half Irish, overly sentimental crying in your beer sap was in her DNA. She felt her heart expand.

Up on stage, Pete joined Dermot singing. Pete was a surprise. Bernie had expected him to look stiff and uncomfortable. But he looked relaxed, and, could it be? Expressive. When he sang he looked like he was feeling it, feeling the truth.

She felt ripped off. How could he be Robocop with her, but show his feelings up there in front of hundreds of people? She also felt a beer-fueled mix of regret and compassion. By the time the chorus came around, she, Sandy and the rest of the crowd joined the entire band, *C'mon people now, smile on your brother* . . .

The band was good. Pete was good. The banjo tripped and danced through the guitar and bass chords, around the fiddle and keyboards. Maybe this reconciliation business would work, Bernie thought. It was certainly working its magic on Sandy, who kept bumping Bernie and putting his arm around her shoulder. She saw Pete look their way a couple times, but she knew better than to think Sandy's flirting would matter to him.

During the break, she sidled over to say hi. "Can I buy you a beer?"

He was sitting on the edge of the stage doing something complicated-looking with his banjo strings.

"Already got one."

She saw, next to him on the stage, the plastic beer cup. "Right." She was at a loss. She watched him tighten the banjo strings. Excessively, it seemed to her. There was an angry pink bruise on his cheekbone. She fought the urge to brush her finger against it, feather soft. Put her hand in her pocket. "What happened to your cheek?"

"Basketball," he said, not looking up.

She waited for elaboration, but there wasn't any.

"So," she said, with sudden inspiration. "You're going to that gun task force meeting tonight in Farmington, right?"

He grunted, seemingly in agreement.

"Can I talk to you Monday or Tuesday about it for a story?"

"Suit yourself," he said, then got up, picked up his banjo and beer, and walked to the back of the stage.

Good talk, Bernie said to herself.

One of the actors dressed in Shakespearian costume sidled over. As though he were telling her a secret, he said, "Oh I have suffered with those that I saw suffer."

"I bet you have," Bernie said, walking away.

"The Tempest, Act 1, Scene 2," he called after her.

She had no patience for people in costume. Santa Claus, team mascots, you name it. It annoyed her when people pretended to be a character, then treated her like she was part of the game. She didn't like playing. Reality was fun enough.

She looked over the crowd. There had to be hundreds of people, despite the overcast day and a threat of rain. Everyone

221

seemed in a good mood. Bring on the reconciliation. Her stomach growled. Across the baseball field, she saw the line for the WACOF buffet. Carol and Vince were serving. She'd say hi and get some food. Potato salad. Just what the doctor ordered after four beers.

Working her way through the crowd, she caught sight of John Carrier, the boy who survived the snowmobile crash. Score!

"Hi. John, right?"

He nodded.

"I'm Bernie O'Dea. I'm a friend of your mom's."

"Oh, hi."

"She says you're loving USM and Portland."

"Yeah, it's great." He looked about as uninterested as a boy that age could look while talking to a middle-aged woman.

"I work for the newspaper and I was wondering if I could ask you a couple questions about that snowmobile accident."

He blanched. That's the only word for it. Went from rosy-cheeked to white in a second.

"That was like, a year and a half ago."

"It's important."

"I gotta go. Sorry." He started walking. She followed.

"What were you guys doing down there?"

He shrugged. "Just sledding."

"You saw a coyote on the bridge and that made Evan crash?"

He stopped. "Yeah. That's right."

Bernie realized Dawna, in uniform, was standing at her elbow.

"Did you guys see Stanley Weston down there that night?" Bernie asked.

One of the Shakespearian actors came up and with a big smile, said, "What if this cursed hand were thicker than itself with brother's blood, is there not rain enough in the sweet heavens to wash it white as snow?"

John, if possible, got even whiter.

"Get lost," Bernie said to the actor, as Dawna grabbed John's arm.

"Hamlet—" the actor began.

222

"Right, Claudius, Act 3, Scene 3. Now get lost," Bernie snapped.

The guy scurried away.

John, staring after the actor, pulled away from Dawna's grasp. "What is this? I'm just up here for my grandma's birthday. I gotta get back to Portland tonight for my job. I don't remember anything about that night. It's not my fault Evan died. If Stanley said he was there and saw a coyote, then he was."

"I thought you said you're the one who saw a coyote," Bernie said.

"You got me confused."

"Is that what you and he were talking about at the post office back in December?"

"I never talked to him."

"Bev Dulac said she saw you two talking. The day you got home on Christmas break."

"She must be mixed up."

"Bev doesn't usually get mixed up," Dawna said.

"I told you what I know. I'm not lying. Geez. Can I go now officer?"

As he walked away, Bernie said to Dawna, "Well, that was interesting."

Dawna nodded. "Guess I better talk to the chief."

. . . . .

For the time being, the chief was busy. The band had started up again and was cooking. The crowd grew, alcohol took hold, people were dancing, singing. Dermot knew how to work an audience. The place went nuts when they played a tribute to Ray.

After the hooting and applause died down, Dermot leaned into the mike again.

"This is for Dragon. I'm told it was his favorite."

Before Bernie, back on her picnic table, could figure out what song it was, a stir rippled through the crowd. "No music for no cop killer," someone yelled. She stood on the table to see if she could see who yelled. It was hard to tell. There was scuffling. The singers and swayers in the front began to turn and push their way to the scrum. The band played on. Well, kind of. Pete stopped singing and dropped his banjo on the stage, vaulting down into the crowd. Bernie saw Dawna sprinting, with Jamie, from the buffet tables. Half the crowd was fighting, the other half was trying to break it up.

Bernie took her camera out of her bag and started shooting. So much for reconciliation.

. . . . .

At the office later, her buzz had worn off and she had a headache. She was turning off her computer to go home when a car pulled up out front. Denise Carrier got out of the driver's side and started walking to the *Watcher* front door. She turned and said something to the passenger side. John got out. Bernie had a mental image of Denise pulling him by the ear, the way the nuns used to when she was in grade school. He looked that reluctant.

"Bernie! Got a minute? Sorry to bother you on a Saturday!" She was all exclamation points, but not with her usual good cheer. Determined.

"Sure, sit down."

"John has something to say," Denise said, not sitting down.

John looked at the floor, his hands in his pockets.

"John?" Denise said. "You have something to say."

He rolled his eyes and didn't look up. "I guess I did talk to Stanley at the post office."

"Okay," Bernie said.

"Tell her what he said," Denise said.

"Mom."

"Tell her."

He sighed. "He wasn't there the night of the crash. Didn't see a coyote. Me neither. No one did." He looked at his mother. "Okay?"

"He told me this today," Denise said to Bernie. "I heard him on the phone telling someone you were asking about it. Justin Mercier. Turns out he's staying at John's down in Portland." She gave John a long look before continuing. "Well, I don't think it's right for him to lie to you or that lady officer."

John snorted. "Yeah and they got one of those guys in tights to come over and hassle me with Shakespeare. Like that was going to make me fess up. Stupid."

"You can't pin that one on us," Bernie said.

"Anyway," Denise continued. "That old buck Cal told my Bud and John that Stanley told him he saw a coyote on the bridge and that's why the sled went off. Neither of them shared that with me."

"Hard to get a word in edgewise," John muttered.

She went on as if he hadn't said anything. "John saw Stanley that day he got back from school and asked him about it. Stanley told him he was never there and saw no such thing."

"The old guy was out of it. I bet he just forgot," John said.

"Stanley was not out of it," Denise said. Then to Bernie, "I thought you'd want to know."

"Sure, thanks," Bernie said, trying to sort it out. "Did you tell the police?"

John jerked his head up. "They're the ones who said Stanley said that in the first place. Tell them they're wrong? Yeah, right. I just want to go back to Portland. I told Evan not to go down into the bog. My hands aren't the ones thick with brother's blood— What? I'm minoring in English," he said to his mother's incredulous stare.

Then to Bernie, "That dude whose property it is doesn't take any prisoners. Look what happened to Dragon."

CHAPTER 22

Local Man Faces Jail for Illegal Junkyard

Wayne Daggett, of Pond Road, is facing 30 days in jail unless he cleans up his property, which county officials are calling an illegal junkyard.

The town and county have been after Daggett for years to clean up his five acres. "Every inch of that property is covered in garbage," said an official with the county health department. "It's a health hazard and an eyesore."

Peaks Weekly Watcher, July 16, 2009

Bernie got the press release about Wayne Daggett from the county the day before Pete gave her the task force memo and Bev ordered her to do a story on the reconciliation festival.

She hadn't had time, with everything that was going on, to do much about the Wayne Daggett story except try to call him. When she didn't get an answer, she figured she owed it to him to go over to his house to get his side of the story. Anyway, there was something about hoarders that fascinated her. Something sad and desperate. Everyone had some bad stuff going on in their head. She had a curiosity about people who went over that line, but she knew part of it was to add to her list of ways not to become like that herself. We're all just a couple bad decisions away from living under a pile of shit, she reminded herself.

Monday afternoon she took a ride out there. He lived down Pond Road past the bog. Bernie thought that when she had time to think she'd try to figure out if the fact that every story seemed to lead her down this road was a coincidence or a pattern. Or she had just entered hell and it was Pond Road. She always knew hell wouldn't be the inferno. It would be something so familiar it would take a while to realize you were there.

Bernie saw Downwind had graded the tote road that had led to Stanley's. As she drove by, a truck coming from the other direction turned in, a huge piece of a wind turbine on its flatbed. Bernie made a mental note to do a wind farm update. The shootings had taken over everything. She'd never followed up with the county on Ike's illegal gate, either. She'd called one guy, he called her back and left a message at the *Watcher*, then she never got back to him. I need more reporters. It was on the list, right up there with fixing the door and getting an air conditioner. Either that, or put the paper on the market and get a job with the state, work forty hours a week and go home and not think about work or what a failure she was until she clocked in again the next morning. The more she turned that idea around in her head, the more it appealed to her.

Wayne's house was about two hundred yards back from the road. She knew this because she had been told. It was obscured from the street by scattered pine trees, old tractors, rusting automobile hulks, the shell of a school bus and mountains of junk. She did a U-turn and pulled up in the knee-high grass between the road and a row of pines and swamp maples. Almost every inch of tree had a hub cap nailed to it. There were also mountains of lobster traps, both the old wooden kind and the newer green wire. Ah yes, Bernie thought, for trapping the elusive Wesserunsett River lobster. They must have wings and fly here from the Atlantic. Peppered among the vehicles and piles of lobster traps were rusted appliances,

227

old swing sets and playground equipment, shelves from a five and dime store. Rows of old bottles lined rickety picnic tables and benches. Boxes of assorted junk and garbage were piled, tossed, and scattered among the debris.

Nailed between two of the pines was Wayne Daggett's prized possession: a large, hand-painted sign featuring a monstrous, grotesquely smiling lobster and the words "Downeast Curiosity Museum."

All of Bernie's history with Wayne was from public meetings, the last time was the wind farm meeting nearly a month ago. He was what was politely known as a gadfly, but since no one was that polite, he was more frequently known as a nut job. Got a meeting? Wayne would bring a gripe.

She picked her way through the yard to the front door of his sagging clapboard house, notebook in hand, camera on its strap over her shoulder. She knocked. "I really want to tell your side of the story" she mumbled to herself, rehearsing the speech that she had given so many reluctant interviewees over the years. Everyone from the dad whose daughter was killed in the drunken-driving accident to the city treasurer accused of embezzlement. It worked more often than she expected it to. Bernie *did* want to tell their side of the story. No story had just one side. Most didn't even stop at two. The more sides, the better the story. She knocked again.

No answer.

"Hello?" The two tiny front windows showed no sign of life. The venetian blinds, yellowed and spotted with what looked like decades of dead flies, didn't stir. "Anyone home?"

Bernie walked around to the back of the house. She stopped, stunned. If the front was bad, the back was a screaming riot. Car parts. Cars stacked on top of each other. How does he even do that? Then she saw how. A backhoe, skidder, a caterpillar, even a small crane. More tractors. All rusted and listing. A 1960s-era ambulance. Rows of appliances, lobster traps, plastic Christmas lawn ornaments. Animals from a carousel! Seats from a Ferris wheel! Bernie wasn't sure whether she was disgusted or sad. Most of it was muddy, rusted, broken. Destroyed. Not worth anything. Why would someone have all this? Something about all the stuff, all the *crap*, really, broke her heart. The carousel animals, their paint faded, big chips and dings in their bodies, noses and limbs missing. What did Wayne see? Something valuable? Something happy?

Way in the back were two more partial school buses, one painted Partridge Family style and a Greyhound, decades old. Bernie went to get a better look. Giant weeds grew in the few parts of the yard not covered by junk. One of the cars had a small maple tree growing through its roof. Bernie watched her step as she walked back toward the buses. The ground was a minefield of scattered debris, broken glass, small tools, dishes, toys, a lot of it hidden by grass and weeds.

As she approached the bus, she was so focused on not breaking her ankle on some piece of junk it took her a minute to realize what was behind it. In the weeds, at the edge of the woods, all by itself, hidden behind the row of buses. Unmistakable.

The rusty teardrop hump of Stanley Weston's trailer.

. . . . .

Pete got up and closed his door behind Rusty. Another annoying conversation, explaining to Rusty why he had to go on day shifts. He was irritatingly resistant. Pete knew why he wanted to work nights—Rusty was lazy and could get away without doing much. But he had a lot more experience than Jamie and Dawna, and Pete needed an experienced guy on days, which were a lot busier. Also, he could keep an eye on him and make sure he was working, not sleeping or whatever the hell he did in the Suburban. On top of it, he had the nerve to ask to be promoted to sergeant, to fill Ray's old post. Pete told him he was still working on that. He wished he could put all the personnel issues aside and spend some time being a cop.

At least Jamie was full-time now, doing weekend days and filling in during the week. Dawna was still in the office more than Pete would have liked, but he hadn't had time to hire an office clerk. At least she'd received her battlefield commission and was filling in on patrol. And thank god she was working the Stanley

Weston case, because he didn't have the time.

She'd updated him earlier in the day on her conversation with John Carrier and what Denise and John had told Bernie. Apparently, Bernie called her right after the pair left. It annoyed him she hadn't called him, but could he really blame her? He wondered if it was a coincidence John had talked to Stanley about the snowmobile accident two days before Stanley died. Cal apparently told the families of both boys in the accident, at least the fathers, that Stanley saw a coyote on the bridge, saw the accident. So why didn't the report reflect it? Why did Stanley say he didn't?

Things had been quiet, with the exception of Cal's fire, for the first six or seven months he'd been here. He was surprised that it suited him, that community policing without a lot of crime was okay, helped him get his head together. He'd been afraid the panic attacks would start again after the shootings, but they hadn't. They'd fizzled out in Philly after he was taken off the streets. He'd had some nightmares, woken up in a sweat a few times, but since he came to Redimere he hadn't had one full-blown attack. Well, maybe one. That night Cal died he felt like he was having one, but it could have been smoke inhalation and the exertion of dragging a nearly three hundred-pound corpse out of a burning house. That's what he told himself.

Stay sane. That had been his motto. Stay sane. Every morning he ran the three miles to the lake and dove in. Stay underwater as long as he could before coming up for air. It became a game, see how long he could stay under. He was surprised at how good he'd become at it. No sound, all the sweat and heat from the run washed off. Then he'd run home. That hour in the sun and humidity practicing for the two-on-two league with Walt helped, too. It did more for his mental health than any shrink possibly could. He still wasn't sure about the league, though. He got pounded Saturday. Every time he moved, there was an elbow, or hand, or knee, crashing into him. He didn't mind a little back and forth. When he was running the youth program in Philly, he played ball with the kids all the time and they were brutal. But this was different.

Hostile.

He knew he had to suck it up. Just like he did when he got to work one morning last week and the Sgt. Ray Morin memorial adopt-a-roadside sign, battered, twisted, and shot full of holes, was blocking the entrance to the police station. Surveillance cameras for the public safety complex were one of the budget items that had been voted down at town meeting.

"No comment," he said to Bernie when she called about it.

Just suck it up, he said to himself. Stay sane.

He sighed and looked at the stuff on his desk again. Stanley's notebook. Pete thumbed through it, looked at the neat, block pencil print dates. The checklist. Talk to Cal. 1/18/08, shelter, negligent?, R, J!, bridge "coyote bait."

Pete wished Cal was still around so he could talk to him, too. Clear this all up.

He was sick of violence. Sick of death. He thought coming here would get him away from all that. The joke was on him. He was glad the rumble at the reconciliation festival was no more than shoving and name-calling and no one was hurt. Maybe everyone else was sick of it, too.

. . . . .

Bernie opened the door to the trailer. It was warm and dark, trees shading the sunlight from coming in the milky little window. It didn't take much light to see the Army-neat cubby she had poked through in March had been trashed. Cabinets ripped off the wall, the sink ripped out, the bunk and table on the floor in a pile.

"Cop said I could take it."

Bernie jumped and turned around. There was a short, chubby silhouette in the sunlit doorway.

"It's mine. Loren didn't want it and the cop said I could keep it." Wayne Daggett's voice was querulous.

"Hi Mr. Daggett, I'm Bernie O'Dea."

"I know who you are."

"I'm here about the story in the paper. I thought I'd get your side." She'd start with the easy stuff before she worked her way up to the trailer.

"I get that newspaper, but I'm behind in my reading. Was down to Togus most of the summer with a leg infection." He started to pull up a greasy pant leg, but Bernie waved him off. He let go, disappointed. "Anyway, got 'em all up in the house. Takes a lot of time. I clip out the articles, file 'em. I'm in January. January 2001."

She wondered fleetingly if he knew about 9/11 or the recession. "We got a press release from the county saying you have to clean this up or you're going to jail."

"This is my property. This is investment for my retirement. I can sell it for a lot of money. They can't make me get rid of it."

He was still in the doorway and Bernie was sweating, the air thick. She had to get out of the gamey trailer. "Mind if I come outside?"

He moved away from the door.

She had never been this close to Wayne Daggett before. He looked like a garden gnome, one with food-flecked stubble, a stained T-shirt and overalls and very few teeth.

"So you'll go to jail?"

"The hell I will. This is my property. They can't take it. They want to take everything. Government interference. Fascists. That president wants to take our guns away," he said. So he *does* know who's president. Bernie hoped Wayne didn't have a loaded gun squirreled away and was planning on exercising his Second Amendment rights by shooting her. He had launched into a rant, but seemed more cranky—defensive and whiney—than hostile. She could relate.

She interrupted. "What cop?"

He stopped in mid-sentence. "Huh?"

"You said a cop said you could keep the trailer. Which cop?"

"That cop after they found Stanley." Wayne looked annoyed, like she should know. "I asked Loren what he was going to do with Stanley's stuff. He said that girl took it." He looked at Bernie. "You. You took it."

"Some of it."

"So Loren said I could take the trailer. That cop was there. Ripping it apart."

"What cop?"

"The asshole. You know, the one who hassles me. The asshole."

"Ray? The one who got shot?"

"Someone shot that son of a bitch? Good riddance. Waste of tax money, that guy was."

CHAPTER 23

Bernie tried calling Pete at the station when she got back to the office, but got no answer. She tried his cell and got voicemail.

She left a message saying she was at the *Watcher* until ten and needed to talk to him. She wondered if he would bother. Maybe she should have said it was about the trailer.

She was trying to get an early start on the pages, but was hot, jumpy, and unfocused. She tried to concentrate. It didn't help that she'd been hunkered down in the newsroom all afternoon and now well into the evening and hadn't eaten. Food would help, but the Country Grocer was closed and there was nothing in the office fridge but beer and curdled half-and-half.

She pressed her beer bottle against her head. It was wet with condensation. When the hell was the heat and humidity going to break? This was Maine for chrissake, at the foot of the mountains. Ski country. It's not supposed to be this hot for this long.

She sat back in her chair and considered her page dummies, but her brain wouldn't hold. She was thinking about the trailer. And Ray. And the fact that he wasn't here anymore to ask about it. She wondered if Dawna told Pete about Stanley and John Carrier. She wanted to ask him herself, but didn't want to step on Dawna's toes. She wished the puzzle pieces would sort themselves out in her head.

It wasn't going to happen tonight.

A cloud of moths swirled in the doorway. She slapped at a mosquito. She could close the door, but it was too friggin' hot.

The office phone rang.

"Hello, sweetheart." It was Harry. "I knew I'd find you burning the midnight oil."

"Some things never change. What's up?"

"I didn't want to fuel the fire if it doesn't mean anything. But something's been bugging me. The more I thought about it, the more I thought I should say something."

"Okay."

"The last time I talked to Cal, he mentioned Stanley and it seemed, I don't know, odd."

"How so?"

"I was saying to Cal he'd be down here in Florida if the deal on that winter place he was going to buy back in '08 hadn't fallen through, you know, he just couldn't afford it. He seemed so down in the dumps, drinking and all. I was trying to cheer him up."

"Sounds like you were doing a great job."

He ignored her sarcasm. "I'm getting to that. He'd told me before about Stan going down south, and I said, 'Well, maybe you could go down and visit Stanley.'"

"And what did Cal say?"

"He said, and I quote, 'Harry, that's the funniest thing you ever said.'"

"Did you ask him what he meant?"

"Yeah. He said he couldn't even take care of himself, was all. But it seemed like there was more to it."

"When was that?"

"Right before Cal died. Couple days, week at the most, before Christmas."

Bernie didn't know what to make of it. Harry didn't either.

"I know you're out straight with everything else going on up there, but I thought I'd just add that into the mix."

Harry's call shot what was left of Bernie's concentration. She gave up and concentrated on her beer instead. She put her feet up on her desk, took a swig, and closed her eyes.

The sound of car coming down the street broke through quiet hum of crickets and buzzing bugs. She opened her eyes. The cruiser pulled up out front. The car door slammed and Pete came in, official and serious in his uniform and full duty belt.

"You had something you wanted to talk about?" Not friendly, but not unfriendly either. The bruise on his cheek had graduated from pink and purple to a nice blue and black. Matched his uniform.

"You guys were great Saturday."

"Thanks."

"I didn't know you played the accordion, too. You're really good."

"Thanks."

She could see how this was going to go.

"I don't know how much reconciliation there was," Bernie said. She wasn't going to give up on trying to make him talk. Perverse, she knew, but she couldn't help herself.

"Yeah," he said. Then, after a pause, "You looked like you were having fun."

Ha! A breakthrough. "It was fun, right up until it wasn't."

"So what did you want to talk about?"

Okay, back to business. "Stanley Weston's trailer is in Wayne Daggett's yard." She decided she'd just come right out with it.

"What?"

"I was over there checking things out, the county—"

"Right, yeah."

"And there it was, way out in back. Thought you'd want to know."

"I suppose you had to go in and look around again."

Bernie felt her face get hot. She gave a big, exaggerated shrug, palms up. "What else was I gonna do?"

He looked at her, considering. A muscle in his cheek twitched.

"Do you wanna know—"

"I can take it from here," he said, wheeling around. The cruiser door slammed.

"—what Wayne Daggett told me?" she continued to herself and the mosquitoes and moths.

. . . . .

The next morning Bernie realized she'd never asked Pete about the gun task force meeting. She wanted an excuse to talk to him more about the trailer and see if he knew the Carriers' news yet, so that was a good excuse to go see him. She wondered if she should say something about what Harry told her. But it was almost nothing. So amorphous she could barely keep hold of it herself.

When she stopped by the police department, he was at his desk, his head bent over paperwork.

"Knock, knock," she said, standing in the open doorway.

He looked up.

"I never asked you about the task force."

"It was just a public forum. We wanted to let people know they weren't going to lose their guns, as long as they were legal. But to look out for illegal sales, anything hinky."

"Okay. Routine. Anyone I know there?"

"The usual. The Sportsman's Club gang, Carrier, Loren, Miller and his bunch."

"They say anything?"

"Just listened. Didn't know I was supposed to take notes for you," Pete said, already looking back down at the paperwork on his desk.

Ouch. Okay. Moving right along. "You go see the trailer?" She was hopeful that she'd given him a gift, with the trailer. Hoping he'd look at it that way and ease up on her.

He looked back up. Gazed at her. That old, familiar unreadable green laser stare. Waited a beat. "No comment." Then he looked back down at his paperwork.

Bernie smiled through the familiar burn of humiliation. No asking about the Carriers, then. No friendly chat, even, about the Red Sox, or the casual jokes they used to share. That was gone and

237

never coming back. It wasn't easy. Painful, really, to be dismissed like that. But she'd sinned and she had to do her penance. "Okey dokey. Talk to you later."

. . . . .

Pete kept his eyes on his desk until he heard her walk down the hall. He wondered how long he'd be mad at her. It wasn't easy talking to her, but it wasn't easy being mad either when she looked at him, flushed and rosy with the humidity, big hurt eyes shining. He had a flash of her sitting on the picnic table with Sandy the other day, flirting, giggling. Looked like Sandy was having trouble keeping his hands to himself. Pete couldn't blame him, she looked like a rosy sweet peach. He kicked himself for the flash of jealousy. No, it wasn't easy to stay mad at her. It got easier, though, when he reminded himself why he was mad.

He was relieved she wasn't that interested in the gun thing, was just putting in the press releases like he wanted her to. After the task force meeting the other night, Jody Mercier told him his kid said Kenny Paquette got the gun he used for the drugstore robbery from Evan Wentzel. Kenny had been carrying it around, showing it off, for almost two years before he decided to put it to use. All Pete needed was Bernie getting hold of that and making hash out of it in the paper.

Then there was the trailer. Right after he talked to her the night before, he'd gone over to Wayne Daggett's and roused him out of bed. "Don't know why you folks don't just leave me alone," Wayne mumbled as they picked their way through the minefield of junk in the back yard by flashlight. Being woken up didn't improve Wayne's disposition. No surprise there, Pete thought, shuddering at the chaos in someone's mind that would create such a mess.

"Cop said I could have the trailer, now you want to come snooping around it after you cops already ripped it apart once. I seen him do it. That girl took what she wanted, then he came and trashed the place."

"Which cop?"

"Didn't leave nothing for Wayne," Wayne said sadly.

"Which cop?" Pete repeated, nearly tripping over an unidentifiable piece of rusted metal.

"The asshole. Ray? I told the girl. Don't know why I have to keep telling people."

"Well, *the girl*, isn't the police. *The girl* has no business nosing around."

The trailer yielded nothing. Pete knew it wouldn't. Ripped to shreds, the inside a mess, not helped by spending the wet spring and humid hot summer among the weeds in Wayne Daggett's yard.

What was Ray looking for? Pete felt like yelling with frustration. Dammit Ray, what the hell was going on?

CHAPTER 24

Thursday after lunch, Bernie got in her car and headed south down Route 27 toward Augusta to get the just-released records from the shooting, including the much-awaited cruiser video.

The ninety-minute drive gave her plenty of time to think. About Ike Miller and Ray and Dragon and Stanley. The Carriers. The trailer. Harry. She kept getting the things mixed up in her head. Stanley's death, last December, found in March. The deaths of Ray and Dragon on the Fourth of July. The deadly snowmobile accident, more than a year before Stanley was found.

Common denominator? Ike Miller.

Coincidence? She didn't know. There's an old saying about there being no such thing as coincidence. Bernie didn't believe it. Coincidences happened all the time. Just the other day, she had just read the word "Latvia" in a book at the same moment someone on TV said "Latvia." If that wasn't a coincidence, what was? How often does anyone say Latvia, for chrissake?

As she sped south along the Wesserunsett River, through the woods and farms toward Farmington, she tried to get her thoughts in some kind of order. Driving usually soothed her mind. Maine's two-lane roads were like a drug for her, the trees and mountains could make the state seem claustrophobic, car bombing along almost in a tunnel, then all of a sudden she'd come out on a ridge, and there'd be a vista of mountains, woods and lake as far as the eye could see. It blew her away every time. Today she had too many things to juggle to enjoy the ride, though. For instance, the meeting that Dawna had told her about. Cal was mad about something having to do with the accident. Rusty claimed it was because he was meeting a woman, but Bernie found that unlikely. It was almost zero degrees that night. What woman is going to not only meet with Rusty—shudder—but do it in a car in the middle of nowhere in single-digit temperatures?

She sat at a light in downtown Farmington, drummed on the steering wheel, shifted in her seat, trying to keep her blouse from sticking to her back. With the humidity, it was hard to remember how cold it had been that night. Everything kept coming back to the bog. Did the snowmobile accident have anything to do with Stanley's death? Did Stanley tell Cal he saw a coyote on the bridge? Or did he mean it when he told John he said no such thing? What could the three cops have been arguing about a year and a half ago? Only one of those cops was still alive—another coincidence?

But first, the cruiser video.

The land leveled out after she left Farmington and the mountains behind. More farm fields, ramshackle houses and trailers, rusty farm equipment, as Route 27 followed the Sandy River, then south through idyllic Belgrade Lakes village, the speed limit an annoying 25. Once through there, though, she pushed the pedal to seventy-plus, the two-lane road widening, flattening, toward her childhood home, Augusta. Fortunately, the Department of Public Safety was in the north end of the city. No need to navigate Augusta's crumbling, byzantine maze of streets and death-defying traffic rotaries today. Good thing. Her patience couldn't take it.

When she made the right-to-know request, the state emailed her a form. Hers was the first formal request, but obviously they knew it wasn't going to be the last, so they streamlined the process. The form listed all the crime scene information with prices: cruiser

DVD, $6; autopsy photos $10; interview transcripts, $2 a page. So much for freedom of information, Bernie griped to the clerk after emailing her form back with everything checked off. "Processing fees," the clerk said.

She crammed into the small conference room with the rest of the press. Everyone who'd made a request was there. TV stations from Maine and Boston, reporters from all over the place. Bernie didn't even recognize most of them. Nick from the *Sentinel*, who gave her a nod and wave across the room. Andy from *Lewiston*, who sidled up with a big smile.

"Look what we wrought," he said.

"Nothing like a video of a couple guys getting shot to bring out the hard-core journalists," Bernie agreed, pretending she didn't see his wet hot dog hand offered for a handshake.

A secretary came out of an adjoining office.

"Bernadette O'Dea, *Peaks Weekly Watcher*?"

Bernie raised her hand.

"Come with me," the secretary said.

"Why does she get to go first?" the Associated Press guy asked.

"First order, first served," the secretary said over her shoulder.

Bernie went into an office where Lt. Leary from the night of the shooting stood with a cardboard box. He looked at a sheet. "Bernadette? *Peaks Watcher*? Okay, DVD, autopsy photos, interview transcripts," he went down the list.

The secretary held out her hand. Bernie gave her a check. The secretary gave her a receipt and Leary handed her the large carton. It was awkward and heavy.

"Thanks," Bernie said as Leary opened the door for her. Weirdest shopping trip she'd ever been on.

She couldn't get back to Redimere fast enough. As usual, Route 27 north in July was a lesson in frustration, especially with the weekend approaching. Crowded with traffic, few places to pass. Belgrade Lakes' afternoon farmers market was in full swing, the road a parking lot as summer people and tourists wandered out of the gift shops, drifting into the sidewalk-less road, narrowed by their SUVs mixed with central Maine's unofficial fleet of dented pickups with ladder racks and dusty Subarus, slowing traffic through the village to a crawl. C'mon, c'mon. She pounded her steering wheel, finally bursting out of town and flooring it through the farms, woods and over the hills north toward home.

As she careened down Main Street, she remembered her DVD player at home wasn't working. Fritzed out during a power outage in the last thunderstorm. Shit. She parked in front of the office, where she'd left her laptop on her desk. The day had become hotter and more humid. She was soaking wet, hungry. She didn't care, she had to watch that video. The office was empty. It was nearly five on a Thursday, no reason for anyone to be around. She was glad of that, she wanted to watch the DVD alone, too impatient to bring the laptop home and watch it there.

She popped the DVD in. As an afterthought, she went to the front of the room and pulled down the blinds above the big picture window, bringing down an avalanche of dust, cobwebs, and dead flies.

She pulled up a desk chair and hit play. The recording, transferred from the cruiser's recorder, flickered, followed by a few seconds of snow. Then there was Pond Road through the windshield of Ray's cruiser. Ray had turned the camera on as he began following Dragon. The ice cream truck was barely visible in the distance. Bernie guessed Dragon didn't even know Ray was there.

"Going down the Pond Road," Ray said into his radio. The familiar slightly annoyed cadence jolted her. The road was deserted. Everyone was at the party or at the beach. The ice cream truck pulled down the bog road. A minute later Ray turned in, too, past the stone wall that Carol, Bernie, and the others had sat on that night, past the meadow, down to the dirt patch. Dragon's truck was parked near Ike's gate, no sign of movement, no Dragon, Justin or Ike Miller. Just meadow grass and trees swaying in the breeze. Some birds circling overhead. A calm, perfect summer evening in Maine.

Ray stopped behind the truck, so that the driver's side was in view, but not a good enough angle to see inside, or see in front of it. He got out of the cruiser and walked toward the truck.

There was no longer audio. Bernie checked her computer volume before realizing it was the recording itself, not her machine. That's right, the mike on Ray's belt that recorded audio when he was out of the car was among the many pieces of police equipment that wasn't working that night.

Dragon leaned out the driver's window. It looked like both he and Ray were talking at the same time. Bernie could tell even on the low-quality tape and from the distance of thirty feet or so that Dragon was agitated, his hand punctuating his words. No gun in that hand yet. Ray, at least in the profile view on the tape, was calm, collected.

The bile charged from her stomach up her throat. Just another day in their lives, their stupid feuding ritual. Yet within a couple minutes, they'd both be dead.

She swallowed.

Dragon got more animated, but Ray stayed calm, as if it were any routine traffic stop.

Dragon leaned farther out the window. Bernie could see spit coming out of his mouth as he yelled. Ray turned to walk away, then turned back, grabbed the pepper-spray canister from his belt and with calm precision sprayed Dragon in the face. Dragon jerked back into the truck, no longer visible.

Ray reholstered the canister, then looked up as though something on the other side of the truck caught his attention. He said something short and quick, then turned back toward his cruiser, angry and determined. He stopped and turned back. Looked at the truck. Walked back toward it. Talking, or maybe yelling.

"Don't go back," Bernie said to the screen.

There was no movement from the truck.

Then, a gun's barrel through the truck window. It jerked. Four times. Ray fell back, staggering to the rail fence, falling against it, sliding to the ground.

Bernie's stomach heaved.

Seconds later, Ike Miller came into view from around the front of the truck, ran to Ray and grabbed Ray's gun from its holster. Ray had been reaching for it as he fell and it was partially out. Ike went over to the truck, put his gun hand in the window. Calmly, like he was at a firing range. His arm jerked. Twice.

Bernie gagged.

The whole thing took less than five minutes.

. . . . .

She hadn't been out for a run in days. She couldn't get the video out of her mind. The lack of audio had given it a weird dream-like quality. Or nightmare-like. She didn't know if it would have been better if there had been sound or worse. Even the truck, stupid lime-green truck with the dancing popsicles on it, made her want to cry.

There was something about the tape that bugged her. She had watched the recording a second time but couldn't put her finger on it. Running helped her sort things out and she hadn't done much recently. It was a little after six and she had to go. Not even a choice, a physical craving. If she went now, she could get a good one in before dark.

It was still hot and sticky out even though it was past late afternoon and into evening, but she was going to pretend it wasn't. Mind over matter. She bobby-pinned two dollars and her driver's license together and put them in the key pocket of her shorts. She'd run the two and a half miles to Pondside Convenience and buy a nice cold Gatorade. Always good to have a reward to run to.

She set off down toward downtown. She realized she also hadn't put on any mosquito repellent. This was going to be a lot of fun. How many times had Pete watched the tape? She guessed probably a million. She should talk to him and see what he thought. She'd probably get that now familiar no comment. Every time he said it, it felt like a slap in the face.

She jogged through downtown, quiet at the day's end. A couple cars in front of the Country Grocer, no others in sight. She ran out

Main Street to Pond Road toward the mountains without one car passing her. The loudest sound was her feet slapping against the pavement. She felt slow and heavy. Maybe it was because she hadn't run for days or maybe it was the humidity. Or maybe it was the weight of that tape. Slow as she was, her head was going a hundred miles an hour. Over and over, she saw Dragon's hand come out of the truck, Ray jerk back toward the fence. Saw Ike calmly shoot Dragon.

Earlier in the day, she'd gone down to the bank and asked what she'd have to do to sell the newspaper, no, not just the building, the whole thing. The loan officer, surprised, said he'd look into it and get back to her. She tried to muse on that for a while, whether she'd really do it, to get the tape of the shooting from running through her head, but it didn't work.

As she approached the bog road, she glanced down it, almost expecting to see the ice cream truck shining in the early evening sun.

What she saw was the navy blue Redimere police cruiser.

She turned down the road.

CHAPTER 25

Bernie passed the stone wall and the meadow, then the rail fence that marked the property line that Ray had sagged against as he died. There was no sign now of the shooting. Nothing left in the dirt patch to show what had happened there almost three weeks before.

There was still some time before dusk. Bernie didn't want to meet up with Ike Miller, but she wanted to see what Pete was doing. Given the time of night, she assumed it was Pete, since he was doing an evening patrol now. She knew he wouldn't be happy to see her, but her curiosity had her by the throat.

She went past the empty cruiser and around the closed gate. Once she got inside the trees, the road through the bog was damp and the air was hothouse dense. She was coated with sweat within minutes. She thought about that Gatorade she'd planned to buy. No Gatorade in here. With every step, she felt more uncomfortable. Both sides of the road sloped down to brackish water or black mud. It smelled like something dead. The trees were tangled with reeds, vines, and leggy shrubbery, towering over her now in mid-summer, the setting sun filtering through. Why had she thought this was a good idea? But something was going on, she knew it. There was no sign of Pete. She looked down at the road to see if there were footprints in the damp earth, but it was too dim to tell.

She got to where the washout had been that spring. It had been repaired. A bright silver culvert guided the stream, no longer rushing, but sluggish and clogged with growth, under a new earthen rise in the road. Logs were laid horizontally across the dirt for traction. They were new, fresh-looking. Bare, white and shiny, except where they were lined with muddy tire tracks. She crossed and jogged on, slapping at mosquitoes, an almost welcome distraction from the humidity. The road became more uneven after the repaired part—roots, potholes, jagged rocks, tufts of weeds making it an obstacle course in the dim light. She listened for Pete. All she heard were bullfrogs, cicadas, birds, a loon. Then something else. She stopped. What was it? She walked, listening hard.

She stopped again.

Voices. They were louder now. Pete's calm rumble and a louder, higher voice. Nasal. Twangy. Ike Miller.

She crept closer. She knew they'd be pissed if they saw her, once again sticking her nose in where it didn't belong. The road curved and she could see the bridge through the trees, a ray of sun reflecting off the metal gate. She hunkered down and peered through, feeling silly about sneaking, but doing it anyway. Pete was by the gate; branches obscured some of her view, but she could see his navy blue back. Ike was facing him, his trusty ATV at his side. She shifted to see better, rattling some branches. She held her breath, afraid they'd hear, but they kept talking. She leaned forward some more.

Holy shit. With a sudden lurch, a huge rock drop in the pit of her stomach, she saw that Ike was holding a gun. Not his usual shotgun, but an ugly looking handgun. It was aimed at Pete.

"Discuss this rationally," Pete was saying. His hands were up, but his voice was normal, conversational.

"How about you just show me your warrant?" Ike replied.

"Put down the gun. Let's go into town and figure it out."

Ike let loose a big guffaw. "You ain't goin' anywhere, now I've seen you under that bridge."

"Put the gun down."

"Too late for all that. This is a big swamp. Body could disappear easy. Flatlander police chief got lost, slipped and fell. What a tragedy."

"That's not how it would play out."

"I'm a hero in this town. I put away that kid. You're a fuckup. I can get away with it."

Bernie realized with certainty, with dread, that Ike was not going to let Pete out of the bog alive. She had to go get help. She never carried her cellphone when she ran—nowhere to put it. The tiny key pocket in her shorts was barely big enough for her driver's license and money. She calculated. She knew she was more than a mile in. It was already getting dark in the bog as the sun went behind the trees, the mountains. She'd be even slower getting out, with the rough terrain, no light, the narrow road with the brackish water on either side. She didn't know if Pete's cruiser was unlocked. Even if it was, it would take her some time to figure out how to get the radio to work. It would take her even longer to run to Pondside Convenience to get help. Either way, help would have to get there—state police or sheriff from who knows how far away. Then they'd have to get back through the woods to the bridge. Best case scenario? Fifteen, twenty minutes, or maybe even half an hour or more for her to get out of here, get help and for it to get here. Ike wasn't going to stand there jawing with Pete for that long, or even a fraction of that.

She could throw a rock or a stick, distract Ike. Bernie looked around, found a thick, short stick. Hefted it. She'd always had a lousy arm. The likelihood of hitting him was about zero. Distract him? Maybe. But then what? Rush him and grab the gun? Hope Pete was quick enough to realize what was going on and grab the gun? With her luck, she'd just startle both of them enough that Pete would get shot.

She had to play to her strengths. That left one option.

She stepped out of the woods. "What's going on?"

Ike made a noise. Like a growl.

Pete didn't turn around as he spoke. "Get out of here." His voice was calm.

"What's going on?" She repeated, trying to sound as calm as him as she walked toward them.

"Bernie, please."

"No." She couldn't have left if she wanted to, her legs were rubber. She was surprised she could walk. Surprised at how matter-of-fact she sounded. She was scared. Really scared. But she was also pissed off. Ike Miller. He blew away Dragon and now he was going to blow away Pete?

"For once, I think me and the little lady agree on something," Ike said. He gave her an ugly smile. Kind of like the Grinch, Bernie thought. He gestured with the gun, still aimed at Pete. "Step up here next to your boyfriend and put your hands up where I can keep an eye on them, like his are."

Bernie stepped forward. She never knew how scary a gun could look. But then she'd never seen one that close and aimed at her before.

"Little Miss Cop. I'd ask what you're doing here, but it's obvious. Real question is, what am I going to do with the two of you?"

The cicadas and birds chirped. A loon cried and another answered back. Something splashed in the water. Probably a frog, Bernie thought. A mosquito bit her calf, then another. She didn't slap at it. She didn't move. She had a fleeting idea that she could barrel into Ike's legs, like on TV or the movies, knock him over, grab the gun. Or grab Pete's gun out of his holster and blow Ike away. She pictured trying to knock Ike over, but then falling backwards herself because he was so much bigger than she was. On top of it, she'd never held a gun in her life, so even if she got it from him, she'd probably just end up shooting her toe off.

"You can get out of this," Pete said to Ike, still calm. "At least let Bernie leave. This isn't her business."

Ike turned to Bernie, all fake friendly menace. "No warrant. Typical cop, thinks he owns the world. You, I think you're just plain stupid."

Bernie shrugged. What could she say?

"Get his handcuffs," he said.

Bernie looked sideways at Pete. He was staring straight ahead.

Ike gestured with the gun. "Maybe you haven't heard, but when I shoot, I don't miss."

Bernie was out of ideas. The snap on the cuff pouch slid in her shaky, sweating fingers, not cooperating as she pulled at it.

"Hurry up," Ike said.

Pete didn't speak or move, but she could feel him breathing as she wrestled the cuffs out.

"Put one end around his wrist," Ike said. The cuffs rattled in her shaking hand. She took Pete's left wrist in her hand. It was warm and dry. The cuff slipped in her hand, across his wrist, the metal gouging him. Pete still didn't move. When Bernie clasped the cuff shut, Miller told her to thread it between the vertical pipes of the gatepost. She poked the loose end of the cuffs through. The post was welded at the top. No way to slip them up and over.

"Now you," he said.

She did what he told her, cuffing her wrist, sneaking a glance at Pete. He hadn't moved, was still expressionless. She wished he'd do something, say something. Not that there was much he could do or say. They stood, backs to the gate, facing Ike, their cuffed hands nearly touching like two teenagers on a shy date.

"Hands up," Ike snarled. She put hers up, her right hand jerking Pete's left, the chain rasping on the metal pole. Pete put his up more slowly, halfway.

"Don't get any ideas," Ike said to him, the gun trained on Bernie. "First shot will be for your girlfriend." He undid Pete's duty belt. Pete made a sharp noise and Ike laughed, stepped back with the belt, unholstered Pete's gun, and flung the belt far into the bog. "Ain't much of a soldier lets his gun get taken from him," he said. "Give me your keys." He pointed with Pete's gun to the ring of keys attached to Pete's regular belt. Pete didn't move. Miller stepped closer, one gun aimed at Pete, and pressed the other to Bernie's temple. She felt her bowels loosen.

Pete unhooked the keys.

Ike tucked Pete's gun into the waistband of his pants, took the keys, searching the ring until he found what he was looking for— the handcuff key. He unhooked it and put it in his pocket, tossing the rest of the keys into the bog in the direction the duty belt had gone.

Then, so fast Bernie didn't realize it was happening, he moved, shifting his gun so he was holding it by the barrel and smacked Pete across the side of the face. Pete sagged back against the gate. Bernie lost her balance, landing on the ground.

"Both of you on the ground," Ike snarled. Fine with Bernie, she was already there. Pete slumped against the gate, bent over.

"Down," Ike yelled, karate-kicking Pete in the ribs. He went partway down, but grabbed the top of the gate with his right hand and stayed there, suspended, braced against the metal.

"Pete," Bernie whispered.

Pete shook his head.

Ike karate-kicked him in the stomach. It made a sickening sound and Pete gasped, but still didn't let go.

"Let go," Bernie said, not so much a whisper as a terrified croak.

Pete clung to the gate as Ike, purple with fury, grabbed Pete's arm, wrenching its grip from the gate, braced himself with a boot against Pete's torso, and pulled the arm forward, twisting it. Bernie wasn't sure which she heard first, the bone snap or Pete's shout of pain.

Ike pulled Pete by the broken arm and he fell forward, his face hitting the dirt, the cuffs rattling against the pole.

Ike laughed, then turned to Bernie.

Her whole body clutched.

"Now for you."

"No," Pete gasped, the first word he'd spoken since before Bernie had handcuffed him. Ike kicked him in the side, hard. Another sickening thud. Then he leaned down so his face was almost touching hers. She could smell aftershave, tobacco and his breath, harsh and dark. "I was going to kill this asshole and just dump him in the swamp. Two of you is a problem, but not much of one. It's a big swamp. But two of you showing up here also poses a question. Someone's been talking about what's going on down here and I want to know who."

Bernie couldn't speak. Her mind raced, but came up with nothing. Anyway, what was she supposed to say? No one had told her anything. Except Stanley, in a round-about way.

"I don't think our hero here is going to say much," Ike said, straightening back up. Pete was face down, his breath sharp gasps. "But you're quite the little talker, aren't you? So let's talk."

Bernie felt her bowels loosen again, then grip. She tried to concentrate on keeping that together instead of thinking about what was coming next. He bent down again. Close enough this time that their faces were touching, his breath wet and hot against her cheek. "What'll make you talk, sweetheart?"

"No," Pete said again with a groan as he tried to lift himself up. Ike kicked him hard in the ribs again. Bernie's arm jerked as Pete bounced back into the dirt. Ike grabbed her ponytail and she closed her eyes and waited. The cicadas were louder now. Somewhere an owl hooted. Then a loon again, a long wobbly song that died off into the growing night. With her eyes closed, she could almost pretend she was on her porch, safe at home. Not here, paralyzed with terror, the one guy who could help her a broken mess, chained and helpless, retching at her side. Her scalp ached where her ponytail pulled, she felt Ike move, but she wouldn't open her eyes, couldn't. She gripped the dirt at her side, felt her fingernails break. Her other hand, cuffed and useless, jerked and hit the pole with every spasm from Pete. She braced for a blow, some kind of pain, wondering where it would hit.

Then a miracle happened. A good old twenty-first century miracle.

Ike Miller's cellphone rang.

And in true twenty-first century fashion, he let go of her

ponytail, took the phone out of his pocket, stepped back a couple feet, answered. "They can't come down here. Tell them I'll meet them at the house. Ten minutes." He swore and clicked the phone shut, then looked at the two of them. "I ought to just kill you now. But you'll keep. Give you time to think."

Bernie's scalp tingled, every muscle in her body ached. She couldn't believe she was spared, at least for now, that easily.

He smiled at her as he got on the ATV. "Don't go anywhere till I get back," he said, chuckling. He spit off to the side and regarded Bernie and Pete. The smile disappeared. Then he roared down the road in the direction of his home.

Bernie tried to relax, unclench. Her shorts felt wet, she wasn't sure from sweat, the damp ground, or if she'd peed herself.

"Shit," Pete said between gasps. He grabbed the pole with his cuffed left hand, pulling himself back, struggling to sit, his breath ragged and wet, his right arm dangling at a grotesque angle.

"Are you okay?" Bernie asked. Stupid question.

"You should have left." Pete spoke in gasps.

"I couldn't."

He sat back against the gate. The effort made him wheeze. He leaned his head back against the metal, wincing, the side of his face caked with blood and dirt. He took a deep breath, then another, each one a groan.

"We have to get out of here," he said. He looked at the cuffs, then the pipes they were cuffed to. There was no way out. He banged his cuffed hand against the steel.

Bernie's armed jerked. "Let's not break any more bones."

He looked around as if the answer were in the tangle of trees and reeds. Dusk was gone and darkness was setting in. In the past few minutes, grinding fear and panic and anger had been all that Bernie felt. She realized it had kept her from feeling the mosquitoes that were chewing every exposed part of her damp body. Her bare limbs were clammy and wet, the ground gritty against the back of her thighs. Is this how I'm going to die? A sweaty, grimy, mosquito-bit idiot? She wondered how long it would take Ike to get back. The loons were in full throat now. Frogs or maybe bugs danced in the water, making happy splashes. An owl—the same one as earlier or a different one?—hooted, then hooted again. Bernie was tired. Wiped out. She closed her eyes and slumped back against the gate. This is what giving up feels like, she thought.

Pete wasn't giving up, though. "I can pick a handcuff lock. I just need something to pick it with."

Bernie opened her eyes. Pete was looking around again, as if a lock pick would appear in the dirt.

"The pin on your badge?"

"It's too thin. Too small and round. You're on the right track. Something flatter. Metal." He was still wheezing, but the task had given him a surge of energy.

Right, Bernie thought. *Let's Make a Deal* flashed into her mind. All those people in silly costumes, with their shopping bags full of useless stuff. Where's my shopping bag? All I have is—

She straightened her legs and reached with her free hand into the key pocket in the waistband of her shorts, pulling out a damp wad of dollar bills and her driver's license. Held together with a bobby pin. She held it up. "Ta-da!"

He made a noise that almost sounded like a laugh.

She detached the money and license, stuffing them back into her pocket.

"Take off the rubber end," he said.

She started picking at it with her finger.

"Bite it."

Bernie chewed the rubber off and spit it out.

"Stick the end into the hole, bend it into an L."

She could barely feel the bobby pin with her wet fingers. They slid, the edge of the metal cutting ridges in her skin, but finally got an L. Pete talked her through, his voice, between wheezes, was patient. She tried to match his calm, but couldn't. Her hands shook, her fingers swollen sausages as she stabbed at the hole, fumbling with the pin, then dropping it.

"Shit!" She couldn't see it in the dusk. "I can't find it." She was embarrassed to feel her voice near that about-to-cry pitch. She dragged her hand around in the dirt, grime covering her fingers. Back and forth, over pebbles and ants. Twigs. "Shit. Shit. Shit."

"Slow. Gotta be there."

She dragged her fingers more slowly, lightly. The only sound Pete's labored breath. She felt her finger touch metal. "Thank god," she said, as she stuck it in the keyhole and jiggled it around.

"Slow, easy," he said.

She took another breath, slowed down. His lock popped.

"Good girl." He took the bobby pin from her and popped hers in seconds. "You're going to have to help me." He grabbed the gate with his good arm and pulled himself up. He tried to stand, but doubled over at the effort.

She put her right arm around his waist and he put his good arm around her shoulder. He staggered forward. She gripped his forearm and they began shuffling down the road. "Slower," Pete gasped.

She shuffled slower. Her shoulder and neck hurt from the vice grip of his arm. Her mind kept racing forward to the road, the edge of the bog, the light that she was sure hadn't gone away outside of the trees. "Stop a second." she said. She rolled her shoulder, adjusted her grip on his arm. "Sorry. Is this okay?"

"Let's just go. I'll be okay when we're out of here."

They began the shuffle again. She tried to match her pace to his, slowly moving one leg forward at a time. The mosquitoes feasted on every exposed part of her, and even some of the unexposed ones. With neither arm free, she couldn't slap at them, as futile as that would be. She tried to focus on moving. Pete was doing his best to hold himself up and walk, but he was badly damaged. He leaned heavily on her, his soaked uniform clammy against her bare arms, each breath ragged with pain. She kept up the shuffle, one foot in front of the other, trying not to stagger under his weight. One foot in front of the other. One foot in front of the other. Ike's gun, his hot harsh breath. One foot in front of the other. The menace in his voice, his eyes. Just concentrate on getting out. They shuffled in silence until she couldn't take it anymore.

Words would make this better.

"What were you doing down here?"

Pete didn't answer and she thought, despite the situation, he was going to continue the cold war. Then she realized, stupid, it's hard for him to talk, or breathe.

"The notebook," he finally managed. "John Carrier. What he said." Each word seemed an effort. "Kenny Paquette said Evan Wentzel found gun under the bridge. There's a locker under there. Checking it out when Miller came."

"I don't get it."

"Miller's selling guns. He's the connection." Pete coughed and stopped, Bernie halted a half step too late and staggered forward. "Right under my nose," Pete said.

"Why would they be under the bridge?" She felt like she was missing something. Maybe it was the heat and fear, but she didn't get it. They started shuffling forward again.

"Dunno. Private. Secluded. Better than from his house," Pete said. "I think Stanley knew something. Could see the cars going in and out from up at his trailer."

"You think Ike killed him?"

"Dunno."

He was breathing harder from the effort of the conversation. They slowly made their way in silence, his weight was beginning to make Bernie's legs buckle. She lost her footing and teetered sideways, grabbing him tight around his ribs to keep from falling. He gasped in pain, then swore.

"Sorry, sorry, sorry," Bernie said.

"I'm okay. Keep going."

They did, but even slower.

The chorus of bullfrogs, crickets and bugs was loud. Chirping. Sounding to Bernie like they were laughing at them. The shapes of the trees and vines, already menacing in the daylight, seemed alive in the near-dark, ready to attack. The tote road was rough and crumbly beneath their shuffling feet, and hers kept catching, making her stumble. Pete's breath was punctuated with groans. She could feel his heart pounding against her ribs. She tried to count the beats, anything to distract her from their slow march. She chewed over what he'd told her, trying to make it fit. The humidity and darkness pressed down. Suffocating. Bernie had never wanted to get home so desperately in her life. She strained to see ahead. Were they close? There was a blink of light. Headlights from the road? They couldn't be that close. Was she seeing things? There it was again.

"Did you see that?" She stopped, straining to see through the dark.

"What?"

"I thought I saw a light."

Bernie had convinced herself they were outrunning, or at least out-stumbling, the terror she'd felt at the bridge. As long as they kept moving forward she could feel salvation. Pete's body, as broken as it was, as heavily as it weighed on her, felt solid against hers, reassuring her, his heartbeat pacing her. She had faith he wouldn't let anything happen to them.

Now the terror crept back.

The light came again, winking through the trees.

"Ike?" Bernie whispered. The thought was even more chilling now that she realized he might have killed Stanley.

"He'd come from the other direction."

Bernie's instinct was to hide, but Pete wasn't moving. Silly me, police chiefs don't hide. But then they usually have guns. And two working arms.

The light was strong and bright now. Definitely coming toward them.

Bernie's legs trembled. Pete must have felt them.

"It's okay," he said.

Yeah, right.

The light was on them now. She could feel him straighten up a little, accompanied by a painful intake of breath.

"Chief?" Rusty's startled voice.

Bernie felt a huge surge of relief.

"I saw the cruiser down by the gate. What's going on?"

"Ran into some trouble," Pete said.

Rusty shined the light into their faces. He seemed to be considering. Bernie shielded her eyes, wondering what there was to consider.

"You mind getting that out of our eyes?" Pete asked.

"Oh, sorry." Rusty turned the flashlight away.

"You going to help us or just stand there looking?" Bernie asked.

Rusty grinned. "Just surprised to see you guys."

"Here," Rusty handed Bernie the flashlight, a big heavy Maglite. It felt good in her hand, like that salvation she'd been moving toward. Rusty took Pete's arm from around her shoulder. "I'll take him and you lead the way."

She was grateful. They were coming to the part of the road with the culvert and she wasn't sure she'd be able to navigate those wet logs with Pete's weight. Better yet, she had a free hand to swat mosquitoes.

She was several yards ahead, around a curve, before she realized how slowly Rusty and Pete were moving and how far ahead she was. "Let's get the hell out of here, guys," she muttered, slowing to wait for them to catch up, surprised they hadn't called out. She waved at the mosquitoes. She was happy for once to see Rusty. Too bad he wasn't in uniform. A radio and gun would really come in handy. He was such a goofball. Pete looked like death walking, you'd think Rusty would press for details about what happened. Maybe he was and that's why they were taking so long. She couldn't hear their voices. She slapped at a group of mosquitoes on her neck, then another on her thigh. The night sounds weren't so menacing now, the chirps and splashes cheering them on. Almost home, almost home. Well, relatively. What was taking them so long? Oh yeah, she had the flashlight. Duh. She'd turned to go back when she heard a yelp.

"Okay guys?" she called.

Something—a big frog maybe— made a loud plop and splash.

"Guys?" she began walking back. Her running shorts and T-shirt stuck to her uncomfortably. All she wanted was to get in the shower and get the sticky grime off. What the hell was keeping them? She moved faster.

"Guys?" she called again. The only answer was the frogs going nuts in the water.

She felt him before she saw him. Rusty barreled out of the darkness, knocking her down.

"What the hell?" Bernie dropped the flashlight. Rusty picked it up.

"Where's Pete?" she said, getting up. He lunged at her. She managed a half-duck, but the flashlight glanced off the side of her head and hit a tree. Rusty body-slammed her and she went over the embankment, sliding on her back into the bog water.

She heard his retreating feet, the light bobbing away down the path.

Her head hurt the way it did when she banged it on the kitchen cabinet. She felt the bump and looked at her hand. No blood. "What the hell?" she said again.

The brief glimpse she caught of Rusty's face registered. White, stunned—and scared shitless.

Pete.

She scrambled up the muddy embankment. Without a flashlight, she could only make out the outlines of shrubbery and the road as she backtracked.

"Pete?"

Nothing but buzzing, peeping, bullfrogs, splashing.

"Pete?" Desperate now.

Still nothing. Wait. The splashing.

She inched toward the edge of the road and peered toward the noise.

A sapling in the water moved. She looked closer. It wasn't a sapling.

She grabbed Pete's arm and pulled. It was too far away for her to get footing on the slippery path. He grabbed her wrist and she got down on her knees and pulled harder.

"Jesus," he gasped, his head coming out of the water, he was twisted around, his back to her.

"What happened?" Bernie asked. She tried to pull him out more, but couldn't get leverage. She lay down on her stomach and, still holding his arm, tried to get her other arm around his chest. "Can you push off with your legs?" she asked. She could just barely hold him out of the water.

"Ankle's caught."

"What happened?"

"Bastard pushed me in, tried to drown me," Pete said between gasps. "Where is he? You okay?"

"He took off. I'm fine." Fine except for the fact that her arms and shoulders screamed with pain as she lay on her stomach trying to hold Pete out of the water.

"Pushed me in," Pete said. "Held me under. I went limp and he took off."

"He tried with me, too. Didn't stick around to see if it worked." Her grip on Pete loosened. He slipped into the water and she grabbed the back of his shirt, leaning out farther, catching him around the shoulder again.

"Shit," he said, spitting out water.

"Sorry. I'm trying to hang on." Bernie realized neither of them would last long like this. But if she let go, he would go under. She didn't think he could survive many more dunkings.

"Can you push against something with your other leg?" she asked.

"There's no solid bottom," he said, gasping for breath.

Keeping hold of the back of his shirt, she wormed backward so more of her body was on solid ground. Her grip wasn't firm enough and he slipped, almost going under again and she grabbed his arm, trying to pull him closer so she could circle both arms under his arms and around his chest. He jerked as her hand went under his broken right arm. "Sorry." She stretched out as far as she could, tightening her arms around his chest, her face on his shoulder, his hair wet against her cheek. She could smell his soap smell, faint but there. She took a deep breath.

"I'm going to push again, pull my leg out," he said. "Try to pull me. On three."

He counted off and pushed, but she couldn't get any leverage to pull.

"Dammit," he yelled, slipping farther down.

"Sorry." Bernie shifted again and tried to grab him tighter. He gasped as his broken arm jerked again. "Sorry."

They both said nothing for a minute, his breathing a wet groan.

"We have to get out of here," he said.

"I know." She felt like crying.

"Let's figure this out."

She wondered how, between ragged breaths, he could sound so calm. She tried to be calm, too, and think. "We need a tree branch or something. Something you can lift yourself up on with your good arm and then I can get back and get some leverage to pull."

"Yeah."

She looked around. No handy tree branches within arm's reach.

"The logs," Pete said.

"What?"

"The logs by that culvert."

Bernie guessed they were about fifty yards away. They might as well be a mile. No way she was letting go of him, letting him slip under again.

He must have known what she was thinking.

"I'll be okay if you go fast."

"You'll drown."

"Not if you go fast."

"I can't," she said, feeling hysteria rising. "I can't let go of you."

"You have to, or we'll both die." His voice was a painful rasp.

"I can't," she said. Can't came out as a sob.

"When I count to three, let go."

She didn't say anything.

"Bernie, we get out of here or we die. I know you can do it. On three." It was an order.

Her grip slipped again. She knew she didn't have the strength to hold him above the water much longer. Any second she expected to hear the ATV or Rusty's footsteps.

"Count to three," she said.

On three, she let go. She heard him go under, but was already moving down the road to the logs. Focus, she said. She could see a little now she was used to the dark. She got to the logs in less than a minute. She grabbed the first log she saw and tried to lift it. Nothing. Her hands were wet, the log was wet. It was embedded in the mud, pushed down by the weight of vehicles.

"Shit."

She tried prying an end with her fingers, trying not to think of Pete under the water. The skin on the tips of her fingers skidded across the log.

"Shit shit shit." She tried the end. How much time had gone by? It felt like an hour. She wiped her hands on her wet shirt. She gave another tug. With a loud sucking noise, the log popped free, sending her back on her butt. It was about eight inches in diameter and ten feet long. She hoisted it on her shoulder and staggered sideways, caught her balance, started moving, back to Pete.

Rounding the curve in the road, she realized she hadn't marked the spot. She looked for a familiar shrub or clump of reeds. In the dark everything looked the same. She tried not to think of him under the water. Stuck, hurt, drowning.

In desperation, she laid the log down on the road, most of it extending over the water, and began rolling it.

"Please please please please. Hail Mary, full of grace, please please please." She wondered if God was laughing at her. Good Catholic turned bad. All the sudden you think Mary's gonna help you? Too late for that. Please please please. I'll be good, just please please please.

The log hit something. Pete's arm came up and looped around the wood. She laid her full body weight on it to anchor it.

He pulled himself a few inches out of the water, hanging on with his left arm and taking huge pained gulps of air.

"Want me to pull it?" Bernie asked when his gulps slowed.

"Yeah."

She got up and the log dipped back into the water.

"Shit," she said, diving back onto it before he went under again.

"Pull," Pete said. Bernie got on all fours, inches above the log so it wouldn't see-saw again, put her arms around it and pulled. Pete gave a shout as his leg came free. She pulled harder and grabbed his belt, helping as he heaved himself onto the road.

He lay on the ground, retching, a grunt of pain with each retch.

"Sorry it took me so long." She squatted next to him, wondering how to help. It was only dumb luck he was still alive. He took a couple deep breaths, groaned again. "Please be okay," she whispered.

He rolled over and smiled, more like a grimace. "It only hurts when I breathe."

She tried to smile back.

"Let's get the hell out of here," he said.

She took his arm and he struggled up and leaned his weight against her.

"Do you think Ike sent Rusty down here to kill us?" she asked.

"Maybe." He took a deep, pained breath and they began to move. "Or keep an eye on us. He didn't have a weapon. Lucky for us."

They shuffled a few yards, the only sound their feet in the dirt and Pete's labored breath.

"Rusty. Shit," he whispered. "What next?"

Bernie felt faint. Tears stung her eyes. She matched her step to his slow shuffle, grateful for his wet, solid weight against her, feeling his heartbeat, his chest heave with each breath. They stumbled wordlessly through the dark back to safety.

Bernie was surprised to see that outside the bog it was still dusk. Pete leaned in the open window of the cruiser and radioed county. Done with the call, he sagged to the ground.

Bernie looked down at him. He was sodden. His right cheekbone was swollen, purple and, despite the time he spent in the water, blood and dirt was caked onto his face, neck and shirt. His right arm hung at an impossible angle. His eyes were closed. But he was still breathing.

She realized how close they came to dying.

"Jesus," she said. Her legs gave way and she landed beside him, sobbing. Without opening his eyes, Pete reached over and gripped her hand. She gripped back.

They waited like that until help arrived.

CHAPTER 26

Bernie hadn't wanted to go to the hospital. She wanted to go home and take a shower. A nice long one. Long enough to wash off the sweat and the dirt and the grime and the mud and the blood and the mosquito bites and if she was lucky, the confusion and the panic and the terror.

But Jamie, at Dawna's insistence, rushed her in the cruiser to the hospital in Farmington behind Pete's ambulance. Bernie could see Dawna tending to him through the back window.

At the hospital, she was treated for dehydration and given an antiseptic for the cuts and scratches that she didn't realize she had. They checked out the bump on her head and determined it was just that, a bump, not a concussion. They also gave her ointment for her mosquito bites. She was covered with them; she doubted it would last the night.

Pete had a torn rotator cuff, a broken upper arm, several broken ribs, a punctured lung, and a broken cheekbone and was taken into surgery.

She had to give Jamie a report. Then she had to repeat it all to the state police. She had a feeling she was going to be telling the story over and over in the coming days. All the cops had a lot of questions and Bernie wasn't sure what to tell them. She was trying to get her head around it herself. She needed some quiet time to think, but the rest of Thursday night was plastic chairs, fluorescent lights and questions, questions, questions with no answers.

. . . . .

When Bernie finally got home long after midnight, she had trouble sleeping. She kept jerking awake, feeling something coming after her. The mosquito bites didn't help. The police were looking for Rusty and Ike. Bernie didn't think either one was going to show up at her house, but given the events of the night, who knew what the hell was going to happen? Scenes from the bog kept playing over in her mind. Ike with a gun on Pete, that first, gut-gripping sight of it, the realization that something terrible was going to happen. Pete in the water, Bernie sure he was going to drown. Rusty, his face huge with fear and panic as he barreled her over.

She fell asleep as the first light of dawn was coming through her window and the morning symphony of birds was rising. The last thing she remembered was getting up to shut the window. Stupid birds. She'd had enough wildlife for one night.

Her ringing phone woke her close to noon. She picked up the landline and said hello a few times before realizing the ringing was her cell. She stumbled into the living room to find it.

It was Carol. "I'm bringing over lunch and I want to know everything."

Bernie felt good for the first time in twenty-four hours.

"So Rusty was in cahoots with Ike?" Carol, sitting at Bernie's table, was still trying to untangle the story, or at least as much as Bernie could tell her. While Bernie was showering earlier, Dawna left a message on her machine saying state police found a cache of weapons, guns of all kinds at Ike's place. Rusty, in his precious Ford pickup, had been arrested a couple hours before in New Hampshire.

"Pete was right, Ike was selling guns," Bernie said. "The bog was his drive-through window and he had his own personal police officer to make sure everything went smoothly."

"I'm still not sure that I follow everything," Carol said.

267

"Me neither, but we need to straighten it out. I can't write the story for the paper, 'cause I'm in it. Guy will do it. You can help."

"Great." Carol grimaced. "Not really my shtick."

"You'll do fine," Bernie said through a mouthful of macaroni and cheese. "We know Ike was running a gun ring. Rusty was his lookout man, gopher, whatever—"

There was a knock at Bernie's door. Dawna.

"I have to go," Carol said, giving Bernie a big hug. "I'm glad you're okay." To Dawna, she said, "I'm handing her off to you. Make sure she rests and doesn't get all hopped up about the newspaper part."

"I have updates," Dawna said after Carol left.

"For the story?"

"Well," Dawna looked half apologetic, half wary, "Why don't we just have this conversation off the record and let the state police give you the official information?"

"Okay." Bernie was too wiped out to argue.

"Rusty's looking for a deal to make things easier on himself, so he's talking. He said Miller put the guns in a locker under the bridge when a buyer was coming. Rusty did the exchange."

"Seems kind of half-assed."

"According to Rusty, Miller was paranoid about people coming to his house, thought the bog would be private. Cal found out from Stanley after the snowmobile accident."

"Cal was covering up for Ike? All that time?"

"Yeah," Dawna shook her head. "I never would have thought that of Cal."

"You never know about people. As much of a doofus as he is, I never would have thought it about Rusty, either."

"Rusty said Stanley had evidence about the gun sales. It turns out it was Rusty who ransacked Stanley's trailer, not Ray. Wayne Daggett didn't know them apart. Rusty said he didn't find anything. Then the chief put him in charge of checking where the trailer went and Rusty just said it was sent to the scrap yard in Mass. Total lie."

"Ike killed Stanley? So why'd they wait until the body was

found to look for the evidence?"

"Don't know. Still trying to figure out how everything fits."

"Could have been Rusty," Bernie said. "Although, seeing how he botched the job with Pete—thank God—it doesn't seem likely."

"They're checking Rusty and Miller's DNA to see if it matches what was under Stanley's fingernails."

"Well, that's a hell of a story. Or could be once everything begins to make sense," Bernie said. She didn't feel triumphant, just sad and tired.

. . . . .

She thought of going to see Pete in the hospital, but when she called they told her he was being discharged the next day. She wasn't sure what she'd say anyway. The night before had been a strange, frightening experience, as intimate as sex. She wasn't sure if it changed their relationship for better or worse and didn't know if she wanted to find out.

She spent the rest of Friday hanging around the house, watching TV. She tried to read, but couldn't focus. It was hard enough focusing on the TV. Every once in a while she'd get up and look out the window. Not that she was nervous or anything. She finished off the entire casserole dish of macaroni and cheese and wished she had more food in the house, but she didn't feel like going to the store. She didn't want to deal with the questions, the looks. Aside from a quick check-in with her folks, she didn't answer either phone, just let her voicemail fill up. She knew her four sisters, three brothers and a variety of friends were calling, but the thought of explaining everything all over again exhausted her. Rusty's arrest and the hunt for Ike were all over the TV news, but so far only the bare bones of her adventure with Pete seemed to be public.

She was sitting on the couch with the cats, scratching her mosquito bites and watching TV, waiting for a time that seemed reasonable to go to bed so she could lie awake, tossing and turning, when there was a knock on the door.

She turned on the porch light and looked out the window.

Justin Mercier.

"Come in."

He stepped in, cringing at the porch light.

"I don't want no one to see me."

"Your folks know you're around?"

"I talked to them after you told them I was in Portland. But they don't know I'm here. I'm laying low. Were you going to bed?" She was in a T-shirt and sweat pants, grateful the night was cool for a change or she would have been in tank top and boxer shorts—something no boy Justin's age should have to see, especially with the crazy quilt of mosquito bites, scratches, and cuts. Could put him off women for life.

"I'm fine. Sit down and tell me what's up. Sorry about blowing your cover. They were beside themselves. They had to know."

"Yeah, I know." One of the cats jumped into his lap and he stroked her head, triggering a room-rattling purr. "I have something to tell you, but I need to know I can trust you."

"This is between us. I promise."

He opened his backpack and brought out Stanley's Audubon field guide.

"Did you take that from my house?"

"Dragon did. He called it his ticket to ride."

Justin opened the book to the back. The list of numbers and letters. "Know what these are?"

Each listing had no more than seven figures, the letters mostly MA, PQ, NB, NH, with a few RIs and NYs thrown in. She got it now. They were license plate numbers. MA for Massachusetts, NB was New Brunswick. PQ Quebec. Why didn't she see that before?

"Stanley wrote these down," Justin said. "He could see the lights from his trailer, so he started hunkering down by the stone wall and writing down the tag numbers. One night Dragon was having a smoke up to the trailer with him and saw lights going into the bog, too, and Stanley told him about it, showed him his system. He wrote the tag in the book, numbered them, then he had another list in his notebook, where he'd have the dates, numbered and so forth. So it was double-blind or whatever. In case someone had one

270

list, they'd need the other. He had his own lingo—the customers were coyotes. The guns were coyote bait."

"What was Dragon going to do with this?"

"He didn't know. He and Stanley knew it had to do with guns, because Evan Wentzel found one under the bridge, in a locker down there. He picked the lock. There were a bunch, but Evan only took one. Dragon figured there were big bucks involved."

"Did Dragon kill Stanley?" Dragon didn't seem like a killer, but he'd killed Ray. She'd learned over the past day or two that life was full of surprises.

"No way. But when Stanley's body was found, Dragon said he needed the notebook and the bird book. He knew the cops were involved with the guns, too, but didn't think they had that stuff, or he would've gotten wind of it. He wanted all the evidence. He was going to either get in on it or blackmail Miller, whichever felt right."

"Doesn't sound like a good plan."

"I know, it was fucked up. When he couldn't find the notebook—he looked in your office and everything—he figured the bird book would be enough. That's what we were doing down there when Miller shot him." Justin looked down and kicked at Bernie's rug. "Stupid idea."

"What did Ray have to do with it?"

"I don't know. Dragon figured he knew about the gun thing, because the other cops did. But I don't know. He didn't seem to be one of the players. Maybe wrong place at the wrong time? Messed the whole thing up."

"So why did Dragon shoot him?"

Justin bit his lip and looked at the ground. "I don't know what happened. There was a lot of noise, yelling and stuff. It happened fast. I was hiding. I had my head like—" he demonstrated, his head tucked into his arms. "I was down behind the ice cream machine."

"I want to show you something." Bernie put the DVD of the shooting in her laptop.

They silently watched the recording. Was it only the day before that Bernie had first seen it? It seemed like decades.

Justin watched, emotionless. When Ike shot Dragon, he winced, but kept his eyes on the screen.

"Is that what you remember?"

"It shows what happened," he said, shrugging, "I already watched it on YouTube once. That was enough."

"Sorry. I can't figure it out. Why does Ray walk to the cruiser, turn around and walk back? What was going on? You can't see the front of the truck. Where was Miller?"

"Like I said, it was confusing. Stuff was happening. I don't know what."

"I wish the recording showed everything," Bernie said.

Justin looked at her like she was stupid. "What about the other camera?"

CHAPTER 27

Bernie got dressed while she waited for Dawna to arrive. She'd tried to convince Justin to stick around and talk to Dawna himself, but he was skittish. She can't say she blamed him.

Turns out that Ike had security cameras by the entrance to the bog. Bernie didn't know why she never figured that out. Every time someone went down there, he showed up. But why didn't anyone find them after the shooting?

Dawna had the answer. "The chief had Rusty guard the area that night. Rusty must've got rid of the cameras." She looked disgusted. "I guess we know who his real boss was."

"Did state police find any tapes from the camera at Ike's place?"

"I don't know. I talked to Lt. Leary a little while ago and he didn't say anything about that. He said they found a ton of guns. But no records of sales, not even a computer, if you can believe that."

"Knowing Ike, he had a secret bunker. You know, like Hitler or something," Bernie said, laughing.

"He did have a bunker." Dawna started for the door.

"Where are you going?"

"The old Millers had a bomb shelter in the backyard, out

behind the barn."

"I'm going with you."

"No way. The chief would kill me."

"C'mon. State police are there. I can't possibly cause any trouble. After what happened last night, I need this." Bernie tried her best pleading look.

Dawna looked like she was going to say no again, but then said, "Come on."

The Miller residence looked deserted. Police tape crisscrossed the front door of Ike's big ranch-style house behind the stockade fence, but there were no police around.

"Wonder if they're done for the night? It is almost midnight," Dawna said. "Leary said they were almost done here, anyway. They're concentrating on trying to track down Miller."

She called Leary on her cell while Bernie wandered toward the barn, out past the back of the house.

"Hold up," Dawna said. "They're coming back. We'll wait for them."

Bernie was already halfway around the house.

"Wait for backup," Dawna said, running up behind her.

"I just want to see. I won't touch anything. It's probably locked anyway." Wait was never a word in Bernie's vocabulary and it sure as hell wasn't going to be now.

Dawna shook her head, but followed as Bernie went around the back of the barn. She could smell the cows and hear their snuffling and low moos, they blended with the comforting warm summer smell of hay. Her flashlight caught thick summer grass, night bugs and mosquitoes. Just a night walk through a meadow, worlds away from the nightmare in the bog. Bernie knew Ike was long gone. Even so, she was glad Dawna was behind her and packing a gun.

About fifty yards behind the barn, off to the side of a pasture and near dense woods, was a hillock, with a grove of shrubbery, blueberry bushes, rugosa, a few birch trees in front. "That's where it is," Dawna said, several steps behind Bernie. As Bernie got closer, she could see a gap in the shrubs, and deeper in, light. Closer, she realized it was an open door. Her stomach gripped. A dark shape farther in began to form into a familiar one. Ike Miller. He had his back to the door, apparently at the top of the steps leading down to the bomb shelter, fiddling with a box.

Dawna grabbed her arm and pulled her back, catching Bernie's eye and signaling her to get behind some nearby bushes. She didn't have to tell Bernie twice. That sweet hay-smell feeling had dropped straight through her gut and out the other end the minute she saw Ike. The bog didn't feel so far away after all.

Dawna pulled her gun from the holster. "We're waiting for backup. They should be here any minute," she whispered, so quietly Bernie could barely make it out.

Bernie strained against Dawna's arm to see more. Ike straightened up, lifted the box, and walked out of the shelter. Bernie's breath caught, even though she knew he couldn't see them in the dark. He took a right and it was then she noticed his pickup parked near the fence of the cow pasture, near what must be the other end of the bog road coming out of the woods. A happy yelp broke through the quiet night sounds. Maybe Ike didn't see them, but his dog did. Dubya came bounding over to Bernie from the bushes near the door to the shelter.

Bernie froze.

"Don't say or do anything," Dawna whispered.

Dubya cocked his head to the side and sat, staring at Dawna and Bernie through the brush, with a loopy dog grin, waiting for them to play. Don't bark, Bernie prayed. Go to Daddy.

Ike had the passenger side of the pickup open. "C'mon, boy. Dubya. Come."

Dubya's ears wriggled back. He heard Ike. But he was having fun with the game. He gave a yip, then smiled wider. Let's play! Bernie sucked in her breath, closed her eyes.

"Dub. C'mon." Ike was getting impatient. "Leave it. Come."

Dubya turned and looked at Ike, who was still standing by the pickup. Then stood up and barked at Dawna and Bernie.

It got Ike's attention. He strode toward their hiding place, his hand reaching to the back of his waistband.

Before Bernie could react, Dawna was already moving.

"Stop!"

Ike stopped.

"Mr. Miller, you're under arrest. Put the box down."

He stared at her, then started laughing.

"C'mon Pocahontas, you ain't gonna shoot me. I gotta hit the road." He stopped reaching, showed his hands, gave her a big grin. "C'mon Dub." The dog looked quizzically at Bernie, then trotted over to his master. Ike started walking toward the truck.

"Damn straight I'll shoot you."

Ike turned around and looked at her, his smile fading.

Dawna stood in full firing stance, her gun steady in her hands, aimed directly at him. No dimples, no smile, no self-conscious blush. It was a Dawna Bernie had never seen before. A warrior.

"I. Will. Shoot. You." There was no mistaking the menace in her words.

Ike put the box down and his hands up. When backup arrived a few minutes later, he was on his face in the grass, in handcuffs.

. . . . .

The state police uncovered Ike's monitoring system in the bunker. It was very state of the art. All his recordings were in digital computer folders, enough to take the investigators months to sift through.

For now they skipped to the one dated July 4, 2009. Leary even showed Bernie the video without her having to ask.

Dragon Dube wasn't a killer.

Ike Miller most definitely was. The tape showed him watch Ray and Dragon's confrontation from the seat of his ATV, then go into the ice cream truck on the passenger side, the side not visible on Ray's cruiser tape. Dragon, undone by the pepper spray, was easy prey for Ike, who grabbed the gun out of his hand and bashed him in the head with it.

"Must be a favorite move of his," Bernie said to Dawna, the

3

picture of Ike slamming Pete across the face with his gun still playing in her brain.

"Yeah, the damage to his face from the gunshots erased any damage from that hit," Leary said.

Ray turned around and went back to the truck when Ike hit Dragon, his shout to stop clearly visible. The recording also clearly showed Ike shooting Ray with Dragon's gun. Then Miller got out the passenger side again, ran over to Ray, grabbed his gun, and shot a still-groggy Dragon.

It was all there in nice high-definition color. State of the art.

CHAPTER 28

Bernie was still in hermit mode late Saturday afternoon when Pete called.

"I wondered how you're doing," he said, sounding so normal it was hard to believe the last time she saw him, just two days before, he looked more dead than alive.

"How about how you're doing?" Bernie asked, realizing she should have been the one doing the checking up, but still unsure of her footing with him.

"I'm okay. Are you?"

"Yeah. Considering."

"Considering."

There was a long pause.

"Hey, I meant to visit you in the hospital—"

"I wasn't in long," he cut her off. "You could lose all your limbs and they'd still hustle you out in two days."

"Do you need any help? Cooking? Housework?" Bernie asked, thinking of the broken arm, the broken ribs.

"Nah, I'm a lefty. But I wondered if you wanted to come over. To talk."

"Sure." Bernie was surprised. "I'll get pizza."

Pete answered the door a while later with beer in hand.

She could see the outline of the wrapping around his rib cage under his T-shirt. His arm was in a cast suspended by a sling, with a foam wedge holding the cast out and away from his body. The right side of his face was swollen and purple, with a row of stitches across an angry gash on his cheekbone. Dawna told her they had to put a plate in his arm, screw it in, to fix his broken bone. He was unshaven, his face flushed.

"You look like hell," Bernie said.

"You don't. Bring that into the living room and get yourself a beer."

She put the pizza down on the coffee table as he lowered himself into a recliner. There was a half-empty Jack Daniels bottle on the table next to his chair.

"Are you on painkillers?" she asked. He was at least a little drunk.

"Nah. I don't like that stuff." He held up his beer bottle and grinned. "Doctors Sam Adams and Jack Daniels have their own prescriptions for me."

Bernie wasn't sure how good an idea that was, but he was a big boy.

She sat on the couch, took a swig of beer and leaned back, looking around. The last time she'd been here was a month ago, the horrible conversation about the notebook. She'd never made it into the living room that night. The room was comfortable. Old furniture, nice TV airing the Red Sox pregame show, a couple banjos and a guitar, the accordion in its case. An elaborate sound system with piles of CDs and—Bernie was impressed—vinyl records. Several shelves of books.

Something was missing.

"Are you really okay?" Pete asked. He was trying to maneuver a piece of pizza one-handed without dropping the toppings.

"I guess I should have gotten plain. I'm okay. I'm not the one who got hurt."

He eyed her as he chewed his pizza, but didn't say anything.

"A lot has happened in the past couple of days," she said.

"I'll say," he said. "Rusty, Miller. Dragon. And Ray. Ray. Jesus."

"I know."

"Hey. We're just talking as friends, okay? No reporter?"

Her face got hot. "On my honor." She crossed her heart.

They silently ate.

"I had to see that damn tape of Miller shooting Ray myself. I didn't really believe it when they told me," Pete said, breaking the silence. "How could we have been so wrong?"

Bernie shrugged. She wasn't going to point out that she thought there was a rush to judgment from the start as far as Ike's role went.

"I have a question."

He looked at her.

"Why didn't you just sit down when Ike told you to?" It still made her recoil, how savagely he had beaten Pete.

"Dunno." He looked like he was going to say more, but instead he struggled up out of his chair. "Want another beer?"

"Sure." She wasn't going to push it. She examined the living room again. She knew what was missing.

"You don't have any pictures," she said when he came back with the beers.

"Pictures?" he looked around, then pointed with his good elbow, the arm that held the beer. There was a large watercolor of a sailboat over the couch. Obviously done by an enthusiastic amateur. "It was part of the décor when I moved in."

"I mean, family pictures. You know, mom, dad, junior, sis. Everybody's got them."

"Not me."

"You have family."

He shrugged and picked up a piece of pizza.

"But no pictures."

"What's the problem, Bernie?" He seemed annoyed. She wasn't sure if it was at her or the pizza, which lost half of its toppings as he lifted it. She was thinking maybe her. She didn't want to spoil their renewed camaraderie, but she couldn't help herself.

"It just seems a little," she searched for the word. "It seems...blank."

He chewed his pizza. "Blank?"

"That sounds different than what I meant." She felt herself flush again.

He kept chewing, giving her the old familiar green laser gaze, compromised a little by his purple, swollen cheek.

She let it drop, concentrating on her beer and the Red Sox. Neither of them spoke for a few minutes. Then he grinned at her, impishly. An expression she'd never seen before on him.

"Soooo," he said, drawing it out. "Why's a nice girl like you single?"

The question startled Bernie. It was one of her least favorite. She went through the Rolodex in her head of her standard smart-ass answers, but decided the best defense was a good offense.

"Soooo," she mimicked him. "Why's a nice guy like you divorced?"

"You first."

"I got laid off and decided to buy the *Watcher* and my boyfriend didn't want to come along, and that was it." The not-so-truthful *Reader's Digest* condensed version.

"As easy as that," Pete said.

"I didn't say it was easy. It's just how it was. Now you."

He took a minute, taking a big swallow of beer.

"Just one of those things. Grew apart. We're still friends."

"Copout," Bernie said.

Pete looked surprised. "That's the truth."

"Yeah, but that's what they all say. You have to give me more."

Pete shrugged.

"C'mon, did you cheat?"

"I'm not that kind of guy." He seemed genuinely hurt.

Bernie was surprised to feel relieved. "Then what did you do?"

"Why do you think I did something?"

"Come on."

He picked at the bottle label with his thumb. "She got tired of me."

They sat in silence for a couple minutes.

"What about your girlfriend?"

"Girlfriend?"

"The blond Portland lawyer."

Pete laughed. "Jesus, this is a small town. We went out a little. Nothing serious. Portland's a long drive."

"Oh."

"Oh," Pete mimicked, with the impish grin again. He studied her, the smile fading. "It's not that I don't have feelings. I'm not...blank."

Bernie flushed again.

"I show my feelings. In different ways."

They both drank silently.

"That's all you're going to tell me?" Bernie asked, her beer bottle empty. She went in the kitchen and came back with two more.

"Yep," he said, taking a beer from her.

"Okay. So tell me why you don't have any pictures."

"Nope."

"C'mon," Bernie gave him her best don't-give-me-a-speeding-ticket-smile. She felt a little drunk herself. "I almost drowned you. The least you can do is tell me your intimate secrets."

"Nope."

They finished their beers and watched some of the game, not talking much. Even though the Red Sox were winning for a change, after the fourth inning Bernie got up.

"I gotta get going. I'm beat."

Pete walked her to the door.

"Thanks for having me over."

"Thanks for coming." He looked into her eyes. She thought he was going to say more. Instead, he touched her cheek, then cupped the side of her face in his hand. Before she could protest, he kissed her. It was what she imagined when she let herself imagine that type of thing: warm and soft and sweet. A little beery. Which she hadn't imagined, but didn't mind. She'd been around the block enough to be on the receiving end of a few drunken kisses, but it still caught her by surprise. His hand was hot against her cheek and neck. His cast pressed against her. She put her hands on his chest and felt the tape from where his ribs were wrapped. She could feel his body heat, his heart pounding. Smell that warm soap. She felt a jolt of compassion that made her stomach drop.

"I guess I should go home," she said, pulling away, trying to sound like she meant it.

He didn't say anything. Their eyes locked and he leaned his forehead against hers and brushed his thumb along her cheek. He slid his hand down her cheek, his thumb tracing her lips, her jaw line, her neck and finally resting in the hollow of her throat.

She felt a tightness deep in her stomach.

"I show my feelings in different ways," he said, his voice soft wet gravel.

Bernie backed away. He didn't take his eyes, moist and red, off hers.

What she wanted to say was: "You're incredibly drunk. You've got a broken arm, broken ribs, and a broken face. And you're the police chief and I'm the newspaper editor. Other than that, I'd rip your clothes off and do it right here on the linoleum."

What she said was: "I gotta go."

And then she did.

. . . . .

Pete woke up the next morning with a killer hangover and pain screaming from every part of his body. He couldn't find a position that was anything close to comfortable in his bed, so he'd finally given up and slept in the recliner.

"That's about what I deserve," he said to himself while he shaved. He'd picked the wrong day to look and feel like shit. He was expecting Dave Marshall and Lew Kinney, who wanted to talk to him about what happened in the bog. And everything else. He wondered how much of a mess they saw it as. Gun trafficking right

283

under his nose. One of his cops involved. Cal had known all about it, or at least Rusty said he had. Pete was still trying to figure that part out. A bunch of people dead. The whole Ray-Dragon shooting had been totally botched. State police's case, but still. And there he was on the gun task force. What a joke. What a mess.

He looked at his bloodshot eyes in the mirror and sighed. "You gonna have a job when this is all over?" He was already on probation. He bet Redimere didn't have double-secret probation.

He wondered if any of the selectmen—Gert Feeney, maybe—had tipped Bernie off about what the board was going to say to him. He felt stupid about last night. There weren't many people in his life that had his back, that's one thing he and the shrink in Philly agreed on. Sid, Cal—at least at one time he thought Cal did, goddam Cal—his ex-wife, Karen, before things went bad. After Thursday, Bernie. He knew that now. But he still felt stupid about last night.

When she asked why he didn't sit down for Miller, her eyes huge with compassion, he was so tempted to tell her that he'd learned young how the only defense was to pretend it didn't hurt. But the whole thing made him sound too pathetic and he already felt pathetic enough. Forget about that anyway, the beating he took was nothing compared to the way he felt lying helpless on the ground as Ike closed in on her. If that phone hadn't rung, they'd both be dead. He couldn't have saved her. The thought twisted his gut.

That kiss. He cringed. Not that he hadn't meant it. He'd wanted to touch her for a long time. His recent girlfriend, the Portland blonde Bernie was so curious about, was beautiful and model thin. Nice to look at, but all planes and hard angles when he held her. When he talked to her, too, for that matter. Bernie was soft and warm, no hard angles there. What he would have given for two good arms last night.

"Jesus, you're an idiot," he said to his reflection.

His reflection looked back, mournful, pale, and battered.

He made a one-armed attempt to iron a shirt and dug out a pair of khakis. He had briefly toyed with, then rejected, wearing his uniform. He had two, besides his dress uniform. One was still the moldering mess that the hospital had given him in a plastic bag. He'd briefly taken the other out of the closet, then put it back. It would be too much. Reek of desperation, a little clownish. Still, he wanted to look like he was taking the meeting seriously. No T-shirt and jeans. An occupational therapist at the hospital had shown him how to thread his broken arm through a sleeve with his torn shoulder. It was painstaking, but he wasn't going to be one of those guys with the sad empty sleeve hanging down. He wanted to look strong and in control. The police chief. Somehow hide that same sinking feeling that he'd had in Philly every time he'd had to talk to someone—his boss, IA, the shrink, HR—after his breakdown.

He'd screwed this up, too. It was his town, his people, his duty to keep them safe. He had to convince Dave and Lew that he was still the guy to do that, if it wasn't too late.

He was still pulling on his pants when the doorbell rang. Getting dressed with one arm was going to get old fast. He pulled a piece of toilet paper off his chin, forced an expression that he hoped looked more like a smile than a grimace of pain, and answered the door.

Dave and Lew stood at the top of the stairs. Lew, in what looked like his church clothes, held a casserole dish.

"Wow, you took a beating," he said. He shifted the dish and reached out to shake Pete's hand, realizing halfway through shake approach that Pete's right hand wasn't going to be doing any shaking. He shifted the casserole dish to his other arm and tried again, and they executed one of those unhappy left-handed shakes.

He pushed the dish toward Pete. "Maggie made you a tuna casserole."

It was Dave's turn to look embarrassed. "Sorry, I didn't know we were bringing anything."

"Don't worry about it. Want some coffee?"

The two men fidgeted next to the kitchen table, looking anywhere but at him.

"Sit down," Pete said. This was going to be harder than it

looked. Now I'm going to have to try to put the two guys who are going to fire me at ease. Jesus.

He busied himself with the coffeemaker, another complication with one arm, as the two sat down.

"I guess we have some things to talk about," Lew said.

Pete nodded as he measured out the coffee.

"That was a hell of thing in the bog."

"It was," Pete said.

"Bernie, too," Dave added.

Pete turned and looked at the two. Lew was fascinated by the pepper mill. Dave was watching Lew. "She saved my life."

"Lucky for you she came along," Lew said.

"Yep," he said, wishing they'd get to the point.

Dave cleared his throat and looked at Lew, who was cranking the top of the pepper mill. Some pepper shot out and he jumped back. "Down to business," Lew said, wiping at the pepper with his hand.

Pete sat down, trying to find a position that was comfortable with his sling. They both watched. Almost as fascinating as the pepper mill.

"We can talk to you more about what happened later, when you're feeling better. We just came here—with Gert and Rene's blessing—to let you know that we're behind you one hundred percent and you're off probation," Lew said.

Pete was dumbfounded. Surprised at how relieved he was. The two looked him in the eye for the first time since they got there.

"Thanks. I appreciate your support."

CHAPTER 29

Bernie tried to make up for lost time at the office. After spending all day Sunday there, with Guy and Carol's help, by Monday, she was feeling more on top of things. Guy wrote the story about what happened in the bog, sticking to the bare facts, leaving out the soul-curdling terror. Bernie handled the gun trafficking story. She was glad for the distraction. But there were still so many pieces that didn't make sense.

After Dave Marshall's weekly press conference—how mundane that seemed now, although the announcement about Pete was good—she stopped by the police station to see if she could get more details on the Ike-Rusty arrests. She hoped she'd see Pete, but also kind of hoping she wouldn't, after that kiss on Saturday.

Dawna was sitting at her desk, eyes glued to the computer.

"Chief in?" Bernie asked.

Dawna rolled her eyes. "He's been holed up with the state guys since six. At least they came here, since he's having so much trouble getting around. He's pretending he's okay. He shouldn't even be working, but he insisted. They said at the hospital he's lucky he's in such great shape, probably saved his life when he was under water. But still, he's not Superman."

"How are you guys doing?"

"We're okay. Chaotic. State's doing nights and weekends now, since it's basically me and Jamie. The chief can't drive, although he'd try if we let him."

"How's Dubya doing?" Bernie asked.

Dawna smiled. "He's at the county shelter. They're going to sort him out for adoption. He's a good dog, and cute. He'll go fast."

"He is a good dog," Bernie said. "Despite his master."

The silence hung. Bernie had a ton of questions, but didn't know where to start. "Have they figured everything out?"

"They're still trying to figure it all it out. I guess we'll never know everything. Miller isn't talking, Rusty has shut up and everyone else is dead." She said it matter-of-factly, but her voice broke on dead.

. . . . .

Later that afternoon, Bernie's cell rang. It was a collect call from the Franklin County Jail. Rusty. She accepted the charges.

She wasn't sure what to say. How's jail? Nice way to screw up trying to kill Pete? Nice way to screw up trying to kill me? Her head spun.

Fortunately, she didn't have to say anything.

"I'm calling from jail," he said. No shit. "Pay phone. Almost forgot how to use one of these things." He chuckled.

Was he really going to be chatty? The whole thing seemed unreal.

"I know I'm not too popular right now, but I need to talk."

Bernie found her voice. "What about?"

"Can you come for visiting hours tomorrow? Around ten? They're transferring me later in the day. So it's gotta be tomorrow. You have to set it up."

Bernie had done a few jailhouse interviews in her day. "I know the drill. What's up?"

"I have some things I need to say. I don't trust the police, so you're my protection. I tell you first, they can't twist around what I tell them."

Bernie wanted to scream at him. Protection? After what he

did? But she knew that would kill the interview. "Here are my ground rules. If you tell me something that's going to get you in trouble, you have to promise me you're going to tell the police. I don't want to be on the other end of a subpoena."

"That's my plan. I'm gonna tell you first, so you know the story, then tell them everything and get a deal. I gotta go. There's another guy waiting to use the phone."

"I'll see you tomorrow morning."

"Hey Bernie?"

"Yeah?"

"I know you probably hate me right now. But I want you to know, I'm a victim, too."

She hung up.

. . . . .

She got to the jail early the next morning, a low-slung brick building off Route 27 in Farmington. She pulled into the narrow parking lot beside sheriff department cruisers and the paddy wagon. Funny thing about jails. It didn't matter if it was an urban jail in Massachusetts or a rural one in Maine, they all had that same antiseptic smell that her Catholic grade school had. There was also another underlying smell. A reek. Poverty and despair. When she walked into the waiting area, the sad sack disenfranchised group waiting to visit family members looked like every group she'd ever seen in a jail waiting area. Poor, dirty, hopeless.

One thing she wasn't prepared for was seeing Rusty. When he sat down across from her at the table in the visiting room, she felt a wave of revulsion, underscored by fear. Yet it was just dopey old Rusty in orange jail coveralls, pale, with bags under his eyes, his red mustache drooping more than usual.

He smiled. "Hey, Bernie. This is a hell of a thing, huh?"

Bernie didn't smile back. Last time she saw this idiot, he was trying to kill her. "How's jail?"

"Cooking's better than my wife's," he said with a wink. Unbelievable. "But, there's a lot of scum here. Sex offenders, druggies."

Gun traffickers, attempted murderers. "I know you have some things to tell me," Bernie said. "I have questions for you, too, and we only have an hour. So let's get going."

"Okay," Rusty said. He looked nervous now. "First of all, I want to say that I didn't think anyone was going to get killed. I didn't know any of that was going to happen. That was all Ike. I was just trying to make some money."

He outlined how he'd stumbled on Ike's operation a few years ago and offered, for a price, to help him out, turn a blind eye, help keep people away. Ike increasingly had him do the gun exchanges at the bridge, liking the level of separation it gave him.

Bernie was disgusted—Rusty actually sounded proud.

Then they found out Stanley knew and was going to tell.

"Guess he told Cal he knew a while back, but me and Ike only found out in December. Ike was pissed. Then he went south—or I thought he did. When they found his body, Ike wanted me to go over to the trailer and find out if he had anything incriminating. But you beat me to it." He glowered at her. "Anyway, I had Wayne take the trailer, tore it up later to make sure you didn't miss anything. Told the chief the scrap yard took it."

"If Ike killed Stanley, why didn't he look for evidence in December?"

Rusty shrugged, as though it didn't matter. "He never said. But he kept me in the dark about a lot of things. Like how he had me set Ray up."

"Set Ray up?"

"Well, Dragon found out about the guns, so he was meeting Ike down at the bog to blackmail him, or he wanted a cut or something," Rusty's voice began to shake. "Ike told me to call Ray on my cell, not use the radio, and get him down there. I didn't know he was gonna kill him." He started to cry.

Bernie wasn't moved. "I thought Ray followed Dragon down there on his own. You guys set him up? To kill him?"

Rusty shook his head so hard Bernie thought his mustache was going to fly off. "No. No way. Not *us guys*. Ike set him up. He just had me call him."

Bernie felt another wave of disgust. "So Ike wanted Ray down there, because he was going to kill Dragon to shut him up, but make it look like it was another Dragon-Ray thing?"

Rusty nodded.

"And you never saw that? That he'd have to kill Ray to make it work?"

Rusty shook his head.

Either Rusty was soulless or the stupidest person Bernie had ever met. "What were you doing in the bog when you ran into me and Pete?"

"Ike said he had you two tied up on the bridge, wanted me to keep an eye on you while he redirected some traffic. Boy, was I surprised to see you guys walking out."

"So when you tried to kill Pete, why didn't you finish the job? Why didn't you try harder to kill me? Why didn't you disable the cruiser or its radio?"

He shrugged. "I don't know. I didn't go down there to kill anyone. It all happened so fast. I thought the chief was dead. I just wanted to get the hell out of there. After I hit you, I didn't want to hang around. I just wanted to get out of Dodge."

No surprise, Rusty wasn't any more competent a criminal than he was a cop.

"I want to tell you about Cal, too," Rusty said. "He wasn't just covering for Ike, he was in on the whole thing. That's the thing I'm afraid they're going to try to cover up. I figured you were on to it when you kept asking me about the snowmobile accident. Ike had me put a cable across the bridge when we weren't expecting customers, because kids were coming down there so much and one of the guns was stolen from the box. One bad accident might scare them away."

Or kill them, Bernie thought.

"So it worked. That night of the accident, Ray bought the story I was down there with a girl, but Cal didn't. He went down to check on me and figured it out, then got in on it. He and Ike are buddies from way back. Cal said he'd keep his mouth shut in exchange for the planning board doing the deal with Dunkin's to build the new police station. He wanted that station so bad. He'd lost that winter place in Florida, too, because he didn't have enough money in the bank. So he wanted to make some dough. Buy a place, spend six months a year in Florida. We kept Ray in the dark.

"That's why Cal got Novotny in here instead of making Ray chief." He spit out Pete's name. "Cal said he wouldn't figure out what was going on because he was from away. Wouldn't catch on to the mountain politics. It'd all go on over his head. Wasn't familiar with the terrain, the folks, no one would tell him shit. Cal said he had a lot of influence over him. Novotny would never suspect anything."

"Didn't work out too well."

"I guess not," Rusty said. He looked sad. Bernie wanted to smack him. "Didn't expect Cal to pay the price."

"What do you mean?"

"Oh, yeah. That's the other thing I wanted to say. Cal started having second thoughts about everything. Those kids were a problem, after that gun disappeared. Then the thing with the cable—"

"The thing? You mean Evan dying?"

"Look, cut me a break. I'm trying to tell you what happened. Cal told the kids' dads Stanley was there and saw a coyote. Got everyone off everyone's back. He never figured the Carrier kid would talk to Stanley, kid was happy to stay out of town. I helped with that." He sounded briefly proud again. Bernie wanted to slap him again. "But Stanley talked to that Carrier kid in December, found out the truth and went all nuts. Like we killed the kid on purpose. Um, like Ike did. Stanley knew the whole thing was going on, turned out. Was just watching, whatever, but got pissed when he realized that kid didn't die in no accident. Stanley and Ike and Cal had that big argument at the Christmas party about it."

"Not Vietnam."

Rusty snorted. "Naw. Stanley was upset that the kid was killed because of the cable, not a coyote. After that, that border guard had died in November, shot by one of Ike's customers. Stan went to his cousin's—that's what we thought, me and Cal—so I figured things would quiet down. But then Cal got all antsy about it, too, and started drinking night and day. I have it figured out now. He was covering for Ike killing Stan and maybe that was one death too much. You know he got gallons of booze as retirement presents and he was drinking his way through it. Ike had me over there checking on him 'cause he was losing it. I went over Christmas Eve and Cal was shitfaced and babbling about how he was going to state police, tell them everything, about the Wentzel kid, about Stanley. Didn't know he meant Stanley was dead, though. Didn't know he was dead until he came out of that snowbank."

"So Ike killed Stanley and told Cal," Bernie said, trying to keep up.

Rusty looked at Bernie like she was stupid. "Duh."

She let that go, she didn't want to lose the thread. "So what happened after Cal told you he was going to state police?"

"I called Ike and told him, then went home to bed."

"Okay." Idiot.

"I didn't know Ike was going to kill him." He started to sob again.

"Kill him?"

"He said Cal was passed out. He poured booze around and set the house on fire. He was pissed he came to enough to dial 911, but said he couldn't kill him outright, like shooting him or strangling him because it had to look like an accident."

Ike killed Cal. He killed Ray and Dragon. Stanley. And Evan Wentzel, for that matter. Bernie's heart sank.

"So you knew this? Ike told you he killed Cal? And you never said a word?"

"He told me after. It was too late to say I knew. Why not blame Professor Pete for not figuring it out? And him and Cal such good friends." He sneered through his sobs. "Ike left a vodka bottle on the floor. Someone shoulda picked up on that dumb mistake.

Cal wouldn't be caught dead drinking vodka." Rusty apparently didn't see the irony of his words. He started sobbing harder. "I didn't think anyone was going to die. I didn't think Ike was going to kill anyone."

Out in the parking lot, Bernie dialed Pete's number.

"We need to talk."

. . . . .

Half an hour later, she pulled up in front of Pete's. She was relieved he was home. She'd rather have this conversation with him alone than in the station with Leary and his entourage listening. It wasn't even noon, but he looked wiped out when he greeted her at the door. His broken cheek was swollen and raw and his hair was sticking up as though he'd slept on it. His uniform shirt was unbuttoned and untucked, showing white T-shirt and the outline of the wrap around his ribs underneath.

"Did I get you up from a nap?"

He looked embarrassed. "I had to get up anyway, when you called. I think I fell back asleep, though. Just recharging, have to get back to work."

"Should you even be working?"

"I'm okay. Just tired. What's up?"

"Can we sit down?" Looking at him made her hurt all over.

"Right," he said, leading her into the living room. A pillow and rumpled blanket were on the recliner. She had a sudden memory of watching him at the gym last winter as he did pushups, body plank-straight. One arm. Clap in the middle. Other arm. Clap. Like he was driven. She lost count as she watched, mesmerized, from the treadmill. She thought at the time how like a machine he was. But he wasn't at all. He was just as human as she. She felt that surge of compassion again.

"I wanted to talk to you, too. But I've been busy with state police for the past couple days."

She sat down on the couch, wondering how to start. He stayed standing.

"Sorry about Saturday," he said.

"Don't be."

"I was out of line."

Bernie hated this kind of conversation. She'd just as soon pretend the embarrassing moments never happened and move on. The kiss had confused her and she hadn't been able to figure out how she felt. But she knew she didn't want to talk about it. "It was fine. You were fine."

"I was drunk. I'm not that guy. I have more respect for you than that."

"It's okay," Bernie said. *Is this what he thinks I want to talk about?*

"When you came over I meant to apologize, but never got around to it. A couple weeks ago I said some cruel things to you that I didn't mean." He was looking right at her, green laser, making sure she looked in his eyes. "I was under a lot of pressure. No excuse. I'm sorry. You were doing your job."

"Don't apologize. Please." Bernie wanted him to stop. Thinking of the whole thing made her burn all over again with humiliation. Made her think of her possible plan to sell the paper, get out. It was about more than him and what she'd done. She didn't want to tell him that, but it was about her and the fact she didn't have it anymore. She was glad they seemed to be friends again, glad her spinning desperate wakeful nights had ended since the night in the bog. Still, she wished he'd sit down and change the subject. She didn't want to be reminded of her worst moment and how she'd hurt him and where it was taking her.

"I was an ass," he said.

Bernie was mute with shame.

"I also wanted to thank you," he said.

"For?"

"Thursday night. I'd be dead right now if—"

"If I hadn't stumbled in like a nosy idiot?"

"You did more than that. When you saw Miller with that gun, you could have left and saved yourself. You didn't."

"What else was I supposed to do?"

He smiled, as dimpled and crinkly as he could with his banged up face. "Anything but what you did."

"Thanks, but I don't deserve any of this." She dreaded the next part. He started to say something, but she kept going, rushing it out. "Anyway, why I'm here. I was just at the jail. Talking to Rusty."

Pete didn't look angry, just more tired. "And?"

She took a deep breath. Pull off the Band-Aid.

"Ike killed Cal." There were so many things, but she figured that was the lead.

Pete turned a little whiter and sat down on the recliner, on top of the pillow and blanket, as if he didn't notice they were there.

She told Pete everything Rusty had told her. She tried to be methodical and matter-of-fact. When she was done, he said, "Guess I better tell Leary." He took his cellphone out of his pocket and went into the kitchen.

Bernie sat on the couch, wondering what to do next, whether she should leave, when she noticed something new on the table next to the couch. A picture: an old square snapshot, yellowish and faded, from the '70s. It was forlorn in a wrong-sized frame that still had a $4.99 sticker from Redimere Drug stuck to the corner. The photo was tattered, a corner missing, creased as though it had been folded and spent time in a wallet. Two boys sat on crumbling concrete steps. One obviously a young Pete, about thirteen—head of curly brown hair, the same square face and tilted eyes, unsmiling, his forearms resting on his knees with a baseball glove gripped in both hands like a shield. The other boy was a few years younger, tow-headed, with a bowl cut, mugging for the camera. Bernie wondered if it was the only picture Pete had. She'd asked about his pictures, then called him blank. She wasn't sure if it was the photo that was so heartbreaking, or that he'd put it out because of that.

She heard him ring off. She put the picture down and went into the kitchen. She knew better than to say anything about it.

CHAPTER 30

Wednesday afternoon she pushed the computer button and that week's paper went winging through cyberspace to Waterville. Rusty, for once, was true to his word and repeated to police everything he'd told her. She got her scoop and the police got their man.

Good for me, she thought, with less enthusiasm than she would have expected from herself.

She went home and changed into her running clothes. Her last run, two weeks ago, had ended badly. The night in the bog. This one would be redemptive. A new start.

She took off down the hill. The humidity had finally broken. It was a beautiful day. Even though it was early August, she could feel fall in the air, riding down from the mountains. Summer ended fast in Maine. Today was cool compared to the last several weeks. She felt light and fast.

She went through town and turned onto Pond Road.

More than four months ago, Stanley Weston's body was found here. A lot had happened since then. Stanley's death still gnawed at her. Ike denied killing him. Other than that, he wasn't saying anything. Police took his DNA to see if it matched what was found under Stanley's fingernails. No result yet. They had bigger fish to fry. Once it was all official, then she'd be happy.

Funny how things work out, Bernie thought. Everything came back to Stanley. She passed the entrance to the bog road and felt a chill. She wouldn't be going down that road again.

She neared the spot where Stanley's body had been found. The dirt-covered waste of the previous winter was still in the road, along with some new trash from the summer. The inevitable Mountain Dew bottles, crushed and dirty, their labels faded after months in the sun, cigarette butts, sand from last winter, clumps of leaves, and unidentifiable gobs of muddy crap.

Bernie paused. There was no roadside memorial. It was like no one even remembered. A patch of black-eyed Susans bloomed next to the tree line. She picked some and made a bouquet. Something for Stanley. She wondered if she'd recognize the exact spot. Someone died here, you'd think there would be some sign, she thought, scanning the shoulder of the road.

Something glinted in the afternoon sun. A wedding ring, a large one, a man's. She picked it up. It was scratched and dirty from spending more than eight months by the side of the road. But not so dirty she couldn't read the engraving. Celeste & Calvin, June 21, 1971.

She put it in her pocket and headed for the police station.

. . . . .

The next Tuesday, Pete stopped by the *Watcher*. It was early evening. Bernie was alone, getting the paper ready.

He sat down next to her desk without saying anything, shifting to find a comfortable position with his cast and sling.

"They got Cal's DNA test back." His voice was flat. "It matched the stuff from Stanley's fingernails. They did a rush on it. All of a sudden it's a priority."

When Bernie gave him the ring, he didn't want to believe it. It was easy to get some of Cal's DNA—there were still hairs on his dress uniform cap that held a place of honor on a shelf in the new station.

"Cal's DNA won't match," Pete had said to Bernie after the hair and ring were taken away by state police.

Now he said, "Cal killed Stanley Weston."

She didn't say anything.

"Rusty says he saw some deep scratches on Cal's arm the day after that party. Cal said it was from a cat that came up on his porch. Cal must've tussled with Stanley out on the road. Lost his ring. His car's still over at the gas station, where they towed it after the fire. Out back. They were waiting for his nephew in Massachusetts to come claim it. We did a search this morning. Tire iron had blood on it." He paused. Bernie had questions, but she didn't ask them.

"You'd think a cop would be smart enough to get rid of that," he said, the same flat voice. "I don't know, maybe he wanted someone to find it. Anyway, best guess is he beat Stanley and left him in the road for the plow. It was snowing hard enough. Don never saw him."

"I'm sorry, Pete."

He shrugged. "State's putting out a press release. But I thought I'd tell you in person."

"Thanks."

"Jesus. Cal. Don't know how I could've gotten a guy so wrong. My friend—" His voice broke.

He leaned his head back and put his hand over his eyes. He was crying. Bernie wasn't sure whether to hug him or run from the room. She shuffled papers around and waited.

"Are you okay?" she finally asked.

"Fine."

Bernie pictured him with that little girl in Philadelphia. "Honest?"

"I'm just really, really tired." He dropped his hand to the desk and gave her a half-smile. "Don't look at me like that. I'm fine. Honest."

"Tell that to your hand." It was clenched in a fist, knuckles white. She put her hand on top of his and gently pried it open. It was hot and still wet from his tears. Their fingers intertwined. She hadn't planned to touch him like that, and she didn't know why she did. She wouldn't have done it weeks ago, before the bog, but now it seemed right. Necessary.

They sat in silence for a minute, his hand gripping hers like a lifeline.

The phone rang and she glanced at the caller ID. The loan officer at the bank. She disengaged her fingers.

"Sorry."

She kept her eyes on Pete as the loan officer told her that after doing a lot of digging, because Harry had sold her the paper at such a discount, she may be able to make a small profit from a sale. The market wasn't great, but the paper was doing well enough—surprising for a newspaper—to be an attractive commodity despite the recession and the state of the newspaper industry. Bernie murmured responses, but realized the information wasn't that interesting to her. Her eyes were locked with Pete's, the green laser gaze just as intense, but sad, seeking. Her mind, she realized, was not on selling the paper. Partly it was on Pete, but also on tearing up her front page and getting to work on the Cal story, that frission of excitement that she hadn't felt since the night of the shooting jumping through her.

When she got off the phone, Pete stood up.

"I better let you get back to work."

Bernie sighed. "Yeah, I've got to write that story." The hugeness of it staggered her. "Just when it finally got quiet, this place is going to be crawling with press again. Will there be a press conference tomorrow?"

"Probably. I'll let you know." Pause. "Thanks."

"No problem," Bernie said. Dumb response.

He focused back on her, silent, the laser look, rimmed red.

She smiled. Her hand still burned from where his had gripped it. She knew she'd be feeling it for the rest of the night. "I'll talk to you later."

"Okay." He stood for a moment, then left.

She turned back to her computer, the outline of the story, the layout of the page, already forming in her head.

. . . . .

After an hour or so, she went back to the refrigerator for her bag dinner, glancing out the grimy back door. It looked nice out. She opened the door and stepped onto the rickety wooden steps. Past the dirt parking lot a flight below was the fork of the Wesserunsett River where it turned into rapids. Stanley used to sit on the grass there, watching the water, gazing at the mountains to the west. Sometimes Bernie saw him out there and wondered what he was thinking. Then she'd go back to her work and forget him. It was a beautiful evening. The kind that's a gift in late summer. The humidity that had hung through the last couple months was gone. The air was mild, smelled like hay with a twinge of fall coming down from the mountains, glowing with the setting sun. The golden hour before dusk.

Bernie grabbed a beer out of the fridge to go with her dinner and went down to Stanley's tuft of grass.

"C'mon, Dub," she called. The dog bounded out from under her desk and joined her at the door.

The paper could wait another half hour.

—30—

Coming Soon

NO NEWS IS BAD NEWS
Another Bernie O'Dea Mystery

A body found in the woods in Redimere, Maine, turns out to be a troubled youth involved in the case that first brought Police Chief Pete Novotny to Redimere three years before, when he was a Philadelphia homicide cop on leave for mental health issues. The tangled murder that he never solved now comes back to haunt him and newspaper editor Bernie O'Dea.

Are any of us who we say we are? As fall turns into winter in Redimere, Bernie, Pete, their families and friends, all must confront demons that will uncover ugly truths, shred relationships and cost lives.

About the Author

 Maureen Milliken is a columnist and news editor of the daily newspapers in Augusta and Waterville, Maine. She grew up in Augusta and worked for a variety of newspapers in New England before returning to Maine in 2011. Her Bernie O'Dea mystery series debut novel *Cold Hard News* reflects not only her love for all that is Maine, but also her lifelong affection for the newspaper industry and fascination, of course, with the darker side of life. She lives in small central Maine town, where she keeps a wary eye on the snowbanks.

For updates on her next book, go to www.maureenmilliken.com or follow Maureen on Twitter @Mmilliken47. Like her Facebook page facebook.com/maureenmillikenmysterywriter.

23964277R00196

Made in the USA
Middletown, DE
09 September 2015